On Tuesdays at Eleven

A Novel

Isabelle Scharfenberger

Dedicated to

the Light, to Love,

to God

"I said: what about my eyes?
He said: Keep them on the road.

I said: What about my passion?
He said: Keep it burning.

I said: What about my heart?
He said: Tell me what you hold inside it?

I said: Pain and sorrow.
He said: Stay with it. The wound is the place
where the Light enters you."
— Rumi

Contents:

A few days after settling into my new flat with Harry, I was dragged along to meet his long-time psychiatrist, Dr. Hugo Bourke. Doctor Bourke felt it important that I understand Harry's recent manic episode, so that I would grasp the complexity of his manic-depressive behaviour and know what to expect going forward.

But when I walked through the door and into Harry's session, I couldn't keep it together. How comical it was – here was my 59-year-old boyfriend, his psychiatrist, and my 24-year-old self – trying not to smile as Dr. Bourke is describing the reasons for Harry's erratic bi-polar behaviour. I pictured the whole scene as if floating like an angel from above, imagining this as another humourous chapter in my life story here.

After struggling to try and look serious through nearly the entire session and having to explain that this was not indicative of me having a lack of care, I asked Dr. Bourke to recommend me my own psychotherapist. He said he knew of "just the one," as if he were Ollivander – the wandmaker from Harry Potter – selecting the perfect wand for me. Little did I know how perfect that wand would indeed be.

I decided to trust his judgement, which led me back to the same olive-green Victorian house, where I climbed the oak spiral staircase to the 5th floor. I'd only been in London for a week. I hadn't returned since living there with my family in my mid-teens, but it felt more like home to me than anywhere else I had lived.

The rain was pelleting down on the pavement as I walked there, umbrella-less, from the tube. When I arrived, I must have looked like a drowned rat, soaked through and through. My heart raced as I knocked on the door to Scarlett Bennett's office. She opened the door to greet me.

"Samara, right?" I nodded and smiled as I made my way to a brown leather chair. My head was running with first impressions of her, her first impressions of me, and how I would explain my life story. I felt an intensity between us and knew I wouldn't be able to hide myself within the maroon walls.

She had a statuesque figure, and her hair was wavy, chestnut coloured, and just past her shoulders. Her eyes were a penetrating sea green. I was drawn to her hands, her long, slender piano fingers that made me think of antennas seeking to understand the outside world. Something about her seemed otherworldly. Her eyes held an expression of ancient wisdom. It felt like they could reach into the depths of my soul, unearthing what I thought I had lost within myself. I guessed she was in her late forties.

Her demeanour spoke of a no-bullshit approach, and I couldn't tell which of us was psychoanalysing the other more. Silence filled the room. It was clear she expected me to speak first, an action I avoided at all costs. I liked to hear strangers speak first, so that I could figure them out, and then adjust myself accordingly.

I realised the silence had gone on too long and muttered a comment about how Dr. Bourke had recommended me via my boyfriend, Harry Roberts.

"Yes, alright then," she said. "Why don't you tell me why you are here?"

Finally, her first question.

"Well, I suppose I'll begin by telling you about my family. That's usually the root cause of all our problems, isn't it?"

She looked at me expectantly, studying me with those electrifyingly green eyes of hers, that looked upon further inspection to be a mixture of green and blue. Perhaps they changed colour depending on her mood.

"I spent most of my life living around the world, moving every few years because of my father's career. I was born in New York City, and am American from my mother's side, and German from my father's side. My father was a German diplomat. I felt that I constantly had to change who I was, in order to adapt to different cultures, new friends, new living situations, while in a turbulent family. I'm now afflicted with what I perceive to be a lack of a fixed identity, and confusion as to who my true self actually is."

I always knew there was a piece of the puzzle missing, a riddle to be solved in regard to my identity.

"And what do you feel your true self actually looks like?" she asked.

"I didn't always feel so split off from myself. I actually felt content with my life for a while, but somewhere along the lines, everything went pear-shaped."

She didn't respond, only continued looking at me coolly, waiting for me to continue.

"I was a highly sensitive child. I was extremely shy, and I was always hiding in my house, under the table, any sanctuary I could find. My sensitivity amplified a life that was harmful for me. I didn't know how to cope, and so I became a living ghost. The wounding in my family runs deep, and no one has been immune to the relentless criticisms. The controlling forces I grew up with made it difficult for me to access my natural state during those formative years. I was too busy trudging through the trials of childhood to connect with my inherent self. Growing up in a family like mine has shaped me in a way that I haven't recovered from, yet."

As Scarlett stared intently into my eyes, a memory flashed in my mind's eye, a memory that had been lurking in the shadows for too long of a time.

"I was seven, and my mother Oona was driving me and my sister Inez to our Saturday painting classes. We lived in Paris at the time. It was mid-October, and the rain was pouring and exploding in heavy splashes on the sky windows above me. Heavy grey clouds filled the Parisian sky; seagulls could be seen flying by. It was one of those lazy and dreary, yet mystical urban weekend mornings. A dense fog saturated the air which made me feel safe and protected. Somehow, the world seemed less harmful, less biting, in the rain."

"Feeling enveloped by the weather outside, and free in my creative state of mind, I got started on my assignment for the day. We were told to create whatever we wished, to let our creativity run wild, unencumbered. I worked tirelessly, but in an exhilarated fashion, as I watched my creation come to life. I drew an enchanting forest. I drew glowing green fairies. I drew unicorns sliding down rainbows. I drew beautiful, goddess-like women with full and plump breasts. I drew lurking shadowy figures that plagued my dreams. It embodied all that I was feeling that day, the places I loved to dwell in my imagination. Painting filled a void within me. I looked forward to sharing my work with my mother. When I showed her my painting, she had a look of disgust on her face.

"'What is *this*, Samara?' She wasn't happy with the fully formed breasts I had painted. I couldn't understand why. I'd always been enchanted with boobs. Why would this be looked at with rejection? A tear rolled down my cheeks, reminding me of the rain pouring down from the skies. I recall thinking that the sky was weeping with me. How I longed to hide away in those puffy clouds! I swallowed my pride. I threw my feelings aside. And that was the last day of art class that survived."

Silence descended upon the room again. Scarlett wasn't much of a talker, I surmised. Anxiety ran through me. I found it difficult to express myself when there was no feedback. Maybe this was one of her methods, to feed her patients as little information as possible and see how they handled it.

"My mother was always too wounded to know how to be a mother to me or my sister. I longed for a nurturing mother who validated me, who would show me it was alright to just be myself, who wouldn't try to change me. I didn't know how to love myself because I felt unlovable. I still do, and I don't know how to change it. I have done a lot of healing work over the years, working on self-love and learning how to love my imperfections. Unfortunately, I still expect perfection out of myself because my mother always did.

"And James, my father, took us on trips around the world, sending us to the finest summer camps, allowing us every opportunity to take lessons in anything that struck our fancy, teaching us the wisdom that he had accumulated in life, and most importantly, how to be free thinkers in a world that demanded submission to group think. But I felt like I never really knew him, and because of his sudden death, I never had the chance to understand him. Though I learned much from him intellectually, there wasn't much of an emotional connection, even though I knew he cared. I don't think he knew how to be more present emotionally, so he was somewhat of an absent father figure, until he truly became absent."

"A light shines in your eyes when you speak of him. How did he pass, if you don't mind me asking?"

"All of my life, I sensed his sadness. I wanted to help him, to bring light to his dismal eyes, to remind him of the joy of living. It was like something irrevocable had switched in him, and I didn't know how to turn back on the light. I had several dreams that he was going to die from a heart attack if he didn't start looking after himself better. Well, my dream turned out to be prophetic."

"I was in Switzerland, studying at university on the day he died. All morning and afternoon I couldn't breathe properly and felt extreme anxiety. I couldn't shake the feeling that something bad was going to happen. I went for drinks at the bar on campus with some friends. It was there that I received a text from my mum saying to call her and that it was an emergency. She didn't have to say anything more, because I already knew. The day happened to be Thanksgiving."

I gazed out the window, observing my soul as it departed the room, observing my thoughts as they strapped me on a boat, rowing gently down a stream. Merrily, merrily, merrily, merrily, life is but a dream.

Although already surprisingly comfortable in the silence with this stranger, I felt uncomfortable that she was processing my feelings with me, maybe even for me. Of course, I was well aware that it was part of her role, but I wasn't used to sharing my feelings with another. Scarlett, perhaps beginning to sense the uneasiness the direction of my thoughts was taking me in, brought us both back into the room.

"There's much to unpack in everything you just shared with me, though I'd like to start with the part about your mother. What is your relationship to her like now?" Scarlett asked me.

"It's very strained. We're hardly in touch and she hardly has a clue about me," I said.

"I think it will be important during our time together that we focus on the feelings that you were never able to express as a child. I'm sure that memory of your painting class came up for a reason, and I think it will be a good starting point for us to examine that more."

"Right. How could I have had feelings when I had to be the chameleon, constantly adapting to my surroundings in order to survive?"

"In this room, we'll work on finding out who is really itching to be acknowledged and accepted. It will take some chipping away at these layers to find the true and natural self within you. It was a coping mechanism for you to tuck her away, in order to win love or be accepted, but you can free yourself once you realise that this emotion of being unlovable is just that – an emotion, not a truth."

I let that sink in for a moment.

"Thank you for your wise words, Scarlett," I said.

She half smiled at me, looking quizzically into my eyes, probably to gauge whether or not I was being sincere. She seemed to register that I meant my words genuinely. I liked the way she looked at me. I wondered if she looked at all her patients in that deeply penetrative way. I didn't feel like I had to defend myself to her, and, for once, I didn't feel like I was being misunderstood. We stared at each other until she broke my gaze and looked to her right at the clock on the red velvet chair beside her.

"Well, that marks nearly an hour. I think it would be good for us to see each other once a week. Do Tuesdays at eleven usually work for you?"

I told her that would be fine. I thanked her for the session and told her I was glad to meet her. As I gathered my belongings, I was aware of her studying me.

When I stepped outside, I felt as if the anchors holding me down were slowly lifting. The sun was shining, and the droplets of rain were beginning to evaporate. The healing gift of being seen is not to be underestimated. I had plenty of time before I was meeting Harry for dinner and wanted to fully digest my first session with Scarlett. I took a right down the next street and decided to walk straight from there, endlessly towards the sun.

The sun was just beginning to set, casting a tangerine glow that rippled across the puddles on the street. The remaining rays of light enveloped my body in warmth, nurturing and soothing me. Tonight was the night of the full moon in the sign of Pisces. I often noticed a tangible shift of energy when the moon was full, as if people were attuned to a different wavelength, in harmony and rhythm with celestial events. It was only natural, after all.

As I walked, I realised I cared less about the reflections of the therapy, and more about my reflections of Scarlett herself. I liked her style, that *je ne sais quoi* about her. Though I had only known her for fifty minutes, I felt we had an understanding. The connection felt palpable, as if I could touch the threads of energy running between us in the air. I wondered how accepting she would be of me when I shared the rest of my story, but I knew this wasn't the time to filter. She would have to witness my entire self. Whether or not she would end up liking me would have to be an irrelevant factor.

I was somewhat intimidated in Scarlett's presence, but I figured that was not such a bad thing. I needed someone to push me out of my comfort zone and something told me Scarlett would be just the one for that.

My thoughts turned to Harry. We had only recently started living together, but I already felt stagnancy in the connection. There was part of me that yearned for more, a sort of divine discontent – for a deeper passion, a deeper purpose. My priority was the growth of my soul.

It was time to make my way over to meet Harry for dinner at a Japanese restaurant in Hampstead. I called for a taxi, and as we drove along, my thoughts wandered back to Scarlett. What was it about her that drew my attention, almost commanded it? There was something about the way she looked at me as we were closing the session. It was as if I saw myself in her, like I was meeting myself for the first time.

Chapter Two – Is this a Figment of my Imagination or an Ordinary Sensation?

As I entered Jin Kitchi, I breathed in hints of jasmine by the doorway, and found comfort in the Zen ambiance: Noren curtains dividing the rooms, paintings of Sakura blossoms in spring, the refined style of preparation in the cooking. It felt like a place to hide away from the troubles of the world, especially as the sky continued its weeping outside. Harry spotted me and waved me over.

"Hello angel," said Harry.

I noticed he was on his second bottle of sake. At least he kept himself busy in my absence, I thought. I kissed him and apologised for being late. I explained that the weather caught me in a bit of a bind, as I helped myself to a glass of sake and started picking at the edamame.

"Have you ordered anything else to eat yet?" I asked.

"No, darling. I've been waiting for you," Harry replied, a hint of annoyance in his tone. I scanned the menu for my favourite dishes. Once I had made up my mind, I called over the waiter. Harry and I had met him in Japan a year prior and he was the reason we knew about the restaurant's existence. The circumstances in which we met were more absurd than I care to share, but let's just say it led to an intimate understanding between the three of us.

"Hello Shin! Great to see you again."

"And you, Samara, Harry! I'm happy to see you again."

We'd seen each other a week ago, the night I arrived from Thailand to move in with Harry. We'd stopped by the restaurant on the way home from the airport.

"What can I get you?" Shin asked.

"We will have one order of the Wagyu beef to share, one garden salad, two miso soups, two orders of wild salmon sashimi, two fatty tuna sashimi, two yellowtail nigiri, two scallop nigiri, and one black cod special entrée."

"Certainly, and would you like any other drinks?"

"Well, we're running low on the sake, so another bottle of the premium, and a bottle of San Pellegrino please, with lemon."

Shin set off to put in our order and I slid next to Harry on the bench, fingering the whisps of his silver-grey hair. The alcohol was lifting my spirits towards him. When it came to Harry, I could be as fickle as a cat. There were days where I felt overwhelming love for Harry. And yet, on other days, I questioned what on Earth I was doing with him. Such was the nature of our relationship. Perhaps such was the state of confusion for any twenty something year old. I wondered – was I living out some kind of serious daddy issues in being with Harry? Did he represent a fatherly figure in my life that I was longing for? And if that was the case, if it was fulfilling the need for a father, was that so wrong? I figured that if it felt right for the time being, that's all that mattered.

Harry asked about my session with Scarlett.

"So, was Dr. Bourke on to something when he predicted you two would be a right pair?"

"I believe so, though time will tell. I think she may be one of the very few people that will be able to understand me in the way I need to be understood."

"Well, it is her job to understand you, or at the very least, listen to you without judgement and hold the space for you to better understand yourself. I wish you could see how loveable you are," said Harry.

Harry was right; on some level I didn't fully accept myself, and I hoped that was something Scarlett would be able to help me with.

I kissed Harry on the cheek. He often told me I was doing well and reminded me to not be so hard on myself. He would tell me things like, "Be kind to Samara." In a lot of ways, he was like the father I never had, maybe even the mother I never had, encouraging me even when I felt like I was good for nothing. I patted Harry's leg and rested my head on his shoulder.

"We can't be so afraid of drowning that we never let go of our life raft. Our purpose in life is not to be safe, to always be comfortable, but to take risks, to learn, to experience, to grow."

"This is why I'm always telling you to stay in the present, to not get too caught up in thinking about everything so deeply. Life only exists in the *now*. Always trying to figure out the future is a sign of fear," Harry said.

"I don't like the idea of shutting off my brain. We have thought for a reason, and it's a beautiful thing."

Harry frowned at me, as he did any time I shared my own opinion. I noticed myself leaning away from him, as if to retreat into a place where my identity would not be lost.

Harry was always pressing me to just be. It felt like an encouragement to become a mindless zombie.

Harry took my hand and pulled me closer to him. "I love the bedtime stories you conjure up. You're a well of creativity. Maybe once you come to understand yourself, you'll get started on that book that's waiting inside of you."

And he was right. My fear of not being good enough was so ingrained that I tended to give up before I gave something my best shot. I hoped Scarlett would be able to help me get to where I needed to go.

I spotted Shin making his way over to our table. The rain was pouring even harder outside. The occasional rumble of thunder could be heard in the distance. It was my ideal weather for eating sushi and making love, which would be next on the agenda. There were many qualities unique to Harry, one of which was that he was a tantric master and was widening my sexual horizons. Sex with him was different from anyone I had been with.

I indulged in the beautiful food before me. We ate and drank in silence.

"Where did you go just there?" Harry asked.

"I was thinking about how to put my dreams into action and find a way to overcome my fear of not being good enough at anything."

"You're doing so well. When I was your age, I was on drugs and far from a spiritual path. I wish I'd been aware of the things you already know. But I still ended up where I needed to go. Try to have more fun and not take yourself so seriously. You'll get to where you need to be."

"Thank you, Harry. That's reassuring. Sometimes I think you're too easy on me."

Harry's hand grazed my thigh. He looked into my eyes deeply, lustfully, and he kissed my neck. Before we got too carried away, we paid the bill and headed straight for our bedroom.

Chapter Three – Child Runaway

I woke up around 7 am with a mild hangover but felt happy. I could have done with more sleep, but I preferred waking up with the sun. Harry had already left for a meeting with his attorney. I savoured my alone time.

I sat in sukhasana facing the outside world, watching cyclists pass by, as I recited my morning prayers and finished my meditation. I made myself a lemon, ginger, honey, cayenne pepper elixir to clear my system for the day, the ultimate hangover cure when my body wouldn't even ingest water.

I pulled an oracle card from a deck written by my beloved spiritual teacher. The card was about acceptance, which I found to be one of the most important spiritual lessons. To me, it was connected to patience and trust, two qualities I had certainly struggled with in my life in moments of doubt.

What was it, I wondered, that I was having the most trouble accepting at this time in my life? I was still in the process of finding my raison d'etre, which I was ever so impatient for. I felt I would know when I found it.

My stomach grumbled. I boiled two eggs and brewed the French press. I looked forward to reading and journaling, loafing around, and checking out a meditation school Harry had told me about. I started meditating regularly in Thailand and wanted to keep up the practice. The school hosted crystal sound bath sessions, reiki, breathwork, and yoga.

I took a shower, brushed my teeth, and opted for a black and white checkered dress, red ballet flats, and red cat-eye sunglasses.

I walked from our home in Notting Hill to the tube. I put on my headphones and played a rainy-day jazz playlist. I wanted to hold on to my pleasant mood. Gone were the glory days of university, I thought, where I would glide through the day laughing in bliss, operating like a high-functioning alcoholic who could take on anything with grace. All the same, I still often felt that alcohol, in general, did me more good than harm.

Hangover fogginess was actually stark clarity for me, where I could just ride the wave of my thoughts into an infinite abyss of revelation after revelation. Sometimes I would cry in bliss and gratitude, the gift of life ever so present.

Harry seldom drank and as he was my main company, I was hardly drinking. Last night had been an exception for us.

Perhaps other spiritualists would not agree, but I felt that sometimes we needed to get a little 'fucked up' to come back into our own truths of what we need.

I arrived at Victoria station and got off in search of the Re:Mind Meditation studio. I was feeling about a kilo lighter from the summer heat and alcohol detoxification.

A woman in a black sun hat, black choker, black nails, and a long black dress registered me for meditation classes. I felt agitated, and in a rush to get to a tranquil place where I didn't have to interact with anyone. Dealing with people was giving me anxiety.

I decided to hang out in Hyde Park, laying in the grass and getting grounded, soaking up the summer sun. As much as I loved the stimulating energy of living in a city, I never did too well near crowds of people. I could only take city life in small doses.

I was grateful it was summer as I started my life with Harry, as I felt more inclined to explore. Just thinking about the winter made me feel hollow and sad. Generally, I loved the change of seasons, but after a solid month of biting cold weather, I couldn't take much more of it, and would hardly go outside.

At home, I made a stir fry of miso ginger tofu, courgettes, carrots, and baked chunks of aubergine. As I cooked, my thoughts wandered into vague memories of my childhood. My hangover was starting to get the best of me. By the time my lunch was ready, the past was causing me unease.

When I was six, my sister and I planned to run away. She was eight. It was my clearest memory. Although this memory was somewhat sorrowful, I loved bringing myself back to it, because of the flicker of hope of getting out of childhood's snare.

We were living in Paris at the time. My mother was volatile that afternoon. It was one of her usual outbursts, which I had grown accustomed to by that age.

I tried to crawl under my desk to escape her, but she dragged me out and hung me upside down by the foot as she spanked me, over and over again. Afterwards, my sister Inez and I decided we weren't going to put up with it anymore.

Once our mother left us to our own devices, we planned our escape. The rain was pouring outside, but nothing could derail us. I didn't care about safety, because anything felt like it would be safer than my current circumstances. I just wanted to be free.

My yellow backpack was packed and ready, with my monkey stuffed animal for comfort, a whistle, a roll of toilet paper, a rainbow umbrella, and a few pairs of warm clothes. I didn't think about packing long term. I just figured everything would sort itself out on the road, that life would take care of me.

To my dismay, at the eleventh hour, my sister decided we couldn't go through with the plan. Maybe because she was older and had to be the more responsible one, but as I've aged, I feel the real difference was just in our spirits. I was more inclined to run away and escape, and she was more inclined to work through it by sitting right in it.

Remembering my first runaway attempt reminded me that even at that young age, I knew what I was doing. We always know what we are doing, in truth. The mind may run us in circles, but ultimately, we make the choice that we were always going to make.

I was in alignment with that curious six-year-old self, the girl that wanted to venture into the unknown with the trust that she would be divinely protected. We have to trust that life is not trying to catch us out but instead lead us exactly where we need to go. We may not be given what we want, but we will always be given what we need.

I let much of the rest of the afternoon roll by in contemplation – journaling, reading, working on a story, meditating. I was in a much better space. I watched the late summer sun lowering beneath the pink clouds.

Harry returned home around eight. I could hear him fumbling with his keys. I went to the door to greet him.

"Hello, my darling," I said. I gave him a kiss. "How are you feeling?"

"Hiya," said he, brushing past me with his briefcase.

What happened to the loving intimacy we shared last night?

I retreated to the sofa and let Harry settle. I supposed if I were to spend the entirety of a gorgeous day hungover in an attorney's office, I might not have been so happy either.

Harry stepped in front of me. "Are you hungry, darling?"

"Yes. Are you craving anything in particular? There isn't much in the kitchen, but I can bake sweet potatoes, boil peas, perhaps a tuna salad? Or we can order take-out."

"That will do just fine."

I headed to the kitchen. He stopped me and asked if I was interested in hearing how the divorce proceedings went.

"Tell me all about it," I said, returning to the sofa and curling up next to him.

I was working on becoming a more attentive partner and staying present in conversation, after a life of disassociation.

"Well, until we sell the company, splitting up our assets is tricky. And some of the companies looking to buy us are interested because we're married."

Here we go. It was always some excuse or another. I doubted Harry had any intentions of getting divorced.

I headed into the kitchen to start boiling the peas. He followed me.

"It isn't so simple really," he said, sensing my irritation. "It's a waiting game to see which companies will take the bait first. At least we spent the day taking account of our assets and how they will be split up, so once we decide on a buyer, it will all be fast moving."

I oiled and salted the sweet potatoes, put them in the oven, and took out the ingredients for the salad – albacore tuna, organic tomatoes, carrots, avocado, celery, spinach, rocket, and beetroot.

"Well, I hope it doesn't drag on for years. Claudia shouldn't be so involved in our relationship. I don't think you'd like it if I was still married and constantly in contact with my husband."

Harry stroked my hair and put his hands on my shoulders, looking at me with his arctic blue eyes.

"I understand and I'm grateful that you've been so understanding and patient."

He seemed sincere and I wasn't looking to argue. I wasn't okay with the situation, but for the time being, Harry was part of my journey. It might have scared me if Harry actually did get divorced. I could feel obligated and bound to him. At some point, we would have to discuss having an open partnership. I had a tendency towards polyamory.

"How are the girls?" I asked, changing the subject.

"They're visiting relatives in Scotland for the week. I spoke with Charlotte on Facetime. Chloe turns three on Monday, so I'll be flying over to visit them on Sunday. They seem like they're having a great time and enjoying spending time with their cousins."

Harry was no angel when it came to love affairs and commitment, either. In that regard, we were like two peas in a pod, which is perhaps why our arrangement seemed to work so well. Claudia was wife number three, so I was surprised he insisted that we stay committed to each other, given his own history. Still, somehow it felt like being with him stabilised me.

The sweet potatoes were ready to come out of the oven, the peas were boiled, the tuna salad ready to be consumed. We mostly ate in silence, lost in our own thoughts. It was a contemplative day for me, but I felt at ease in his presence.

Chapter Four – The Sandman Is Coming

Harry flew to Scotland on Sunday, my least favourite day of the week. After he left, my soul was craving isolation, and so I lived like a hermit – reading, writing, meditating, relaxing with sea salt baths by candlelight and taking solitary walks in the park as I enjoyed the last days of summer.

Wednesday was my first meditation group gathering. There were ten of us in the class. The primary focus was on the importance of presence, which was perfect for me. The first thirty minutes were spent in meditation, then we shared Buddhist teachings, followed by a group discussion.

I met Vighnesh, who was from one of the oldest tribes in the jungles of Sri Lanka. Our energies seemed to have met before we did. We shared a sense of familiarity.

He walked up to me in the tea break, placing his arm around my shoulders, and said, "Fancy meeting you here," as if we were the oldest of friends. I felt a wave of peace circulating through my body as we sat down and chatted. We shared tales of our wanderings around the globe. His mission was to celebrate, enjoying this gift of life, not feeling like he had to *do* anything in particular. I admired that about him.

"I've been to Sri Lanka a number of times to visit my friend Asha," I told him.

Tea break ended too soon, and we returned to our group for a final meditation. After the session, I retrieved my light summer coat. Vighnesh caught my arm just as I was heading out the door.

"Hey, Samara, can I invite you for a drink? I'd like to continue our conversation. There's so much I want to know about you," he said, his gleaming eyes locked on mine.

"I'd love to, but I have a commitment." Harry was returning from Scotland. "How about this Saturday?" I asked.

His smile told me the answer. We exchanged numbers. We bid each other farewell with an odd handshake and warmth in our hearts.

There were a few things I had to do before Harry got home. I picked up my dry cleaning, stopped at the bank to take out cash for therapy the following day, and picked up some groceries. When I got home, I put the groceries away and had time to read for half an hour before Harry arrived.

He strolled through the door around eleven, looking exasperated from traffic. I kissed him hello and helped him with his luggage.

"Did you have a nice time visiting the girls?"

"Why are your shoes here? They're in the way of everything," he said.

I sighed. "It's nice to see you. Welcome home."

I retreated to the spare bedroom to sleep there for the night. I'd hardly heard from him during his trip. He'd spent the last few days with his wife. Was he keeping something from me?

I awoke the next morning feeling well-rested. Harry came into my room, looking apologetic. He started stroking my hair.

"My angel, listen, I'm sorry I was being a bastard last night after not seeing you. I haven't been sleeping well. I just didn't have the patience to repeat myself about things."

"You asked me *once* before to keep my shoes in the closet, and I apologise for not remembering. However, it would've been nice if you'd been a bit more considerate when I stayed awake to see you. You barely called while you were away. How do you think that makes me feel when you're sleeping in the same house with your wife?"

"I was busy with my girls. The au pair was back in Germany and Claudia was dealing with a lot at the office."

I doubted he couldn't find a spare moment to call or write me, but rather than argue, I listened to my bodily needs. I was feeling very horny since it had been almost a week since we had last made love. I put my finger to his lips, took his hand, and guided him to our bedroom.

Feeling revived, I threw on a white summer dress and red shades and walked down to my usual coffee shop on the corner to pick up breakfast and an iced coffee.

It was such a hot morning that I could smell the heat. Smoke was rising from the asphalt on the roads, the air was dense with humidity, and I was perspiring by the time I reached the coffee shop. Fortunately, there wasn't much of a queue at that early hour.

At home, I sat on the sofa feeling the sun pouring in on my skin as I ate a lox and capers bagel. Harry was in the shower, so I left his croissant in the kitchen. I took my coffee and notebook upstairs to the rooftop. I brought my Balinese sarong to shield my skin from the steamy rooftop surface. Once I found a shady spot, I sat down to journal and reflect. Writing was my primary outlet when I didn't know what to do with my conflicting emotions. It helped give me clarity.

How crazy was it that I was living with an older man in a domestic situation. How had I gone from childhood to this? It felt as if a sandman had come and robbed me of my youth, so I wrote a poem about it.

'The Sandman'

Time, isn't it fine?
Does it make you lose your mind?
Or hold onto something with trine?
Longer than last winter's eerie shrines?

The clock ticks, the clock tocks
I am feeling like all is lost
The sandman is coming
He's waiting for morning
To come and swallow up all of your prolonging

Footsteps shuffle, dust lifts off
My heart is beating like a hummingbird's wings
Ready to take flight, ready to swing
The sandman is coming
The sandman is coming
Maybe my dreams will actually start running

Force is what I need
Something stronger than myself
That inner strength, that is missing from my belt
If the sandman is coming,
I will start running,
Straight first into my magical running world

When I finished writing, the sun had swallowed up my
shade, just like the sandman swallowing up my precious life. I
retreated back into the cooler temperature of the flat. I found
Harry sitting in the nude on the sofa as he read a newspaper
and ate breakfast. He looked up and thanked me for getting
the croissant. I nodded, left him in peace, and went to brush
my teeth and spritz myself with my signature perfume, Sole Di
Positano by Tom Ford, before heading off to my appointment

with Scarlett. My scent made me feel like I'd just rolled out of
a bed of lush citrus flowers along the Mediterranean coast. I
bid Harry farewell and set off for the day. I wanted to stop at a
yoga studio a few streets away to get the schedule and focus
more on my grounding.

It was time to get comfortable with descending my
power into the lower realms of my physical body, so that I
could feel connected enough to make my dreams a reality. I
figured yoga would help with that, that it would unlock
something trapped in my body. And I wanted to have a
routine and be a little more involved in a community.

As I peered into the studio, I had the impression that
it attracted a cool crowd and left hoping I would make some
conscious connections there.

After a twenty-minute commute, I arrived at 113
Sumner Place to meet what felt like a reflection of myself. I
didn't yet know whether feeling like Scarlett and I mirrored
each other was a technique she had mastered as a
psychotherapist, or if we were strangely similar.

I greeted the receptionist who called Scarlett to let
her know I had arrived. I found Scarlett at the top of the spiral
staircase. She had a rather intimidating presence. I felt my
chest tighten at the sight of her, and my heart started to race.
I decided to try my best to put my perceptions of her aside.
What I thought of Scarlett shouldn't matter. What mattered
was whether we could work together.

"Hi," I said as I brushed past her. "How are you?" I
asked, shy of how to begin without any kind of warming up.

"Yes," was her response.

Okay, no messing around with her today, straight to it
then.

"I don't have much to share. Harry's mostly fine. He's
the man I'm living with. We moved in together as soon as I

landed here from Thailand. He's nearly sixty, still married, and has three children, two of which are practically still babies – three and five. Maybe I have daddy issues, but the truth is we fell in love instantly. I was detoxing from my life, fueled with alcohol and drugs, empty and unprotected sex, feeling lost and lonely. I knew I had to reel myself in before I fell too far down the rabbit hole. Harry seemed to come into my life just at the right time."

"How did you meet?"

"I checked myself into a place on the island of Koh Chang where I intended to do a juice and liver cleanse, practise yoga, get myself back into some healthy habits. He happened to be there the same week, solo, as his wife had already flown back to London for work. Funnily enough, before I met him, I told my best friend, Asha, that I had a feeling I was going to meet someone on that trip. I initially avoided him like the plague."

Mentioning the word 'avoid' seemed to strike a chord within Scarlett. I saw a spark of recognition in her eyes as I paused, waiting to see if she had something to say.

"When we're children, we develop certain attachment styles – some healthy, some unhealthy, and completely dependent upon the type of relationship the child has with their primary caregiver. Given what you've shared with me about your mother and other significant relationships, it's clear to me that your attachment style is avoidant."

"And what does that mean?" I asked.

"Well, if a child had a loving and caring relationship in the first years of life, then this stable way of relating would be carried over into their adult relationships. If, on the other hand, there was a lack of secure attachment, and a lack of trust and reliability in those primary years, as seems to be the case for you, then the attachment style would manifest as anxious ambivalent, avoidant, or even disorganised."

I wondered if Scarlett had already touched on why not everything felt right in my world.

"How can you already tell that I'm an avoidant? Is it based off our interactions, or from what I've told you?" I asked.

"It's a bit of both. The resistance I feel from you in delving into vulnerable emotions, the way you intellectualise what's happening in your life, almost as an outsider, like it didn't happen to you, the unreadable poker face and the sense of aloofness about you," she said.

"Seems like a lot to get from knowing a person so little."

"When you've been doing it for nearly two decades, it comes rather quickly," Scarlett replied.

Maybe I was coming across as aloof because I didn't feel at ease around her. I was only mirroring what I felt about her, unless she was mirroring me. Therapy could be a rather confusing house of mirrors.

"And what about my life indicates avoidant attachment?"

"You're self-reliant, independent, there's a sense that you have one foot out the door, and in the way you described numbing painful emotions. You grew up feeling that you had to be independent. Not having your needs met time and time again led to either a conscious or unconscious fear that any dependency on another, or expression of vulnerability, would lead to disappointment. Thus, you've ended up *avoiding* anything in life that would trigger these earlier traumas."

Scarlett had a point, and I knew all of this, but sometimes avoiding facing how wounded I felt made me feel that I was okay, and everything was flowing well in my life. I never wanted to come across as if I needed help.

"Thanks for sharing that insight. It puts perspective on where I feel unfulfilled in my relationships. I often hide in the shadows, but I suppose I can't expect others to get to know me if I don't share more of myself. Harry was the exemption to this rule. I opened up to him more than I perhaps ever had before."

"Tell me more about it," said Scarlett.

"Harry and I met on 11/11, my life path and destiny number. I felt his eyes on me during the entire yoga class. I avoided him. Yes, an example of my avoidant behaviour, perhaps, but I just wanted to be left alone. A day later he approached me by the pool. He was a good conversationalist, so I opened like a flower in spring. I desperately wanted connection. I'd never had a man interested in me like that before. I was hooked pretty quickly."

I paused, taking a moment to trace back my memory and visualise myself in the moment.

"Before getting into the pool, I started unbuttoning my dress. He turned away, as if to preserve my modesty. He made me laugh, which was rare for me in those days. I agreed to meet him for dinner. He convinced me to come to his room for something called a 'timeline therapy healing.' He'd observed that my life revolved around my spiritual path, and he told me he'd taken self-development classes and was experienced in transcendental meditation. He was exactly what I was searching for – a deep spiritual connection."

"I can see how you could feel drawn to him when he resembled everything you were looking for, a sense of comfort at having found someone when you felt so lost," Scarlett said.

"Yes, well, still I saw right through his 'timeline therapy' offer and why it needed to be in his bedroom. He lit candles and incense and asked me to lie down on the bed as he took me back to moments in my childhood. Hardly five minutes later he offered a tantric massage. The sexual tension was very high. I allowed him to kiss me, but told him I had to go. I won't deny I wanted him, and the attention excited me, but I felt I couldn't sleep with him that first night.

"The next night, we took a tai chi class together at sunset, and he invited me back to his room. We discovered we had a similar taste in music, which made me like him more. I played Thievery Corporation and we started slow dancing. When I looked into his eyes, I had a feeling that I had seen those eyes before. They were so familiar. Where had I seen them before? And then it hit me. He looked exactly like my deceased father.

"The feeling was eerie, and I wondered if I was in a dream. How was I suddenly dancing with my dead father in this candlelit room in the jungle? Did he just take over Harry's body and decide to greet me with his presence? The whole experience felt like being in a trance. I was a puppet in a playboard, and I didn't have the strength to interfere with what was going on. All I could do was participate in the act.

"Everything about our night together was surreal. We shared everything about our lives as we lay in bed, with great joy. It was as if we were coming back together after having been separated for lifetimes. There was no shame, no judgement, just complete acceptance of each other's souls. In the end, it wasn't just sex. It felt like so much more."

Scarlett looked engaged by my love tale.

"How would you describe your relationship with Harry today? Did he live up to your expectations from your initial meeting?" Scarlett asked.

I got the sense that Scarlett was somewhat jaded when it came to love. Maybe she had been through too many heartbreaks. I got the feeling that the tale amused her, as if she was waiting to hear how Harry turned out to be a disappointment only to validate her own ideas about love.

"My relationship with Harry is turbulent. There's a lot of love there, which keeps me hanging on, but he recently went through a psychotic episode which was difficult for me to handle. I have difficulty trusting him. The initial façade he wore, the infatuation, the love bombing, all ceased only a few months after we got together, maybe even a few weeks. I understand every relationship has its honeymoon phase and then comes the period of reality where limerence ends, but the contrast between the two was so sharp that it shook me. A lot of the deep love I once had for him has faded and now I often finding myself wanting to spend time away from him so I can reconnect with myself."

"Do you feel you can't connect with yourself when you're with him?" Scarlett asked.

"I suppose. He takes up so much space that I find it hard to find myself in his company, like I lose myself in his presence."

"Do you feel there's a connection between Harry and your father?"

I gave Scarlett's question some thought, looking out the window at the solemn grey sky. I hadn't yet thought too deeply about the parallels between Harry and my father. Yes, they were the same age, yes, they looked similar, yes, their mannerisms were the same, yes, they were both businessmen, yes, they both had multiple wives and affairs, yes, they liked the same music, yes, they had similar family dynamics. Check, check, check. There wasn't much that wasn't alike, the more that I thought about it. I considered how we are all working something out in our relationships.

I found myself rocking back and forth as I thought, a self-comforting ritual from childhood which I resorted to when painful emotions were bubbling to the surface. I caught myself and wondered if I had perhaps been disassociating because Scarlett seemed about to repeat herself. I interjected before she could.

"It feels more like a spiritually destined, karmic relationship we were meant to live out, with certain lessons to be learned."

Scarlett didn't press me further, and I was grateful for that. But because of her look of understanding, I felt I could trust her a little more. We had a few minutes left, so I figured I may as well bide my time somehow.

"Harry knows how to push people to extremes. I was no exception. If I didn't stand up to him, he would push further and further. I need someone who will challenge me to step into my power. I'm growing through the challenges."

"I trust that you do know what you're doing. I'm getting a better idea of Harry's character. Have you heard of the book, *Love's Executioner*? I think you might like it. It's about a psychotherapist's tales of his experiences with various patients. In one of the tales, he says he doesn't like to be love's executioner, crushing the fantasies of his patients, but how that was all he could think about with one love-struck patient who couldn't get over what he decided was infatuation," Scarlett explained.

What was Scarlett trying to tell me? That I was in a sinking relationship?

"I'll check out the book," I said.

There was something about Scarlett, something peculiar that I liked. It drew me in. Maybe, she too, possessed something I needed to integrate into my life.

We stared at each other, comfortable in the silence. I couldn't tell if she was a million miles away, or right there with me.

She looked at the clock at the same moment where I wondered what the time was. At that moment, the clouds broke open, no longer able to sustain their weight, and the rain started pouring down, splashing like stones against the window. All in a trance, I paid her, thanked her, and stepped outside of her office, re-entering the unforgiving outside world. I found myself hoping the sandman would come and vacuum up the time until I saw Scarlett next.

The rest of the week passed smoothly. The first hints of Autumn were in the air. I'd had enough of the sticky urban summer weather and looked forward to the shift of energy. Just as the sun-kissed leaves fall off the trees as winter approaches, I hoped to shed the skin of my past to make way for transformation. I knew things with Harry were out of alignment. I was holding on to something that was perhaps no longer serving me.

Harry was focused on selling his pest control business, which could take another year or two. Harry had a habit of telling me we'd agreed to something that I would have no recollection of at all. He would always use that word – agreed, and it would leave me questioning my own memory, my own sanity. He'd recently told me that we'd *agreed* that he would be spending another weekend sleeping in the same house as his wife and children.

I wasn't even sure Harry was conscious of gaslighting me. It was perhaps just his natural way of dealing with people – manipulating them.

Until I had a plan, I would try to keep the peace with him. He expected me to take on the role of a domestic wife, adhering to traditional roles, but he wasn't providing the protection and support one might hope for from a man.

I focused on getting into a regular routine for my writing, meditation, and physical exercise – like yoga and tai chi. It was important for me to become more grounded in order to spiritually ascend further. I needed to settle in one place for a while and build a foundation, cultivate the feeling of being 'at home' that I was always searching for.

I started going to yoga twice a week which helped me become more embodied. I needed to be more in touch with my feelings, too. I attended meditation again, though Vighnesh wasn't there. I wanted to at least see familiar faces regularly and be able to speak my own language for once. After years of living in foreign countries and not fully adapting to the native language, I felt damage to my throat chakra and free flow of expression, not to mention my own childhood memories of being silenced.

Another week passed and then I was riding the vintage birdcage elevator up to Scarlett's lair.

Like a ghostly figure, Scarlett was waiting for me at the door. I greeted her and walked past her, feeling in a trance. Surprisingly, she was the first to speak this time.

"You left something in the wake of your departure last week," Scarlett said.

"Oh, yes? And what was that?"

"There was a symbolic presence of a moth in the room. It flashed before my eyes in a vision, but it was crystal clear. I felt it was communicating a message that was left unsaid. Moths tend to signify secrets and what is hidden beneath the veils of illusion, lurking in the shadows. I found it rather curious."

"I find it as curious as you," I said. I made a mental note to research moth symbolism later.

She sat there waiting for me to continue.

"Last week's session was about my dysfunctional relationship with Harry, childhood patterns, my avoidance."

"Well, is there anything you're avoiding telling me, Samara? Did you reflect on the homework we discussed?"

It wasn't quite time to dive into the gap of my memory, the missing years of childhood, the disassociation, the dreams that haunted my sleep every night.

"There is a lot more ground to cover. Everything will reveal itself in time. When you try to chase something, it tends to further elude you."

"And likewise, what you resist, persists," Scarlett replied.

"What is your relationship to secrets?" she asked.

"I suppose I don't see anything wrong with them. I think it is in everyone's nature to enjoy a bit of mystery. Of course, I understand you'll have to be an exception to that rule."

Scarlett stared at me expectantly, waiting for more.

"I prefer to keep things to myself. Exposing my innermost thoughts and feelings kills the fantasy, almost like it infiltrates its essence."

"And what if I were to propose that sometimes giving up the fantasy can set you free?" Scarlett asked.

"Who says I'm not free?"

"Samara, there must be something you're trying to work out, or you wouldn't be here. Don't you think that holding on to secrets keeps you from accessing the truth?"

"Therapy should be about empowerment, right? There is a time and place for open discussion. Not everyone can handle the truth, especially if it's unconventional or controversial. I have to ask myself if I'm I willing to allow someone else to infiltrate my intimate insight. We have to be our own greatest source of authority.

"To play the devil's advocate, though, one might consider the nature of the existence of pearls. The precious gem is formed only when a foreign particle, has worked its way into the oyster's shell. The pearl defends itself covering the irritant with its inborn fluid. Eventually, the exquisite pearl is formed. One could then argue that, in nature, when something pure is mixed with something potentially dangerous, it can create something more magnificent through the process of alchemical bonding.

It reminds me of a quote by Rumi - "Everyone is so afraid of death, but the real Sufis just laugh: nothing tyrannizes their hearts. What strikes the oyster shell does not damage the pearl."

The real transformation happens when one allows the death to happen without resistance, to allow the purity to be struck by a foreign entity, to have the courage to face the death of one thing so it can become another. Something initially uncomfortable and unwanted actually ends up serving evolution.

One has to decide if they want to take that risk of exposure. I guess my answer is yes, there are times when I feel secrets are necessary, and may help us access our true nature. The world isn't always ready for our personal truths."

"Samara, you're avoiding looking deeper at yourself and your history with secrets. I hope with continued patience and trust in the process, eventually, you'll feel more comfortable exploring your deeper truths regarding relationships. Perhaps next week you can tell me what your family's history with secrets is. How have things been with Harry?"

It was true; I wasn't fully willing to meet Scarlett halfway today. I felt fortunate to have Scarlett in my life. Perhaps she'd be able to draw my truths out of me.

"Things with Harry are not so great. The relationship lacks the intimacy I need. Great sex isn't going to cut it. And the sex is erotically fulfilling, but I'm beginning to feel like I'm being used. I certainly don't feel like there's love in the love making."

"And how intimate would you say your previous relationships were?"

"I'm somewhat ashamed to say Harry has been the most intimate yet. I've had passing flings. I guess the most 'normal' relationship I have had was my boyfriend when I was 21, which lasted almost two years, and was mainly long distance. He was like a first love. He came into my life when my father died. Our relationship was more friendship but somewhat lacked romance and deeper intimacy."

Scarlett considered this. "Would you say your relationship with – what was his name, actually?"

"Luca."

"Would you say your relationship with Luca was healthier than your relationship with Harry? Do you prefer friendship as the root to romantic relationships? And what makes a relationship intimate to you?"

"Starting with a friendship is maybe the best for long-term success and stability. Sex can't be everything. With Luca, it was more like puppy love, which was tender and precious, but as I aged, I needed more, so we eventually parted ways. And with Harry, it started off as sex and spiritual connection. We can have a blast together in our shared off-kilter approach to life, but the chemistry is dwindling."

"What other qualities do you look for in a partner? And what would you say is the most important to you?"

"A spiritual connection is the most important, feeling deeply connected to each other's souls. Vibing with each other so beautifully that explanations aren't needed. An emotional and intellectual connection is important too. I want to be with my intellectual equal, to challenge and learn things from each other. A telepathic connection too. Sort of like knowing your lover better than you know yourself. And I want my lover to be playful and with a dry sense of humour, always making me laugh. Those are some of the ideal qualities I look for."

There was a long silence, as Scarlett seemed to be processing what I'd shared. We peered directly into each other's souls from across the room. There was something loving and tender about her gaze...at times anyway. Other times her gaze could be intimidating and scrutinising. I never knew what to expect. I admired how beautiful she looked on this day. Her flowy lilac dress suited her. I admired the way her sage green hair clip was placed in her wavy chestnut hair. I admired the way she sat, perfectly poised with one leg crossed over the other. I figured I should stop with my thoughts of admiration before she picked up on them.

But the thoughts didn't stop. Once the flow started, it was like a tsunami. I couldn't focus on therapy anymore. Everything about her was drawing me in. She was all that I could see. I found her voice to be sensual. It transported me through time and space, and into a candlelit bedroom in a medieval castle with red velvet curtains. Fuck, was I falling for my therapist? No, those thoughts really don't deserve a place in here, I thought. The rational part of my mind shut the thoughts away. It was probably just transference. I was starting to think Scarlett preferred watching me think, rather than hearing me speak, when she finally spoke and declared that it was time.

I took one last, deep look into her eyes, piercing beyond the veil with a final, unyielding gaze.

Chapter Six – The Heart, The Head, and Lové

After a soak in a candle-lit sea salt bath, I drifted off to sleep. I woke up around five in the morning from a vivid dream involving my father, James. He was still alive in the dream, and we were having dinner at his apartment in New York. He was cooking us a feast. The scent of garlic brought a wave of nostalgia, mingling with the familiar smell of tobacco and whiskey on his breath.

One of my memories from when we lived in South Africa was James' daily ritual of whiskey at ten am. He must have been going through a rough time, but he kept everything to himself. He was probably the most secretive of us all. He must have felt as isolated as I sometimes did, with no one to trust with his true feelings.

In the dream I registered that my father had long been dead.

"I had an interesting dream about you a couple of weeks ago," I said in the dream. "It was pouring rain and the landscape was barren. Everything felt abandoned. All I could see was a house. I peered through a window in the basement and there you were, but you weren't yourself. You were purple, kind of looked like a monster, and appeared to be alone, crying out for help. It was like you were the freak and being kept away from the world because you were, in your own mind, too ugly for anyone to look at. It was disturbing," I told James.

"Starting our dinner off on a light note, I see." He laughed. "Remember how much fun you had in the summers as a kid? How worry-free you were? That's what I want for you for the rest of your life. You should've learned by now that summers can disappear if you aren't careful. If you like what summers have to offer, you can keep it that way – if you use your head."

And that's when I woke up from the dream. It almost seemed as if my father was visiting me from the afterlife, wanting to get an important message across.

I contemplated the dream as I lay in bed. Was I really so carefree in the summers? He didn't understand what was going on in my heart, how hollow I felt in childhood. And yet, there was also real truth in what he shared.

In our last memorable conversation, he said, "By practicing the power of thought, you will be able to keep the freedom, fun, and excitement of life alive. That is why you have a head on your shoulders – to use it, to make life the way YOU want it to be.

Watch your thoughts, they become words. Watch your words, they become actions. Watch your actions, they become habits. Watch your character, it becomes your destiny."

"I value the power of thought, but what about the power of the heart?" I asked my father.

"Samara, the heart certainly has its place, but it doesn't take the place of the mind on a practical level. If one was to follow their heart when it comes to risky investments, how far would that take them? The heart can bring passion to our desires, but focus too much on it and it will likely lead to pain," my father replied.

"But isn't pain part of the game when it comes to love? One can't love deeply and expect to not ever get hurt. Wouldn't you say your best moments in life came when you were truly living in your heart?"

"I'm not discounting the heart, but the mind can get you where you need to go."

He was too set in his ways to hear me.

I thought of the homework Scarlett gave me regarding family secrets. My father kept his son a secret from everyone. I felt sad that my father didn't feel comfortable sharing such a big piece of news with us. I felt disappointed when I found out about his other child, because it was a reminder of how little I knew about my father. And how little he knew about me. If he'd known me, he would've known that I'd have unconditional love for his 'mistakes.' Mistakes are just learning experiences and nothing for us to be ashamed about.

Harry still hadn't stirred, but soon I would have to get up and get ready for our weekend trip. I remembered Scarlett's comment about the presence of the moth in the room. From my search on the internet, I discovered that when a moth presents itself to you, in physical form or a vision, it can be a sign of concealment. Moths are masters of disguise, able to blend in with their environment. It can mean that you are hiding aspects of yourself from others and yourself. I couldn't help but make the connection to secrets that we had touched upon. Also, moths are drawn to the light, as if they want to draw something out of the shadows, to reveal what has been hidden. I wondered—was I hiding something from myself, or, perhaps even more, was Scarlett concealing something from me?"

My alarm went off. I kissed Harry good morning and we rolled out of bed. I brewed coffee in the French press, ate a slice of avocado toast, and then we headed out the door, weekend bags in hand.

In the car, I was mostly quiet, blissfully in my own inner world.

How are you feeling?" Harry asked.

"Fine, thanks, but I could use a bathroom break and coffee. Then I'll take over driving the rest of the way."

"So, Fucked up, Insecure, Neurotic, and Emotional," he said with a laugh.

And I might have laughed, too, if it hadn't been the 50th time he'd made that joke. I wasn't in the mood to talk about my feelings. We pulled into a rest stop and I told Harry I would meet him back at the car. I felt like I could use some physical space between us. The air was crisp and fresh — a nice change from London. I picked up an iced coffee and was swiftly behind the wheel. My mood lifted as I drove further north, away from the city and deeper into scenic landscapes.

We reached our destination just after noon. It was more beautiful than I'd anticipated. The cosy log cabin was surrounded by colourful autumnal leaves — reds, oranges, yellows, greens. There wasn't a soul in sight, only lush nature. The cottage was clean, spacious and well stocked. Chopped wood was available for our campfire and barbecue. After unpacking the car, we agreed that a nap would do us well. We had sex before sleeping and moments after, I drifted off into dreamland.

I slept soundly and longer than I intended to. My body needed rest.

I heard Harry outside and the logs crackling in the fire pit. I stayed in bed to read. After a few chapters, I went to the kitchen and took out the grass-fed steaks to thaw and marinate with salt, pepper, and garlic. I chopped up celery, tomatoes, and avocado to add to organic rocket leaves for a salad and then tossed it with the pumpkin seeds Harry had prepared back home. I cut long slices of carrots and drizzled honey onto them, finely chopped more garlic to scatter over the carrots, then placed them in the oven to roast. Just as I finished the cooking preparations, Harry came in.

"Did you sleep well, angel? I didn't want to wake you. I got a fire going."

I was surprised Harry knew how to make a fire. I sometimes felt like the man in the relationship, and that was really saying something.

"Bravo. I did sleep well, thank you. I marinated the steaks and they're ready to go on the barbecue."

"I was about to open a bottle of rosé. Can I get you a glass or are you laying off the alcohol tonight?"

"I'd be happy to have a glass, but I won't be drinking much tonight. Thank you, honey."

I lit the torch stakes around the table outside to keep away the mosquitoes and set the table. I sat outside watching Harry grill.

"You cooked these steaks perfectly. This is just what I needed today, absolutely fortifying."

"You know how I love to please you, my angel."

Harry had finished nearly half the bottle of rosé.

"Samara, you seemed far away when we made love. Have any sexual experiences made you feel disconnected when it comes to sex? I felt like you were having sex because you felt you *needed* to, not because you *wanted* to."

I looked at him, my eyes like daggers in the moonlight.

"Why would you ask that?"

"There are signs that indicate something happened to you. You have dreams of being raped. You shriek if I touch you in that particular spot. Your lack of periods before we met. Your hypersexuality and disconnection. Your avoidant nature and difficulty being present. And it's not usual to be dating someone nearly three times your age. Not that I'm complaining," Harry said.

I appreciated that he was aware of me, but it wasn't something I wished to discuss. It was more suited to be handled with Scarlett.

"It's not like I uncovered anything new since the last time we spoke about it."

"I figured maybe you were working through it with your new therapist. You've seemed distant lately."

He was right; I had been more dismissive lately. I didn't like that Harry was probing into what I was discussing with Scarlett. It felt intrusive. I kept finding myself comparing him to her. It appeared that Scarlett's care for me was genuine. For better or worse, they were both quickly becoming the two most important people in my life.

I was realising there was something off with Harry. I felt resentment towards him because I felt like I was being used for his own selfish purposes.

A few weeks after meeting him, I had a dream where we were making love, but as he moved over me, a sudden wave of anxiety washed over me. It was then that his face turned into a raging lion mercilessly fucking me. The eyes looked vacant, with no emotion, just a dark void of nothingness. Like he was Hades, and I was Persephone being taken into the underworld, my innocence being vacuumed away with the last rays of daylight. That dream was still as clear as day in my mind.

I had another dream a week later that Harry lived in a red farmhouse surrounded by hay weeds, like something out of a horror film: tumbleweeds swirling by, scarecrows standing eerily in the distance, voodoo dolls pinned to the farmhouse door. I was peering in through a window of what was supposed to be his family home, except there was no family there. I saw him inside and there was a feast laid out. The seats were filled, but not with people. Instead, there were life-sized dummies posing as members of his family. It registered that he had murdered his whole family and was in an extreme state of psychological denial, pretending they all still existed. I woke up with a sharp scream.

He would always need and want more. Eventually, I knew I would run dry, until there was nothing left to take, until all of my light was swallowed, and I became a hollow shell of nothingness myself.

The next morning, I woke up relaxed and emotionally grounded, perhaps due to being out of London. I felt like I could enjoy where we were, and put my reservations about Harry to the side, at least while we were here. I slipped out of bed quietly so that I could have some time alone. I didn't like being disturbed in the mornings because it was my most sacred time of the day – my time for prayer, meditation, yoga, tai chi, my time of peace before the chaos of the world set in.

I stepped outside the cabin into the crisp, cool autumnal air and sat at the wooden table, where the sun was shining brightly upon me. I spent the remainder of the early morning on a blanket spread over the dewy grass, praying, meditating, and practising gentle yoga.

I brewed a pot of my daily elixir and then sliced golden kiwis, fresh pineapple chunks, and local blueberries. I sat in the fireplace room before waking Harry to do a morning reading. The card that I chose was about trusting in the Divine timing of events in my life, that I'm exactly where I need to be, doing exactly what I'm meant to be doing. It was encouraging to remember that we all have our own unique timing, and it is only futile to compare ourselves to the timing and blossoming of those around us.

I suspected patience and faith were two virtues I was meant to master in this life. Keeping the faith in the absence of little to no evidence was no easy feat. For most people, trusting without assurances seemed like a sign of being out of touch with reality.

And so what if people thought I'd lost my mind? Perhaps that was part of the point – to lose my mind and trust in the Divine so unconditionally, that no matter what, my faith would never waiver, even in the moments where it felt that I had hit absolute rock bottom. That was the only way to allow the Divine unrestricted access to my life – by trusting unconditionally, letting go of control, and absolutely surrendering to something greater than my individual self, to a higher power, to God.

I believed that God could take any form meaningful to each person—whether that's the Universe, eternal light, Love, Jesus, Buddha, Allah, one's higher self, spirit, or something else entirely.

As I sat in contemplation, a vision of the Tarot card *The Hanged Man* appeared to me. It symbolises a man in between worlds, like a bridge between heaven and earth. The card can represent wisdom, spirituality, but most importantly, seeing things from a different perspective. I felt that my entire life was defined by the essence of *The Hanged Man*. I was coming to realise that part of my purpose was to go against the grain, to follow my heart and intuition, knowing that, in Divine timing, I would be led to exactly where I needed to go. We are often not aware of just how much we are growing until one day when we wake up, we realise we have transformed from caterpillar to butterfly.

I whipped up crepes for breakfast. Harry shared his recipe with me when we moved in together. I made about a dozen, with caramelized bananas inside, and set out organic maple syrup and raspberry jam. Harry emerged, scruffy-haired and sleepy. He looked rather precious, like my grandfather, and I felt tender towards him.

"Good morning, my love." I kissed him on the forehead, feeling far less like the vicious hyena I had been yesterday. I wasn't sure how long this feeling would last before it might revert to a state of apathy, but I was trying to turn over a new leaf. As long as I was choosing to stay in the relationship, I felt I should at least make an effort to be fully present in it.

"Morning, darling. What a lovely breakfast. You've perfected my recipe. Did you sleep alright?"

"Splendidly," I answered, "aside from when I jolted out of bed from you touching me in the spot I asked you not to …."

"I pulled away when I saw your reaction. Another reason why I asked what I did the other night, but…not to worry, I won't get into that again this morning."

A little late for that.

"Another reason? What might the others be?"

"Honey, I just woke up. Let's park it until the evening. I'm sorry for mentioning it at all."

It was indeed too early for such conversations. I didn't want to spoil the day, especially when I was feeling fond of him. I was pissed off that he couldn't just apologise for touching me in my sleep when I had told him a number of times not to. Being my boyfriend didn't give him one hundred percent access to my body at all times. I would drop it for the sake of peace and attempt to assert my boundaries again in the evening. I brought the pancakes, fruit, and coffee outside to the sun-drenched wooden table.

"So I was thinking we could go on a hike today, leave around one-ish, and be back around five or six to relax and have time to meditate before dinner. How does that sound? The hike is supposed to have some beautiful scenic look-out points and a lovely summit."

"Whatever your heart desires, angel," Harry said, concentrating on his breakfast. "Though, the sky is looking rather grey and heavy with clouds, so I'm not sure how long the blessing of this sunshine will last us," he added.

"I checked the weather and there was no forecast of rain. Worst case, if we get unlucky, we get a little wet. I could use a bit of a cleansing from a weeping sky."

The idea of getting caught in the rain didn't bother me at all; I secretly hoped that we would. Being in the rain made me feel alive, connected to everything around me.

We finished our breakfast in silence. It was my belief that change was often a blessing of protection rather than a rejection or refusal of what we thought we wanted. What is actually happening is that God is bringing us what we want, just not in the way we expected.

I loved the thrill of change, but perhaps so much that change itself might have been something for me to change. I wasn't too concerned with what kind of chaos ensued as a result; it was freedom that mattered. I felt it would soon be time to say goodbye to Harry, and I was preparing myself for the inevitable. I wondered if our karmic contract and the lessons I needed to learn from him had already been fulfilled, or if there was more to come.

I didn't know how to unbind myself from what was beginning to feel like his entrapment, as if I was trapped in his snare and unable to find a way out. I felt as if I was a fly captured in a Venus flytrap, except this was a human level Venus love trap.

After breakfast, I changed into active attire and packed us a light lunch. The drive took about twenty-five minutes, during which I refrained from conversation with Harry, getting lost in my own world once again. So much for my early morning affections. It was safer in my internal reality.

The weather seemed to be holding up well, but when we arrived, there was only one other car there. Odd for a weekend, I thought—perhaps a foreboding sign of a storm brewing in the skies. I looked forward to retreating in nature to clear my head without many people around.

It was a pleasant walk to the summit, spent mostly in silence, absorbing the calming sounds of mother nature. Colourful arrays of trees enveloped us. At the first summit, a view of a seahorse-shaped lake could be seen, with shimmering rays of sunshine bouncing off pools of light. We paused and a ladybug landed on my ring finger. I made a wish for better days and my restored freedom, in whichever way that needed to manifest, according to Divine will.

After a few hours, we reached the summit, and I set out our lunch. Harry decided to read and lay in the sun for a while. I spent the next hour gathering wild blackberries to turn into a fresh blackberry pie.

I allowed myself to get lost in the magic of reconnecting with nature in silence. I tuned into my surroundings and accessed a deeper meditative state. The sounds of nature brought me into a hypnotic daze as I listened to the bees buzzing past my ears, the rustling of the wind, the fluttering of small white butterflies everywhere. The weather was idyllic. I filled two brown paper bags of blackberries.

Then the sky turned dark and stormy. I felt the first droplets of rain and made a dash across the rocks back to where I had left Harry and our things. His mood appeared grim when I found him. He was obviously pissed off with me for not taking his weatherman warning signs seriously, as the rain began to pellet down.

"Don't look so down, love. Come, it will be fun. We'll hurry down and make an adventure of it."

He grimaced at me as if I was to blame for the weather.

"C'est la vie. It's just rain and we can make a fire at the cottage to dry ourselves when we get back."

I walked back into the forest where there was some overhead coverage; Harry followed suit. Fifteen minutes into our descent, it started downpouring. Soon enough, we were soaked through and through. It felt like a true cleansing of body and soul, a reminder that we sometimes have to let the release happen, just as there comes a point when the clouds can no longer bear their weight before having to let go.

As I continued the descent, I thought about one of my romantic fantasies I'd had since childhood. I would passionately kiss my lover in the pouring rain as the thunder rumbled in the sky, feeling our naked bodies against each other. Lightning would strike, creating an orbit all around us. When the rain would let up, the sky would transform into golden rays of light, drying the wet ground and our vulnerable bodies. We would lay down on a blanket and make love as we took in sensations of life around us – the scent of the petrichor after the rain, the sound of the birds beginning to chirp as they emerged back into the light, the wet strands of our hair... As I came out of this reverie, I was saddened as I thought this fantasy would have to wait for the right lover, not the man behind me that was cursing just because we were getting a little bit wet.

I had brought a small bag of marijuana with me, which I would indulge upon later. I looked forward to returning to our temporary home and enjoying a fire in the midst of the rainstorm with a joint, good music, perhaps a bit of wine.

We arrived at our weekend home and Harry continued to be in a foul mood. I poured him a glass of whiskey on the rocks and left him to start the fire as I prepared dinner.

I pan-fried wild salmon and made a side dish of wild asparagus and broccoli. I looked up a recipe for the blackberry pie, whipped it up, and set the pie into the oven to cook. Once all of that was done, I got out my joint rolling supplies. I lit up the altar candles in the dining room, picked a Beatles playlist, starting with the song 'Within You, Without You,' and disappeared into my own world once more. I cherished music and its ability to reconnect me to myself. This song, my 'song of the summer,' as I called it, seemed to do the trick in returning me to a state of peace.

I finished rolling the joint, set the table, and called Harry to the table. I despised domestic affairs, mainly because of the traditional roles still prevalent in society. It felt suffocating to my soul. I would feel better if it was less conventional. Perhaps if I were with a woman, it would feel more bearable? I guess ultimately, I didn't want normalcy as it seemed to come with expectations. I knew I would always dream of elephants with wings, of tigers that could sing.

Harry seemed calmer, in part because I kept intentionally refilling his glass of whiskey. We were both drinking more than usual. I finished eating the salmon with thoughts about when and how I was going to leave Harry. When was the right time? Probably no better time than the present, right? If I wasn't in love and happy anymore, then what was the point? I went into the kitchen to take the blackberry pie out of the oven and set it to cool.

As I returned to the table, 'Yesterday,' was playing. I hoped to chill and just listen to music, but my plan of getting Harry drunk so he would leave me in peace seemed to backfire. He was looking sloshed.

"So. You seem to be irritable and in a distant mood after we make love. Would you care to talk about that?"

It didn't feel like 'making love' anymore. It felt like another one of the duties that was expected of me. I won't deny the sex itself was sinfully satisfying and erotic, but it was not making love. I believed it was a potential replay of past traumatic events that I was trying to work out with him.

Harry was likely referring to the deep sadness that can follow sex, known as postcoital dysphoria. An ex had once pointed out my displays of sadness afterward, which was disconcerting, as I hadn't been aware of it until he mentioned it. But I couldn't deny the feelings of emptiness I had after sex. I didn't know if it was past trauma being subconsciously triggered, or that I was with the wrong sex altogether. Nothing was out of the question in my mind.

I had tried to dismiss the notion, but hearing it again from Harry made it harder to deny that there might be some truth to it. Yet, because it came from a man I no longer felt in love with, I couldn't help but wonder if it was really about me or if it stemmed from his conditional love. I decided to not respond. I excused myself from the table to go smoke my joint in the bathtub and locked the door behind me.

Chapter Eight – 'Are You Having Fun Up There?'

Harry and I headed back to London the next morning, eager to return home and settle back into our usual routines. Gloomy Sunday passed by, Monday was any other day, and then I found myself back in Scarlett's office on Tuesday. Light was shining brightly into her office, and we were both wilting in the lingering warmth of an Indian summer. I dove straight into where we had left off.

"You asked about my family's history with secrets. When I was about sixteen, I was upstairs in my bedroom. Our house had multiple floors, with balconies overlooking each level, so it was easy to hear conversations from anywhere. My ears perked up when I overheard talk of a half-brother who lived in Sweden—this was news to me. I descended the stairs, sat down at the dinner table, looked at my mum and said, "So I have a Swedish half-brother?"

"Sounds like heavy news for an ordinary school night. Where did the conversation go from there?"

"I found out that my mum and sister had known for years. I was aware of all of this until my dad's death when I was 21, but never felt I could ask him about it. My half-sister, from my dad's first marriage, wasn't even aware of our brother until she read my dad's will, and it was only then that she found out."

"I wonder what his reasons were to keep your brother hidden. It seems that his secrets weighed him down, ate at his soul. I wonder if it makes you feel closer to him to keep secrets in your own life. Why not try and design a different framework for yourself?"

I twisted the aquamarine ring on my finger as I thought about that. Scarlett waited, observing my movement. I found it difficult to think when being watched.

"I think my father coped by keeping certain things to himself. I still believe everything happens as it is supposed to. We just don't know the Divine plan. His self-destruction may have been the very lesson, spiritually speaking, that he needed to learn in this life. If he hadn't died then, would I be sitting in this office with you, seeking a different path in life?"

"You say everything is divinely perfect, and I'm not arguing. But if you don't want to continue this same pattern of hiding aspects of yourself, then you'd do well to examine how you feel about secrets in your own life. Are you finding comfort in them, or do you long to be authentically who you are and still be loved for it?"

"It's been a coping mechanism, but I no longer want to hide my true self from the world."

Scarlett gave me a knowing look but didn't pry any further.

"Come, let's sit on the floor. I brought some activities for us," Scarlett said, scattering colored pencils, blank paper, and an assortment of rocks playfully across the floor.

I wondered if she intended this activity to help me open up and shift from my mind into my body, though I wasn't sure if it would make a difference.

"I'd like you to create a family tree with these rocks. Designate each rock to a different family member, then place them in relation to each other, whether that's closeness between them, marital relations, etc. Then we can talk about how you feel you fit into the family tree."

I stared at her, reflecting on what it felt like to be so close to her. I wasn't sure what insight she might procure from such an activity, but I decided to give it a go. I chose a somewhat demented looking rock for myself and laid that to the side. I chose a rock with a crevice in it to signify my father.

I chose an oval, smooth-shaped pebble for my mother, and the rest I chose at random.

I placed the mother rock next to the father rock, my sister's rock just below our parents, the half-sister and half-brother off to the side of my father, and both of my grandparents as pairs above my mother and father. I placed a rock for my father's fiancée off to the side, with the extended family members I didn't have a relationship with any longer. I looked up at Scarlett.

"And where does your rock fit in?"

"Perhaps... here?" I placed the demented rock next to my sister, under my parents.

"Is that where you feel you fit in best in terms of closeness to other family members?"

"I spent the most time with my parents and sister, so they were my direct family. I was never as close with anyone else in the family. I'm not sure I fit into the family at all. The only person I was ever close with was my sister Inez. She was all I had." I moved my rock off to the side.

The sun was pouring in through the windows, creating a hazy hue between us, and I felt silly playing these games. I hoped Scarlett would move on. I was starting to perspire, perhaps either from our proximity to each other or the sun beating down on my skin. We looked into each other's eyes for a moment before she scooped the rocks to the side and placed the blank paper in front of me.

"Now, I would like you to draw your impression of the masculine. What form does it take? Is it a figure of a man, or something else? Try not to think about it so much and just flow with whatever comes to you."

I chose a brown-coloured pencil, to appear as if I wasn't thinking too hard.

"I should warn you; my drawing skills are not the best."

"No matter, whatever comes to you Samara."

I tentatively drew a tall, lopsided figure looming over the blankness of a page, like a phantom in the night. I drew eyes that ended up looking simultaneously possessed and expressionless, a flat-lined mouth, and wild curly hair going off in all directions. That was all I could manage, but looking at the end result, the expression in the man's face made up for the lack of other distinguished features in the body. He looked like a death-eater. I tossed the pencil to the side when I had finished, frustrated.

Scarlett asked what its name was. I picked up a black pencil and scribbled 'Vladimir' above the figure. I felt uneasy with these activities.

Scarlett gazed deeply in my eyes. "That's a scary looking man, Samara."

"I'm not sure why the eyes look possessed, but that's how they always come out. I'm not sure we can call him a man. I know he's scary. He looks like he's about to murder us both with an axe," I laughed.

"I notice you often use humour to deflect uncomfortable situations."

"I'm not so sure how seriously to take this."

"I'd like you to draw yourself, in any way you like. Include the setting. Again, try not to think about it too much, just put the pencil to the paper."

I drew myself sitting atop a grey, puffy cloud with my legs dangling over the side, looking down at a house surrounded by steep, rugged mountains. It was raining big blue raindrops.

"What would you like to say to that Self of yours?" Scarlett asked.

I took a red-coloured pencil and wrote, "Are you having fun up there?"

Scarlett laughed at this, as did I, for we both knew I was half here, half there.

I was now becoming quite comfortable on the carpet with Scarlett. Sitting on the floor so close to each other added a new dimension to our interactions. I realised that it was not the sunlight that was making me perspire, but the proximity of closeness to her. It was almost too much to bear. I toyed with the coloured pencils, zigzagging a red one on the carpet between us, then looking up at Scarlett. I picked up a green-coloured pencil, and then a yellow, repeating the process, each time dragging it a bit closer to where she was sitting. I found myself unconsciously playing with my skirt, my gaze trailing along the cotton as it draped over my long, tanned legs. Scarlett simply watched me as I worked hypnotically to draw her in.

"That's a beautiful skirt," Scarlett said.

I smiled sweetly, resting the side of my head on the palm of my hand, continuing to gaze into her eyes. Scarlett brought us both out of the trance, looked up at the clock, and suggested we return to our chairs. I returned to my seat begrudgingly.

"How have things been with Harry?" she asked.

I sighed.

"We had a bit of a disaster weekend get-away. I find it difficult to be around him constantly. I feel he can't be there for me in the way I need him to be."

"What are you searching for in your relationship with Harry? You continue to stay yet seem somewhat apathetic towards him most of the time."

"I still feel a deep connection to him. My life felt so ungrounded when we met. He was older and established and part of me wanted someone to protect me. Now, my emotional needs aren't being fulfilled."

Scarlett bit her lower lip and lifted her hand from the arm of her chair towards her head, pressing two fingers into her temple, looking at me as if deliberating whether she should share what was on her mind.

"You have this fragility..." She paused. "Fragility isn't quite the right word. It's more like this delicate aspect to you, like that of a butterfly. If someone were to try to capture and contain you, it would destroy the essence of your being. You have this sense of freedom, rebelliousness, inherent desire to not become too attached to anything – perhaps as a means of self-preservation, or a desire to fly free – and at the same time, there's this need to feel grounded and safe. It's like the two sides are competing."

"Well, maybe I'm not meant to have any path, except to float in and out of people's lives."

"If your path was simply to be a butterfly, then I don't think you would be here with me, delving deeper into your life." Scarlett paused, as if thinking this over, before she said, "I had a dream about you last week."

"Oh, yeah?" I asked, perking up. "Tell me about it."

"We were on a beach, standing at the edge of the water. Our plan was to swim across the water to reach another shore that we couldn't see, to venture off on what seemed to be an instinctive, spiritual journey. I was naked and walking into the water, and you walked with me, but your clothes were still on. I suggested you take them off for the long swim, but you were reluctant. The dream ended with me saying, 'Well at least take off your socks!'"

I burst out laughing to the point of tears. Scarlett joined in my laughter. Clearly the message was that if we were going to trek into unknown territory together, we had to be fully in, and I had to be vulnerable with her. The release of mutual laughter also felt like a release of the erotic tension circulating in the air.

After my laughing subsided, I said, "Well, keeping my clothes on doesn't sound like me. Normally, I walk around naked every chance that I get."

Scarlett smiled as if to say she didn't doubt it.

"You have a playful, seductive energy about you, Samara."

I fiddled with my crucifix and gave her a mischievous smile. Her eyes met me in return, glistening with amusement until she looked down at her watch to tell me our time had come to an end. I paid her and walked out the door, but not without one final tantalising smile.

*Chapter Nine – Rapunzel, Rapunzel, Let Down Your Golden
Hair!*

Three days later, Harry returned from work, huffing
and puffing as he opened the door. I was snugly curled up like
a cat reading, *A Flight from the Enchanter*, by Iris Murdoch.
Harry stopped in his tracks, looking as though he was waiting
for an explanation.

"Yes, mon chéri?" I asked.

"Didn't you hear me at the door with the keys? I
mean, it's unbelievable!" Harry exclaimed.

"Apologies, I was engrossed in this book and the
pigeon is exceptionally loud today," I said, gesturing in the
direction of the windowsill where the pigeons cooed the day
away. "Had a bad day?" I asked.

"It was fine until I come home to our flat and get
treated like an invisible ghost."

I scowled at him, then returned to my book.

He ran towards me, knelt next to me, and opened his
eyes alarmingly wide. "Smile a little. You're talking to your
lover, not the grim reaper."

I couldn't help but laugh, which infuriated Harry
more.

"Have you prepared the mise en place for dinner
tonight?" Harry asked.

I closed my book with a sharp thud. "Yes Harry, and
bought all of the ingredients you asked me to, but seeing the
way you're behaving, I'd rather not be around you. You can
cook your own dinner. I'm going out."

"And where might you be heading?" asked Harry

"Far away from you. I'll have a few drinks, smoke a
few joints, see where the night takes me."

My Italian friends were in town. I called my friend Sofia and made plans with her. I headed out the door without another word to Harry and picked up a bottle of Châteauneuf-du-Pape down the street before hailing a taxi. I felt relief at escaping Harry for several hours. I felt like he was destroying my youth and that I was being dragged into old age with him. I wanted to feel young and alive again.

There was the conflict of wanting to free myself, but not knowing how. I was beginning to wonder if there was any feeling worse than the feeling of entrapment, even if it was only an illusion. The feeling of being a prisoner locked away in a castle was beginning to feel all too real. I wondered if I liked to imagine myself like a Rapunzel character trapped in a tower of my own making.

I heard a crackle of thunder and rain started falling. I paid the driver, rang Sofia's bell, and entered her Japanese styled sanctuary. I threw down my coat and dropped on to the leather sofa.

"My love, what's been going on?" Sofia asked me.

"I feel like I've outgrown Harry. I'm unsure of what to do and where to go if I leave him. At least with him I've felt some sense of security. I just keep going back and forth in my mind and he's driving me mad."

I poured glasses of wine for both of us. I was desperate for some girl talk. Thank goodness for girlfriends.

"If I know anything about you, it's how independent and strong you are. You just have to trust yourself. You always land on your feet. Don't let Harry be the first to dampen your spirit like this."

I leaned across the marble coffee table and kissed Sofia on her forehead and held her hand in gratitude. I picked up my glass of wine and we wished each other cheers. I drank a wholesome sip of the wine which proved to be exquisite, and then sprawled across the sofa.

"Will anyone else be joining us this evening?" I asked her.

"Yes, Zena — I believe you met her once when you were visiting me in Rome. She should be here any moment."

Zena rang the bell and came inside dripping wet from the storm. I didn't recognise her, but she seemed to recognise me.

"Samara! How wonderful to see you again!" she said, hugging me affectionately.

I pretended I knew her and greeted her with the same affection.

"So lovely to see you, Zena! Very happy you can join our little impromptu party."

I revel in the company of strangers when accompanied with wine on rainy nights, especially friends of Sofia's. I poured Zena a glass of wine, 'finishing school' values still intact, and we ordered sushi before we became too drunk to remember to eat.

"Zena, I was just catching Sofia up on my relationship. I've been living with a bi-polar, sixty-year-old man for the past year and our relationship is on the rocks. Even though I am scared to leave him, I am realising I just find much more peace in my own company."

"What's holding you back from making a move?" Zena asked.

I refilled my wine and lit the candles on the coffee table.

"My emotions are all over the place. One day I'm totally sure of leaving him, and the next I get wrapped back into it, like a spider being trapped in its own web. There seems to be a strong karmic connection between us. Anyway,

I don't want to bore you. Let's drink this wine into oblivion, shall we?"

I searched in my handbag for my joint rolling supplies and realised I forgot the rolling tobacco.

I asked Sofia if she had some.

"Yes, darling, in that green leather bag."

I took the liberty of rolling three joints so that I wouldn't have to do so later when my hands would likely be shaking. Just as I finished rolling, our food arrived. We ordered salmon and yellowtail sashimi, a variety of different rolls, edamame, miso soup, and crispy black cod to share.

"Sofia, how long are you in London for?"

"Sadly, I am returning to Rome tomorrow afternoon because of my work schedule. I'm opening up a theatre production company with my friend Marco. You must come visit when it's all finished!"

"I'd love to come see it and visit you. And how exciting about the theatre production company! I'm so glad you're doing something that you love."

"Samara, remind me again how you both met. Did you go to school together?" Zena asked.

"I went to business school in Switzerland. Don't ask me why; I just didn't have a clue of what I wanted to do at the time. I don't regret it because I was able to have internships around the world. I worked in Tokyo, Barcelona, Hanoi, and Vienna. Living in Switzerland and going to an international school was an educational experience in and of itself. But in the years since I graduated, I've been following my own spiritual path, learning about sound healing and shamanism, learning reiki, writing poetry, learning about life and love through some insane relationships. We'll see where it all leads."

"I went to fine art school here in London and I was following my passion like you. I had trouble finding suitable work once I graduated and my father was persistent in telling me to find a more reliable source of income, so I let my love for painting slip away from me. I haven't picked up a paintbrush in over a year and it makes me sad to think about," Zena said to me, her voice trailing off.

"Yes, I understand where you are coming from completely," I said.

"I feel very fortunate to not have to depend on a parent for approval. I think that one of the most difficult things about following one's dreams is breaking away from the family, breaking away from what is expected of you."

I clapped my hands together and brought our plates to the kitchen.

"So! Shall we go have a digestive outside? Is there an umbrella anywhere around here?" I asked.

Fortunately, there was one big enough to cover the three of us. Zena refilled our wine glasses and we ventured outside in the rain for the first two joints. We came back inside and put on some music. In my altered state of mind, my thoughts turned to Scarlett. Thinking about her was becoming my preferred pastime.

I could no longer ignore the feelings of ecstasy I felt in Scarlett's presence. It was as if I knew her from the moment I met her. It felt like it was mutual.

My favourite song, I Can Fly, by Lana del Rey started playing on the speakers. The lyrics reminded me that I too could fly away from it all. The door to the cage was open; I would just have to realise it myself.

A text message came in from Harry. It was a reminder that it was ten pm. That's it. And then I remembered – Harry had persuaded me to agree to an eleven pm curfew! I hazily consented to it one night when I vomited after too many drinks. I wanted to impose strict restrictions on myself. I could hear his voice in my head saying, "Samara, we agreed to this…"

I showed my girlfriends the message to give them an idea of what I was dealing with. They urged me to find a way to detach myself from him.

As an act of retaliation, I opened the large bottle of sake we'd ordered. I poured three tall glasses, we said cheers to each other, and I lit up the third joint inside. We couldn't be bothered to move from our places at that point in the evening.

I took a hit, passed it on, and replied to Harry – 'meow meow meow, meow meow meow, meow meow, MEOW MEOW MEOW.' I left it at that and shut off my phone.

Zena and Sofia were engrossed in their own conversation. They didn't seem to mind me lost in my own reveries.

It was after midnight when I decided to head home. I was feeling exhausted suddenly. I kissed and hugged Zena and Sofia goodbye. I hoped the night would end with a heavy thud on my pillow, bringing me into my sweet dream land.

As the taxi pulled up to my flat, I noticed the lights were still on and I felt a sinking feeling. I was feeling a bit dizzy and did not feel like seeing Harry. I paid the driver and ascended the stairs, taking long deep breaths into my heart to try and ground myself.

I unlocked the door and found Harry sitting in our bedroom staring at me. I changed into my nightdress for bed, all the while feeling his eyes penetrating like lasers into my being. I went into the bathroom to wash my face and brush my teeth, but jolted when I spotted Harry's face in the mirror, behind me, still staring. Finally, he spoke.

"Well, did you have a nice evening?" he asked, his voice laced with sarcasm.

I finished brushing my teeth and walked past him to the bed.

"Yes, my evening was fine. Thank you," I replied.

"So, how many drinks did you have then?" he asked.

"Maybe a bottle of wine or two. I lost count somewhere along the way."

"What's wrong with you? We agreed that we would only drink a glass or two of wine once a week, together, and you go off totally disregarding our rules and doing whatever you want. That's not a true partnership. I think you need to go to an AA meeting darling, because you are out of control."

"We never came up with these 'rules' together. What are you, my father? I don't even remember where the hell that absurd eleven pm curfew came from. And then you're telling me to limit my drinking and only drink under your supervision? I'm 25. I don't need my partner telling me when I can or can't drink, or what time I need to be home. Go to your meetings all you want, but don't drag me into it. I'm going to bed. Perhaps you can go to sleep thinking about being a little bit less controlling."

"Being in a relationship requires responsibility. Disregarding all that we agreed to, not honouring the relationship, amounts to being irresponsible. No one would put up with the way you act! You are lucky you are with me because any other boyfriend would have kicked you to the curb by now."

I responded by turning off the light.

"Good night, Harry."

I passed out quite quickly, as I usually do after drinking and smoking, only to be woken up again around 2 am with a terrifying jolt. I started hyperventilating and could hardly calm myself down, only to realise it was because Harry tried touching me and fingering me in my sleep again, provoking the rape dream. We had a serious argument about this before when I told him he was not permitted to touch me sexually in my sleep – it always caused a PTSD reaction for me. When I finally calmed down and my breathing levelled out, I turned to the monster sharing the bed with me.

"What the hell is wrong with *you*? How many times do I have to ask you not to touch me in my sleep?"

"You must have been having a nightmare. I swear I haven't touched you."

"Oh, then did I just imagine your fingers up my vagina? Is that it?"

"Probably. It's not the first time you've woken up from nightmares like this. I was only stroking your hair."

I glared at him and turned over to face the wall, cursing him under my breath. I tossed and turned for a while and eventually fell back asleep, until four am crawled around and the same thing happened again; only this time, I felt Harry's penis inside of me from behind. I shot up again, foggy and confused, trying to catch my breath.

"What the actual fuck Harry!" I yelled in his face.

"Darling, what is it...?"

"You know damn well what it is. Are you now going to tell me I didn't just feel your penis inside of me?"

"You didn't just feel my penis inside of you," he said.

"You are a twisted fuck. Go fuck yourself."

I got out of the bed and stuffed my pillow under my arm to go sleep in the other bedroom.

"Good, please do sleep in the other bedroom. Do you see the effects that your drinking causes on our relationship? I can't be having your toxicity around me while I'm in the process of changing my meds, so please make plans to leave and live elsewhere. I will give you a one-month grace period to make other arrangements."

This wasn't the first time Harry had told me to leave, basically kicking me out and, out of the kindness of his heart, allowing me a 'grace' period. He always tried to play the card as if I was living in his flat, which technically it was, but only because we had to put it under his name for the rental contract. We couldn't put my name on the contract because I didn't have a bank account set up yet, but our rent and bills were split equally.

I finally fell asleep with thoughts that his actions themselves were actually my grace because I had been looking for an excuse to take action and to love myself enough to end this toxicity.

The following morning, I woke up with the sound of my bedroom door opening and Harry peeking inside. He opened the curtains and then lifted the covers to join me in bed. I was too drained to even deflect, so I just stared at him from my pillow.

"How did you sleep?" he asked me.

"How do you think?" I replied.

"Listen, darling. I didn't sleep well either and I'm sorry about last night. I love you, Samara. Let me into your life, as your lover, your boyfriend, your partner."

I couldn't think clearly, and I felt like a vulnerable, emotional basket case. All I could do was cry. I wanted to believe him. I wanted someone I could trust, someone I could rely on. I was looking for tenderness and I was tired of the constant emotional upheaval. I simply wanted to be loved.

"You know, the problems in our relationship aren't as bad as you make them out to be. It's actually very normal. There will always be ups and downs. Look at how much you've grown since we met."

"How do you explain your behaviour last night? Telling me I need to go to AA, and then you wake me up triggering my PTSD not once, but twice, and tell me that it's all in my head?"

"Okay, I have a confession to make. It's true that I touched you in your sleep, but only because I was doing an experiment to see how you would react. I was only trying to help you. I wanted to see if I touched you in that spot again, if you would be again disturbed. Turns out you were, so the experiment was worthwhile. I want to help you to make sense of what happened to you in your childhood and it's best if things come out to the surface with me, someone who can be there with you, someone that can coach you through the process."

"I never gave you permission to test your hypotheses on me. Did you really need to wake me up a second time, to validate your experiment by taking the liberty to stick your cock in me while I was sleeping? It's disgusting, Harry."

"You think all I care about is sex, but half the time, I don't feel safe around you sexually."

I looked at him in bewilderment, lifted the sheets, and got up to move away from him.

"You're always jumping on me when I've got work and other things to do and I'm always happy to comply. It's not accurate to say that I'm the one always pushing sex on you. Do you think that's very fair?"

Another one of Harry's predictable questions he would often ask me.

"Which one of us has already ruined several marriages and relationships because you couldn't keep it in your pants? It's not fair to act as if you were doing me a favour when you were ready to satisfy my needs without complaint. I don't feel like I'm in love with you anymore.

You've been volatile this summer and I've been more than patient. I mean, I even *agreed* to your absurd eleven pm curfew. I don't need my own boyfriend constantly threatening to throw me and my things out on the streets when he's the one acting like an asshole. I'll make arrangements to leave you. Someone else can put up with your shit. it's not going to be me anymore."

Chapter Ten – From Caterpillar to Butterfly

I asked Harry not to speak to me during the remaining time that we would be living together. I didn't need him creeping back in my life as I tried to make arrangements to leave. I slept in the other bedroom, and so when Tuesday came around, I was eager to sort out some of my life with Scarlett.

I spent the weekend focusing on my growing affections for Scarlett, rather than dwelling on where I was going to live. My heart raced as the taxi neared 113 Sumner Place. I pressed the button for the 1950's style bird cage elevator and attempted to level out my breathing as I ascended to her lair.

Scarlett looked brighter, more pleased than usual to see me and spoke first for once.

"How are you, Samara?"

"I've left Harry."

"Okay…" Scarlett replied, dragging out the word. "And what was the catalyst for that?"

"He's holding me back. I have decided I must make a meaningful sacrifice of Harry on the altar of life."

"Yes, but was it a rash decision? Did something in particular prompt it?"

I recapped the events from last Thursday, ending with, "And then he touched me sexually in my sleep without my permission. And a few hours later he actually started having sex with me while I was sleeping, sending me into two separate near panic attacks. I basically told him to go fuck himself. Now I've got a month to sort out where to live."

"And how are you feeling about all of this now?"

I looked out the window and twisted the aquamarine ring on my finger.

"Mainly, I feel a sense of empowerment, of liberation at deciding to leave him. At the same time, I'm afraid because I don't know where I'm going to live if I leave him. I don't know many other people here, don't have a job tying me here, don't have a bank account set up, so what do I do? Head off to Timbuktu again? I have a family home in the states, but I don't feel safe going back there either. I feel like an orphan with no home to go to."

"I think it's best not to let yourself go into a state of emotional overwhelm. Just take one step at a time. Only focus on what you have to do in this moment."

Making a decision wouldn't have weighed so heavily on me if my heart wasn't already tied to Scarlett. Because, more than anything, I wanted to stay here and find a way to have her in my life forever. I was willing to sacrifice myself in order to maintain my relationship with her.

"I had a vision of you, almost as if in a dream, or in a hypnopompic state. You had taken on the character of Golem from *The Lord of the Rings*, and behind you was an impressive pile of treasures. You were wearing the ring of power, but you kept disappearing on me. You would take the ring of power on and off, disappearing and then re-appearing. I told you to put the ring around you as a necklace, to ground yourself within its power. Instead, you tried to give me the ring – presumably in an attempt to give your power away – and so I put it around you as a necklace. Once it was around you, you transformed from Golem into Yoda, into an enlightened spiritual master full of wisdom. You no longer felt you needed to hide yourself, or give your power away anymore, but rather you were now learning to embrace it."

"A powerful omen in relation to recent events with Harry. Perhaps you psychically picked up on me taking my power back from Harry and learning self-respect.

"What was apparent to me was your elusiveness. I want to make sure that you are not projecting seductiveness because you see it as your only sense of self-worth."

"How do I come across as seductive to you?"

"Oh, you've just got the whole thing going on – your mannerisms, the way you look at me, the way you speak, your facial expressions, the sensuality and enchantment about you," she said, with a wave of her hand.

One might imagine how much it pleased me to hear that my beloved found me enchanting. Whether Scarlett was mentioning the enchantment simply for therapeutic purposes or there was more to the story, I considered it progress. Truly, I felt it was she who was doing the enchanting. Her eyes sparkled like fireworks in a charcoal sky.

"If I were younger, and we were at a café together, I would say that you were flirting with me," Scarlett said in her low, sultry voice, inviting a deeper exploration of the energy present in the room.

"Well, I flirt with everyone. It's just the way I am," I laughed.

"Maybe there's something to explore about how your relationship with Harry relates to your relationship with your father. As you said, there are similarities. I think it will be useful to recognise what you were trying to figure out with Harry, so you don't follow the same pattern and attract partners like Harry in the future."

"I do think part of it has to do with my relationship with my father. I believe I may have been sexually abused by him when I was a child. I don't even like to say that because it's not yet something concrete and crystal clear in my mind, but I feel this is the safest place to share that."

I paused, gathering my thoughts.

"I always had a feeling there was *something*, a void where there was once a black hole of pain. As much as I tried to pretend this feeling didn't exist, I couldn't shake the feeling that there was something wrong."

Scarlett appeared to be listening attentively.

"Starting from around the age of six, I had nightmares of being chased and raped. These dreams were so frequent that I just learned to live with them. I wasn't even fazed in the dream itself. Rather than running from the abuser in the dream, as I had for many years, the dreams switched tempo. I would just lie down, close my eyes, detach from my body, and offer up the shell of what was left of me. It was as if the abuse had gone on for so long that the soul had already been lost. Nothing else could be taken from me."

"Only in the last year have the dreams become somewhat less frequent, but the night terrors and screaming out for help in my sleep remain. I think the healing work I did helped to an extent. My inner dreamer no longer had to chase after me to heal what was left unacknowledged. All of that being said, my body still holds the memory of the trauma. When Harry touches me in my pelvic area, near to the sacral chakra, it prompts an unconscious fear response. I think it's a PTSD reaction from what happened. I think, despite my own personal efforts, far more healing on the matter is needed. I've hardly spoken about it, in truth."

Scarlett seemed to be with me.

"It makes sense that you would feel empty without much of a connection to your body. Leaving your body was your way of coping with pain that was too much to bear. You did what you had to do, because very likely, the pain of remembering could have been more destructive for you. It was your way of protecting yourself."

"Perhaps repressing the memories helped me get here today, to be able to discuss this with you without falling apart at the seams, to be able to function in day to day life. But because it's buried so deeply within me, despite my many symptoms and behavioural reactions, I still question myself. Sometimes even to reflect on it makes me feel a sense of guilt, but where else would it be coming from, I am then left wondering.

"I'm humbled by your courage in opening up to me. Repressed memories can be a controversial topic in psychotherapy, but this is your truth, and your experience. I believe you, and I want you to know that," Scarlett said sincerely.

A sense of relief welled up inside of me. Here was someone that could share the weight of my burden, so at least I wouldn't have to feel so alone in it all. I smiled at her.

"Anyway," I said, "though I have no fully formed conscious memory, perhaps that is a gift, a form of obscuring grace. There is a saying that the Divine grants destiny with compassion. The Divine grants us only what we need, what is useful. What is restricted, denied, withheld, is often saturated with grace."

"Samara, you have a beautiful soul. There is something within you that is raw, precious, and full of inner strength. Yet, your sensitivity has led you to hide your true self. That's why you have so many defences, to protect that vulnerable part of you. It's also why you feel disconnected from yourself, as if you lack a sense of identity. You are like a butterfly, but remember, a butterfly's wings aren't just for escape—they can also be used to land and feel at home."

"That reminds me of what my Sri Lankan friend said to me once. 'The butterfly is the only one who lacks the ego because he was a caterpillar before.' In other words, the butterfly only became its beautiful and free self after the humbling experience of living as a caterpillar, going through certain sorrows and pains before it could transcend the confines of its cocoon."

"I sense that within you lies a profound quest, an authentic search for something that is yet to be fully unveiled. You're amidst the journey of discovery, navigating the pathways of your own essence. Though the destination remains veiled, trust that all things come in time. Much like the acorn's transformation into the mighty oak or the caterpillar's metamorphosis into a majestic butterfly, you too shall land upon the destiny inscribed for you."

"Ultimately, we are all just finding our way out of the mud. And you know, *eventually,* we'll make it to the other side," Scarlett said, somewhat apathetically.

That brought us to the end of our session. I muttered something about how I would reflect on what she had said. After the usual exchange, she opened her arms to hug me. I relished in the comforting embrace of her presence, feeling an overwhelming sense of love for her that consumed every part of my being. I glided out the door feeling weightless.

Chapter Eleven – Eventually

Harry presented me with a bouquet of red roses and truffles when I returned from my session with Scarlett, apologising for his behaviour, in attempts to make amends and restrain me from leaving. Thursday it was champagne and a drawn bath of Himalayan salt and essential oils. I tried my best to not forget the underlying unhealthy aspects of our relationship. I had a battle going on within me of trying to stay strong in my decision to leave Harry, and another part of me that wanted to trust in my relationship and believe that this was just a rough patch.

Scarlett was the perceived light that kept reminding me what a healthy relationship is supposed to look like. She made me feel seen for my inner beauty rather than my outer beauty.

I went through the days somewhat mechanically, behaving stronger externally than I felt internally. On Friday, as the skies darkened and the heavy clouds released buckets of rain, tears began to stream down my cheeks. The thought of losing Harry and feeling totally alone in the world felt like too much to bear. Losing him would feel like losing my father all over again. I couldn't imagine enduring another mourning process like that, and yet I thought perhaps that's exactly what I needed to release the grief of what was left unfinished with my father: of not being able to say goodbye, of leaving the mystery unresolved, of feeling like I never understood him, and did he ever, me? It would tear me to pieces, but that was maybe the beginning of the creative, emotional breakthrough that I needed.

The weekend proved to be sunny and perhaps the last stretch of temperate weather preceding winter. I seized the opportunity to recharge in the fresh, crisp air at the park. I told myself to trust that the answers would come in time.

Harry was staying at his other home for the rest of the weekend, looking after the girls.

I walked down the rose garden pathway and had a coffee at a table outside a café. I thought of Scarlett, and the thought felt like ecstasy.

It was like entering another world, every Tuesday at eleven with Scarlett. It was as if time stopped, and nothing else in the world existed. It was more like nothing else in the world mattered, like having a holy communion with God, and stepping out of ordinary reality, into our reality. She was bringing back to life something that had been missing from me for too long, perhaps lifetimes too long.

These blissful musings carried me into our next session. After we both sat down, Scarlett asked how I felt after the last session with her.

"Happy and alive," I told her, the first words that came to me. No point in trying to filter the joy that our session had elicited in me.

Scarlett laughed. "What do you think of the idea of the abuse of power?" She asked me.

I sought to determine the intention of her sudden question. Her inquiry seemed to suggest a curiosity of how an abuse of power might be received by me. There was an air of darkness in the way she asked me, something that felt subtly dangerous. Or simply, her aim was to highlight the existing power dynamic between us.

"I think abuse needs to be defined. But if the person on the receiving end of the 'abuse' does not feel in any way abused, if there is mutual consent, even if it's 'against the rules', perhaps it is more complex to answer. The exception would be if the person giving consent was not mentally stable or in some way unfit to give consent, such as someone who is too young to be aware of what is going on."

Obviously, the dynamic I was referring to was in the context of us feeling free to colour outside the lines, though it was impossible to tell what Scarlett had in mind.

"I think there is a dissonance between what is inside of you and what you project. It's important for us to seek to integrate these two elements within you."

I smirked. How could it be that she was voicing what hadn't quite yet landed about what I felt about her – that there was something paradoxical in her own nature that left me wondering what side she was truly operating from.

"Even the way you smile," she continued, "is part of your allure. And it makes me sad because I think your natural playfulness was taken advantage of when you were little."

"Perhaps," I said, wiping the smile off my face. Seeing her simply brought a smile to my face; it's not something that I could help. Her energy penetrated my entire being.

"I feel that your flirtatious nature became ingrained because you saw it as a way to earn love and affection. I want you to realise that you can form intimate relationships without bringing sex into the equation."

Scarlett paused at the sound of mumblings outside her office. She walked over to the door which opened to a few construction workers doing God knows what to the beloved bird cage elevator. With all of the authority and power in the world, she commanded them to silence for the remainder of our session. I admired her assertiveness.

She re-entered.

"Do you think you use your sexuality as a way to become more intimate and connected?"

"I'm affectionate and I think physical touch helps people break through barriers. My intention is for connection, but perhaps people view it as an intention for sex. In the last year or two I feel I have been more vulnerable and open than ever before. I just think you haven't been able to see that side of me yet. It's difficult for me to be myself in a professional setting when the attention is directed on me. I also naturally feel an attraction to you, so I'm not surprised if my sexuality is 'present' in the room."

I was surprised at the words spilling from my mouth. I didn't expect to tell her that I was attracted to her.

"You can't be *attracted* to me," she said dismissively, as if I had said the most astounding thing in the world.

I laughed internally because here we were discussing the importance of not using my sexuality as a means of deepening intimate relationships, and yet I was commenting on my attraction to her. But someone had to acknowledge what was inevitably floating between us in the room, and it certainly didn't feel like it belonged to me alone. Nevertheless, I was willing to 'take one for the team.'

"There are other ways for us to grow in closeness outside the realm of sex, and besides, I don't think you'd feel fulfilled if I gave in to your seduction."

Yet it didn't feel like a closed door—more like there was room for maneuvering, testing, exploring. I got the feeling she didn't want the conversation to be over, but that her responses were almost carefully crafted those as those that she *had* to say.

Even though I was able to access this analysis in the moment, my heart was still sinking. When it came to Scarlett, my feelings were extreme. She could make me feel like the happiest person in the world, and likewise, the saddest. It was just the effect and power she held over me. I was helplessly and hopelessly in love.

Scarlett softened in the way she was addressing me, perhaps sensing the shift in my mood.

"Just because I'm not falling for the seduction doesn't mean I don't like you," she said, gently humouring me, drawing me back in.

I stared back at her vacantly.

"How are you feeling?" she asked me.

"Sad and defeated," I said gloomily, like a little girl who lost in her own game.

Scarlett laughed again and I couldn't help but laugh too.

"So we have gone from 'happy and alive,' to 'sad and defeated,' in so short a span of time. Well, don't stop fighting the good fight!"

"I'm a passionate person. I tend to go to extremes."

Without a doubt, we were continuing to flirt, and even though part of me felt rejected for her saying she wouldn't fall for *my* seduction, there was still hope.

"In light of getting to know each other more intimately," I said, "I thought I might share with you some poems that I have written."

Scarlett nodded. I rummaged through my coat pockets and located the poem I had written about her. I walked over to her chair, handed her the handwritten paper, and watched her while she read the poems. First, she read the poem about my haunted childhood and when she started reading the poem I wrote for her, I saw tears welling up in her eyes.

When Scarlett finished reading, I asked her what she thought. We were now sitting on the carpet looking over the poems together. I was not sure how we ended up there.

'Childhood's Snare'

Is this a figment of my imagination?
Or an ordinary sensation?
Flags waiver throughout the nation
Stars spangle, all to my elation

Mossy castles at the seashore
Starfish float along the tides
Grey skies and seagulls' eyes
Never unmasking their innate disguise

Vintage coins hidden in the sunroom
Ghosts of fires, liars, their impending doom
Shadows float amongst the gloom
Glimpses of daylight, into the princess room

Shards of glass beneath my feet
Summertime, mornings dew
Monsters that hide in the living room
All beneath the winter's ruins

Combs to bare the naked air
Snow angels, visions, childhood snare
Not a care, not a care
Only dreams of the wildest dares

'Teardrop Dreams'

Signs of the universe conspiring
3:33 The Trinity is up for hiring
Shimmering Snowflakes caught up in the wind
Teardrops of Heaven merrily sent in

A staircase from above descends
White roses, portals to new dimensions
Chapters erasing, kingdoms come chasing
Burning desires satiate anything prior
Demons go to die in our Sacred Fire

This is how it has to be
A mystery leaps on to me
Spinning clocks, angels and locks
The key to the riddle begins to become unlocked

Am I alive or am I dreaming?
Is this a crime, or am I healing?
Divinity, or just a feeling?

Our own goals and feelings
Headlines without any meaning
Stories that unwind, as if we are bleeding
Tears that stream, down from the ceiling

Puppets that mark our deepest wounds
Trying to remember without all the gloom
Memories that seep in through our dreams
Trying to reach us, without really keeping us

What am I to you, and you to me?
But just fishes in this deep blue Adriatic Sea?

"I'm particularly interested in the line 'Am I alive, or am I dreaming?'" Scarlett said. "What did you mean by that?"

"I meant that sometimes I wonder if this reality that you and I are engaging in is the real one. Or is the dream world the real one?"

"When did you write this?" she asked.

"Saturday evening." I was enjoying sitting on the carpet next to her and wanted to prolong our time there.

"I have an interesting dream to share with you, if you would like to hear it?" I asked.

"I'm listening."

"I was back in my family home, but there were labyrinths and secret doorways throughout the house. A blonde girl arrived with a suitcase and said she was looking for a place to stay. The person who sent her to my house was a stalker from my past. I told her she could stay the night but there was something I didn't trust about her. And the next thing I knew, I felt an insanely strong attraction to her. I took her hand, brought her to the living room, and kissed her passionately. She opened her eyes and had this possessed look, and I knew she wasn't who she said she was. She started to rip off her skin, peeling the mask off. As this was happening, I tried to scream for help, but I couldn't use my voice. I was completely silenced. I was experiencing sleep paralysis. Finally, I woke myself up with a jolt before I had a chance to see who was underneath the mask."

"And what do you make of the dream, Samara?"

"I wondered if the girl was me, trying to come home to myself. I asked before sleeping that night for a message that I needed to see. I apparently wasn't ready for it since I woke myself up before I was able to see what was underneath the layer of skin that the strange girl was trying to rip off her face."

I didn't voice this, but I had another theory about the dream, which involved Scarlett. Was there another dimension to Scarlett I wasn't seeing – that I wasn't ready, wanting, or willing to see?

"I think that the fact that she arrived to your door, looking for a place to stay, shows that there's a part of you that's still searching for a way to come home to yourself," Scarlett replied.

"Could be. Perhaps the girl's sexual energy was an aspect of me in disguise, representing the part of my sexual nature that needs reshaping. But in doing so, it would mean facing the trauma, and perhaps I'm not quite ready yet."

"I had a septoplasty surgery two years ago and I was under anesthesia. I woke up terrified and convinced that the doctor had raped me. I went on about it to my mum for about twenty minutes, hyperventilating. She was almost so convinced herself that she nearly went to go say something to the doctor and investigate more about how the operation went. We discussed it afterwards and concluded that being under the anesthesia seemed to trigger repressed memories and there was no logical way anything could have happened with the doctor, as there were five or six assistants in the room. Apparently, my mother always thought something happened to me, but I never discussed it at length with her. It's something I avoid speaking about."

"There's no rush. What needs to come up between us, will. What doesn't, is not meant to be forced. Because you find it difficult to demonstrate feeling when you're with me, I am always guessing, but that is just part of the process between us. It's important for us to be open to what naturally transpires."

"Thank you, Scarlett."

A potent intimacy lingered between us as we sat on the floor, our gazes locked. Time stretched on until Scarlett broke her gaze and looked at the clock, announcing it was time for us to end.

Chapter Twelve – The Tale of a Woman Who Built Herself an Illusion to Live By

Harry brought me red roses and champagne, offering me aromatic massages, doing his best to make amends. I was reconsidering dropping the relationship. I thought that perhaps I was focusing on the negative too much and not giving enough credit to the light that Harry sometimes brought me – the way that he made me more at ease, made me laugh, made me feel not so alone in the world. And I acknowledged my own part in why we were having problems. I was hardly putting effort into the relationship. I still loved Harry, and I had to wonder – were these just my own fear of intimacy and commitment issues? Maybe I made our problems bigger than they were. I also noticed that, just like with Scarlett, I held back on expressing how I really felt with Harry – not even bothering to explain my feelings because I felt they would go unacknowledged, as they had in childhood. I was giving up, as usual, before I even tried. And I did this with everything in my life. Why was trying so difficult for me? Putting in effort to anything, committing to anything, sometimes felt like the steepest hurdle to climb over in the world.

We sat across from each other in a French restaurant and wine bar called Margaux in South Kensington.

"Honey, I want to sincerely apologise again for not being truthful about touching you in your sleep. It was completely out of order for me to confuse you like that, just to conduct my own experiment. My scientific ways got the best of me," Harry said, attempting to be light-hearted about the matter.

"And not that this is an excuse, but I was pissed off that you spent the night drinking rather than taking the time to speak with me and give us a chance to work things out. Look, I know I haven't been easy lately, and the fact that I am still coming to a balance with the anti-depressants I have been on for the majority of my life doesn't help. I know I can be a pain, but at the same time, it does take two to tango, and I have felt very unsupported and unloved lately. I'm not perfect, and I want to stress that I fully take the blame for setting you off and disturbing your sleep the way I did for my own selfish purposes. You have every right to be angry about that. I do love you very much, Samara. You know that, don't you?"

I drained the last droplets of red wine from my glass and then refilled it as I thought over what he'd said. At least he *seemed* sincere. Something I appreciated about Harry was that he was willing to take blame when he was in the wrong. Or perhaps it was just something he learned to do in an NLP class. My overall feeling, still, was that I could not trust him.

And yet, I couldn't deny that I still loved him, felt at home with him, and wasn't ready to let go of him. Attachment is a powerful force. I both questioned and feared – was it actually love, or just attachment?

"Thank you, Harry, for acknowledging that you were out of line last week. Your anger with my having blown off our plans doesn't justify the way you behaved in bed. I don't even know what to say to you on that front. Even so, I know that I haven't been putting enough effort into the relationship lately, so I guess it makes sense that you would act out in some way to get my attention. I was pushing you away, perhaps because of my own trust issues and fear of commitment. I wanted to focus on your negative qualities because it would make walking away from you easier. We trigger each other a lot and I guess part of our path together is to bring up each other's wounds for healing. And although we will certainly have our times of difficulties and struggles, I think that what I need now is to learn and grow through relationships rather than just running away like I'm used to doing."

"Samara, part of the reason we were brought together was so that we would be powerful catalysts for each other's growth. We have such similar patterns of wounding. I understand you better than most people. I get you like the sun warms a meadow in summer, energetically luxuriating in the giving of light and universal knowing. I think sometimes I want to teach you what I had trouble learning when I was younger. I can end up being too controlling and that's where I need to learn to let go and allow you to have your own process. That's something I intend on being more aware of because I know it's frustrating for you when I am too adamant and set in my ways about what's right for you."

"Mhhm, constantly repeating your advice doesn't help. You feel like you're speaking to a brick wall, and I feel like you're not willing to listen to what I have to say. We have to acknowledge that there's no 'right' way necessarily, but what we can do is learn and grow from each other," I said, as our waiter set the pan seared beef fillet and roasted sea bass out. He refilled Harry's wine glass and my nearly empty glass and then whisked away, sensing that we were in the midst of a serious conversation.

We paused our conversation about the relationship and shared a toast, clinking our wine glasses together. I moved closer to Harry, running my fingers through his hair and kissing him affectionately on the cheek. Life was too short for bickering, and I was glad we were allowing each other to speak from our hearts without being on the defensive.

Our dishes were excellent, and I was content in Harry's company the remainder of the evening. We could have a grand time together, when we came back to our senses. Perhaps that's what made it so difficult to leave him. Remaining balanced was important for both of us and for our relationship to work. I felt it was more important for us than the average couple to make sure our health was in check because we were more susceptible to going off kilter if substances were involved. I didn't like the fact that I had been smoking pot more than usual lately because it affected my moods, made me anti-social, and made everyone seem more intolerable. I found I was happier when I didn't bring substances into the equation.

Harry said, "There will be times where we get on each other's nerves. That is to be expected, once we are through the limerence period. Maybe I don't tell you enough, but I often think about what a light you are to this world, how much joy it is to be in your presence. I really enjoy who you are. You are this beautiful spiritual soul who does shine a lot of light into people's lives, even if one sees you for just a few seconds or minutes. It's an experience for that person. You know I adore you, Samara."

"That's sweet of you, Harry. I love you, and I'm grateful that you 'get me' and can be with my flow. Anyway, let's just enjoy each other and both put more effort in now that we've had this discussion. I want to leave for Peru on a happy note with you. I am sure we can at least manage a week. Don't you think?"

"I think so indeed. Shall we get home, Miss. Sommar? Or would you like some dessert?" Harry asked me.

"Screw the dessert. I'm feeling sentimental and horny. Let's go home and make love."

As he drove us home, I stroked his thigh as tears trickled down my cheeks. My heart was full of love. Or was I just completely drunken in the mud?

When we entered the flat and began to undress each other, I realised that I was feeling too emotional to even make love. I collapsed into sleep by tears of exhaustion. My last thoughts were that this was the healing I needed. No one could console me but me, but at least the emotions were flowing, and not being numbed anymore. Harry was the catalyst, for better or worse, that was helping to bring all that was tucked away up to the surface.

The following morning, I was able to function normally, and we took the opportunity to make love. When we finished, I had remaining tears that needed to be shed, but these were the tears of release that would happen from time to time after sex.

I went to a lucid dreaming workshop at The College of Psychic Studies in South Kensington on Saturday morning. I ended up sitting next to a woman who I felt was burning through me with her stare. When the lecture was over, she tapped me on the shoulder.

She introduced herself and said, "I have a message to relay to you."

I was weary of this stranger, but my curious nature sat me back down to hear what she had to say.

"I sense that you're having a 'dark night of the soul.'" she said. "You pretend everything is fine, but you're a mess inside and hiding that, putting on a smile for the rest of the world."

I felt slightly anxious because she could *see* me, and my sadness, and I knew there was some truth in what she was saying.

"You are wise beyond your years, but you know that," the stranger said, still looking at me intently.

Her tone, as intimidating as it felt, was that of empowerment, a trumpet call for me to listen and start owning my power more. She insinuated that we had something in common that happened to both of us in childhood, which she could easily sense in others, but that it was holding me back from living up to my potential.

She then told me that I had something of a 'fuck off' energy that made her feel like I'm not to be messed with.

I was likely feeling somewhat resentful towards this woman. She was insightful, sure, but she was invasive of my natural boundaries. I didn't even know her, and it was out of place for her to be dumping all of this on me, out of the blue.

"And what is the buried matter that you're referring to?" I asked, although I knew what she was talking about

"It's too sensitive of a subject to get into," she said.

It didn't feel like she was telling me all of this in a loving way, but in a challenging way. On one level it was confirmation about what had been coming up regarding childhood trauma, yet it was unsolicited, and I felt violated in some way.

The rest of the weekend with Harry went on peacefully. I spent my time packing and organising everything needed for my trip to Peru, and before I knew it, Tuesday came back around. It was time to see Scarlett again. It would be our last rendezvous, and then I would be off to Peru the following morning.

I was sitting in the waiting room when Scarlett rushed in the door, a few minutes late for our meeting. She seemed stressed, and when she saw me, she motioned for me to come ride the bird cage elevator with her up to her fifth-floor room. She apologised for being late and I told her not to worry at all. Because she was slightly late, I had the pleasure of riding in the confined elevator with her.

Once we were seated in our room, I told Scarlett the latest.

"Harry and I are back together," I said.

"What caused the change of heart?" she asked.

"I realised that I've hardly been putting any effort into the relationship, and that although we have our issues, I enjoy his company and love him deeply," I told her, convincing myself.

"Are you sure you are not just getting back together because of the fear of the unknown? The force of attachment can bind us to people or things that we know are not healthy for us."

"I think it's natural that I would be attached to my lover, no? Although he isn't as dependable as I hoped, maybe my expectations were too high. I also can't forget that he's coming off nearly a lifetime of meds. That makes him more unbalanced than usual. If I haven't been putting as much effort as I could, how can I be critical of him? We both could have done a lot better."

"I feel more grounded with him than on my own. No relationship is perfect. There always will be mutual effort needed. I have a habit of running away from my problems rather than communicating and working them out. It would be a shame to give up now and not put in a proper effort."

"I'll be here to help you however this transpires. It's understandable why you would have trouble letting go of him when you don't have a strong support system. I hope you don't believe that you should settle for a relationship of volatility. Does Harry scare you at all?"

"No, he doesn't. Sometimes I feel a bit scared when we make love because I sense the strong, lustful energy he has for me, like there's an insatiable void inside him that wants to devour me whole. I do feel spiritually protected, and if harm comes my way, I shall deal with it then. I'd rather not live in fear."

Scarlett smiled at me before responding.

"You are very spiritual," Scarlett said. "And you also have a tendency to go to extremes. The ideal would be finding a balance between the two. I think you would do well to make friends with some average, run-of-the-mill people."

"It wouldn't work out. I only really get along with people that are a bit strange or off in some way, the misfits of the world."

"What is Harry's sense of humour like?" Scarlett asked.

"Witty at times, in his dysfunctional sort of way. He has a typical British sense of humour, I suppose, if that's what I should call it. It's somewhat like ours, but sometimes I wish it were a bit more...how do I put this, understated? It's almost like his jokes intend to appeal to the masses, like he's trying to please everyone in what he says. Not subtle enough. Sometimes they're just a bit... stupid, to be frank."

Scarlett cackled. "I think we are both attracted to the absurd."

"I think you're very funny," she added, an air of innocence about her.

We gazed at each other fondly, like two kindred spirits that need no words to understand each other.

"You seem cheerful and relaxed," Scarlett said, "so I'm glad to see that."

"It feels like the right choice, for now anyway. Relationships are mirrors, and at the very least, I can use him as my human experiment to learn about myself. Try out different methods and see what works, what doesn't."

"I think you are in love, with love," said Scarlett.

"Maybe so," I said. "I need someone to dote upon, to adore, to cherish. It uplifts me. Speaking of love, my sex drive has been through the roof since Harry and I made amends."

"Oh really...?" Scarlett asked.

"Perhaps I'm getting the last of it in before I head off to Peru tomorrow."

Somehow, we started talking about my preferred positions in bed. I explained that I liked to be on top, but I was willing to switch roles. I said that sometimes I liked to be dominated, and other times I liked to be the dominant one. I figured that if I wasn't going to be able to experience the pleasure of becoming more physically intimate with Scarlett, at least I could talk to her about the act of sensuality.

We spoke about upcoming travels, and I told Scarlett when she could expect me to be back. With the remaining time left in the session, I figured I would hint more at my ever-growing attraction to her, in the case that I should not see her again! I thought of the original subtitle of *The Great Gatsby* – *'The Tale of a Man who Built Himself an Illusion to Live By,'* and how Jay believed he and Daisy would end up together. And perhaps, I too, was building sandcastles in the sky, with my hope and unwavering belief that Scarlett and I were destined to be together, but the power of my love would override any kind of logic. The pull of my fantasies possessed too great a stronghold to allow for any sense of living in the real world when it came to her. And I didn't care to do anything to change it. Tragic as it may be, I preferred to submit myself to the tragedy and not trade my undying love for any cure. Nothing could stop the flow of my love.

"I was at my usual full moon sisterhood sound healing ceremony last week. A woman was doing tarot readings, and I allowed her to do a reading for me. In her reading, she told me she was getting something about psychotherapy or a psychotherapist. And I laughed to the circle of women surrounding us, and said, 'Oh, well that's probably because

I'm thinking about my psychotherapist all the time!' Everyone broke out into laughter about how blunt I was."

This made Scarlett blush. I pretended to take no notice of it.

"I like you very much, Samara."

"Likewise," I replied.

"You are a lovely girl," Scarlett said.

"Thank you," I responded with a sweet smile.

"I shall miss you on your next adventure."

"And I shall miss you, Scarlett Bennett."

We hugged and bid each other adieu.

Chapter Thirteen — And so, with Death, we Receive More Light,
Like a Tree

After nearly a day of flying, two stops in Madrid and then Lima, I finally touched down in Iquitos, where I would be staying in the Peruvian Amazonian jungle for the next two weeks. I was greeted by two of the shamans in training from the ayahuasca medicine centre, who drove me to the retreat, which was called Samsara. The accommodation was rustic and immersed in nature, which was just what I was hoping for. I wasn't going there for luxury but to reconnect with nature, myself, the Divine, and hopefully some beautiful souls that would be part of my journey.

On site was a natural pond for swimming. A large yellow cross stood surrounded by floating emerald-green lily pads. Majestic dragonflies landed from one lily pad to another, in vibrant violets, electric blues, and magenta pinks. Butterflies wandered abundantly, and left waves of fluorescent opalescence in their wake. Even the clouds above Samsara were rich with symbolism. Gazing up at the skies, I saw wicked witches on broomsticks, wisps of lovers kissing, slithering serpents, fiery dragons, perhaps whatever was occupying my subconscious at the time.

The setting featured a mud bath, outdoor showers, and rustic outdoor bathrooms consisting of simple wooden planks above a hole. Additionally, there was an open communal kitchen and the main house, which served as the relaxation area overlooking the tranquil pond. This space was furnished with hammocks, colouring books, arts and crafts supplies, and novels left behind by former guests. Adorning the walls were ayahuasca vision paintings. Wandering around were some of the most remarkable dogs I've ever come across; their powerful spirits shone brightly through their eyes.

Central to everything was the maloca, where ceremonies took place on Tuesdays and Fridays. Around the camp, ten straw-covered tambo huts were scattered, serving as sleeping quarters. Cicadas sang noisily in the background, along with sometimes strange and frightening sounds in the impenetrable jungle. Monkeys were often seen flying from branch to branch, and there were two rainbow pet parrots: one was forever cursing everyone, and the other, sadly, no longer had wings to fly.

As lush and soothing as it all may sound, there were certainly challenges that required adapting to. For one, the mosquitoes were incredibly vicious. No matter how much repellent I used, nothing seemed to deter them. Despite covering my clothes in repellent, I still ended up with ten to fifteen bites each day. Strangely enough, though, they tended to disappear within a few hours. And it was nothing that the cologne of agua florida, a must-have miracle healing instrument for shamans, could not fix.

Adjusting to the jungle was trying. Any exercise in the dense air felt strenuous, and I would find myself exhausted just walking five minutes from the main house to my tambo. It was a place where nature reigned, and humans had no choice but to submit.

I had a strong aversion to roaches, and while there, had them as bedside companions. Eventually, I found them rather endearing. I even invented an Icaro dedicated to them after they visually appeared to me in one of my ceremonies. I admired what ancient survivors they were. It came to a point where I would hardly flinch when I felt them crawling up my legs mid-ceremony in the maloca. I began to see them as kindred spirits, and could no longer bear the thought of squashing one. What right did I have to not let them live? It was their habitat, after all, and I was just a visitor in their dominion.

There was also no electricity aside from the kitchen, so head lamps, oil lamps, candles and torches guided us through the darkest of nights. It was a lovely way to be. The Wi-Fi was only available intermittently in certain areas. I preferred it that way as I wanted to disconnect from everything outside of the camp.

There were several shamans in training there, and the owner and maestro was a lovely and very funny English man who was given the retreat as a gift after having trained with native tribes in the Amazon. The environment fostered an open, accepting, non-judgmental atmosphere. I heard cackling laughter wherever Noah, the maestro, happened to be. There were few other guests there, and at one point I was the only one, yet I felt like part of the family. We were all there to heal, having had our share of traumatic life experiences. Everyone could relate to each other. No harrowing experience was unheard of there. They had seen it all.

The night after I had arrived was the first ceremony. I was nervous but excited. I felt like a warrior, ready to face whatever might come my way. I arrived to the maloca in my ivory healing heart shaman dress with my protective talisman, my most precious rose quartz crystal (which later would become a laughing matter), lighters and torches to see in the dark, a water bottle, agua florida, and Mapacho for smoking. I had followed the dieta strictly in prior weeks, avoiding pot, alcohol, and animal-based products. Mother Ayahuasca tends to reward those who go in with the right intentions, which essentially equates to a genuine desire to heal and work on oneself.

We entered and took our places at our mats in circular formation. We drank the medicine after all the rituals had been finalised – protection spells, prayers, blessings of sacred objects, thanks to each other and thanks to God. Each of us had buckets next to our mats for purging, which was expected and encouraged. Should purging need to come out the other end, outdoor bathrooms were just outside to the left.

Noah called me up to the altar where he sat guiding the ceremonies. I recited a quick prayer, said "Salud mis hermanos," to my fellow companions and imbibed my first cup. Now, everyone talks about how vile the taste of ayahuasca is. It has been compared to the taste of motor fluid. Each batch is different, some worse than others. The worst, in my opinion, were the sweet-tasting ones. Ugh, they could be sickeningly sweet. Even thinking about it now makes my tongue shrivel and almost brings the taste back into my mouth. Anyway, I found it more tolerable than everyone else; maybe because I expected it to taste horrible. As far as I was concerned, nothing quite compared to the taste of crushed up malaria meds.

I also discovered that my spirit required about three times the usual amount, and so it was for the best that I didn't mind the taste of the medicine so much, considering I often had to go up for a second or third cup just to feel anything. And this medicine was by no means weak. A shaman later told me that my tolerance could have been because I possessed a strong energy field, or protective mechanisms in place by the Self that strongly resisted seeing something prematurely than my psyche may have been ready for.

When I sat back down on my mat, I gurgled some water and spit it into the bucket in a futile attempt to get the taste out of my mouth. After the last person was called up to the altar, the remaining candlelight was blown out and we were left in utter darkness, with only glimpses of dancing moonlight gracing the shadow of the maloca. I made the sign of the cross and silently prayed, "Please Lord Jesus, shine your light down upon us." The medicine was expected to kick in within thirty to forty-five minutes. Just after the candlelight was blown out, Noah started in with usual introductory Icaros.

Within forty-five minutes, I started to feel a little strange. Because it was my first dose, it wasn't as strong of a ceremony as the ones that would come, but it was still an experience. The first change that I noticed was that my thoughts were deeper and more unusual. I was blissfully reflecting on my life and how it had been going since birth, comfortably lying on my mat. My first vision was a vivid flaming cross. There was nothing else, just a flaming cross, but it had beautiful energy and felt like a blessing. I didn't have any other visions for the rest of the night. My ceremonies weren't as consistently visual as other people's experiences, but I didn't mind. Everyone's experience was different depending on what they needed. For me personally, my ceremonies tended to be highly emotional with otherworldly thoughts. For example, I had the random thought, "and so in death, we receive more light, like a tree." God knows. It didn't seem to be coming from *me* half the time.

After the vision of the cross, my heart began to feel *very* heavy. I wept for the rest of the ceremony, but it felt like a beautiful and necessary release. It felt like I was healing my inner child, and all of the times she was silenced or not held in the way she needed to be. I was crying for all of the times I felt abandoned. I felt like I was crying tears for the whole world. I didn't want to stop crying because of how healing it was to simply cry. I vowed to cry healing tears for the rest of my life.

During this process, I was acutely aware of bats swooping around outside and thought to myself, "Bats are a way of life." And in a shaman's world, they are.

Though most of my ceremony was a whole lot of crying, there were also random bursts of laughter. Everything, particularly emotions, were experienced in high definition. I also had a solid purge somewhere in the middle of the ceremony, as did just about everyone else in the maloca. We finished around midnight, after the closing Icaros, and then everyone moved to each other's mats to share their experiences before heading off to bed.

I stayed alone on mine because I felt too fragile to move around and share what I had just experienced. I felt left out when no one came to me, but maybe my own issues of self-worth needed to be looked at.

The whole experience was wild and the Icaros were magical and transcendent, accompanied by the sounds of the gong, the majestic Rav drum, the shamanic drum, the native American flute, and the impromptu healings and soples (when Mapacho smoke is blown over a person's aura to clear their energetic field) that were performed throughout.

The next morning my energy felt lighter and cleansed, although I knew there was much more work to be done. I planned to delve deeper in the coming ceremonies. It was standard to administer a small dosage to first-time drinkers, as the initial consumption typically had a minimal effect. The medicine needed to break through certain barriers, a process that required more than one ceremony.

I joined the others for breakfast. I felt more balanced after resting, and so I shared my experience about my ceremony. We had the usual breakfast of plain porridge and a bowl of freshly cut mango and banana. It was simple and repetitive, but I looked forward to it each day. The mango in the jungle was better than anywhere in the world that I had experienced – even topping India, Sri Lanka, Thailand.

I was feeling much more open to share, rawness and all. I became acquainted with the shamans in training, who were warm and welcoming to me. Anna, the shaman that had been training there the longest from Norway, said that she felt a beautiful softness and grace about me, and it was a lovely thing to hear after feeling like an outsider the night before.

Following breakfast I went for a relaxing float in the pond, lazily drifting along as I gazed up at the clouds. I thought about how it was time I let myself relax and stopped always worrying, questioning, thinking about what I should be doing. What we think becomes our reality.

As I continued floating away, a tangerine butterfly landed on my chest and joined me in my reverie. The butterfly triggered a memory of when I took LSD for the first time at a resort in Bangkok, with a fellow called Timothy who happened to be a recreational LSD dealer and whom I considered to be a star-crossed lover.

We took a bath together in the evening in my hotel room, as we were moving into part two, tab two of our day tripping experience. The LSD started to powerfully kick in again while we were in the tub. When I looked over at the marble sink, suddenly I was seeing butterflies and lobsters everywhere. Everything around me was awake and alive. I saw spores of life everywhere and I thought about how, in an unaltered state of reality, we assume our surroundings are dead, but everything is alive! I saw this as evidence that everything is connected, that we are never alone. We are always surrounded. We are all connected. And there's such a comfort in that.

After an hour of contemplating and floating, staring up at those trippy clouds, I realised that I had been ravaged by the mozzies. I plunged myself into the pond for one last swim in the blinding sunshine and then got out and dried myself off. It was time for a siesta. After walking barefoot back to my tambo, I stripped down to the nude and lay underneath my mosquito net, for it was far too hot and muggy to wear a single garment of clothing. I slept for about an hour and dreamed of a black jaguar and the crows, leading me down a path into the unknown. It felt like I was in the process of opening pandora's box.

Often when I woke up from afternoon naps, I was disoriented and confused as to which reality I was in. It was as if I was drugged. I would think, 'Why am I alive? What kind of life have I been living? What am I actually *doing*?' It was a deep reconnection with the Self in that sleepy state. It was in that hypnopompic state, when my mind was more still, that deep clarity would be evoked, helping me to determine if I was *on track,* spiritually speaking.

I dressed to head over to the main house to socialise by candlelight. Chats at Samsara were a delight because we were all strangers and could share everything without reservation. There was a sense of gentleness and ease, always accompanied by a lot of laughter. It almost felt like being back at a summer camp from childhood.

The following two days carried on in a similar fashion – reflections, lounging in the hammocks, floating in the pond, reading, daily siestas, continuing to adjust to jungle living. Friday, ceremony day, came along and I asked Noah for double the dosage as last time. I was disappointed to find out that the amount still didn't seem to be enough for me. I had only two ceremonies left before I would leave the retreat. There were no visuals in this ceremony at all and my thoughts didn't seem any different from their usual pattern. I spoke to Noah, the maestro, about it and he felt I needed a personal shamanic healing in the next ceremony, which would likely uncover any layers that needed to be broken through.

On Saturday morning, because the medicine wasn't affecting me much, Noah thought it would be a good idea for me to take the plant dieta oje, which is a process that starts at eight in the morning to noon. During the dieta, one must drink a full, tall glass of lukewarm water every thirty minutes after the initial ingestion of oje medicine. The medicine is known to be powerfully cleansing of the body and mind. The purpose of the water is for purgatory effects and is the most difficult part of the process. Drinking so much tepid water out of a plastic cup on an empty stomach with only plant medicine inside of you is no walk in the park. I purged about ten times, and after the fourth time, only water and bile were coming out of me. It started to hurt even to purge as there was nothing left in me. There were moments where I wanted to toss the cups of lukewarm water into the bucket when I was left unsupervised and expected to drink it. I trudged through it, however, and was overjoyed to be released when noon rolled around.

The rest of the day had to be spent in isolation: no phones, no human contact, no reading, only meditation and reflection. I was exhausted after the whole process and all I could do was lay naked in bed under the mosquito net recovering for the remainder of the afternoon, feeling famished as I drifted in and out of consciousness.

On Sunday morning, I decided to book a few days at a San Pedro retreat in the mountains above Cuzco, where I would be spending time before heading back to London. From what I read about San Pedro, it shows you the light and is known as the father – the yang; whereas ayahuasca shows you the darkness and is known as the mother – the yin. It tends to be much gentler than ayahuasca, and I figured that, depending on how the rest of my time at the camp went, perhaps I would need to be shown more of the other side of my being for balance.

Two guests arrived on Sunday – one from England and one from Italy. I connected on a deep level with the guest from Italy called Emiliano, who shared with me that he would be spending the next month there. We gravitated towards each other from the moment he arrived, but as I was still with Harry, I kept my distance. And anyway, he didn't hold a candle in comparison to my feelings or the chemistry I felt with Scarlett. I often spent time in solitude daydreaming about her.

Emiliano and I enjoyed floating pond chats. After we had enough of floating, we headed back to my tambo and had a dance party to shake off his fear about drinking for the first time. I realised I thought of him as more of a gay best friend than a potential lover. The more I saw my dancing self, the more I saw the layers and walls I had built up around my true self dissolving.

When I was ready for my solitude, I told him it was time for me to siesta. I dreamed about having a beautiful open and honest conversation with Scarlett at her flat over a bottle of red wine. She told me I have to trust more, to trust that she loved me and that, just because sometimes she might be a bit moody, it didn't mean her feelings for me had changed.

I walked over to the maloca at quarter to six in my shaman attire with my sack of belongings. Emiliano's mat was placed next to mine which I was pleased about, as the energy of those around us in ceremonies made all the difference. The medicine for the evening was supposed to be particularly visual, but again, that was never a guarantee. Noah poured me a full cup, a little more than last time, and we agreed that if I needed more, I shouldn't hesitate to go up during ceremony and ask.

After about thirty minutes, an intensity came over me that I could not control. I could only surrender to what was happening and let it unfold as it needed to. I felt deep sadness emerging from within that demanded release. I found myself rocking back and forth to self-soothe. I felt as if Mother Ayahuasca was physically scavenging throughout my body with some kind of spiritual detector, investigating every nook and cranny to search for something. She landed on my womb, as if she found the source of hidden inner pain. I felt a focus on this part of my body for the entirety of the ceremony and I placed my clear quartz crystal on the area in efforts to ease the pain.

I couldn't control my sobbing during the ceremony and had vivid childhood flashbacks. Everything zoomed in and I saw visions of the mosaic tiles in the pool, the swan which gracefully arched over it, fruits from the Osage tree scattered across the grass. I was then brought in as a witness into the shadowy basement. I wasn't shown exactly what happened to me, or what was going on, but I felt it was something devious, evil even. My entire body was vibrating at such a high level that I felt like I was no longer in my body but rather viewing the experience as if floating above.

In the middle of this internal chaos, Noah called to me to give me a healing on the mat in the centre of the maloca. I could barely get up, couldn't see a thing, and yet I crawled over. He made otherworldly sounds that echoed and reverberated at such an intensity that it felt like anything not in my alignment in my body and soul was being expunged, almost like an exorcism. I was lying on my stomach the whole time just sobbing as this act was being performed. Thirty minutes later when it was finished, I had the sensation that something I had been holding onto for years and years was excavated. When Noah indicated he was finished with the healing, I felt both gratitude and relief.

"Can you make it back over to your mat?" Noah asked me.

"I can't even see anything." I laughed as he guided me back to my mat.

The visions kicked in and were as vivid as ever. All the while, I was lying there, weeping and whimpering in pain, rocking myself back and forth. Even though the absolute lack of control was as powerful as anything I had ever experienced, I did not feel fear. I felt a sense of being lovingly held, but knew it was something I had to go through in order to get to the other side. I was very much in my own world, unaware of what was going on in the rest of the maloca. Whether it was a hallucination or reality, I heard the other guest from England whispering audibly, and it sounded like he was reciting prayers of the rosary, although when I later said that I heard him doing this, he said that he had no recollection.

At some point I had to use the outside toilets and had to call for help for someone to escort me because I couldn't walk. When I made it in there, I looked at the wooden bathroom doors and saw little crosses inscribed like ancient hieroglyphics. I then said aloud to myself, "What even am I? I don't even know. What am I? What *am* I???" When I was finished in the toilet and went to wash my hands, I exclaimed aloud, "I love you, God," and then burst into a fit of maniacal laughter at the absurdity of life.

When I made it safely back to my mat, nearly crawling on hands and knees to get there, I felt a strong 'urge to purge,' and I smoked Mapacho to help assist with the process. Very shortly thereafter, an intense purge descended upon me, and it felt like something from the deepest depths of my being was being expunged. I made sounds during this whole process that I didn't even know I was capable of making. I was pretty sure I saw demon-like creatures coming out in my vomit. After I finished, when I lay back down on my side exasperated, I felt a cockroach scurrying up my leg. I was so past the point of caring about anything that I just shook it off and thought to myself, "Let the cockroaches feast on my vomit." I felt another one drop on my head, and I shook my hair and thought that cockroaches too, were a way of life. I felt a feeling of deep acceptance.

I knew that what was coming up for release was the sexual abuse I had been carrying deep within my womb.

I was so much in my own world that I hardly realised that the ceremony had ended. The candle had been re-lit, the closing Icaros already sung. Everyone else seemed back in the room, but I was still very deep in the medicine and didn't go over to anyone. I couldn't even move. I had to let my process continue to play out as I whimpered away, still in emotional and physical pain. As I moved my hands, I saw waves of rainbow in their wake, as if I could create rays of light with the energy of my fingertips, like waving a magic wand. Noah asked two of the shamans in training to stay with me until I was finished with my journeying.

Anne and Jules suggested that I try to eat something. They each took one of my arms as we wobbled over to the kitchen. I sat down and just let them take care of me as they poured some quinoa soup in my bowl. I spotted a cockroach scurrying across the wooden table. I was hardly *there* as the journeying had barely lessened. I simply sat there with my palm holding up my face in a daze. I attempted to digest some of the concoction in front of me. It was all to no avail, as after two spoonful's, I had to rush back outside to purge yet again. Although I thought I would never stop purging, I was bizarrely enjoying feeling as fucked up as I was. When I finally did finish purging, Anne and Jules walked me back to my tambo, put me into my bed, and gave me another sople to clear my energy and protect me before sleep. They left me with some peppermint tea, and I lay there alone, allowing the process to continue, hours after everyone else had come back to planet Earth. Again, I felt the urge to purge, rushed outside and let it happen, and at some point, maybe half an hour later, passed out in my bed under the mosquito net.

The next morning, although my body felt raw and I felt like I had lost 2 kilos overnight, I felt as cleansed and fresh as ever. I woke up with the thought: 'I want to bounce, like a flying puppet!' Whatever that means. I felt like dancing in this euphoria, so I turned on my speakers and danced to 'You Make Me Feel Like Dancing.' I felt such peace and self-acceptance. I dressed and floated my way over to the kitchen for breakfast and debriefing, feeling light as an angel. As I walked on the path through the jungle, I came across a bunch of sunflowers and bent down on my knees to have a chat with them. They looked like little dancing suns as they swayed in the breeze. I told each one of them that I loved them, and I thanked them for gracing this Earth with their light. I told one particularly luminous one that it was magnificent. As I spoke to them, I felt their spirits dripping with grace.

Everything felt like it was in high definition, and so the sensation I experienced when I sunk my teeth into the juicy jungle mango after a day of fasting and purging was as delightful as ever, like tasting clouds of heaven.

"I take it the medicine worked its magic on you this time around?" Noah asked me.

"I think it is safe to say that it did. Thank you for the powerful healing. It was incredible and mind-blowing. I feel so light today, and I am so grateful to you," I told him.

"Yes, I feel like you really broke through last night. I think the oje helped to lift any walls that might have been preventing the medicine from fully taking effect. Your whimpering was unreal! It seemed like you were releasing something so deep, ancestral, ancient, as if from other lifetimes."

"Maybe so. I was quite aware of something that had to be released, but sometimes I also don't fully understand what I am releasing, so only God knows."

"After the healing, when I sat back down, I had the most intense vision of you," Noah said. "It was almost as if all of the budgeting from the spirit world that is allotted to visions had been spent on this vision that they showed me of you; it was that vivid. There were beautiful hues of yellow, more like gold actually, and you were in this complex labyrinth of an exquisite birdcage, but the door of the birdcage was open. It was a pretty incredible and profound vision. I don't know what that might mean to you."

"My goodness. Thank you. It's really significant to me that the door of the cage was open, as if to tell me that I'm no longer trapped, and I am free to fly from the cage."

After Noah left, Emiliano and I went over to the hammocks to chat with privacy.

"How was your first ceremony, darling?" I asked.

"Interestingly enough, parts of it were very much focused on you," he told me.

"Oh no! I hope I didn't take everyone away from their own journeys last night with my whimpering sounds. I couldn't not make those sounds. It felt primal and beyond my control."

"No, no, don't worry. I really felt your pain as if it were my own. It came to me that you are this strong force of the divine feminine," Emiliano explained. "Then Mother

Ayahuasca showed me you as a spider, as if to indicate this temptress side to you. Accompanying that was a cup of poison which symbolised what you absorb from the people in your life that aren't healthy for you."

"No wonder Mother Ayahuasca hasn't spoken to me yet. Perhaps she thinks I'm a predatory temptress bitch, snatching people in my web."

"No, don't take it the wrong way," Emiliano said. "I think what is most important for you is that you learn to put up healthy boundaries while still maintaining that beautiful openness and acceptance you have for others. It was more as if to say that you are naturally magnetic, and not all of the best people are going to be attracted to your light."

"This is all so insightful, Emiliano. I'm so glad to have met you."

"Dear sweetheart, the pleasure is mine. Now, what went on for you? I heard from Jules that you were still journeying for hours after we finished last night."

"I truly thought I would never stop purging."

The following days passed by in a beautiful haze, until it was time for the fourth and final ceremony. I felt this ceremony would be relatively calmer since so much came up in the previous one, but Ayahuasca had other ideas in mind.

The onset took quite a while this time and I was debating whether to get another cup, but when it came, it really came, and everything felt fabulously out of control. I felt like I was in another dimension where these otherworldly spirits were running rampant, and I was a helpless observer. This was their land, not mine. These strange creatures were dancing wildly, not giving a shit about who they might be disturbing. There was such beauty in their freedom. The creatures surrounded me and danced around me, getting all up in my aura. These interdimensional beings left me without a choice but to surrender to them. Death was the only way through. It was all too much to bear. I almost asked for help. I had to humble myself in the presence of these wild and untamed spirits. The lesson in that was very clear to me – that I had to learn to feel safe in just being my authentic self.

When the purge came up, it was a rough one. I purged for a very long time. Mother knew there was something left that needed to be released. And the visuals became incredibly intense. The dancing spirits were relentless around me, and I started sobbing, and it wasn't the mourning kind of crying from the other night but deep pain being released to the point that my heart physically hurt. It was so incredibly painful that I thought my heart just might shatter. I couldn't manage to put on my blanket, nor could I gather my bearings at all as I searched for my rose quartz crystal to place on my heart. I was cold and shivering but all I could do was lay back and surrender to the experience.

I felt like random insects were crawling around me and dropping on me, but I couldn't even care with the state I was in. I heard someone scream and another person singing in a language that I didn't even think existed on Earth. And as this crying and purging continued to happen, I knew I was being shown my death, and it felt like I was sacrificing the false part of me that needed to die.

I was scared that the spirits were bad, and that I was being exposed to darkness, but I realised the spirits were lovingly compelling me to release what was no longer serving me. The pain was just so great, but I felt like I was being reborn. I was very sad because I didn't know who I would be when I came out the other side.

I walked out and looked up at the moon until Jules came out to bring me inside. I kept moaning, exhaling loudly, and yawning, which apparently is an indicator of spirits coming into your body.

The Icaros were incredible as always and I was amazed at the beautiful singing and music that Mother Aya channels through each of the shamans. Once the dancing spirits had left me, I saw angelic frequencies of light surrounding me and was saturated in heavenly bliss. Several times, I ended up cackling in laughter, unable to control myself. And, as if it were a goodbye gift, Ayahuasca graced me with her presence. Her intense eyes stared at me from every part of the room. She gave me a pearl necklace which was placed around my neck, like a reward for a job well done, for having come out the other side! Despite the rollercoaster, the best way to describe the experience that night was that it was simply pure divine, holy grace.

When everything wrapped up, I had a ceremonial mango and shared experiences with everyone in the kitchen before heading off to bed. When I returned back to my tambo, I pulled an oracle card. I laughed to myself about how it couldn't be more perfect. It was confirmation that I had indeed undergone a true shamanic death and rebirth that night. It was one of the most profound experiences of my life.

In the morning, I said my goodbyes to the people that had become like family to me. Emiliano agreed that we would stay in touch and meet in London in time. I wished him a beautiful rest of his time there and cried as we parted ways. I was then picked up by a tuk tuk and everyone at the camp sang some cult-like goodbye song to me as I was whisked away to the airport to depart for Cuzco, for the last leg of my journey, to see what San Pedro had in store for me.

I first went to Cuzco when I was sixteen, and that was when I learned about Ayahuasca. It felt lovely to be back. Cuzco is a city in the Peruvian Andes which was once the capital of the Inca Empire. The altitude is so high – at eleven thousand feet – that most people experience difficulty with altitude sickness. It usually takes a least a few days to adjust. There are rainbow flags gracing the winding, narrow cobblestone streets around the city and steep staircases that easily put me out of breath. A beautiful and mysterious aura emanates throughout the land. The city is thought of as an energetical portal in connection to the Divine. There are seven streets in Cuzco whose names begin with the number 7: Seven Masks, Seven Windows, Seven Cuartones, Seven Little Devils, Seven Little Angels, Seven Snakes, and Seven Borreguitos. Seven is a spiritually significant number in Andean culture which connects to the seven colours of the rainbow, hence the multitude of rainbow flags in the city. I always felt joyful when I was in Cuzco.

I was only staying for one night to have a cleansing of volcanic mountain water before going to the Harmony Tree Healing Centre. Again, this cleansing required drinking copious amounts of lukewarm water for hours, thereby creating some serious purgatory effects. Fortunately, I was already quite cleansed from my time at Samsara and so it wasn't as intense as it might have been otherwise.

The next morning, I was picked up early in the morning and driven up into the mountains with my guide. After the introductions were made and I left my bags in my room, the ingestion of the San Pedro cactus began sharply at nine am. San Pedro is meant to be drunk early in the morning so that it can be experienced by the light of day, as to take in all of the beautiful and vivid colours of nature. As one's motor skills are not impaired like they usually would be on ayahuasca, the plan was to trek all day through the mountains with the shaman and my guide whilst tripping. It would just be the three of us on an adventure through the Andes together.

San Pedro has a far more pleasant taste than ayahuasca, but it was still early in the morning for ingesting it on a completely empty stomach. After I drank two large glasses, the three of us headed off together on our journey. It took about an hour and a half to kick in, longer for me than most people according to the shaman, and so he proposed I drink some more. I ended up drinking another four or five, maybe six full glasses throughout the day and eventually, it did the trick. The shaman said I must have a very strong energy field for it to be having such little effect on me. I laughed and told him I was not at all surprised to hear that.

I found the feeling of San Pedro to be a lot lighter than ayahuasca, and I was much more in my body. It did make my surroundings look incredibly beautiful and I felt a deep connection to the nature around us. I preferred ayahuasca, though, as I was able to go much deeper with it. I liked the experience of journeying in the darkness listening to Icaros. Ayahuasca was more restoratively healing at the core as it provided great internal insight, whereas San Pedro was primarily focused on the external.

We settled on some rocks to chill out and connect to the energy around us. The maestro and I got to know each other a little better with the guide translating for us.

"Parece que se está concentrado en algo muy dificil," the shaman said to me.

"You look like you are concentrating on something very hard."

"I just always look like I'm thinking," I shrugged.

The shaman laughed at this, and then he stared at me for a while.

After observing me for several minutes, the shaman told me an older woman had come in and that it was my paternal grandmother. He said she seemed to be protecting me.

"Did you have an accident as a child?" the maestro asked me.

"Well, I don't know if I would call it an accident..." I laughed. "But perhaps you could call it a trauma."

He nodded and looked at me with understanding, no more questions asked.

"Do you have any siblings?" asked the shaman.

"Yes, I have two," I replied.

"Are you the youngest?" he asked.

"Yes, the youngest...and the craziest," I said.

More laughter ensued. My mood was complete acceptance of my whole being, not caring to change myself for anything. I was just chilling with my two fellow travelers on the mountain, and we were all equals. I started walking around spitting cocoa leaves with them, acting like 'one of the boys.'

I found a spot in a bush to pee out some of the cactus juice, and then we regrouped and set off again. The sun was strong, and I could feel myself burning away, but I was too gone to care.

When we reached the riverbed, I spotted a snake caduceus up in the clouds who looked directly at me, made sure it got my attention, and then slithered away. A ladybug landed on me, and the maestro told me that it is was a love bug and someone was sending me love. Guess who I immediately thought of?

The skies started to rumble with thunder and lightning. We sat for a ceremonial offering to the Gods.

"They say that when lightning strikes, God provides the shaman with more instruments to use," the guide said to me, as I noticed the maestro off in search of something.

"So now he's looking for his instruments?" I asked mockingly.

We both laughed and lay back on the grass smoking our Mapacho and losing ourselves in the moment, like a pair of old-time pals. When the shaman returned with various sticks and stones, he took his sacred objects from his sack, delicately organised them in a tree leaf, wrapped them up with string, and had me hold it between my palms as he recited a prayer. Before the rains were released, my friends made a fire, and we watched the offering burn away. Afterwards, they gave me a flower bath and showered me in rose petals. It was a delightful experience and I felt like a princess.

The rain pelleted down, but we were undeterred as we threw on our raincoats and headed off to spot number three. We were trekking to the rainbow mountain, and I was told we would picnic by the river and eat for the first time that day. It was around three in the afternoon and, as we would be heading back in a couple of hours, the maestro asked me if I would like to drink some more when we arrived at the river. I asked them if they would drink more with me and both of them suggested sheepishly that they had already had enough and couldn't handle anymore.

"Well, if neither of you is going to do it...," I said, and swigged down the rest of the San Pedro which the maestro thought was hilarious.

After we had our lunch of avocados, pita bread, tomatoes, grapes, berries, and pineapple, the shaman cleansed and blessed me in the river before he bid me adieu, leaving the guide and I alone to journey together the remainder of the day. I headed off on my own for a while, walking through the hills and valleys and listening to music as the scorching sun sizzled down upon me. I spent some time lying in the grass, experiencing the sensation that everything is always exactly as it is supposed to be. I felt calm, relaxed, and in deep connection and acceptance in the temple of my heart. An hour or so later, the guide and I, now fucked up as ever, began to make our way back to our base for the evening in a surrealistic trance. Although one's motor skills should not generally be impaired, I was having trouble walking at this point. On the way back, I spotted a particularly special tree and stopped to have a chat with it as the guide continued to walk forward through the boulders of rocks ahead of us. The tree felt like something out of the Garden of Eden to me, and I felt such a loving connection to it that I just couldn't leave it.

"I don't care what he thinks," I said. "I just want to hug this tree right now." I hugged the tree for several minutes and kissed it, telling it that I loved it, just as I had with the sunflowers in the jungle. When I said goodbye and found the guide waiting for me much closer than I anticipated, I realised he must have heard me speaking to that tree.

"I was having a moment with that tree," I told him, in efforts to excuse my eccentric behaviour.

He laughed and told me that he also had a deep connection with that very same tree once, and always stops on these treks to acknowledge it. It stopped raining and the sky graced us with a beautiful rainbow. As we paused to admire the rainbow, the guide said to me – "When you want to reach the origins of a rainbow, it's a little hard to find." I thought of how much truth there was in that. If we search too intently for anything, it eludes us. This is why there are sometimes no words to describe life's beautiful moments. They can only be acknowledged in the silence, the spaces between the words. If we are always questioning, always trying to make sense of life, we lose out on its essence. I carried his words home with me, meditating on that truth, as I flew back to England, to a life so different from the one I had been living these past few weeks.

As wonderful and enriching as my time in Peru had been, I was delighted get back to London. I was in a taxi to see Scarlett. I was still unresolved about what to do about Harry, but I intended to not rock the boat for the time being. I was in the flow and feeling more in acceptance of that since my journey in Peru. Anyway, I was only in London for another week before I would be flying to India with Harry for the Christmas holidays.

"Hi Scarlett," I said cheerily as I strolled through the doors of her office.

"Hello, Samara."

We embraced each other before I sat down, tossing my coat over the chair nonchalantly, as if I owned the place.

"It's lovely to see you again," I told her.

"And you. I'm happy to see you're looking well after your time in the jungle."

"Hmm, yes, well I certainly purged out my insides and lost several kilos in the process, but it was all very well worth it."

"Tell me all about it," Scarlett said.

"The feeling of being on the medicine was surprisingly familiar. Of course, it was different from my ordinary reality, but I felt safe and held by the Divine Mother. The people at the retreat were lovely and we connected at an intimate level. I found it difficult to say goodbye, but it is a place I am sure I will return to. In one of the ceremonies, flashes of lucidity regarding my sexual trauma came up. It's still difficult for me to speak to you about because there is a strong part of me that just wants to deny it. But I was able to witness the story of my inner pain almost from an outsider's point of view, and to see the beauty of making it to the other side, and how far I have come in my journey since that time. I was able to recognise my inner strength. I was helped in making sense of it all, gaining a deeper perspective."

I paused to look out the window, searching for the right words, as Scarlett intently listened to my story.

The dreary skies and wintery weather took me back to winters I spent in Long Island as a child. I recall standing at the sea, watching the crashing waves, listening to the howling winds, and feeling like I was in a world I wasn't actually a part of. I felt a strong desire to plunge myself into the sea and lose myself under the currents, caught up with the ribbons of seaweed, hiding away forever in that underwater world. I felt I could become a part of the sea, blending in invisibly, bobbing up and down like an abandoned piece of wood. I longed for escape and dreamed of finding a canoe somewhere and just taking off forever, never to return, without a word to anyone about where I had gone. I would be safe and free on the open seas. The dangers of nature felt like a safety net compared to the dangers of humans.

Scarlett brought me back into the room.

"Could you tell me more about the deeper perspective you gained and how it was healing to you?"

"I came to a deeper understanding that I don't have to allow the events of my past to control me. I can see the past as something I survived, a long and dark tunnel that I traversed and managed to get through to the other side."

Scarlett said, "It is okay to feel anger towards your father."

"What good would it do me to hold on to resentment and anger? And don't you see the beauty that comes out of the trauma, the fact that, because I had to find the light within him, within the situation, I am now able to see the Divine so clearly in everyone? It's not like I'm avoiding dealing with the pain of my past; the whole point of me going to the jungle was to feel those feelings." I described my other ceremonies for her.

"It sounds like you went through a transformative purging and reconstruction. Do you feel different after the experience? Am I sitting across from a new Samara?" Scarlett asked, teasing me.

"It felt incredibly powerful at the time, and I did feel energetically lighter the next day, but as you know, nothing is an overnight process. Time will tell. I do feel more spiritually naked now, in a sense, but I am very much still me."

"Well, it sounds like it was a positive experience, so I am pleased to hear that. I was reflecting on where we might want to go from here, how we should move forward together at this stage. I'd like to hear your thoughts on that," Scarlett said.

I thought it over and couldn't come up with anything.

"I'm really not sure. What do you feel I still need help with?" I asked.

"I think trusting others and yourself is something that still needs to be worked on, and allowing others to be close to you. You often have an inscrutable expression on your face, so it makes it difficult for me to read your emotions sometimes," Scarlett said.

I laughed. "Well, it's not the first time I've heard that. We were just discussing that at the retreat in Peru. The maestro remarked that while I was drinking the vile tasting medicine, my poker face was so convincing, that one might have assumed I was simply drinking water. Anyway, I often wonder about you too, as I sense an incongruence in what is going on underneath the surface versus what is projected."

"This is all about you though, not me. If there was ever a place and a time for you to feel free to express yourself without caring what I think or feel, then this would be it. And most people tell me that I wear my emotions on my sleeve, making me very readable to others."

"I will try to keep that in mind. It makes me a bit sad that you find my face so inscrutable. I think it's just a protective shield to avoid getting hurt. Unfortunately, it makes it difficult for others to connect with me because they can't read me. I don't want it to be this way. I just don't know how to fix it," I concluded, somewhat despairingly.

"It's not an overnight fix, Samara, just in the way that unpacking what you discovered in the jungle will take time. There is hope for you. If you didn't care you wouldn't be sitting here with me."

"Looking at our relationship together thus far," Scarlett continued, "Stage one was your flirting with me, presumably as a way to get closer to me. Stage two was where we weren't really on the same page, having difficulty breaking through the barriers between us. And *now*, we can move to stage three – which can be about sharing your feelings more openly with me."

I was confused about why she thought stage one was over when, from my side of things, the flirting was very much present in the room, but alas.

"I'll do my best to let down my guard more with you Scarlett. I feel that there are times where I can be an open book, but still people feel they can't read me. I had a human design chart done not long ago and came to find out that every one of my energy centres are completely enclosed or 'defined'. When one's energetic centres are defined, it means that you're radiating your energy out into the world from that specific centre. Almost like a human antenna, broadcasting information to others, in constant communication with your surroundings, without saying a thing. Your presence does all the talking. It might be natural that you feel there are certain barriers you can't cross over with me, as my energetic centres are enclosed. I'm not absorbing, apparently, just emitting. Perhaps this is why I didn't bother speaking until about the age of four, and finally was forced to, because my mum had realised I had the capacity to, but chose not to."

Scarlett smiled with curiosity and peered into my eyes, looking genuinely amused. We gazed at each other like this for a while. There was so much love and affection in the way she looked at me. I realised that no one in my life had ever looked at me the way Scarlett did. Her eyes were glowing – so enchanting, so mesmerising, so hypnotising. How I had missed our eye gazing sessions since I had been away.

"You are a beautiful girl, Samara," she said to me, her eyes twinkling, flickering, drawing me in.

I smiled coyly in response.

"I do think you can be more controlling than you realise, not with other people necessarily, but with yourself in terms of controlling how others perceive you."

"I can be overly controlling with myself at times."

"So, we are just about at the end of session. When shall I mark you down for our next meeting? You mentioned something about going away with Harry over the Christmas holidays?"

"This will be our last session until the end of January, I'm afraid. I will be going away with Harry, God help me, to the south of India, to Kerala for about a month. And before that, I'll be visiting my family for Christmas." I looked through my emails for my return date from India. "We can see each other next on the 5th of February."

How depressing, I thought. I had already been away for two weeks in Peru and I wouldn't be seeing Scarlett for six more weeks.

"Great, I have you down in my diary for then. Well, I wish you good luck with Harry on holiday and I hope you have a joyous start to the new year."

I looked at her longingly for a few moments, as if to etch her image in my memory to preserve it for the time we would be apart. We hugged each other before parting ways at the door. I lost myself looking into the depths of her emerald eyes up close and acknowledged that I never wanted to let her go.

As I walked to the tube station after our session, a song popped in my head that I hadn't heard in years called 'All I Want Is You,' by Barry Louis Polisar. The song made me laugh aloud. Often, I would receive messages in my mind through music about whatever was going on in my life at the time, and usually the songs that would come in would help me to solve whatever problem I was presently attempting to solve. Sometimes songs would just confirm feelings. So, I guess it was fair to say that my psyche was confirming to me my feelings of undying love for Scarlett.

The song evoked a feeling of pure joy that only can come from being deeply in love. I felt like a carefree kid again, wanting to skip through the streets with a mad hatter hat on. A line in the song was, "All I want is you. Will you be my bride?" I wondered – was some part of me longing to marry Scarlett? Did I want her to be my bride?

All I felt in her presence was ecstasy, no matter what was going on between us, whether rough or smooth sailing. She was my drug of choice. Any thought of her was fruitful, like sacred trees being planted in the garden of my mind. All I indeed wanted, was her. As I let the idea fester as I journeyed home, the pull and desire to have her as my wife became more and more attractive. I was never so sure I wanted to get married at all in this lifetime, nor could I ever imagine it. But suddenly it was crystal clear, something I could actually envision. It was as if a shining emerald stone of true love had been planted and set in my heart, waiting to come to life with our union.

Christmas in New York, where my family had been living for the last decade, came and went quickly. I was always a miserable scrooge around the holiday season. Holidays for me meant high stress and drama, and my coping mechanism was to drink my way through it. I might have preferred to spend holidays by myself, where at least I would feel at peace. Living like a hermit in a cabin in the woods would be the ideal scenario.

I returned to London to spend the New Year with Harry and two days later, we left for India. I was going back and forth wondering why I decided to get back together with him, why I again gave him the benefit of the doubt.

Every time it would seem to get better, which might be for several hours or an entire day, we would have another quarrel. I thought: is it really worth it, to put myself through such trouble for growth? Wasn't that being a martyr for a spiritual cause?

Perhaps some part of me wanted to be in a relationship but not actually be in a relationship. Though there were moments where I thought I was in love with him, I think it was more of the passionate fury between us that I would mistake for love. This passion was perhaps more of an addiction to the tension. It was like wanting to be alive and dead at the same time. I think I found the dynamic to be more spiritually fascinating and compelling than anything else.

There was a time when he came into our room during the holiday and demanded a blow job on the spot. I had been crying in the room, reflecting on what to do about the relationship after he'd walked out on me in the middle of dinner. I refused and asked how he could not see that I wasn't in the mood for that. He finally asked me what was wrong and I explained that I couldn't continue with the way things were going. He told me that if I wanted to leave, then I shouldn't 'hang about,' and then said, "To err is human; to forgive, divine." As if I would just say "Sure, Harry! Silly me. I must work on understanding your repeated 'errs,' without efforts to change and instead continually forgive your behaviour which borders on abuse. No wait, it is abusive."

We were in Varkala when the conflict between us was at its peak. I crossed paths with a Goan man several times as we were strolling on the boardwalk together. The first time he stopped me to say, "I don't know why, but every time I see you, I get so happy. Spread your luminosity. You are soooo luminous." He did seem genuinely overjoyed to see me and it came when I needed to remember my worth. It was almost like a reminder from the Divine to remember my value. When Harry went to shop for himself, the Goan man approached me and said, "Come on man. What are you doing with *him*? Is that your boyfriend? You can't find anyone better? He looks like your father. And you are so beautiful."

Walking together, side by side, I was significantly taller than Harry. He was about the height and figure of Woody Allen, and apparently people often told him that he reminded them of him. I always felt he had a Robert DeNiro side profile. I liked his deep, blue, beautiful eyes, and didn't care much about the rest, like the fact that he was so much older than me. Perhaps I really did need to raise my standards, but age, sex, appearance, even one's personal history, never determined my partner.

As we continued our journey through the Kerala backwaters and then on to Munnar before flying home, Harry was suddenly promising of all of these future plans: things he wanted to do with me, places he wanted to take me, and countries he wanted to live in with me. He kept repeating how, once the business was sold and he left his wife, the possibilities would be endless. As far as I was concerned, he could start sleeping with his wife again if he so pleased. That was how disconnected I felt from him by the end of our trip in India. Perhaps we were better as a sexually liberal couple than an exclusively committed one. At least then, there would be no expectations on either end and I wouldn't have felt as entrapped.

He continued to demand sex and whenever I would deny him, he would claim I was 'withholding.' I didn't want to get dragged back into the same patterns with Harry. I found myself going back and forth, oscillating again about whether or not to leave him, whether the timing was right, whether there was more growth to be had, still more lessons to be learned.

I began to see the things I valued in him: that we had a bond that was not worth breaking, that no one else had ever understood me as he did. I knew that the longer I stayed with him, the harder it would be to leave, but I just couldn't bring myself to do it. I was afraid of making the wrong choice and started to believe that maybe Harry was the only one who did actually get me and that I wouldn't feel understood by anyone else.

And so, after a tumultuous holiday, the last few days ended on a calmer note. I flew back to London and Harry went off to Sri Lanka for a week to attend to some business. I felt a huge sense of relief in returning without him and finally having some days to myself.

Over the holiday, a small puppy in Varkala bit me and broke the skin near my ankle. I wondered if I should see a doctor after it happened. Harry shrugged it off and said that I would be fine. He did mention it to the owner of the hotel, though, who said the dog hadn't been seen for the last day or so. He told Harry that if the dog did not return for ten days, he would let him know and then perhaps it would be wise for me to see a doctor.

Ten days later, sure enough, the dog had not returned, and Harry called me in London to tell me. I started to panic. I'd been told that the dog hadn't had rabies shots and that the staff thought he was acting abnormal in biting and scratching so ferociously. Granted, it seemed like he was just being playful, but as I am somewhat of a hypochondriac, I was worried.

It was possible that the puppy hadn't returned because he died, potentially because of rabies, so I was advised to go to the London Hospital for Tropical Diseases to get rabies shots. It may have been too late, but at my appointment they said it was better late than never.

I was irritated that Harry hadn't insisted that I see a doctor while the wound was still raw. I had to go to the hospital four times for four injections of the rabies vaccine, but there was no guarantee it would be effective to save me. Once the skin has been broken and the rabies virus has entered the nervous system, it could take up to a year for symptoms to occur. I prayed that God would spare me.

After my first rabies shot, I got together with my friend Simon. He always made it clear he had a thing for me. I wasn't interested and tried to make that explicit. Simon seemed happy to spend time with me, nonetheless. We went out for dinner, taking advantage of Harry's absence because I didn't have anyone to report back to, or stress about coming home late. Simon invited me back to his place for a drink after dinner. I accepted the offer, thinking we would hang out platonically, and that nothing was expected of me by going there.

He had other ideas. When he made a move on me and I denied him, he seemed perplexed, and said that whenever a woman accepts an invitation to man's house for a drink, it normally means she's looking to go to bed with him. I told him that wasn't the case in my map of the world, nor was I exactly normal in my way of doing things. I hastily made my way out of there.

As I travelled home that evening, I wondered why it was so difficult to accept that sometimes a woman simply wants to spend time with a man without being interested in sex. Was it that naïve to think so?

Tuesday rolled around and I was more than eager to see my beloved again after what had been a difficult start to the new year. Scarlett was my only light in the darkness, the only guiding torch of hope that carried me through difficult times. Harry was a phase I would surpass. But my love for Scarlett felt eternal.

I rode the bird cage elevator up to the fifth floor and found my image of perfection waiting for me.

"Hi, sweetheart. Welcome back to the cold," she said, sounding and looking like a striking ice queen with her low, sultry voice and those now arctic blue eyes penetrating into me.

"Greetings, dear Scarlett."

We embraced once I was through the door. Scarlett seemed to be in her element in the darkness of winter, like she thrived in it, while I was more of a summery person. This quality of hers drew me in. It helped me remember that it was okay to drop my sunnier exterior, which was sometimes a false mask, and be more real, expressing the deep sadness and pain I carried inside of me. My deepest wounds were exposed in her presence. It was perhaps our complementary differences that I was falling in love with.

Scarlett's unique beauty reminded me of the white witch, snow queen of Narnia, in the film *The Chronicles of Narnia – The Lion, the Witch, and the Wardrobe*, played by Tilda Swinton. She was an ice queen in all of her aloofness, and I adored it. I envisioned snowflakes of the purest quality dancing around her aura, an icicle crown gracing the top of her royal head, powdery chunks of Turkish delight in offering held up at her hands. I just wanted to lose myself in her ice storm. Thinking in terms of the tarot, the Queen of Swords was a wonderful way to describe her – the no-nonsense approach, the witty sense of humour, the apathetic nature, the highly developed maturity after having seen a lot of shit in life no doubt. These were the thoughts that passed through my mind in an explosion of life, as I made my way over to my usual chair following our embrace. Within instants of seeing her, my soul came alive and my heart pounded wildly and violently against my chest. The energy in the room was electrifying.

Before starting off the session, holding my head up with my hand as I leaned to the side of the armchair, I spent some time dreamily gazing at Scarlett, taking all of her in. Words could wait. She followed suit and did the same, returning my gaze, as we took each other in for an extended period of silence. I felt as if she were undressing me with her eyes. Fatal attraction was all I could think. Fatal attraction.

Finally, after several minutes of this, she broke the silence.

"What are you thinking about?" Scarlett nearly whispered across the room to me, as if anything louder would be disrespectful to the sensual, rainy day jazz mood in the room.

"Oh, nothing much, nothing much. What are *you* thinking about?" I asked her coquettishly, as 'fatal attraction,' kept sounding in my mind.

"Samara, I am just riding the wave with you."

"We are riding the wave together," I corrected. "I'm not thinking about much in particular," I continued, "It's more like I'm just feeling into the energy of the room."

Scarlett asked me what that feeling was.

I was always careful to speak purely from my heart when it came to Scarlett. Sometimes, unfortunately, there just weren't words. This was one of those times.

"It's like a contemplative energy. There is a pleasantness to its intrigue," I said rather vaguely.

"Is there something different about this room?" I asked.

"No, it's the same. Maybe you're just feeling the energy of the other therapist, Christine, who was using this room before us."

The room really did look different to me, but I think it was that there was a shift in energy between Scarlett and I, and that's why it felt so different. It was much lighter, freer, and simultaneously, more intimate.

"You've been on my mind since the time we last saw each other," Scarlett told me plainly.

"Was I? And what was on your mind, precisely?"

I refrained from telling her that there was hardly a moment in the past six weeks that I wasn't consumed by thoughts of her.

"I had time to reflect over the holiday and deep insights were illuminated."

"Distance and time apart from a person often seems to bring about a fresh perspective."

"Tell me about India, your time with Harry? I know you didn't have the smoothest time at home from the email you sent me."

Oh no! I had completely forgotten I wrote her an email while I was in New York. It was all such a drunken haze.

"Home was difficult. I got through it by swimming in alcohol. My mother gave me a letter from my father. She said she kept it hidden for years because she 'had a bad feeling in her gut' when she came across its hiding place in my closet years ago. Anyway, she let me read it, but didn't let me keep it. Strange, when it was addressed to me."

"What did the letter say?"

"My father wrote it when I was maybe eleven and away at this all-girls Scottish summer camp. He wrote about the beauty of summers and how if I play my cards right, I can find a way to make my whole life into a never-ending summer, if I use the power of thought correctly, if I learn *how* to think. He said that he felt I had that ability, and that it's a great power, if I learn to use it well. Reading it again made me burst into tears. I don't see how my mum thought there was anything wrong with it."

"Did you save a copy of the letter before your mum took it away?" Scarlett asked.

"Sure. I took a photo of it."

I found the photo in my camera roll and walked across the room to hand my phone to Scarlett. She read it and then handed the phone back to me.

"It doesn't seem like something a father would usually write an eleven-year-old girl," Scarlett said, evidently already having made a firm judgement on what she read.

I wondered if Scarlett had the same impression as my mother, but from her it felt more like protection for me. I dropped the conversation and moved on to subject number two, father number two – Harry.

"My time in India with Harry was a total flop. India itself was wonderful and is one of my favourite countries in the world. It always feels like I'm going home when I travel there, especially after having spent a summer living there during my years at university. Its magic was somewhat spoiled, though, by Harry's temper tantrums, demands for sex, constant manipulation and gaslighting. I'm on the verge of leaving him again but I won't go too much into that with you because I know I've said it before.

"He's also been unsupportive while I'm in the midst of a rabies scare, and I don't know what's going to happen to me. Harry is still in Sri Lanka and I had to go alone to get my first injection of the rabies shots. I still have three more to go. It may be too late. I just feel really scared and alone."

"I know, honey..." Her voice was nurturing and held me.

Scarlett asked what the situation was with the rabies, and I explained how the skin near my ankle was just lightly broken, but that sometimes all it takes is only a little bit of saliva. I tried to reassure myself that just because the dog went missing, didn't mean he died from rabies, but the chance of infection was still there. There was no cure; once the symptoms start, the disease is almost always fatal.

I envisioned myself heading towards death, transforming into a snarling wild animal myself, aggressively attacking other human beings, foaming at the mouth, hallucinating like a raving lunatic until suddenly my eyes would roll to the back of my head and I'd be gone. What a tragic, tragic way it would be to go.

"Anyway, I'm trying to not think about my potential upcoming death, but if I don't show up one day, you can guess what happened."

Scarlett told me not to be ridiculous and that I would likely be fine. I told her that I did trust that God and I hadn't planned for me to die that way, but it could happen to anyone.

"I went out with my friend Simon. He invited me back to his place for a drink. He tried to make a move on me; I denied him, and he seemed very surprised."

"Were you trying to get revenge on Harry because he wasn't supportive of you and left you alone to deal with your rabies scare?" Scarlett asked.

"Scarlett, of course not! Is it not normal for a woman to go to a man's place for a drink, just as friends?"

"Well, it's definitely suggestive. I mean, what did you think he would expect?"

"I honestly thought nothing. I didn't even consider it. I have been feeling lonely, but I wasn't trying to fill a void by seeing this friend of mine. Do you feel lonely sometimes?"

"Samara, everyone feels lonely sometimes. I live alone but I have people around."

"I wish I lived alone too, or with a lover I was actually in love with."

"Why don't you consider moving out?"

"I have, but I'm not ready. There's still love between Harry and I, even though I don't feel I'm in love with him. If we were to break up, I'm not sure I would want to stay in London, so I can't make that commitment of signing a rental lease when everything is so up in the air. I will in time, of course, but it's not as simple as it seems."

"Yes, you'll leave Harry when you're ready. From what you've shared with me, it seems likely that Harry's attachment style is ambivalent anxious and as yours is avoidant, there is often an interesting dynamic that plays out between the two. It can be very push and pull."

"That it is," I affirmed.

We turned to the subject of sex and intimacy. Scarlett asked me how I become intimate, other than sex.

"Aside from sex, I do best in one-on-one settings. I find it hard to speak in bigger groups and I mostly come out of my shell when I am engaging with only one other person. I like to go very deep with people, and that's easiest with fewer people around. Unfortunately, most people aren't capable of going deep."

"Do you think I'm capable of going deep?" Scarlett asked.

I looked at her incredulously, genuinely confused as to why she would ask me a question to which the answer was so evident.

"Yes," I said with a somewhat frustrated sigh, "I think you are capable of going deep."

"And not just because I am a psychotherapist..." Scarlett added.

"Scarlett, I wouldn't just say that about any psychotherapist. The extent to which I am able to go deep depends on the company I am with. I think that we mirror each other a lot."

"Yes, we most definitely do," Scarlett said.

"I think you are a lovely person, Samara. I like you very much," she added, slightly blushing.

"I like you very much, too," I said.

"There is a book I wrote that I'd like to give you. I'll bring a copy next week."

"That's very kind of you, Scarlett. I would be delighted to read it."

Unsurprisingly, I couldn't wait to get my hands on that book.

Long stares and powerful silences followed, and then Scarlett turned the subject to my trust issues – how I can be either too trusting or very guarded. She said it's understandable why I would have trust issues given my childhood experiences.

"So, how trusting are *you* with people?" I asked Scarlett.

"It usually takes me about five years to trust someone, but once they pass that test, they're in for life."

"Wow. That's really guarded."

I should be grateful if I break any ground with her, I thought.

"That's why I understand you so well," she said, "Because I'm the same."

"Were you always that way? So cautious when it came to trusting, I mean?"

"Not so much as a child," Scarlett replied, her slight smile radiating a child-like innocence.

I gave her a look of understanding, aware that the world's terrors had shattered her ability to trust.

"Likewise," I replied, as we continued gazing at each other knowingly.

There was such a sweetness to our exchange here, something so pure, that I wished I could capture it in a jar to preserve the fullness of the memory forever.

It felt like we were playing an advanced game of chess with each other. We were slowly and tentatively revealing our intentions, our motives, when it felt safe and right to do so. Sometimes she would make a bolder move on the chessboard, and I might retreat, and the next session I would take one step forward, and then have to take half a step back. There was a definite dance at play, but a strategic one. The dynamic was utterly engaging.

"It seems to be that time," Scarlett said.

I nodded dismally and gathered my things to leave. We embraced once more, and then I walked out the door.

Chapter Sixteen – A Date with the Divine, or a Hidden Shrine?

The week after I saw Scarlett, I was in a state of wild love sickness. I hardly had an appetite. I slept only a few hours at night because my eyes would suddenly jolt open, as if I was missing out on precious time that could be spent thinking of her.

It became apparent that I had never really known love until I met her, and she changed the meaning of it. My love for her was changing me at a core level, causing an alchemical transformation.

But how to go about this now? How to get around societal conventions and regulations that would restrain the purity of this love? There was the significant age gap, the fact that we were the same sex, the fact that I had a boyfriend and potentially so did she, the fact that we came from different countries, and the fact that I wasn't sure how long I would be staying in London. The biggest barrier, however, was the fact that it was not legal for us to have an intimate relationship outside of the therapist-patient dynamic. My overflowing cup of love didn't fit into the established dynamic we found ourselves in. Acting as if our sessions were simply 'therapy,' would have been a lie. Every time I saw her it felt like a date. A date with the Divine.

But love is love, and manages to break through every barrier imaginable. And if I should find it in therapy, with an older woman, so be it.

I certainly had the power to make our sacred union happen, I reassured myself. What was needed was patience, time, vulnerability, and practising the feminine way of wisdom. I would gently invite her in, with unconditional faith and trust in the process. I reminded myself that I must not let my love stop me from living like a normal person. I would have to be cautious to not let my undying passion burn me out. A delicate balance would have to be in order.

Sometimes when I would allow negativity to get the best of me, I would become weary that I shouldn't love in this way, that there was something wrong with me, that I was just setting myself up for failure. I wondered if she was just playing games with me, as there were times when she was hot, and times when she was cold. There were times when she was on, and there were times when she was off. What if this was just a cat and mouse game she was playing and was simply having some fun with? It did come to me at the end of the session that it felt like we were playing chess with each other. But I would overpower these moments of doubt and try to bring myself out of it and remember that the desires of my heart wouldn't be there if they weren't placed there by divine orchestration. How could I feel such overpowering emotions if they weren't real, if they weren't 'legitimate,' if they weren't worth exploring?

And then it came to my attention – had I really taken the time to process the part of me that was gay? Or actually fully acknowledge it? Had I suppressed that all of my life? There were signs before, but I ignored them because I had only been in relationships with men, even though I had experimented with women before. I had never fallen in love with a man in the way I had fallen for Scarlett. Had I ever actually 'fallen,' for a man at all? I stored the thoughts away for further consideration when all would make more sense to me. Nothing was quite so clear now. Was anything ever clear with me? Not quite. Not quite. Not quite. Said the flying phantom in the night.

It was the evening before our next session before I knew it. I spent the time thinking that maybe I had to be more forthright that I was serious about Scarlett. All I had done thus far was flirt with her, but maybe I should let her know I meant business.

The last of the thoughts that ruminated through my mind were more like prayers to the Gods of love. Please cupid, shoot your arrows down upon us. Dear Lord, let her accept and love me the way that I do her. And should she not, grant me the right to continue to love her anyway.

I was feeling greater anxiety than usual when I arrived at the Victorian House in South Kensington that Tuesday at quarter to eleven. I climbed the spiral staircase, hoping to come more fully into my body and ground myself before seeing her. My heart was racing faster than usual. When I reached the fifth floor and regarded Scarlett across the way, I knew that today, was not going to be a good day.

Her expression was grave, and her energy was cold. As I walked through the door, I felt as though I had just entered an ice box. I shivered and decided I would be keeping my coat on for the session. I felt like I needed to protect myself. Scarlett had left the book she had written on the chair for me, and I thanked her. As I scanned the book and looked at her name printed on the cover, I commented on how I liked her name.

"Bennett?" she asked, grimacing.

"No, Scarlett, though I see nothing wrong with your last name, either. My cousin has the same Christian name as you and I've always been fond of it."

Silence. That went over well. I suppose that further confirmed that today was no day for flattery or niceties.

"What do you wish to bring to therapy today?" Scarlett asked.

"I don't know. Nothing I can think of at the moment. Perhaps you can just ask me some questions and whatever needs to come up will come up organically," I told her.

I wanted to speak to Scarlett about my love for her, but I didn't feel prepared to come out and say it just then, at the beginning of the session, especially with the mood she was in.

"A good indicator of what might be lurking in the shadow," Scarlett said, "is when something really agitates you and there's not really a reasonable justification for it. Think about when you're out and about. Is there something you really can't stand that you sometimes notice in other people?"

"Not particularly," I said. "I mean, sure, little things annoy me, but nothing to the point where I feel like I'm going to rage because I'm so triggered. Just minor things, like when there's not enough space to have privacy, or breathing room, and yet a person might decide to stand or sit right next to me and doesn't respect my personal space. Or when people laugh in the cinema at something idiotic and I feel like I'm surrounded by imbeciles. Or listening to the sound of chewing. *That* makes me want to blow my brains out sometimes. I'm generally very sensitive to unwanted noise. I understand we all have a shadow, but perhaps I just haven't been able to find mine yet. I suppose it will reveal itself when it's ready."

Scarlett looked frustrated with my answer. "You're going to have to do a little bit better than that. There must be something with more substance that we can look at together. For example, I don't like that look of contempt you have on your face right now," Scarlett said.

"Do I have a look of contempt?"

"And because I don't like that in you, that must be in me too. There are times where I can come across as arrogant, uninterested, apathetic. Recognising it in you brings attention to that quality in myself," Scarlett said.

"Well, perhaps that is just my defence for feeling a little bit put on the spot right now."

I felt like I was being pushed to give Scarlett an answer I didn't have. Wasn't the point of the shadow that it is elusive, anyway?

"Samara, you have to be willing to delve more underneath the surface if we are going to get anywhere and actually make use of our time. Let's look at your dreams. Dreams can also be telling clues as to what is lurking in the shadow," Scarlett said.

"I had a dream last week where I was in a house and it was flooding, everything was caving in on me. There was no escape."

"What was the main emotion you were feeling behind that dream?"

Part of me wanted to tell her it was love, the all-consuming, uncontrollable love that I felt for her. But considering the way things were going, it didn't feel safe to do so.

"I guess I'm feeling like things are somewhat out of control in my life lately. A storm of emotions is brewing and I'm afraid I'll drown in the flood."

"That's rather vague. What is the origin of the fear you're experiencing? Why would it be scary for you to drown in the emotions? What are the emotions that you are finding to be most overwhelming?"

"I guess...I guess it's scary because it's unfamiliar. They are feelings I'm not used to experiencing," I said.

"What is it you are afraid of losing control over? And why do you feel the need to have control?"

"I'm afraid I'll lose something very important if I lose control. It's like, if I let go, I might completely lose myself in the process," I said.

It was she that I was terribly afraid of losing, and yet somehow that was related to me. If I lost her, I would lose the other half of myself. I was trying to tell her in so many words.

"Well, there is that controlling part of your nature we spoke about, but it's more about your own self-control, wanting to make yourself appear in a certain light."

"Here is an example of a dream that I had some time ago: I was in a basement cellar. I was cradling a kitten in my arms, and through the basement window, behind the metal rails, were all these other vicious cats hissing with their pointy fangs, ready to pounce and attack the kitten. I experienced a strong impulse to throw the kitten to the wild cats, into the lion's den," Scarlett said.

"Mhmm, I can see how that might be more foretelling of the shadow. I can't think of any dreams offhand where I had malicious intent, but I am sure I can find something from my past dream material. I'll have a look at it over the coming week and see what I can find."

I thought about Scarlett's dream. Cats resemble the feminine. So, what was it about the feminine that she wanted to toss away? Was it something about feminine power? Feminine sexuality? Malicious intent?

"On the note of being malicious, maybe this is random, but I do remember being mean to a girl when I was like nine about her glasses. How bratty of me. Maybe she provoked me or something. I don't remember, but looking back, I feel like a jerk for it. I mean, I like the look of glasses, but God only knows the rationale of children sometimes."

"You need to focus on going into your own darkness more. I'm trying to give you some examples of my own to help you, but it's like meeting a brick wall. It's not going to get you anywhere if you're only preaching love and light all the time.

Facing and integrating the shadow is what leads us to wholeness," Scarlett said.

"Do you think I don't want to find my shadow? I wouldn't be here if I weren't interested. And I'm not sure where you got the idea that I'm going around preaching 'love and light' all the time. I acknowledge darkness as a necessary means to self-discovery, just as much as the light. Perhaps more so. I'm sure it will reveal itself when the time is right. I'm not just going to conjure up some flimsy answer in order to satisfy you," I said.

"There are other ways of becoming aware of the shadow by examining your daily life. Humour is another example; what strikes us as funny might give us a clue. Exaggerated reactions or feelings about others is another. Negative feedback from others who serve as reflections of ourselves. Situations where we have the same distressing effect on multiple people. Impulsive or 'unintended' acts. That's a starting point for you," Scarlett said.

I felt like she wasn't hearing me or didn't want to hear me.

"What do you think the purpose of me going to the jungles of Peru was? I wanted to make sure I was in a situation where there would be no escaping when it came to understanding the entirety of my core self."

The room became as cold as ice. I felt defenceless, vulnerable, perhaps just like that baby kitten that was about to be thrown into the lion's den.

"You can't expect to go to Peru every time you need to look within. What you need is not outside of you. Hopping from place to place is not going to help you escape your head. It will follow you everywhere you go. Intellectualising and analysing everything will only get you so far. The real work is in the feeling. You must get more in touch with your identity that you consider to be your core self — including the aspects of your personality that you deem as negative. If you are dedicated to your spiritual growth, I want to encourage you to take some time to find out what makes you, you," Scarlett said.

I nodded. I was already too shut down to engage. I needed to be spoken to gently in order for us to get anywhere. I continued to stare at her vacantly and silently let her go on.

"You don't always have to present a 'good,' or acceptable face to society, to me, to anyone. It's important you express and act as you feel. I know you better than you might think I do. It's just that I keep hitting walls with you and then I don't know how you're really feeling. It's never pleasant to confront the darker aspects of ourselves, but if you truly want to know yourself, there's no way around it."

I was doing the best I could to help give Scarlett what she was looking for, but her stern approach wasn't working on me. I felt I'd always been real with her, even if sometimes a bit reticent. I knew she was coming from the right place, but the sudden change in the way she was treating me threw me completely off guard. I couldn't even speak. I didn't even know what I was feeling. I guess numb would be the best way to describe it. Of course, this only frustrated her more. We were completely out of alignment. The attunement just wasn't there.

With my lack of response, Scarlett likewise ran out of fuel, and we just sat in a silent stalemate until the session came to its close.

I wept as I descended the spiral staircase. I wanted to work with Scarlett, be as cooperative as I could be, but she wasn't allowing me the space to explore my shadow with her. The energy wasn't right; it felt too directive, and it caused me to shut down. I wondered how there could be such a shift in her so suddenly. Was she just having an off day and projecting on to me? Dark and crushing thoughts swirled through my mind as I journeyed back to the flat.

Harry was at work when I returned, and I was grateful to have time and space to cry and try to make sense of what had just happened. I thought Scarlett and I had an understanding, but now it seemed that she didn't get me at all. Was the sweetness I'd seen in her just a façade? Were all the months we'd spent together a lie? Had I been completely deluding myself?

What was the point in continuing to work with Scarlett if she didn't even know me by now? Couldn't she see that I was doing the best I could? I implied that I felt pressured, but she didn't let up. Now I was just left feeling hurt. I decided to write Scarlett an email to say that I felt we were no longer suited to working together.

Dear Scarlett,

It is with sadness I must tell you our psychotherapy sessions have run their course. Thank you for all that you have helped me with. I understand that in learning to love all parts of myself, and in continuing to grow in self-love, I have to be cautious to not place too much emphasis on the reflections others have of me. I see now that it's necessary for me to both trust and take into greater consideration my own perceptions of how I feel about myself.

I have the tendency to sometimes take the feelings of others more into account than my own. I've learned that, and am still in the process of learning that, the reflections of others often have much more to do with them, and their own state of being, rather than the truth of how we are. People can sometimes distort, unintentionally, rather than accurately reflect. And so rather than becoming further confused about who I am, I now have to make the conscious decision to honour my own truth.

I truly wish you all the best, Scarlett.

With love,
Samara

After I sent the email, I moped around the flat for several hours and closed all the curtains, not wanting to see the light of day. To say I was depressed about our sudden ending was an understatement, but I saw no other way. It would only lead to further disappointment and hurt if I were to continue to see her after my illusions were shattered.

Harry wrote me that he would be having dinner with his wife and the children. I thought, 'all the better,' I shall go out and fetch some wine. Shortly after I stepped outside, it began to drizzle. Fortunately, my usual wine shop in Notting Hill was only a few streets down. And anyway, I welcomed the idea of being caught in the rain.

My soul needed a cleansing from the grace of Mother Earth. It was the perfect night to drown my sorrows. After choosing a bottle of Montepulciano, I hurried home to make the most of my sorrowful situation. I turned on a jazz playlist, corked open the bottle, and attempted to escape my reality. The warmth of the red wine sliding down my throat somewhat numbed the pain. At least the alcohol would help me to get out of my head, perhaps see things in a different light. But it only exacerbated what I was already feeling. I felt like the biggest fool for having such high hopes in our connection. Who was Scarlett, anyway? I had ignored all the signs again and only focused on the light. Maybe my heart racing before seeing her was actually internal alarm bells going off that something was amiss, rather than flutters of love. Maybe there was a reason I felt I couldn't open up to her as effortlessly as I sometimes could with others, and that it was not – as I had thought – just a reaction of a lover deeply in love. A word of wisdom from my spiritual teacher came to mind, about not seeking darkness if you are really after the light.

I felt a sense of betrayal on behalf of the Divine for placing us together in the first place. Why should this happen to me when I was seeking help? The last thing I needed in my life was more confusion, more pain. I was only half to blame, but I was equally responsible for attracting this situation to myself.

A quote by Rumi came into my mind: "A deep silence overcomes me, and I wonder why I ever thought to utter words."

Scarlett replied to my email, thanking me for letting her know. She said it's usually better to have a final session than to end via email, however, it was entirely up to me. She also said that sometimes things get difficult in therapy, but that often signals the chance for breakthrough. She said that she thoroughly enjoyed working with me and that if at any point I changed my mind, she would be happy to see me again.

I mulled over her words. Had I made the right decision in saying goodbye to Scarlett? Was it too much of an impulsive reaction? I felt at a loss. The way I was feeling now couldn't get much worse. And perhaps that was a sign that it wasn't the right decision to finish just yet.

One way or another, this was feeding my soul growth. I poured myself another glass of wine and started to calm down. Possibly I was being melodramatic about this whole thing. I knew therapy wasn't supposed to be smooth sailing. Yet even in the intense times, there should still be mutual understanding, and that just wasn't present while we were together. Even so, just as I was not perfect, I could not expect perfection out of her, and maybe she was simply having an off day. Was it the shadow in me that I was rejecting by rejecting her? Of course, it was curious that I should attempt to end on this day of shadows lurking in our midst. Could Scarlett have been the direct manifestation of my shadow, sitting right there before my eyes in our session?

After draining another glass of wine, I was feeling rather sleepy. I forgot about dinner and got into bed. I wanted to be fast asleep before Harry returned. I was in no mood to converse with him.

In my dream, I was on a ship with my mum and sister. I kept trying to get in contact with Scarlett but there was no service. I was trying to tell her that I wasn't ready for us to end.

I woke and wrote her, saying that after giving it some thought, I decided I would like to continue working with her and see how things go from there. We agreed to meet as normally scheduled next Tuesday at eleven.

I endeavored to spend the rest of the week taking seriously what Scarlett said, making the best effort I could to give her a better answer, to satisfy her. Like I said, though, the shadow is not exactly something one can go on the hunt for.

I decided I would make an effort to reconnect with Harry and not shut him out as much. There had been a great distance between us since our holiday, but as long as we were living together, we may as well use our relationship as an opportunity for growth like I had initially intended. Conflict was becoming a regular in my life lately, anyway, so what did I have to lose?

I briefed Harry on my exchange with Scarlett and told him of my confusion. I asked him if he had any insight. He reminded me that I'd committed to a year of therapy, so that even though things were difficult, I should follow through with my commitments. I explained that I had already decided I would stick it out.

I made us tea and he offered me fresh insights.

"As I was doing some reflecting, all I could come up with is that you are too self-oriented. We have been having this conversation for half an hour, but not once have you asked me about my back. I mentioned the other day that it's been hurting me, and it didn't cross your mind to offer me a massage or anything. You've just been talking about your therapy problems the whole time. What about my needs? I feel uncared for. Other than that, darling, I see you as this angelic being."

"Thank you. I'm sorry I haven't thought about your back pain. I came to you to discuss what came up in therapy as it's been weighing heavily on me. We've hardly been in contact for days, so I wanted to hash this out before anything else. Anyway, I now give you the floor. Speak of whatever you wish. I am all ears."

"I'd rather not speak at this point, but a massage would be nice," Harry said.

"Of course. I'll get the oils and shall do my best to ease your pain."

I longed for an intimate emotional connection, but I knew that I wasn't going to get that with Harry. Expecting him to act differently would just be a drain of my energy. And so, I gave Harry a thorough full body massage and entirely devoted my thoughts to Scarlett once more.

Harry and I strived to be closer to each other in the following days. He was much more loving with me after I gave him a massage and told me that actions like that are his love language. I understood him perfectly well.

I spent Friday evening by myself while Harry went to squash practice. I took a sea salt bath and contemplated life by candlelight. I then crawled into bed and read Scarlett's book. The context was quite impersonal, to my dismay. I was hoping to get to know her more on a personal level through her words, but nonetheless, I found the psychological aspects to be engaging.

I thought of how Scarlett would often repeat that she cared more about my intrinsic qualities, rather than the exterior superficiality that people could sometimes get caught up in about me. It was a healing gift for me that she emphasised this, that she cared more about my true self than the way I presented.

By the time I finished reading, Harry had still not returned and so I shut off the light in hopes of finally getting a night of sound sleep.

Regrettably, he returned around midnight and tried to wake me from my slumber to take me from behind. I shrugged him off me. It was sketchy that he was returning so late, but I had bigger fish to fry.

Sunday was Valentine's Day and we had plans to dine at Launceston Place in the evening. I picked up a card for him and wrote what loving things I could say, in hopes for better days. I even wrote him a poem, I once sang to him in Rome. He made efforts too, and threw red roses at my shoes. Dinner was a pleasure, and we toasted to all of life's fair treasures.

The following morning, however, was something else altogether. Harry was irritable, but fortunately, he had to look after the children that afternoon, leaving me some time to reflect in peace. I went for a walk in Holland Park and thought about how I would handle Scarlett the next day. I would ask for God's support beforehand and do my best to hold nothing back on how I felt in our last session. I'd say that if we were to continue together, we needed to come to a better understanding and create an environment where I would feel I could speak more openly about my feelings.

When I returned home from my walk, I started preparing dinner as Harry had requested. He came sooner than expected and was obviously overwhelmed from having been with the children most of the day. He wasn't pleased with the way I cut the vegetables. I hardly reacted and just let him blow off his own steam. I didn't need to be dragged into his whirlwind of emotions. I had done that far too often in the past. I was determined to preserve my energy. I kept to myself the rest of the night. I focused on Scarlett to keep the energy light.

Chapter Seventeen – Convalescence, at its Essence

It was unusually warm for the middle of February as I stepped outside at twenty to eleven to hail a taxi. Despite my anxiety, I felt a sense of hope. There was a supermoon, and my emotions felt very much at play.

When I reached the fifth floor, I said hi to Scarlett at the door. She greeted me and soon we were sat facing each other. The energy was tense, and I knew we would have to climb to make it over the fence.

I placed the book I was reading, *Meeting the Shadow,* on the little glass table next to my chair in clear sight of Scarlett, smirking all the while. I wanted to emphasise that I wasn't kidding around about my determination to put in the work as much as she was. I had no idea how to start the conversation, so I just took a whack at it and dove right in.

"We finished the last session with you wanting me to go into my feelings. So, let's start with that, shall we?"

Scarlett nodded.

"When we saw each other last, I felt like I couldn't access my feelings because I shut down at some point. Afterwards, I realised it was anger that I was feeling because I felt the way you were speaking to me was out of order. I felt like you were trying to project this darkness on to me. It felt very aggressive, which is why I felt we couldn't continue to work together."

"I wasn't projecting anything on to you. I've been a therapist for a very long time. I've been in therapy myself. I'm in supervision. I'm able to recognise my own transference. I find it hard to believe that you've integrated *every* negative aspect of your personality because I've never known anybody, including myself, that's been able to do that. And nothing in my relationship with you has led me to believe that you have, either. I think you're quite good at avoiding it, but that's not the same as having addressed it. And if you avoid something consciously or unconsciously, you project it out on to the world, and it comes back to you. And it will come back to you in difficult relationships. And that's why I would rather you looked at it than lived in the belief that you had sorted out what none of us have ever sorted out."

"Yeah. Well, I understand that, and of course there's always going to be stuff that I have to work on. I was never negating that. It was just the way you were coming across that made me feel like I was being attacked. I was trying to explain to you that I was giving you everything I could."

"Which is problematical, Samara, because everything you could give me was, 'I was rude to some girl when I was nine about her glasses.' I mean, I was aware that you were angry at the end. Even if you weren't aware of it yourself, I was certainly aware of it. Therapy is about looking at difficult stuff, and if I stayed only with the part of you that you like, it would be a waste of time for both of us. Ultimately, it won't help you. Sure, it would give you positive reinforcement. And you know, I am there for you, if you want to come back and continue. I am very fond of you. I like you, you know. I like *all* of you. I even like the part of you that isn't that nice. And I can see it, even if you can't."

"And what is that part of me?"

"I would say it's the gamey part of you that steps back and won't engage. It's the part of you that struggles to be fully present, that only wants to show selected parts of yourself to the world. It's easier to be around someone who is more difficult and angry and shows how she's feeling, rather than someone who steps away and doesn't engage. That's harder. That's much harder to be around. I think you are able to meet people in a place which is very loving, but I think you find it hard to be fully who you are."

"Yes, well, from the start I've told you I felt cut off from myself in a sense, like there are disparate parts attempting to find a way to work together. I haven't gotten there quite yet, but it doesn't mean that I am not trying."

"And if I were to continue to reinforce that aspect of you that doesn't engage, we wouldn't be getting anywhere. If I were to say, 'yeah that loving aspect of you, Samara, you're comfortable with it, I'm comfortable with it, too, let's both sit here being comfortable in it together,' I wouldn't be helping you."

"Scarlett, I don't expect you to do that. I'm happy that you seek to challenge me. You wouldn't be doing your job if you didn't bring these things up. But my point is that it felt very aggressive."

"I'm sorry if I was aggressive."

"That approach doesn't work well for me. I mean, I don't expect you to sit here and praise me and tell me I have nothing to work on. I'm not here for that. I just need to be addressed in a softer way. Otherwise, I'll shut down. It's not that I'm trying to be difficult, but that's just how I operate."

"And how do you imagine I felt from reading your last email?" Scarlett asked me.

"Surprised, maybe?"

Why did I say...surprised? It was a rather bizarre response, like, 'heyyyy, surprise! I am quitting and I'm never coming back to therapy again with you. Goodbye, fair-weather friend!'

"That's what you would think my response would be? What did you want my response to be?" Scarlett asked me.

I knew she would catch me on my choice of words.

"I didn't have a want. I just wanted you to understand where I was coming from. You know, your emotional responses are up to you. I wasn't looking for a reaction out of you. I was looking to express my truth, and hopefully shed light on what wasn't working for me. What was your response?"

"I was hurt, because I only act out of your best interest. I felt misunderstood because you were saying things that didn't really make sense."

"Like what?"

"All of this stuff about 'people tell me things that are actually just about them.' I mean, don't you know me? Don't you have any trust in me?"

"I was trying to say that the emotional state of the person reflecting back to you is something to be considered. I didn't feel that what you were reflecting to me was an accurate reflection of who I am. From the moment I saw you last Tuesday, your energy felt a bit off, to be honest."

"Well, I wasn't feeling angry towards you. I was in a good mood while I was with you. I wasn't in a place where I would have attacked you for other reasons."

"It was not my intention to hurt you. It was obviously an emotional email, but I tried to be as straightforward as I could be. I did reflect a lot in the last week, and I spoke to Harry about my shadow side. He told me I can be too focused on myself and end up ignoring his needs. Then I had a dream after I emailed you that I was on a ship trying to get service to write you to tell you that I wanted to continue working with you. In the morning I realised I wanted to at least have a final session with you to discuss this."

"Yes, we at least need to have a final discussion about this. But there's no point asking people what they think of you because you won't get a straight answer. No one is going to want to hurt you."

"I thought of that, which is precisely why I asked Harry. He doesn't hold back at all. He likes to give it to me in any way he can."

Scarlett laughed at that.

"Anyway, I don't think you're too self-involved. On the contrary, I think you over-give to your own detriment."

"Well, I guess I can see why Harry might say that because I haven't paid much attention to him lately and have been focusing on myself more. I mean, I am a bit obsessed with self-reflection. In the beginning of our relationship, I was overextending myself all the time with him, but he pushed me past my limit, so now my effort is rather minimal as I bide my time to figure out what to do about our relationship."

"I think what you do need to be aware of is how attacking *you* are," Scarlett said.

"In an indirect way, you mean?"

"In an indirect way, certainly. You didn't attack back in the session, but then you attacked in the email. So, I guess you need to know that you can be very attacking."

"I think it's a good quality, when necessary," I said.

"I'm not so sure about that," Scarlett said.

"I think being assertive and speaking one's truth is important. I was asserting myself and speaking up about the fact that I wasn't pleased with the way *you* were attacking me in the first place."

"I experienced it as attacking. Highly attacking. Because if you do it in the outside world and think you are expressing your truth, the other person will experience it as attacking."

All this talk about 'attacking.' It was like we were waging a war with each other.

"Well then, I too am sorry if I came across that way to you."

"That's okay. We are having a discussion. Likewise, I am sorry I came across as aggressive to you. I am sorry you felt that my energy was off. I didn't feel it was off, but if you experienced it as off, then that's your experience," Scarlett said.

"And it's necessary for us to have difficult times."

"This is therapy," I said.

"This is therapy. And it's not always going to be nice," Scarlett affirmed. "So...what do you want to do? What else do you want to say to me?"

I mulled the question over.

"I guess I just want to further my point that when we're bringing up tougher subjects, when it's not going to be 'nice,' as you say, I'd prefer if you would be more careful with your approach. More like constructive conversation rather than leaving me feeling like I'm having daggers thrown at me."

"If you experience me as attacking you, it's up to you in the session to say, 'I feel attacked.' That's more constructive than having me tiptoe around. You have to bring your emotion into the session. If you aren't frank with me, and I am not frank with you, right here, right now, don't expect anyone to know what's going on for you."

"I guess it didn't even occur to me to tell you that I felt attacked. In my past it didn't feel like an option to say how I really felt. Instead, I just froze."

"It will come out anyway. Either you'll end up internalising it, and then you'll get sick, or it will come off in emails like the one you sent me, or in passive aggressive behaviour," Scarlett said.

"I was taught that my feelings weren't important, so I got it into my head that feelings don't matter. Sometimes I just wouldn't feel *anything.* It was eerie. This feeling business is all relatively new to me."

"Samara, it's totally natural that you disconnected yourself from your feelings because of what you went through. I understand that. It's a common effect of women that have been sexually abused to shut off from feeling. So, when it comes to us, don't worry about processing so much. Be present and say what you are experiencing right at the moment without a filter. If you start to bring that more into your awareness, it will happen less in the end."

"Yes. It takes time to change our ways," I said.

"It takes a lot of time," said Scarlett.

"Well, this conversation is an improvement for me because in the past I likely wouldn't have said anything."

"Yeah, you would have walked out the door," Scarlett said."

"It's more that I wouldn't have even sent you the email in the first place and would have swallowed it and silenced myself. It was almost like it was my way of gaining power in childhood – showing that I was unhurt, unaffected externally when internally I was crying. I didn't realise I was losing my power by losing my voice."

"Whenever I have supervision, I ask what I can do to get you to go into your emotions more."

"And what were the suggestions?" I asked.

"They were all fairly lame. I've tried everything," Scarlett laughed.

"We can try to get you to express what you feel in here, in a contained setting. I think we both have to be honest about our feelings, for your benefit. It is up to me to express how I feel as well, in order to try to elicit, so we are both in the truth of it together," Scarlett said.

"Mhmm," I replied.

"How are you feeling right now?"

It took me a good minute or so to come up with an answer.

"Pleased, I guess." What a lame response. It was all I could come up with in regard to a feeling.

"What about? What was your fantasy?"

"I guess I'm pleased that we were able to come to an understanding. Maybe I didn't expect you to be as cooperative as you have been, after the way you were with me last week. And as for the fantasy, I didn't have one…"

"*Everybody* has a fantasy. Everyone plays through scenarios wondering what might happen."

Scarlett looked like a person who fantasised a lot. I felt I was more of a daydreamer than a fantasist. What was the difference though, anyway?

"If I must give you an answer, I guess you could say my 'fantasy,' was that I just didn't think you would even understand where I was coming from at all, in the sense that I felt you were being aggressive. Well, you actually still don't see where you were being aggressive, but…"

"I didn't see where I was being aggressive because I wasn't aware of being aggressive. Because I knew I wasn't angry with you, it is hard for me to then imagine that I was being aggressive to you. But you are perfectly entitled to your feelings, as I am to mine. We are responsible for our own feelings, and we feel what we want to feel. We feel what we are feeling. And we are constantly all having misunderstandings in this world."

"We don't have to justify our feelings," I said.

"We don't have to justify our feelings. I don't have to justify my feelings to you, and you don't have to justify yours to me. But if *neither* of us expresses how we are feeling, that will be a problem for both of us," Scarlett said.

"Mhmm. Right," I said.

"It's just not an overnight process for me."

"What does it take? How does the trust develop? What has to happen for you?" Scarlett asked me.

"Well, it takes time, for one…. Hmm, what else? It takes self-expression, on both sides. Truth. Transparency. I think transparency is the big thing."

"So, in other words, for you to open up, you need the other person to lead the way. Is that right?" Scarlett asked me.

"Right."

"And what happens in life, when they don't lead the way? What if they can't trust either, and they're scared?"

"Maybe I would take the lead in that case."

"Would you?" Scarlett asked me.

"Depends. It's very much so contingent upon the person. How do I put this? It's more of a feeling for me, more than anything else. I mean, I can say time and transparency are important factors, that sort of thing, but it actually comes down to a feeling that I get. So, if I feel that a person struggles with that, I would probably then be the one to step up."

There was a period of silence here, where I supposed Scarlett was mulling over my words. It felt to me that Scarlett was speaking in third person about herself. We were speaking about hypothetical circumstances as if they were outside to us, but it felt very much all about us.

"So… *my* thought is that the feeling you get, I would hope, is an awareness that the other person in some way has got your back," Scarlett said.

"That's it. You've understood me well."

"It's like the difference between someone not liking you and somebody liking you for being pissed off. Right? That's my personal experience. That when I know somebody doesn't really like me, it makes me weary to be around them. But if I know that they do like me, if I can sense that they like me, then it's just a matter of wading through the shit."

"Well, I started to think last time you didn't actually like me," I said.

"Because I didn't say, 'oh you're all...'"

"I didn't expect you to say that. It was just your behaviour, your attitude towards me."

Scarlett sighed.

"I *do* like you," Scarlett nearly whispered, "which is why it's quite troubling to me that you should feel that. That I didn't like you, because it's contrary to the truth of what I feel for you. Sure, I get pissed off, and frustrated, but that was only really last week because you were continually stone walling me. So last week I thought we could try and look at something other than what's easy. And then I could see you were getting angry, and you weren't saying it, so then I was getting angry because I could see it, and you weren't saying it, and so it was just like a cycle of frustration."

"Well, I don't want to repeat myself but all I can say is that I need a softer approach, or the walls will go up."

"But you put up walls anyway. All I can speak of is my experience with you and that I often do feel that I am facing walls that I am trying to get to the other side of to meet you. I get frustrated when I am trying to find a way through to you and not finding a way through, but I know that I fundamentally like you. I understand that you are defending yourself, protecting yourself, and I think on the other side, you're nice, I like you, you're fundamentally *okay*."

"Oh, I'm glad. Glad to hear that!" I said laughing.

"So, when you say that you started to get the opinion last week that I didn't like you, wow..."

"It was more like I couldn't trust you."

"What? Because I'm not nice to you all of the time?"

"No, Scarlett. I just feel confused sometimes when I feel your energy shift so much and I experience a very different side to you."

"I probably have about twenty sides to me, Samara, as do you. You know, we are not one thing."

"No, we aren't. It was simply the lack of consistency that threw me for a loop," I said.

"Welcome to the world. You are inconsistent with your own emotions, and you'll experience that with everyone. Emotions aren't constant. They are everchanging."

I didn't voice this, and perhaps I should have, but wasn't there supposed to be some sort of consistency in therapy?

"Well, clearly I have some work to do in feeling safe when it comes to expressing myself emotionally. I suppose that is what we can continue working with."

"Well, if you do decide to leave today, and you don't come back, and if you take anything from our time together, take away that I really liked you. And I don't like everyone I see. Know that even though I don't think you're a perfect person, I don't care. I like you. So that is something to bear in mind. I'm not going to just sack you."

Scarlett then explained how therapy is an extremely difficult journey and looking at the difficult aspects of oneself is tough, and that if we are going to do it, we have to be fully in it.

"It's not like I enjoy floating around in a state of disassociation, Scarlett. It's not exactly a matter of choice. I have become more present at least in the last year since I have been with Harry."

"Well Harry's a sketchy guy, isn't he? You know he's..."

I laughed.

"Sketchy he may well be, but even with his difficulties, with our difficulties, working through it has been beneficial to my healing."

"Well, I certainly think you are working something out with him, and I think you are working something out with me too. I think you and I are like…."

Scarlett trailed off, holding herself back from saying whatever was initially on her mind.

"Dr. Hugo Bourke was very careful with how he referred. He is a clever man and has been doing this a long time. He didn't just land you with anyone, right? He landed you very much with me. And he knows me very well."

"I think you and I are like shadowy reflections of the moon."

"Oh! It's five past, so we need to end."

There goes the clock. Tick tock.

"Sure thing. Thank you, Scarlett. Thank you for everything."

"You are very welcome, Samara. I look forward to seeing you next week."

I tied up my emerald green wool coat and walked out the door only to be summoned as I was about to walk down the spiral staircase.

"Samara, your book!"

I twisted around on my heel and a smile beamed across my face because I realised what book I so conveniently forgot. 'Don't want to forget that!' I thought. It was my *Meeting the Shadow* book, which apparently, I wanted to leave behind. I supposed my shadow preferred to stay with Scarlett.

"Don't want to forget this," she said, a teasing smirk written across her face.

I was left speechless as I heard my words being plunked straight from my mouth. I met her eyes deeply, smirking back at her as I snatched the book from her hands, turning on my heel once again, and gliding down the stairwell in a cloud of love.

Although it was a difficult session to get through, I felt elated at our newfound level of understanding. Not all hope was lost. The song 'Tuesday Afternoon,' by The Moody Blues started playing in my mind.

Ah yes, the sweet, sweet beauty of Tuesday afternoons. I was on cloud 9, chasing the clouds away, leaving myself behind, the shadowy reflections of my mind. Come with me, dear children of the sea. And you shall see, the beauty of Tuesday afternoon. Sway along with me, as we venture further along in the fairyland of love.

I seemed to be buzzing like a bee. It was the supermoon, after all, and I was feeling very much in a thrall. And so, when I arrived at my flat, I thought of what I would say. It was time to write Scarlett, how I loved her ways.

Dear Scarlett,

I just want to tell you I love you. I am sorry if I haven't made that clear enough recently, and I am really sorry that my last email hurt you. I find psychotherapy difficult with you because I like you too much and I feel very restricted in being able to express these feelings given the situation we are in. That's also part of the reason why I am very sensitive to any kind of criticism from you, and why I can't fully open up to you. I can't help how strongly I feel about you. I've only ever really felt loving towards you, and it is coming from a genuine place within me. I am not sure how we are to continue working together, because my love will just get in the way. Of course, I am open to hearing your thoughts.

Samara

Sent. And now it was just a waiting game. I had to get the words out of me, or I felt like I would explode. Even so, I was somewhat internally panicking about how she would take it. Anyway, there was no way around it. I had to be transparent. As I waited to hear back from her, I wrote a poem.

'The Artist and the Dreamer'

I lie awake in the dead of the night
Reciting all of your beautiful lies
Vague answers, insightful as dancers
Twirling into delicate rhythms and rhymes

The pearl threaded into a lesson
A shining opalescent crescent
Its intricacies of allure
Tempting me…please bring me some more

We are the masters of disguise
Before our very eyes
Into the mermaid's mirror, we align
Like a snow globe lost in space,
In time

Distant shores mark spaces between words
A floating compass without a direction
The needle spins to and fro'
Wondering which way it is, I must go

Shadowy reflections of the moon
Distortions begging to be fine-tuned
Why is it so cold when you enter the room?
Feed me some ice cream; I'll give you my spoon.

Dreamers dream into the night
Artists fly their eagle eyes
Untold stories whisper of their glory
Open the page; it's time for the stake.

In an effort to calm down, I took a long afternoon bath, then I fell asleep for several hours. I had a powerful and vivid dream.

I was walking in the forest with another psychiatrist, and we were looking for something which led me into a classroom. The unknown psychiatrist disappeared. Inside of the classroom, there were maybe fifteen bathroom stalls, and Scarlett was in the centre of them all, with each stall circling around her. The class was to be taught with each of us behind the closed doors of the bathroom stalls. She had tarot cards in front of her, and when she was guided to call on a student, she would shuffle the cards and pull out one card with an image that would provide her information regarding what they needed to hear. She worked with two students and called on me as the third.

Scarlett asked me how I was feeling. I felt calm while speaking to her. The dynamic between us felt healing and full of understanding. She then pulled the card for me that said 'concealment,' or 'secrets;' it was one of the two. She said I had reached a new stage, but the roses that bloomed had thorns. She then relayed a vision of the roses crumbling, the petals falling away. It was as if they were trying to bloom but something was stopping them. She said there were too many masks, too many faces.

I was not sure if she was saying my life and my love was a secret, or that she was picking up on me concealing my feelings for her, or that she was concealing her feelings from me.

It then became apparent to me that I needed to acknowledge the thorns with the bloom, both of the rose. I was presenting only my roses, not also my thorns. I was searching among branches for what only appears in the roots. I would have to surrender into the pain, into the depths of despair, in order to fully blossom and bloom. I would have to face the darkness in order for my light to fully manifest. If I were to only present my roses, it would be a false façade, a mask. I wondered if perhaps I was the only one that had fallen in love with my flowers, and I needed to fall in love with my roots.

After I finished writing down the dream, I checked my emails. Scarlett had replied.

Dear Samara,

Then what it is to love is exactly what we need to work with next!

Scarlett x

I looked down at the clock. It was 11:11, on the dot.

Chapter Eighteen – Love is Both Real and Imaginary

The rest of the week passed by uneventfully, aside from the fact that Harry once again touched me without my consent in my sleep.

I went to a sound healing ceremony, and they mentioned a sound healing retreat in Egypt in April. It would last eleven days with seven of those days spent on the Nile and four in a hotel in Cairo. I decided to put down a deposit. Sound healing had become an important part of my journey, especially since using my voice freely and openly while singing the Icaros – the plant medicine songs sang during ayahuasca ceremonies in Peru. I felt that it was essential to use my voice again after too many years of keeping myself silenced.

I reflected on Scarlett's email but tried to not get too caught up in it. I couldn't help but wonder what she meant by 'working with' what it is to love. I was all for exploring the concept of love with her, but I hoped she wouldn't try to dismiss my feelings and tell me that my love wasn't justified.

It had been eight months since I first met Scarlett. It was as if our meeting was pre-destined before we incarnated here.

I didn't get much sleep Monday night. Harry was very much on my side of the bed, and snoring, though my mind was preoccupied with Scarlett anyway. I woke up at five am with the song, 'This Door Swings Both Ways,' playing in my head, a quintessential bi-sexual song.

I felt more alive than ever before since I met Scarlett. My moments with her were the happiest of my life. Before I met her, my emotions had been controlled, contained. And after I had met her, they were uncontrollable, and I was afraid of drowning in them. But maybe that was the purpose of this fated meaning: to come to life. Maybe I was dead before and hadn't really been living. Maybe she was supposed to shake the ground from underneath me and have me dive off a cliff, only to find out that I would come out still standing. Scarlett *is* my lover, I thought, and we are soon to come together in sacred union.

A couple of hours later, Harry emerged from his slumber and joined me in the living room. I was reading when he entered.

"Good morning, dearest," Harry said.

"Morning," I said, not looking up from my novel.

"Do you think we might have a chat this morning about our relationship and living situation?" Harry asked.

"Sure, let me eat something and get some coffee in my system first before we sit down together."

I finished my chapter, cut up some kiwis and ate them with scrambled eggs for breakfast. I drank my first coffee of the morning in an un-leisurely fashion, wanting to get the conversation with Harry over with as quickly as possible. He must have been nervous about me leaving him. He likely picked up on my disconnect from him and could feel that my heart had moved on. If he asked me, I wouldn't deny that I hadn't been making the effort because my heart and soul were one hundred percent focused on Scarlett.

I sat in the chair by the desk for our chat. I took an apathetic approach to his qualms and just agreed where I needed to agree, nodded when I needed to nod. He said something about me not being cut out to live with people, and if that were the case, that I should move out by Friday and not pay my March rent to him. I saw his timing as quite fortuitous. I needed a little push from him. I could always rent an Airbnb for a few months until I figured out the next plan long-term.

After about fifteen minutes of listening, my thoughts started to drift back to Scarlett. It was beginning to feel like nothing mattered in the world outside of her. I was so pulled into her orbit that at some point Harry asked me who I was flirting with, evidently noticing my dreamy expression as I was mindlessly smiling about her. I told him I was only lost in thought about a funny memory from a silent meditation retreat some years ago. He told me I needed to mediate more. I nodded.

An hour later, I reached the fifth floor of Scarlett's office, as usual, pulling the bird cage elevator to the right as I worked on equalizing my breathing in anticipation of seeing her. How would it be, now that I had revealed my feelings to her?

I was wearing all pink, aside from my shining red ballet flats: fuchsia checkered trousers, a magenta long sleeved shirt, large gold hoop earrings, rainbow beaded bracelets, and a large gold cross necklace with an Australian opal in the centre that I bought in Jerusalem some months prior. It was a rather flamboyant outfit, if you ask me, but that seemed to be my mood of the day. I remembered my friend from Nepal once telling me that I reminded him of a stylish monk, and I felt that image somehow suited me that day. Scarlett, on the other hand, was wearing all black.

As I approached the door and grew nearer to Scarlett, I noticed the intensity of expression in her eyes. It was a look that a lover might give her counterpart when she is not happy about something. She looked somewhat repelled. This will be a fun day, I thought. I glided past her obsequiously, meeting her eyes once I sat down with a stare of due respect.

"Are you going to be love's executioner today?" I asked, in hopes to lighten her up.

"You can't email me like that again. Everything that needs to be discussed must happen in the room, when we are in person together."

I nodded.

"What did you *mean* by that email you sent me?" Scarlett asked me, still unsmiling.

I responded with my eyes, intensifying and widening them as if to say, 'What ever do you think I meant? Isn't it self-explanatory?'

"We have to keep our relationship professional. Anyway, you can't love me when you don't even know who I am outside of therapy. You know nothing about me."

"Really? Is this a clone of Scarlett that I am staring at?"

She quickly dismissed that without a word.

"I know who you are from what I've seen. I can feel the essence of you, your soul's nature, without knowing much about you. And from my experience, sometimes the more you know a person in terms of facts about their lives, the foggier and more shadowy the truth of them appears to be. We can sometimes know a person most intimately when we know nothing about them."

In Scarlett's commentary that essentially my loving her would have to equate with knowing something about her, that was like saying the true basis for love was merited in precise knowledge of one's life details and character. And if that was the case, then that would be suggesting that love was in some way measurable. And how dull would that be. How grim. How dreary. It was certainly not the type of love I would ever accept to be part of my reality, and if that was what Scarlett's version of love was, well then, something would have to be done about it!

I didn't love her because of what she was doing for me. I didn't love her because she was listening to me. I didn't love her because she was paying attention to me. I already read her soul and that was what I loved. That was all that I needed to love. It was not love based off attachment and dependence; it was love based off purity. It was indefinable. It was inexplicable. It was eternal. It was unconditional. It was uncontainable. It was an ocean of every love I had ever known, wholesome in every way.

"Anyway, now that you've mentioned it, that is what we can work with, *in here*," Scarlett said.

I nodded compliantly.

"What is love to you? What does love mean to you?" Scarlett asked me.

"How does one put into words the pure feelings of the heart?" I said, like an exasperating romantic, keeping my cool whilst attempting to hold it together.

She scowled at that and shot my words down with a single, powerful glance.

Although it was taking great inner strength to not fall apart and trust that my feelings had value, that they were worthy of being shared, honoured, respected, that I had indeed made the right decision in expressing my love for her, I also couldn't help but be deeply saddened on *both* of our accounts. As much as I might have liked this to be the space where I could express myself openly, and as much as Scarlett's wanted this to be the place for me to do that, the truth of the matter was that it wasn't. Half of the matter had to do with Scarlett's problem with receiving my love. And maybe that was why I continued to hammer it home.

"Love is, at its core, the ability to see the Divine in everyone and everything. Love allows another to be who they are, and that's what's so free about it. It has nothing to do with possession. It's the feeling that you don't need anything from anyone in order to love – that, is unconditional love. It is without expectation. Love is unselfish. It is selfless, deep, pure. It makes one realise they are alive."

And that was how I felt with Scarlett – alive, in just relishing in the gift of knowing that I was existing in the same time and space as her, on the same planet.

"And when it comes to your supposed love for me, where are the foundations in that?" Scarlett asked.

"You might think that my love is not founded in reality, but if it nourishes me, then does it even matter if it's real or imaginary? All that matters is that it is real *to me*. Love is where reality surpasses the imagination."

"Sure, but we are together in here, right now. If you are so wrapped up in your own world half the time, how am I supposed to enter that world with you?" Scarlett asked.

"By accepting my love. By honouring my love. By respecting my love. You question if this love is real, and maybe it doesn't align with what you've been taught about love, but it's simply a different sphere of love."

"I have trouble accepting your take on that because we live on a planet where it is difficult to get by if you are fully immersed in your own world. I want you to be able to function in society, Samara. Your idealism is beautiful, but it's not pragmatic."

"Well, we are talking about love, not practicality, aren't we? This is how I was built. Anyway, the world needs more dreamers and idealists. We have far too many cynics and pessimists as it is."

If thriving on something that was deemed an illusion by others made me happy, then who was to say there was something wrong with that? Only those I empowered to do so.

"And how are you so sure this is not infatuation by means of transference rather than love?" Scarlett asked.

"Oy vey! Even if it *was* transference, then so shall it be! If my unconscious will chose you as my object of romantic love, then that is something to be worked with. The Lord knows Harry isn't cutting it. If we are to really work with 'what it is to love,' then perhaps you need to be my subject, as I am yours, and by working with it, you must allow it. Allow it to be, free.

Even Freud struggled with whether all love in a therapeutic setting could be attributed to transference. He questioned that there were perhaps times that the love stemmed from the actual, real relationship between therapist and patient. The misconception that love in therapy is always simply 'transference' is a hoax. It's outdated."

"We can work with the story that your proclaimed love tells. So, what it is to love is the name of the game, then," Scarlett said. "You mention unconditional love and balance as necessary in love, but you won't feel balanced if you're constantly giving and not receiving. You'll end up drained."

"On the contrary, Scarlett, my love sustains me. I don't need you or anyone to reciprocate my love."

"If you are giving too much of your heart all the time, you won't have anything left to sustain yourself."

"I think you underestimate the boundlessness of my love," I said.

I knew that Scarlett had a point, but I also had to get through to her in my own way, too.

"I know that I have to work on loving myself as I love others. But not having my love returned will not cause me to stop loving. We cannot have the expectation of reciprocity, even though that is the expectation according to society. We need to abolish the idea of love being transactional."

The love that I had for Scarlett, even though I would have obviously liked to have it returned, never in any way felt wasted.

"All I can say is that from my experience, anyone that has given love and not received love in return will, in due course, pour their energy elsewhere," Scarlett said.

"Well, they didn't know how to love, then," I said. "Love is worth fighting for, worth practising, worth driving our energy into," I said.

"And that love has to start with the self. You cannot truly give to another unless you have found that same level of love within you," Scarlett said.

I knew that I needed to work on being more compassionate and loving towards myself. Then I would only be doing things because I wanted to do them, not because I felt like I had to do them in order to win approval.

"Sometimes we need another person to awaken that love within ourselves," I continued.

Scarlett gazed at me, leaving me no place to hide. It made me feel like something was melting within me, whilst simultaneously switching on a light. I could have been speaking about either of us in what I said. Even if my hope to be with Scarlett was unfounded in reality, it brought me joy.

Scarlett's energy had softened. I hoped I was succeeding in getting through to her.

"Well, I do feel you throw the word love around a lot, but I hear what you're saying."

"Perhaps I do 'throw it around a lot' but that's only because I mean it a lot."

"Anyway, what's the latest with Harry?"

"He's threatened that if I don't start catering to him more, then I should move out by Friday before I pay him the March rent. As you can tell I'm not so concerned about it as I haven't even bothered to mention it and likely wouldn't have, had you not asked. Out of sight, out of mind, you know. I'm tired of his jokes."

Scarlett laughed a little too hard.

"I forgot to mention that when we were sharing a bed, he tried to touch me in the part of my body that he knows causes a startling reaction in me, and so I ended up jolting out of bed hyperventilating again, barely able to breathe."

"Well, what are you going to do?"

"I think I will likely end up moving out," I said.

"Where will you live?"

"On the streets," I joked. "I guess I'll look for an Airbnb until I figure something else out."

"Hmm, well that's probably for the best. Take care of yourself this week."

I nodded and took her in with delight for another minute or so before she uttered the dreaded words.

I put on my coat to leave and gathered my things.

"I hope the rest of this Tuesday afternoon is splendid for you," I said.

"Likewise, Samara," she said.

As I made my way home, I reflected on our session. It was a rocky start, but I was pleased with myself for holding my ground and keeping my flame of love burning bright.

Scarlett and I were like polar opposites when it came to our ideas of love. If she wasn't willing to budge on her ability to let love in, I could be the positive example of the possibility to continue to love despite surface rejection, and maybe her witnessing my lack of shame could help her accept all parts of herself, too. It was not an easy task, though, because every time I tried to meet her with love and affection to heat up the room, she would melt it away, vanquishing the flames with the spell of winter.

It was a strange law of the Universe how opposites attract and need each other. Every yin needs its yang. Maybe she needed to integrate more of my feminine energy of love, softness, and nurturing and I needed to integrate more of her masculine energy of self-assertion, self-protection, and boundaries. In order to be whole, one must have both well integrated, which is why I felt we needed each other.

I was brave, but I was also scared. Scared of not being held, not being received, not being loved, having my heart broken, having to examine the fact that it was possible this was all in my head. I was in an incredibly vulnerable place, with my heart more open than ever before. I had never allowed my heart to come so alive because I kept myself guarded from getting hurt in the past.

For some reason I felt safer to put my heart on the line with Scarlett. I just hoped I wasn't placing my faith and trust with the wrong person.

When I reached home, I had to address more pressing concerns, such as where I would live if I was moving out. I only had a matter of days if Harry meant what he'd said.

When I entered through the door, I greeted Harry and then walked into the living room. I sat on the sofa and started reading my book. Harry disturbed my peace to moan about the way in which I wrapped something up from a dinner one night, and he wasn't pleased with the fact that I left the drawers in the dresser slightly ajar, and that there was a little bit of incense left on the table that hadn't fallen into the incense holder. After about thirty minutes of these interruptions, I slammed my book together and asked him to sit down so we could have another chat.

"Look, I can't live with you if you're going to be behaving like such a child. It's exhausting. Nothing is ever enough for you. You always have something you're unhappy about. Why don't we just both agree that I'll be gone by Friday, as you requested, and then just live in harmony for the next few days until then. Do you think you can manage that?" I asked him.

"I can see that you're exhausted, as you have massive bags under your eyes. You're acting as though your world is crumbling. Remember, what happens in your outer world is only a reflection of your inner world," Harry said.

"Why do you think I'm so exhausted? Putting up with you is emotionally draining. I have to check out half the time just to be around you."

Although Harry was a source of my emotional exhaustion, the dark shadows under my eyes were due to my lovesickness. I wasn't losing sleep over Harry. The lack of sleep was due to the relentless thoughts about Scarlett. I couldn't turn them off. I hadn't really relaxed for months, holing myself up in the spare bedroom for hours upon hours, journaling sometimes ten pages a day on what I was going through.

"If you're checking out half the time, if you're not present with yourself, how can you love yourself?" Harry asked.

"For Christ's sake, don't make this about me. I've only been checking out when I'm around you so I'm not brought down by the emotional frenzy you try to wrap me in. I'm not interested in rehashing the details of what is going wrong in our relationship. I haven't seen you change at all, except for maybe a day or two after we have a row when you make an effort, then it's back to the same old story again. If you want me out of here by Friday, then I will leave by Friday."

"Where will you go?"

"I don't know; I'll figure something out."

"Darling, I didn't mean I was going to throw you out by Friday. You're going to Egypt early April. Why don't we just see how things go until then? It would be difficult for you to move in somewhere for only a month before heading off on your trip, and then, where would you leave all of your things?"

"Yes, it's inconvenient, sure, but it's more inconvenient to have to live with you when you're acting like this. I don't have the energy for it anymore."

"Just please think things through and don't act so irrationally," Harry said.

"I'm going to go back to reading my book now."

I went back to reading my book, until fifteen minutes later, I received a message on my phone from Harry, who was sitting five meters away from me at the desk.

Harry –

"My darling Samara, please don't go. I love you more than you know. I can't bear the thought of losing you! Let's open a bottle of Bollinger Rosé tonight and talk things through. You are my one and only true love. We have been through so much together. I'm begging you, please don't go! You are the most beautiful girl in the world with creative intelligence like no other. I never have and never would find anyone remotely like you. Why don't we go away before you are off to Egypt, so we can have a break from our usual routine? Your undying love, Harry." <3

Oh brother, I thought. Classic Harry. When I finished reading his message, I looked up to find him staring at me expectantly. I just shook my head, laughing at his absurdity. It was all too dysfunctional for words. Nonetheless, I decided to take him up on drinking that evening, because why the hell not have some champagne to take my mind off things after a day like that?

We took the car to go fetch some ingredients for dinner and pick up the Bollinger. The weather was crisp with the coming of spring and I felt like I needed to loosen up a little, stop taking everything so seriously, lift a bit of the weight off my shoulders. We smoked a joint in the car by the park before grocery shopping, and then had quite a bit of fun picking out a few treats for dinner. I picked up my favourite champagne truffles.

When we returned home, we played sixties music on my speakers and had a bit of before preparing dinner, which was a walnut, pear, blue cheese salad, as well as pita bread, falafel, and freshly made hummus we picked up from a Turkish deli not far away. As the alcohol in my blood did indeed loosen me up, I started to rationalise that maybe I should just stick it out for the next month or so and then make the decision once I was back from Egypt. Moving right now would be terribly inconvenient, but I wasn't going to stick around if Harry didn't make an effort to get his act together with me. We needed some ground rules. I decided to bring them up at dinner.

"I'm not going to sugarcoat the fact that I'm no longer in love with you, nor do I have high hopes for our partnership. However, it's terribly inconvenient for me to move just now, scrambling to find a temporary place, then having to figure something out again after I return from Egypt. It is all really short notice. So, if I stay here until then, we have to set some relationship requirements. How does that sound?"

"That sounds fair. What might those requirements be?"

"I'm going to sleep in the spare bedroom until Egypt because you wake me up with your snoring, and you try to rape me when I'm sleeping."

"Okay, fine."

"We'll have sex only once a week, maximum. I'm already dealing with heavy stuff surrounding my sexuality and I don't need you worsening it by being so demanding about sex. I feel like I'm just an object of your lustful sexual desire and it's degrading."

"You know that I love and adore you, Samara. If I was only interested in you for sex, I could find anyone for that. But I too could use a break from sex as I have a lot on with work this month and squash championships coming up."

"Great. And the last thing is that I won't tolerate your emotional outbursts. If you have a grueling day at work with high stress, it's not fair for you to come back here and dump that on me. I don't expect a miracle from you but if I don't feel like you're truly making an effort, I won't hesitate to leave. I'm on my last legs. As far as I am concerned, we more or less act like flatmates who fully respect each other, live in harmony like friends, and have sex once a week. Are you agreeable to all of that?"

"I promise I'll make every effort to have harmony with you. I don't want us to be having rows every other day, either. Sometimes I'm only trying to get your attention because I want you to be present. I feel like you're not here enough, and I think part of my mission with you is to help you come into the present."

I was surprised at how compliant Harry was to all of my requirements.

"If that's the case, then find a better way to do it than tantrums. Talk to me rationally. The way you've been going about it will only disassociate me more."

"I hear you, darling. I'd also like you to try to loosen up a bit. I think you need to take it easy on the writing. That's all I've seen you doing lately. Now let's try and put this behind us and make a better effort to enjoy each other's company again. We've had a lot of fun together in the past, so let's try and get back to that, shall we? Life is too short."

Harry turned on the song, 'We Can Work It Out,' by the Beatles and started singing to me.

As much of a pain in the ass as Harry could be, he did often know how to lighten me up and make me laugh. He was toxic, but there was something irresistibly devilish about us being together that made it hard to detach. Part of me enjoyed dancing with the devil, though I didn't want to admit it. Perhaps I was my own worst enemy and really needed to be protected from myself. Although I didn't want to examine it further and convinced myself I was making the rational decision to stay with him because it was very short notice to move out, I was also just scared of feeling utterly alone in the world again.

Chapter Nineteen – A Divine Play of Creation

It was the beginning of March, and the Sakura cherry blossoms were beginning to bloom in London. My and Scarlett's love for each other bloomed in tandem, growing more fully with each passing day. As I walked to the Victorian house at 113 Sumner Place, I took in the delicate scent of the gold and lilac flowers that had begun to sprout, the dewy and earthy aroma of freshly cut grass, the hint of petrichor on the pavement after the morning rain, the feeling of the crisp air and the gentle breeze touching my skin. Love was in the air, and all felt heavenly and Divine that late Tuesday morning as I approached my beloved. I was in a dreamy, romantic world and I hoped that Scarlett would be in alignment with my energy.

I opened the bird cage elevator doors with gusto and spotted Scarlett waiting by the door with a much more welcoming and inviting expression than the week prior.

"Hi, sweetheart," she greeted me as I stepped through the doorway.

What a beautiful feeling to hear her call me sweetheart. I reveled in it.

"Hello," I sweetly replied.

Her energy was much more receptive after her scowling at me last session. We took our seats, and she spoke first this time.

"So, what is your living situation like now? Have you severed ties with Harry?"

"Not yet. He begged me to wait until after I return from Egypt. He said he didn't really mean it when he said I should move out. I don't expect things to change, but I feel it would be more convenient to give myself more time. I can survive another month. I also gave him a list of relationship requirements."

"I didn't know you were going to Egypt. When's that?"

"A little over a month from now. I'll be staying on a boat on the Nile most of the journey with the sound healing sisterhood from here in London. I look forward to it."

"Sounds lovely, which reminds me, I'm not going to be around on the 19th. I'll be in Greece with an acquaintance, visiting *ruins*..." Scarlett said with an apathetic expression, as if she were being dragged there against her will.

I laughed. "You don't seem very enthusiastic."

"It seems a bit far to go just to visit some ruins."

I loved her aloofness. I imagined she was going with a boyfriend, but she of course wouldn't tell me that. At least she wasn't all that excited about the idea of a trip with him, if that were the case.

"And what are your new relationship requirements with Harry?"

"Until I return from Egypt, we are to act as flatmates. I'll have no tolerance for tantrums, and I'll be sleeping in the other bedroom. We won't be 'sleeping together' more than once a week."

"And how did he respond to that?"

"Surprisingly agreeably. I'm not expecting a miracle, but he knows I'm serious about leaving if he doesn't improve. That's all I can hope for. That relationship really isn't my priority as I've been focused on other matters."

"And what are the other things you've been focused on?"

"Well, things like therapy, for example...," I said.

"I see. I've committed myself to you, Samara," Scarlett said, then added, "To our work."

I nodded.

"I hope you can see the shift in me," Scarlett said.

She did seem different. She looked lighter, as if some weight had lifted off her. Maybe my love was becoming infectious. Praise be to the Gods.

"You're very enchanting, Samara," Scarlett said to me, her eyes glowing, hypnotising me.

"Enchanting I may be, but I am only a reflection of thee."

"Your energy has a magnetising quality to it, and your eyes, they draw people in. It's very seductive," Scarlett said, in a rather seductive way herself.

Scarlett didn't seem so opposed to my apparent enchantment. It was said with admiration, with awe, with intrigue.

"Eh, what can I say? I'm only a source of prey."

Ignoring my comment, Scarlett said, "You're too good at it, for it to be this natural, this ingrained in you."

"Well, I can say the same about your eyes, and the general way you operate."

Ignoring my comment about herself, she continued.

"Part of that enchantment is your playfulness, and I think you also use it to test people," Scarlett said, looking at me quizzically, "to see who has the capacity to look beyond it, into the real you."

Did I use it to test people? I couldn't say. If Scarlett felt that she was being presented with a spiritual test, despite any temptations she might have felt, she was passing it, to my dismay. I wondered if her resistance made me love her more.

"How are you feeling?" Scarlett asked me.

"I'm feeling the spirit of spring in the air. Maybe the same shift that you're experiencing. This weather delights me.

As I walked here this morning, I felt like I was floating on a magic carpet ride."

"Yes." Scarlett laughed. "The blooming blossoms are a ray of hope after a long winter." Scarlett smiled at me for a few moments, still penetrating into me with her gaze. "And how are you feeling about last session?" she asked.

"I feel like we've reached a state of equilibrium, after a lot of ups and downs."

"Yes, I think it had to happen that way, to get to where we are now. You once said in regard to Harry, 'the conflict serves.'"

"Speak of the devil, I don't think the Divine is a big fan of Harry."

Scarlett laughed. "Yes, indeed. That is most probably the case, Samara."

"I'll have to figure something else out when I return from Egypt but at least I have some time to think about it. I have been playing with the idea of moving to Sri Lanka for a while, where my friend lives on the beach."

"Have you ever been there before?"

"Yes, three or four times. It's like a second home in a sense, and I was thinking of doing a yoga teacher training and maybe helping another friend of mine with a hotel he's starting up. I'm just not sure what the right choice is, whether to stay here or move there."

"What is your heart more drawn to?" Scarlett asked.

"Hmm, well, although the idea of living at the beach and chilling out in Lanka for a while has its appeal, I've already lived that kind of lifestyle, and I'm seeking something more. I need more depth, and I've had that depth in London, even though it's certainly been tumultuous. My heart is more drawn to staying here."

"What specifically is it about here that makes you feel centred in your heart? What's keeping you here?"

"Oh, I suppose just some of the connections I've made..."

"Yeah," Scarlett nodded, seeming to grasp that perhaps it was she that was keeping me.

"On another note, I'm writing a story for a Stanford online writing programme, and I read one of the required books about storytelling. The author spoke of the importance of the protagonist having a misbelief about themselves that is running the course of the story. So, my question to you, what do you think my biggest misbelief is?"

"That you think you're unlovable," Scarlett promptly answered.

"You think I think I'm unlovable?"

Scarlett nodded.

"Hmm, I've never thought that. I can see what you mean, though."

"It's not surprising given the complex environment you grew up in, and that you have trouble trusting that people actually care for you."

"I think I've realised in recent months that my trust issues are greater than I previously thought. I remember sleeping in my mum's bed, and in the middle of the night, I would search her face frantically with my hand to make sure it was her. Every night I had to check it was really her in the bed with me, and not someone else. My memories of trauma playing out, I guess. I can't imagine how she never found that odd."

"Yes, it perplexes me, too."

"Anyway, obviously the self-protection and trust issues started early on, and have stayed with me, which is why

I find it difficult to trust that people actually do love me sincerely."

"I don't blame you. It's rare to find people we can truly trust."

"I wrote a poem after sending you that email and I brought it with me. I don't want to read it or discuss it but just thought I'd share it with you to have a look at in your own time."

Scarlett motioned for me to bring it over.

I walked over to Scarlett's chair and handed her the poem written on a post card I bought in Sri Lanka.

Scarlett thanked me and then told me that it was time. I nodded somberly. I was sure she was not blind to my subtle withdrawal. She looked at me, deep in contemplation, as I glided past her, trailing down the stairwell in a hazy blur.

On Friday evening, I had a private ayahuasca ceremony led by my friend and shaman, Anna, whom I met in the jungle. The ceremony was held at the home of a woman called Luciana, someone Anna had done private ceremonies with before, and whom she felt I would get along with fabulously. A man named Orlando joined us for the evening. When I arrived, the four of us chatted for a while and got to know each other, lying in our sleeping bags as if we were preparing for a slumber party. Anna told us the medicine was fresh and stronger than usual, and I looked forward to it.

After about thirty minutes, mild visuals began to kick in and I curled up snugly in my blankets preparing for the journey. Another hour passed and not much was happening for me. I went downstairs to use the loo and found Luciana having the same problem. She told me to have a sneaky bite of a banana from the fridge as it tends to enhance the medicine. I took her advice and then Luciana and I went up to Anna for a second cup. Orlando, on the other hand, seemed to be very deep in the medicine, already purging up his insides. Once the second cup kicked in for me, and perhaps with the help of that banana, darkness presented itself to me for the first time. Red and black sinister shapes invaded my sight, creepily crawling into my awareness, almost tentatively, to see if I would allow the creeping to continue. I made the firm decision I wanted nothing to do with the darkness that was testing the waters and banished it consciously from my sight.

After that, I wept for a while, as I do in every ceremony, on the subject of feeling like an orphan, having never had the support of a family to hold me, to encourage me, to provide me with a sense of grounding and nourishment. I held the space for myself but then also concluded that if I'd had a childhood that was nourishing and supportive, I may not have taken the path that I had, which led me to immense self-discovery and world exploration. It was the path my soul had chosen, and even though I would always feel a disconnect from a family support system, there was always a positive spin to be acknowledged.

Once I had gone through the weeping and purification process, Luciana seemed to be having a really hard time, barely able to stand up to go downstairs to the loo. Anna helped her down the stairwell, and she remained on the floor of the loo for the remainder of the ceremony, having a breakdown of sorts. Whilst Anna was helping Luciana, Orlando started to chat me up, telling me that he was feeling me strongly in his ceremony. Our conversation was otherworldly, and I hardly felt like we were still on planet Earth as we spoke, until Anna returned and silenced us, telling us to go back within.

Everything seemed to turn at this point in the ceremony. I was full of laughter and bliss. I cackled several times. I saw rays of rainbow light and angelic frequencies in the air, feeling warmly embraced by grace and light. I had visions of Scarlett and I together in the future, laughing, adoring each other, feeling euphoric in each other's presence. I thought of Rumi's quote – "Lovers don't finally meet each other. They are in each other all along." It was a sweet, delightful melody that I never wanted to end.

When the ceremony did end, we all shared our experiences and these two strangers as of several hours ago turned into close and intimate friends, all social barriers torn apart. Luciana and I had a tremendous amount in common as Anna had expected. We must have covered one hundred topics in thirty minutes, filling each other up to the brim with knowledge, mainly regarding holistic therapy and healing. She seemed full of life experiences and tales to tell. She and Orlando were both in their fifties and I felt much more at home in their company than I did with anyone my own age. After we talked ourselves out of steam, we crashed in our sleeping bags.

When I left Luciana's house the next morning, I decided I wanted to spend the morning immersed in nature. I dropped my things off at the flat and then walked to Holland Park.

The ecstasy lingered on. I sat on a bench overlooking the fountain. One of the peacocks walked by. The sun was shining with the mildest of spring breezes. All of life around me was thriving: birds flew in harmony with the wind, clouds drifted lazily across the sky, branches and flowers danced in the breeze, and a plane jetted across the vast, clear blue sky, heading to some distant shore. How wonderous was this life, threading everything together in poetic harmony.

As the morning drew on, I thought about the darkness that presented itself in my ceremony. I found it interesting that I had the power to say no to the darkness, and just like that, it went away. I think there was a lesson in that. Even in our darkest times, just as the light and joyous times are fleeting, so too will the darkest of our nights break through into the dawning of a new day. Often, it's what breaks us, what cracks us open, that leads to our Divine awakening.

I walked home around noon and thought about the Rumi book of love poems I had planned to give to Scarlett. Perhaps that was a bit much. I laughed, thinking about how unimpressed she was about her upcoming trip to visit ruins. As a joke, I thought it would be funnier to give her a crystal purifying water bottle I'd recently ordered. Something to help keep her hydrated as she was dragged along to visit those ruins.

When I was back in the flat, I had a bath and then fell asleep on the sofa for several hours, exhausted from minimal sleep the night before. It was dark by the time I woke up, and Harry was nowhere to be seen. I sat down at my desk, still feeling the post ceremony euphoric bliss, and wrote a poem about Scarlett. I spent the remainder of the weekend resting and recuperating, locked away in the spare room of my personal Narnia.

Chapter Twenty – Tales of Heartbreak Spinning Through My Head

I arrived to Scarlett's lair in elevated spirits, looking forward to expressing my unconditional love and sharing my gifts.

When we sat down, I told Scarlett that I attended a private ayahuasca ceremony over the weekend.

"You came up in my ceremony very strongly," I told her.

"Oh yeah? What happened?" Scarlett asked.

"I saw visions of us in the future."

"What was going on in the vision?"

"It was blissful," I said, still feeling the euphoria from ceremony, feeling totally unashamed to speak from my heart about the deep love I was experiencing. After all, what was the use of the therapy if I were to hold all of that inside of myself?

"I brought a gift for you," I said.

Scarlett did not look pleased in the least.

"It is very rare that I would accept any gifts, but as we haven't discussed that before, I will allow you to present it to me and then we can discuss it."

I felt terrified and my idea was suddenly blatantly lame. But there was no going back at this point.

"Well, one of them is a gift, just something I thought would be of use to you, and the other is a poem."

I handed her the poem and the gift and returned to my seat sheepishly. I could barely look at her as she examined the crystal water bottle in her hands.

"What prompted you to give me this? There's usually a reason a patient decides to give a gift."

"I thought about your trip to Greece next week to visit those ruins you were so enthused about. I figured you might need something to keep you hydrated."

How odd, I thought, that gifts in therapeutic settings should cause such disruption.

"Even so, Samara, there must have been a deeper, underlying intention as to why you felt the need to give this to me."

She was unwavering in her austerity, frowning all the while, making me feel like a worm squirming under her penetrating eyes.

"Well, you were on my mind, and I wanted to express my affection."

"You're over-giving. I think this is something that must carry over in your other relationships. Part of your desire to over-extend yourself stems from feeling that you have to win my love and affection, as if you're not enough as you are. Do you remember what we spoke about last week regarding your misbelief?"

"Yes, that you think I think I am unlovable."

"Indeed. You have to look at where your desire to give comes from. Does it come from a sense of unworthiness? Does it come from a sense that you *need* to give, in order to be received? There is a big difference between wanting to give and feeling like you need to give; if you are giving with an expectation, because you expect something from your giving, it lessens the value of the gesture for both the giver and receiver."

"I do understand the importance of only doing something because I want to, not because I feel like I need to. There have been times when I have said yes, when I wanted to say no. I wanted to win approval, perhaps specifically love. It's still a struggle of mine. This gift, on the other hand, didn't come with expectations attached. To be fair, I expected you to receive the gift, without this kind of discussion coming forth as a result. Perhaps I shouldn't have expected you to receive at all and that was where I went wrong."

"Do you want the gift back?" Scarlett asked. Her expression was stern. It very much felt like she was looking for a reaction out of me.

"No, I'm not resentful towards you and I don't want my gift back. It was a gift. I didn't expect you to make this into such a huge thing. That poem in your hands probably has deeper meaning than that water bottle."

Scarlett hadn't even gotten to the poem yet, and I knew this would open up an entirely new can of worms. I watched her as she glanced over my words. It was probably my most daring to her yet.

"The handwriting is too small for me to read right now. Please read it to me," Scarlett said.

Scheisse. It was much easier to hand over a love poem to be read than to read it aloud. I wondered if Scarlett just wanted me to read it to her for her own guilty pleasure. Nonetheless, I did what I was told and recited away.

'Sacred Fool'

In the midst of winter, I found
An eternal summer, there waiting for me
It smiled at me through the mists of snow
It laughed with me in the howling winds
It cried with me, as the rains of heaven
Spilled out from the skies,
Enveloping me, deeper inside

The flowers retreated into the Earth
Closing their faces, preparing
For next summer's birth
Their petals disintegrated into the mud
Allowing the lotus to float in with the floods

The flame in my heart is what kept me alive
It burned like a torch, through the darkest of nights
A living temple in which I could dwell
Away from the sorrows, away from the hell

When I thought I was deaf, her whispers,
Became louder than sound
When I thought I couldn't see, her vision,
Burned brighter than sight
And when I thought I couldn't feel?
When the numbness was too real?

She came to me and said,
It's time to peep your head, out from the shed
It is only your fear
Keeping you a prisoner, locked up in here

Come with me beloved, into the night
Where I can show you, pure joy and delight
The moon shined upon us; the nightingale called
The stars dropped down from above
Coming to accompany, our union of love

I looked in her eyes and sailed far away
To a distant shore, where rules were no more
Where her presence was its religion
Where sacred convergence burst flames through its citizens
Restoring me to wholeness, again, and once more

I looked up at Scarlett to hear what she had to say.

"That's beautiful."

"Thank you."

"What inspired it?" Scarlett asked.

"You inspired it. I wrote it the evening after my ayahuasca ceremony, and it flowed through me rather quickly."

"Being loved by you is like being bathed in rose petals. I can say that because I've experienced it with you before, felt it from you before."

"What a lovely thing to say," I replied. "I think of the quote by Rumi – "When the grace of love is revealed, be a mirror to reflect it." I am only reflecting the love inside of you."

"What happened to all of the rage towards me from last session?"

It was quite clear that Scarlett wanted, expected me to be angry. I felt that she was waiting for me to break.

"What rage?"

"Well, it was quite clear to me you didn't really want to be here, didn't want to talk about yourself."

I couldn't understand how she perceived my slight withdrawal of energy to be feelings of rage.

"I was a bit wounded after our previous session and didn't want to feel like I was bothering you. I wasn't rageful in the least; I was just somewhat withdrawn."

"Well, I don't want you to feel like you have to withhold," Scarlett said.

"Sometimes you don't make that so easy for me," I said.

"I just want to know the real you, the you that doesn't have to withhold what you think is unacceptable, the parts of yourself that you have rejected."

"Don't you see I'm trying? Is it not being vulnerable writing you an email expressing my love? Is it not vulnerable to read you a poem I wrote about you? I try to express my feelings but it's hard to get them through when the door is hardly ajar."

"But that has all happened *outside* of the room. The real work has to happen in here, with me."

"Maybe you'll have to do things a little bit differently with me. Sometimes I feel we're completely on the same wavelength and other times I'm a bit dumbfounded. I have trouble going into the depths of my sorrows with you present, with anyone present."

"I questioned your gift because, as a child, you were taught that in order to be loved, you had to be accommodating of others, putting your own needs aside. I don't want this to be a place where you feel you *need* to do anything."

"It's something I need to be aware of, I guess. If we truly want validation, we need to learn to validate ourselves and just be who we are. We become our own validation."

"That's where trust comes in. I want you to trust that my core feelings will not change, and that it's okay to show any range of emotions, especially in here – anger, sadness, rage, depression, whatever. I don't care. Whatever comes up, my feelings won't change," Scarlett said.

"And even when we are not on the same page, Samara, that's where the potential for growth between us lies."

"You're right. I have to get it out of my head that there always needs to be harmony between us."

"On that note, it's time to end," Scarlett said suddenly, cutting off the possibility for any further discussion on the matter.

"Sure," I replied.

I counted out the bills and handed them to her.

"I wish you a wonderful journey to Greece and I look forward to seeing you in two weeks."

"Thank you, Samara."

We embraced at the door for a little longer than normal. A positive ending to a rocky start, I thought.

As I began to descend the spiral staircase, I felt Scarlett staring after me, and I looked up. She was there at the door, watching me. I continued down the stairwell, feeling her eyes on me. I had a strange feeling, a strange effect, you could say, as I continued walking away. As I reached the bottom of the stairway, a song popped into my mind – 'I Try' by Macy Gray. I thought it made perfect sense for what I was intuiting, that Scarlett was holding herself back from saying something.

The song was about choking, stumbling, when you want to get certain words out. It's about playing it cool and hiding it, when you're infatuated. It's about putting up a front, despite feelings of longing, fearing the expression of true feelings. It's about holding yourself back, when you want to take a risk. I felt it was more about Scarlett's feelings as it wasn't like I was choking back on my words. I was spelling out my love as plain as day.

I went into the loo when I reached the first floor, and when I came out, I saw Scarlett by the second receptionist's desk in the back of the olive-green Victorian house.

When we set eyes on each other, she seemed to be motioning for me to follow her. I felt like I was in a trance and my feet were carrying me forward, but I didn't know what I was doing or where I was going. Scarlett seemed to be murmuring. I couldn't make out the words. She went up the stairs. I didn't know whether she expected me to follow her. The receptionist told me to follow Scarlett up the stairs.

I approached the spiral stairs tentatively and, from the first flight, Scarlett said, "I need to have a word with you."

Uh oh.

When I reached her, I said, "What is it?"

"You didn't pay me the full amount. There is ten missing from the bills you gave me."

"Sorry. I'll get the other ten then."

I pulled out my red wallet, fingered out another bill, and handed it to her. I thought, that would be that, issue resolved, over and done with.

Scarlett, on the other hand, was still acting abnormally. I didn't even feel like it was her. Had another soul entered Scarlett's body after I left the room? She was still looking at me as if she expected me to say something more. She was speaking so softly, nearly at a whisper, that I wasn't getting it.

"Scarlett, *what* are you saying? I cannot understand you," I said vehemently.

Another murmur followed. Accusatory stares.

"Subconscious revenge," two words I was able to make out.

"Huh?"

"Think about it," she said.

"Think about what?" I answered.

Finally, it clicked. Scarlett was assuming I was seeking revenge for the fact that she wasn't reciprocating my unashamed expressions of love, just like she thought I was rageful last week just because I wasn't as forthcoming as usual.

"You must be joking. Do you actually think I intended to not pay you ten pounds to seek subconscious revenge on you?"

More murmuring.

The whole situation was making me feel embarrassed that she would accuse me of this and upset that she had such little trust in me.

"Scarlett, I wouldn't do that! Come on!" I stormed down the stairs and out of the door, completely flustered.

There was a lovely black man called Marc just outside the door of the house who had chatted me up in the past. He started chatting me up again now, and I felt I had to be polite. Again, the feeling I *had* to be polite and *had* to give him my attention, rather than taking care of myself and the fact that I was about to have an emotional breakdown. I felt strong and confident and at ease the entire session, but Scarlett succeeded in breaking me in the end.

Marc asked me if I wanted to get a coffee with him sometime. I told him sure. He seemed to be an interesting man. He felt like a kindred spirit. I figured it was a blessing to accept his kindness after what I just went through. After we exchanged a few more words, I ordered a car to get out of there.

As soon as I was in the taxi, the tears began to spill out of my eyes. Scarlett emphasised the importance of trusting each other, but where was her trust in me? It was almost like she couldn't fathom in her own mind, that I could still continue to love unashamedly without reciprocation, without being brought down by her judgements. It was almost as though, if she were to accept that, and acknowledge that there was that possibility to still love despite pain, despite unrequited love, then perhaps it would crumble and shatter all of her own perceptions and conclusions about love.

If she had convinced herself that love was ultimately cruel, and that by expressing our love, we are going to get hurt in the end anyway, well then, that would be self-satisfying and validating for her own conceptual understanding. It would fit in with her prophecy like a hand in a glove if I were to crumble before her eyes at not receiving the response she expected I expected. The solace that perhaps brought her comfort to not make herself vulnerable when it came to love and honest self-expression was that it all ultimately hurts in the end, so better to save oneself the trouble and come out on top, not wound the fragile ego, not run the risk of getting hurt. Better to be the first to leave or avoid altogether. Yet, "tis better to have loved and lost than never to have loved at all."

Scarlett's email came to mind, "then what it is to love is exactly what we need to work with next." Well, we were certainly working with it now, although I wondered if I was in for this still, if I was prepared for this. Would I ultimately come out of this like a wounded bird and walk away with a scarlet letter forever etched onto me? Would this experience taint the purity of my love? Would Scarlett's wounds become my wounds, or would there be a balance and equilibrium reached, as I had hoped, with the natural process of alchemy?

When does one know when to pull out and retreat, or to keep going despite a seeming loss of hope? Yet that wasn't what my spirit would allow, and I had to keep going, for "faith is the bird that feels the light and sings when the dawn is still dark." If I were to stay true to myself, true to my faith, true to God, I had to keep 'fighting the good fight.' What I understood about alchemy is that it comes down to extracting the Divine from the seemingly impossible, and I planned to stop at nothing to acquire the most distilled and pure essence of love.

Of course, as Scarlett rightly pointed out, I 'knew nothing about her.' Indeed. I didn't know her history. I didn't know anything personal about her in actuality. But I knew her soul and I somehow felt like I knew her wounds. It was all intuitive speculation from our interactions so far, and of course I couldn't tell her this, but I felt that this was what was going on underneath the surface in her subconscious world. It was as if my ability to continue to love and continue to stay happy within that love had triggered her. And if it were the case that she was vulnerable in expressing herself in matters of love, then perhaps the incident that felt like an eruption of emotions on the stairwell, was the release that she needed from having to bottle up her own emotions for me, given the context of our therapeutic alliance. One way or another, what happened in the stairwell wasn't coming from me and it hurt and didn't feel fair. She got the reaction that she wanted in the end. She hurt me, deeply.

Although I said I would stick through it, continue to ride the wave, I was finding it very difficult to see how we were going to get past this one.

When I finally made it through the door of my flat, I broke down, an ocean of tears streaming down my face and dripping down to the floor. I felt utterly wounded.

Ten minutes later, I received an email from Scarlett.

Dear Samara,

I have just finished my notes and checked your payment before putting it into my wallet.

Two of the notes were stuck together so you actually gave me the correct payment in the first place, and I now have too much. Many apologies for this. Please pay me £10 less at our next session. I look forward to seeing you on the 26th.

All the best,
Scarlett

I started wailing harder. I felt betrayed and insulted, and yet also relieved that the truth came to light. What was most confusing for me was the inconsistency in how Scarlett treated me. I felt I couldn't speak to Scarlett about what I was going through. I felt like a spiritual orphan. Did she have any awareness of the effect she had on me?

I no longer knew what I was going to do about Scarlett. I trusted her blindly, assuming I was at fault for underpaying her and immediately handing her another bill, when I should have trusted myself. I didn't second guess her for a second. Why couldn't she just accept that my love was without agenda?

Although I considered quitting, I knew I would end up taking the high road. No one was perfect and I didn't think Scarlett wanted to intentionally hurt me. After all, we had just discussed that the challenges were where we could find growth.

Putting myself in Scarlett's shoes, if she did in fact have feelings for me, having to bottle those feelings up, knowing it was impossible to act on them, was just as difficult as what I was going through.

Why was Scarlett acting so odd? Why was she lingering at the door in a way she never had before, when she hadn't yet counted the bills? Did she intend to say something more personal to me when she found me at the downstairs reception, and then when I followed her up the first flight of stairs, changed her mind, held herself back? Were the bills actually, in fact, stuck together? Or was that just something Scarlett came up with, like a magician, because things didn't go to plan. Or was I just trying to find an explanation to bring solace from the hurt I was feeling? If I could rationalise and reason that there was more to the story, then it wouldn't be as painful. Perhaps I was just insane, delusional, reading into it all too deeply. I was the patient, after all. Maybe I was so deluded I could no longer distinguish fantasy from reality. Was I alive, or was I dreaming? Was this a crime, or was I healing? Divinity, or just a feeling?

I was too upset to reply to Scarlett that evening, so I decided I would sleep on it and make a decision about what to do the next day. When Wednesday morning came around, I wrote Scarlett my reply.

Dear Scarlett,

Thank you for letting me know. Speak to you then.

Samara

I needed Scarlett to clear up how she could accuse me of subconscious revenge and jump to conclusions about me after we had spoken about the importance of trust.

I tried to not focus on the incident, which felt like a lover's quarrel. I would wait and see how things panned out. The ups and the downs were becoming exhausting. But wasn't that what love was all about? To be willing to sacrifice getting one's heart broken?

Believe it or not, and this may have been a sure sign I was crazy and delusional, but if I was sure of one thing, I was intent on keeping the faith. It was now my heart that was leading me. If I allowed my mind to run the show, the logical and mental aspects of me – perhaps to some, the remaining sanity – then I would have let go of Scarlett by now and moved on, rationalised that I was just going to get hurt. But like I said, I was past the point of caring about getting hurt. That was not the primary concern. My will was indestructible. My heart was now the star of the show, urging and pushing me to listen to it, to follow it, to allow it to guide me despite all the odds or any concrete evidence. We don't need *evidence* that our love is being reciprocated, in order to continue to keep on loving.

The following week, my beloved Sofia was returning to London for a few days, and we agreed I would stay with her. The timing couldn't be more perfect as a distraction from everything. Her friend Naomi was visiting from Scotland, and we decided we would all stay together.

Although my time with them was indeed a beautiful distraction from the hurt I was feeling in relation to Scarlett, and although I enjoyed their company as the three of us drank and smoked our way into oblivion from start to finish, I was melancholic in my energy, hollow in my expression. Tales of heartbreak were spinning through my head. I wanted to be swallowed up by a tidal wave, like a ship lost at sea. No matter how much red wine I might have drunk, it only led me deeper into feeling. And the depth of that feeling was difficult to convey to anyone. Fortunately, as the law of natural attraction would have it, all three of us were going through a rough time in our love lives. We were able to offer different perspectives, commiserating with each other's pain in our parallel realities.

We were in the midst of Mercury retrograde and I thought to myself, it was no wonder, given all of the misunderstanding and confusion of last week. It had already been a hell of a retrograde and I felt like I was going through emotions that didn't even exist. There was comfort in blaming it on the planetary aspects.

One rainy evening at the hideaway, I spent the night alone with a bottle of red by the bed, candles lit around my head. I fantasised about a romantic renaissance world, a golden world. I wrote a poem to release the pressure from my crown of thorns.

'The Golden World'

As summer approaches,
My mind fills with encroachment
Intrusion of confusion, perhaps just disillusion
The lines slither and wither
Like snakes in the Garden of Eden

An hour to two, I sing praise to you
Bring me a flute; I'll sound out the tunes
Read me a rhyme, the ancient voice of the Divine
Melodies listen, interpreting the system

Intricate flowers bloom, their appointed hour
Chimes twinkle; it's time
Break out of the vines, open the doors
Tentatively touching the Golden World

A smile for a dime
Two cents, and I'll give you mine
Indigo pearls feed into my core
Filling the holes I have longed for

Rain clouds dissipate by
Tears of a clown in my eyes
Traffic lights turn to red
Tales of heartbreak spinning in my head

I was feeling back to my usual optimistic self the next morning. I woke up from an intensely passionate lesbian dream, set in a magical waterfall oasis, kissing nude nymphettes and their plump breasts in the sunshine amidst vibrant green lily pads and tropical palm trees. It was like a scene out of the Garden of Eden.

Walking back from picking up coffee and croissants for the girls and I, I saw a quote on a building: "There is nothing stronger in the world than gentleness." It was like I had been trying to harden myself in the past few days, but that quote reminded me that my gentle nature would always serve me. I could lean into softness to achieve my dreams and desires.

Chapter Twenty-One – The Turkish Delights that Wade into Our Life

Harry and I spoke about going to a monastery the following weekend, Douai Abbey, which would also be the weekend before I left for my sound healing retreat in Egypt. We were chatting about it before bed, and I started to fall asleep while I was in his room. I started getting out of bed to retreat to my bedroom, but Harry told me to sleep there that evening and rest, and so I surrendered. Part of me did miss falling asleep next to him and our evening ritual of the essential oils he would prepare on tissue paper and put under our pillows – a mixture of frankincense and lavender oil. It was comforting in a fatherly way.

The next morning, Harry and I had sex for the first time since the 'relationship requirements' took effect. In the middle of the night, he attempted to touch me in the part of my body where I hold my trauma. I couldn't understand why he would do that to me repeatedly. It was a bit of a blur as I was just so exhausted, and so I let it be, and fell back asleep. After our sex, I felt a deep sense of melancholia and emotional withdrawal.

I thought about how different I felt in Scarlett's presence as opposed to Harry's. There was a feeling of enhancement in being in each other's presence, as if we were conduits for each other's soul awakening, unless I was under some kind of spell. What was I seeking in Scarlett? Myself, of course! I was seeking to restore what was lost.

On Tuesday morning, I woke up around four am hearing the song, 'Our Hearts Are Wrong,' playing in my mind's radio. It was an amusing song to hear, in its irony, and a reminder that our hearts are never wrong, and it is futile to deny when we are in love with someone. It is overthinking it that is wrong. When we overthink something, we create webs and entanglements of confusion against what we know to be true if we just listen to the rhythms of our hearts. The song also spoke of a powerful relationship where there is an undeniable connection that can be almost too intense to reach an equilibrium. But as we spoke about in our previous session, when there is a great energy and power as two contrasting elements seek to collide and converge, eventually, after all the volatility, there would be a merging that takes place and an equilibrium that is reached. The back-and-forth energy would eventually settle into harmony.

And if I really wanted this, my commitment to sticking with it, would have to be my priority above and beyond anything else. I would have to be willing, if necessary, to give up my life for our love. Just like the tortoise that eventually crosses the finish line, slow and steady, would win the race. I would have to make it clear, by whatever means necessary, that this was not just a passing fancy, a schoolgirl's dream, but a true desire of my heart to be with her and only her. No worldly success could satisfy me more. Our love had the capacity to make me the happiest person in the world or lead to my destruction and suicide. I wondered if this was all a grand spiritual test – to never give up on what I believe in, to always trust in the feelings of my heart, to honour that my heart was 'not wrong.' Or was I simply a fool? A fool for love.

I arrived at eleven o'clock. I found Scarlett standing at the door, looking sun-kissed by the Grecian sun. We took our seats.

"Well, I suppose we should get into our stairwell incident right off the bat then," I said.

Scarlett nodded.

"I'll start with my feelings. I felt hurt by the way things ended in our last session. We spoke about the importance of trust, and then minutes later, I was being accused of shortchanging you for 'subconscious revenge.' How am I supposed to trust you if you have no trust in me? And was it really necessary to chase after me over the ten pounds? Couldn't that have waited until now?"

"I wanted to come find you because I knew we wouldn't be seeing each other last week. It wasn't about the money."

I looked at her with a raised eyebrow, expecting her to say more.

"You're giving too much," she said simply, as if that cleared it all up.

I looked on, waiting for more of an explanation. She seemed self-assured, smug even, as if nothing important had happened.

"You still haven't addressed the issue of trust. I trusted you blindly and you proved to me that you're always ready to assume the worst in my behaviour. It was like you were looking for a reaction out of me. Well, guess what? You got it. I sobbed in the taxi all the way home, and even more when I received that email from you."

I had intended to take a gentle approach, but I felt she wasn't willing to meet me halfway.

"I didn't know it would have such an effect on you."

"Well, I didn't email you about it because, as you told me, everything must happen in the room. So, I'm telling you now, yes, it hurt me to the core."

"I guess I didn't see it as such a big thing because I'm dealing with conflicts like this all the time as a therapist."

It didn't seem that Scarlett was going to give me the apology I was hoping for.

"Well, I forgive you," I said gently.

She smiled at me.

"I think you find it difficult that therapy is one-sided. We work together, but the focus has to be on you, and you're too used to placing your focus on others."

"It is difficult. In order for me to feel like there is harmony, I have to feel like I'm holding the other person."

"You are holding me," Scarlett said.

"Anyway, how was your trip?"

Scarlett shrugged. "It was okay. The person I was with wanted to do like five things a day and I wanted to do maybe two."

I laughed. That was so much like her. I could picture her lack of enthusiasm perfectly.

"I had a dream I was viewing some ancient Greek ruins, but then I had a craving for Turkish delight and manifested a Turkish bazaar. Did you know I'm fifteen percent Turkish, by the way? No one knows where from. Anyway, I sat there having tea and indulging in the scrumptious Turkish delight."

Scarlett laughed aloud.

"What's so funny?" I asked her.

"Well, you know the story of *The Lion, the Witch, and the Wardrobe*? Have you read it?"

I affirmed that I had.

"Well then you know the symbolism of the Turkish delight."

Ah, why of course. I got it now. I laughed too.

"Yes, in the story, Edmund was mesmerised and enchanted by the Turkish delight to such a degree that he was willing to do anything to satisfy his desire."

"Was it good?" Scarlett asked me.

"Delicious. Sinfully so. Satisfying to my heart and soul," I said.

"Some of the ones you get around here are not the best. There are some good Turkish delights out there, some bad ones. You really have to know where to go to get the good ones," Scarlett said, laughing.

I agreed. To find just the right Turkish delight was a rarity, but once it was found, it must be captured and savoured and never let go of.

"I'm allergic to nuts, or at least I used to be. Now I'm only allergic to cashews and peanuts, but I used to not be able to revel in the pleasure of the Turkish delight because of that."

"It takes great strength to resist the temptation of the Turkish delight," I added.

"Just like Adam and Eve in the Garden of Eden, the forbidden fruit from which God commanded man to not indulge," said Scarlett.

"The true forbidden fruit, which was actually a pomegranate, not an apple, is meant to be plucked and eaten just when the time is right. Indulge in it too soon, and you run the risk of being cast out of the Garden of Eden," I said.

"Was it a pomegranate? Where did you learn that?"

"A tour guide of mine told me a few summers back when I was visiting Israel."

Scarlett and I stared at each other for some minutes, each in our own reflective thoughts.

"Anyway, I woke up after that dream and I had a message that came into my head. I heard, 'Seek nothing, and all shall come to you.'"

"In regard to your Turkish delight dream, what is it that you most desire? If you could have anything in the world, what would it be?" Scarlett asked.

It didn't take me more than half a second to know the answer, but I didn't feel like I could go through any more pain or outward rejection, so I gently shook my head from side to side, implying that I wasn't willing to answer.

"What is it?" Scarlett pressed further, wanting to draw it out of me.

"What do you think it is, Scarlett?"

"You know we can talk about anything in here," Scarlett reassured me in a lower, sultry voice.

Really? Because when I told you I loved you, you tossed me aside, I thought.

I used my body language to express that I wasn't willing to budge.

"Okay, what would your second choice be then?" Scarlett asked.

"Nothing," I replied. "Only the first choice."

"Ahhh, so it's all or nothing I see." Scarlett teased.

I shrugged. I was not the type of person who settled for second choices.

"I feel like you're keeping a lot to yourself," Scarlett said.

"I could say the same about you," I replied.

Scarlett smiled wearing an expression of knowing that she couldn't argue with that.

"I think it's important we find a balance between giving and receiving. I want you to understand you don't have to win love," Scarlett said.

"If we don't have trust going forward, it will be difficult for us to find balance," I said.

"Touché," she said.

"Do you think if you were to let people into how you were feeling, that it would be like letting go of your father, since he was like that, always keeping so much to himself?"

"Maybe," I said, staring out the window.

It was possible that I didn't want to let go of that part of me that connected me to my father. Maybe it was time to be more of my own person, share more of myself, let the world in.

"Have you seen the film *Performance*?" Scarlett asked.

"I haven't. Is there a message in that for me?" I asked.

Scarlett gestured as if to indicate that there was something she wanted to convey, but that she couldn't say it in words.

"Well, that brings us to the end of session," Scarlett said.

I nodded and carefully took out the bills, one by one, with a smirk.

"Here you are," I said.

"Thank you, Samara," Scarlett replied, smiling with hypnotic eyes.

When I reached home, I thought about temptations, and how they seem most alluring to us when we are most weak. And I thought about how that applied to my relationship with Harry, and could there not be some aspect of that too, with Scarlett?

Every time I was feeling vulnerable and seeking external comfort, I was drawn to him. When I was not feeling secure within myself, I felt closer to Harry, felt I needed him more. But when I was hopeful, I was attracted to what was healthier for me, what was life-sustaining. Harry was, in a sense, like a 'bad' Turkish delight. When I wanted to indulge in dark fantasies, the darkness in me was attracted to the darkness in him. My self-destructive side would want to come out to play. Ultimately, though, it wasn't serving me in the long run, and there would come a time when I was ready to break away.

Scarlett, on the other hand, presented as the 'good' Turkish delight, but perhaps one I would have to wait for, allow Divine timing to dictate. But there were so many uncertainties with her too, so much ambiguity, and I was left wondering what her role was in it all, where was she placed within *The Lion, the Witch, and the Wardrobe?*

I played around with my shamanic drum for the rest of the afternoon as I watched a brilliant display of colours on the London skyline bringing another spring day to dusk. I wrote a poem in rhythm with the beat of my drum.

Later in the evening, I made sure all the necessary documents for travel to Egypt were in order. I printed out the confirmation that my Egyptian visa was approved, made copies of my passports, and printed out my travel itinerary. I thought about how I at least had made it this far with Harry. I would do all my packing on Monday after Harry and I returned from the monastery, or on Tuesday after my session with Scarlett. I was nervous about how I would handle being in a group setting around fifteen other women for nearly ten days with not much privacy and constant activities. I was someone that mostly needed to be alone.

I remembered Scarlett's mention of the film *Performance* and watched it before bed. The film, being right up Scarlett's alley, was perfectly absurd. It was difficult to even know what was going on half the time, what was fantasy and what was reality, and I then came to realise, that was the point. It was meant to be confusing. It was also erotic, psychedelic, hedonistic, and took place in London in the sixties. When I finished the film, I wondered what message Scarlett wanted to convey. Identity was core to the story, and one of the main characters, Chas, goes through a transformation whilst on a trip, and has an epiphany about the striking resemblance between himself and Turner, despite the fact that they are polar opposites on the exterior. So perhaps Scarlett wanted to emphasise that she also saw the parallels between us.

Harry and I left for Douai Abbey on Saturday morning. We'd been getting on rather amicably and things seemed at an equilibrium for the time being. On the ride up, he asked me if we were still a couple.

"I guess," I replied.

"I like being committed to you," he said.

"Do you," I replied.

"I think the world of you, Samara."

I looked over at him in the driver's seat dubiously. We rode on.

I knew that it was far too easy to fall back into patterns with him. I did love him, even though I wouldn't always show it. I wasn't even sure why. There was a resonance between us that was hard to define. I knew he wasn't playing with a full deck, but I almost found it humourous to be part of the act. There was something psychologically stimulating about it. I was no longer in love with him, if I ever was, but there were aspects of him that I found to be truly special. He was one of a kind, if nothing else.

The monastery itself was a bizarre experience. Harry cracked it up to having five-star cuisine, enticing my culinary mind, but there was actually hardly anything served to eat. I munched on the occasional apple and piece of toast the whole time and looked forward to returning to London where I could properly nourish myself after a weekend of deprivation. I was scolded for wearing shorts that were apparently too short. The nuns looked judgmental about the age difference between me and Harry. I found it amusing when people would look dumbfounded, perhaps even disturbed, at the two of us together. We went on a few walks in nature that were quite lovely, although the chill of winter was still in the air. I didn't say no to Harry's thrice appeals at having sex. Each time though, I was unable to orgasm with him, something I never had a problem with in the past.

I tried to make the best of our weekend away, but I would have been better off staying at home. I was not acting in my integrity by letting things happen in order to avoid confrontation. I did feel the end was nigh, though, and I would take action to part ways upon my return from Egypt. I knew it was only a matter of time, and the clock was ticking away. The sandman would soon come out to play.

Chapter Twenty-Two – If a Few Branches Wither and Dry, the Rest Will Bear Fruit

On Monday morning I woke up grateful to be in my own bed, sleeping apart from Harry again. I meditated for twenty minutes, then got out of bed feeling well-rested. After I had my morning elixir, I got dressed, put on my spring jacket and a pair of shades, then headed out to get an iced coffee. Upon my return, I found Harry sitting in the living room on the sofa, legs crossed, staring at me expectantly. I was surprised he was up so early.

"Good morning, Harry," I said.

"Is there something on your mind?"

"I received an email from Douai Abbey," Harry replied.

"And?"

"And, they told me that we are no longer welcome there."

"Why is that?"

"They said we weren't respectful in front of the monks when you wore those short shorts, so they won't accept us back."

"You must be joking. I mean, the monks said something to you about it and we weren't even inside the monastery. We were on the grounds going for a walk. And it's not even like my shorts were that short."

"I did tell you to put on a pair of trousers for the walk."

"Yes, but only because you thought I would be cold, not that the monks wouldn't be happy with my attire. You were as surprised as I was."

"Well, one way or another, I'm not happy about this. I've been going there for years, and now I won't ever be able to return."

"You're not missing much anyway; I'm sure there are plenty of other places you can find for your monastery weekends."

"You could show some remorse; it's not my fault that we got kicked out."

"Look, they probably just didn't like our presence there and had their own judgements about our age difference. I'm sure they just saw me as your mistress, which I suppose is what I am, and taking one's mistress to a monastery for a weekend away is not that common, I should imagine."

"They also mentioned in the email that the monks had to approach you several times, both outside and inside of the monastery."

"You were with me everywhere I went, so it's not like I was sneaking off, roaming around the monastery in my 'short shorts' when you weren't looking. I think you should explain to them that after they told me to not wear those shorts on the grounds in front of the monastery, I changed right afterwards. They're obviously misinformed and aren't aware that it was only once. I'll write the email for you if you'd like. You can read it afterwards."

"Yes, please do."

I locked myself in the spare bedroom. I read for about an hour, and then I drafted the email to the monastery admin. I had no intention of returning but I was doing it on Harry's behalf, feeling responsible because he wasn't the one wearing short shorts. I figured an email of explanation could perhaps open the door for him to return to his beloved monastery.

I came out of the bedroom and showed the draft to Harry.

"So, what do you think? Shall we send it off?" I asked.

"We can't send this to them, Samara."

"Why not? What's wrong with it?"

"What's wrong with it is that we were never being kicked out in the first place."

I looked at him, waiting for further explanation.

"April fools," he grinned.

"Ohhh you little pest! You actually had me feeling guilty and stressed about this all morning and made me go through the trouble of crafting this email for nothing."

"I got you good," Harry snickered.

I laughed, too. I had to admit, it was a rather clever April fool's joke. The email he showed me did seem legitimate, and I never would've thought he'd go through the trouble to concoct a scheme like that, so early in the morning. Although Harry drove me insane more than half the time, he really did know how to lighten me up sometimes.

The rest of the day I was in a light and carefree mood. I went for a walk through Hyde Park and listened to music on a particularly warm and sunny early spring day. Before leaving I rolled a joint which I smoked on the grass under a tree in the park. I brought my Rumi *Little Book of Love* and flipped through the pages, dreamily reflecting on the beautiful sensation of what it feels like to be truly, madly, deeply in love.

The reminder of how transformational love can be is what kept me going through the darkest moments with Scarlett, in the moments where darkness would have me in its hold and I would start to think it was just a hopeless fantasy that would never come to fruition, that I was setting myself up for ruin. But I would bring myself back to the knowing that love is the only thing truly worth fighting for. If we are ever to 'fight the good fight,' then let it be for love, if nothing else. Because even if we think we have become broken beyond repair, and we have to live through the darkest of despair, at the very least, it brings us back into our hearts. And that, more than anything, is what humanity needs. I think there is a misconception, or at least there was for me for some time, that to live with the heart leading us would be impractical, perhaps even foolish, but the heart is as intelligent as the mind, if not more so. It is the heart that connects us to the eternal within us and to the Divine. God knows in ways that we could not possibly conceive, as much as we may try to with the mind.

As Rumi says, 'if a few branches wither and dry, the rest will bear fruit.' And so it is with love. If we attempt to hold on to those withering branches for too long, we are only holding on to fear, with the assumption that there is no other way, not trusting that there is something more, something better for us, something for which we feel we don't have to 'settle' for. What about living to feel alive? If we were to just trust a little bit more, we would see that the Divine has and always will guide us to where there is true safety, which is in the sanctuary of living from the temple of the heart.

And so, we must be willing to accept the gloom as much as we accept the bliss, because if we are willing to keep the faith alive, even if we feel like we have been wandering in a desert for years to no avail, on an endless search for that oasis that we dream of, eventually, in Divine timing, it will lead us to the deepest desires of our hearts, whether or not that is in the form we expect. It is there that we will find our truths. It is there that we will find our satisfaction. It is there that we will no longer be yearning with Divine discontent and a shallow satisfaction that life never amounted to what we once hoped it would be. If we are willing to strap ourselves in for the wild ride and see that our life here is really just a journey that is leading us deeper into our Divine awakening, if we can take a step back and see the bigger picture by letting go of the trivial, the eventual fruit that bears with our commitments to ourselves, will be more scrumptious than the most tantalising of Turkish delights. And so, we mustn't be afraid to let it all go and surrender it into the sacred fires of death and destruction, because with death, always comes new life. We just have to be willing to be raw, cooked, and burned sometimes along the way.

It was five minutes to eleven on Tuesday morning when the receptionist told me that Scarlett was ready to see me. My heart was pounding against my chest more than usual, perhaps because it was the last day we would see each other until I returned from Egypt.

I found Scarlett, as usual, towering over the doorway. She was wearing an azure-coloured blouse, unbuttoned just the right amount to reveal her bare chest. It beautifully complemented her eyes which were a glowing indigo blue. It was always a surprise what colour they might be, everchanging like a chameleon.

We greeted each other and I strode past her to my chair, attempting to gain my composure. I wondered if other people found her as intimidating as I did. It was like being in the presence of a diety.

"I had an interesting weekend," I said, starting off the session.

"Oh yes? Tell me about it," Scarlett replied.

"Harry took me to a monastery called Douai Abbey. Do you know of it?"

"I think I've heard of it before."

"Yeah, well, I figured it would be a good idea to get away for a few days, but I should have just spent the time alone in London. It wasn't terrible or anything, but it felt forced because I'm not in love with Harry. He asked me if we were still a couple. I told him 'I guess,' not wanting create conflict. We slept together, and I just wasn't present during the sex at all."

"Well, it's good that you're going to Egypt for a couple of weeks. You can decide how you want to handle your relationship with Harry upon your return."

"Yes, I definitely intend to part ways when I'm back. Yet I do think we were brought together by the Divine for a reason. He was the link that brought me to London. And I've seen a change in him from how he was in the beginning. But the karmic cycle is now complete."

Scarlett didn't respond, and instead tenderly gazed at me for several minutes. I stared back, resting my chin in my palms.

"What day are you leaving for Egypt?"

"I leave tomorrow."

"I think it will be good for you to be around some people in a group setting. Those kinds of situations tend to bring up some of our own unresolved issues about feeling seen and valued, so it will be a learning experience at the very least."

I nodded.

We then spoke about the resonance we felt with each other. I mentioned to her that we seemed to share a similar energetic vibration, and that our ways of engaging with the world around us felt strikingly alike. Scarlett agreed with this sentiment.

"I had a dream about you last week," I told her.

"In the dream, my spiritual teacher was taking a photograph of us. She took the photo and then pointed to you and then to me, bringing to light our twinship."

"Was that all that happened?" Scarlett asked, insinuating I was holding something back.

I was holding back that my spiritual teacher was indicating we were a perfect match, meant for each other.

"What is it about me that you think your teacher wanted you to see in the dream?"

"That we are mirrors to each other, that what I see in you is a reflection of me, and vice versa. Perhaps that the aspects of you that I have trouble with are aspects of myself that I struggle with. And likewise, the qualities about you that I admire are qualities that I have yet to acknowledge that lie dormant within myself."

"There's another film I thought of that I think you should see, called Persona."

I told Scarlett I'd look into it.

"What are the qualities in me that you admire that you feel you haven't integrated within yourself?"

"Probably the self-assuredness and the self-respect you possess. Also, the way that you protect yourself."

"Well, I think the self-assuredness comes with age. As for the self-protectiveness, I see that in you too, but in the sense that you are guarded with feeling your emotions and sharing them with others."

"But that is precisely how I feel about you!" I exclaimed.

Scarlett looked at me affectionately.

"When we first started seeing each other, you seemed more open and fragile, but I have seen a fierceness develop in your energy. A bold assertiveness does come out at times. I think it is a result of your progress in developing comfortable boundaries with others. You have a tendency to give your power away, but I feel you are learning to contain it more in recent months."

"Thank you, Scarlett."

"What is it that you want from me, Samara?"

I hesitated to respond. Surely, by now, she knew exactly what I wanted with her? I longed to say 'everything,' but what came out instead was, 'connection.'

"I think it's safe to say we've already established that we are connected, Samara," she replied, her tone dry and laced with amusement.

"Well, it's difficult to truly connect in this professional setting. We can only get so far if the focus is always on me. I also feel I am more avoidant with you because I feel you are withholding from me."

Rather than answering, we fell into another five-minute session of staring deep into each other's souls. The way she looked at me was with such love, such tenderness, such affection, that it melted my heart, leaving me feeling as if I had dissolved into sweet nothingness.

It was nearing the end of the session. Scarlett broke the trance.

"It can be difficult to reach a deeper level of connection when there is mutual avoidance in the room. Someone has to take the initiative. Do you remember our conversation about how, when one person is scared or struggles to trust, the other has to step up and take the lead?"

Knowing what she meant immediately, I said, "I remember it well. I said I would step up in that case."

Scarlett let out a sharp, rather witchy laugh and replied, "Oh, yes. Yes, you certainly did."

It was as if as to say 'Well, that answers that; what are you waiting for?'

"We have to end on that note."

It was another example of us talking about our personal relationship in a round-about, indirect way, dancing in spirals, in our third person scenario specialty. Everything in the abstract. Scarlett staying true to her nature, I was left in suspense for the next two weeks until we would see each other next. 'High and Dry' by Radiohead started playing in my mind as I descended the spiral staircase leaving Scarlett Bennett's office.

The next morning, as I flew to Hurghada, a seaside resort town where I'd spend two nights before the retreat, I found myself reflecting on the parts of me I wanted to heal during my time in Egypt. What was causing me anxiety in my life that I most needed to let go of? Harry would have to be the first to go. That was a given. And then there was the internal conflict and confusion I felt about Scarlett.

There were three other women who joined me for a few days by the sea before the retreat began. I instantly connected with a woman named Lara, and we decided to be roommates for the rest of the journey. She also happened to be a psychotherapist in her forties.

At dinner on the second night, I sat with two women, and we started exploring the subject of truth. Was there ever one truth? I explained that I believed there can be many perceptions and individual 'truths' – which may be more rooted in our feelings, our past, our worldviews – but ultimately, there is always one higher Truth.

Interestingly, the conversation shifted to the subject of transference in therapy. This shall be fun, I thought. I had done enough research to understand that the feelings I was experiencing would not be seen as something different.

The extremity of my feelings was something that could only come from the Divine. It was so much more than simply 'transference.' I found it to be disheartening that every time there were feelings of love experienced in a therapeutic space, it was so easily pinned down, stamped, and thrown into the box of 'transference.' Wasn't *that* what was actually limiting? The human need to label everything, to make sense of everything, when sometimes things just didn't need to make sense. If it was possible for people to find love anywhere, and often, in fact, in the workplace, then why should it not be perfectly rational to think there would also be the potential to find genuine love – transference aside – in the therapeutic space. There are moments where one has to make one's own judgment call on whether to follow the conventional rules of the psychotherapeutic world or to be guided by one's heart and soul. God doesn't determine, or rather, place rules, on where or how love can and cannot be found.

I stayed mostly quiet during this part of the conversation, not wanting to be misunderstood and have my feelings tossed into that dreaded box labeled transference. It felt like the odds were stacked against me if I even attempted to open up to anyone about it. Given my trauma history, given the lack of concrete evidence of reciprocal love, given the ubiquity of transference, given that a dual relationship was a big 'no-no,' I was up against some pretty powerful opposing forces. But nothing was more powerful than love – unconditional love.

I bid the girls good night and went for a walk on the beach under the twinkling stars, mulling the matter over further. Although I knew I would always return to my own truth, time and again, I would be lying if I were to say I didn't have my moments of doubt. We all have our blind spots, and it can be hard not to not lose heart when our ways of thinking and being are not understood by others – perhaps even by no one but ourselves. Perhaps others might think that what you are reaching for, that seemingly impossible star, is unattainable, and you would be fooling yourself to think otherwise. That star might be unattainable in *their* mind, but that doesn't mean it has to be in yours.

How sad of a world it is that we live in a place where people are so eager to crush and dampen out the imagination, the dreams, the yearnings of the heart, of our fellow human beings, rather than encouraging each other to shoot for the stars. And living in a dream is not the worst place to dwell, anyway, if that dream brings you a sense of passion and purpose. Without the dreamers of the world, where would humanity be today? Everything starts with a dream. *Merrily, merrily, merrily, merrily, life is but a dream.*

If we fall, we fall, but at least we tried. Why is it that the world is like that? Because many of us have had our own dreams crushed. Why have they been crushed? Because we allowed them to be. Because we gave up. Because we allowed the opinion of another to hold more weight than trusting in our own hearts. Because we didn't hold on to hope and faith and just wait a little bit longer. And so then, we learn that that is the way of life, and go ahead crushing on everyone else's hopes and dreams after having given up on ours.

I hoped that Scarlett would see beyond the typical assumptions of our relationship. I knew she couldn't take action, but perhaps that hope lay dormant within her too, that once it was legal and the allotted time had passed, there would be nothing wrong with exploring the connection more intimately. I certainly felt it was worth the wait.

Two days later, and after a four-hour drive, I arrived at the luxury boat on the Nile. I was assigned to cabin number six, named after Thoth, the God of writing.

Our itinerary included a visit to several iconic sites in Egypt. We would begin at the Dendera Temple Complex, featuring the Temple of Hathor, followed by stops at the Luxor Temple and the Temple of Karnak. We'd then explore the Valley of the Kings, home to the tombs of Twosret/Setnakhte, Ramesses, and Tutankhamun, as well as the Temple of Hatshepsut. Next, we would stop at the Valley of the Queens before heading to the Temple of Horus in Edfu. The journey would continue with a visit to Aswan, including the Temple of Isis and Elephantine Island, and would conclude with the Great Pyramids of Giza, where we would stay for the last three nights in a hotel offering a breathtaking view of the pyramids.

On the first day, we spent time getting to know one another, sharing a bit about ourselves, and discussing our intentions for the journey. This took place during a sound circle ceremony where we sang, chanted, and immersed ourselves in the healing sounds of crystal bowls, shamanic drums, flutes, and a gong.

The following morning, most people rose with the sun for yoga on the upper deck. I needed some alone time, so I relaxed on my private balcony reading, journaling, listening to music, and admiring the majestic Nile River. It was surreal to be in a place I had dreamed of going since I was a child. I wanted to pace myself with the social interaction so that I wouldn't become too overwhelmed. I felt I had to act a certain way, as if I didn't want my eccentricity to be found out, but I knew I had to let go of the fear of judgement. Before heading out to mingle for the rest of the day, I told myself, "It is safe to act naturally."

When we joined together in a sound healing sharing circle, we discussed with one of the group leaders, Christine, which Egyptian God we would individually be working with for the journey. I learned that my 'story' in Egypt was associated with Horus, the Divine sun child reborn out of impossible circumstances, by Isis and Osiris. He is said to have significant resemblance to the Immaculate conception and Christ Consciousness, the concept of rebirth and the golden light after death. He is the pure soul that survives, the self – reborn. Horus is the product of magical reunion, with the right eye as the sun representing power, the left eye as the moon representing healing, and a golden solar disk that crowns above his head. He is also said to represent the colour red and loyalty.

After understanding his significance, we reflected on what this meant for me personally. It was about learning to let my inner light shine regardless of the company, claiming my royal space, and trusting it was safe to expose my authentic self.

As a little girl, I would hide in the corners of classrooms, behind the aisle boards in elementary schools, beneath my mother's dress. I was always a shy little creature, but part of that stemmed from not wanting to be seen as different and feeling unsafe in revealing that to the world.

The night finished with a gong bath and a deep meditative session under the stars of the Egyptian sky.

We visited Dendera Temple complex and the exquisite Hathor temple. Hathor was known as the Goddess of the sky, fertility, music and dance, sexuality, femininity, beauty, and love. She was worshipped in the form of a cow with stars above her, symbolising nurturing and maternal energy. Love radiated from her temple, and simply stepping through it, absorbing the palpable energy, was an extraordinary experience. Each of us spent time individually wandering through the site, meditating on the hieroglyphics that resonated with us most. Later, back on the boat, we delved deeper into their meanings.

Next, we visited Luxor Temple and the Temple of Karnak, traveling by a small boat on the Nile at sunrise. I played the shamanic drum alongside our group leader, leading us into the temple at dawn. Karnak was considered the 'most select of places' by Ancient Egyptians. It is a city of temples and chapels surrounding its own sacred lake. We spent many hours exploring, meditating, and chanting together where the guides allowed us to do so. Whenever I managed to escape from the group, I prayed in every temple, pyramid, portal, and tomb I visited, asking for the stars to align so that Scarlett and I could come into an intimate union.

In the late afternoon, we had a group session where each of us was assigned specific roles to be responsible for during the remainder of the trip.

Initially, Christine, the group leader who lived in Egypt, asked me to take on the role of blue lotus bearer, ensuring that the sacred blue water lotus extract was shared at each gathering. The blue lotus, a mythical flower dating back to Ancient Egypt, was known for its ability to put one into a dream-like and meditative state. It was also known for its aphrodisiac qualities and to induce a mild sense of euphoria.

After we had a more intimate conversation, she decided I would instead be responsible for overseeing the temple arts. In other words, I became the sacred scribe, documenting the events of our journey. After Christine changed my role, she remarked that she sensed my entire being light up, as if it was a more natural fit for me. I felt a deep sense of gratitude for how supportive and uplifting the sense of sisterhood was. It felt like being back at the summer camp I attended when I was a child, where there was no competition, only freedom to be ourselves, and to love and support each other.

Amidst busy yet fulfilling days, we sailed down the Nile River, renowned as the longest river in the world. After visiting the Valley of the Kings in the scorching, relentless Egyptian sun, I felt ready to crash. There were more group activities scheduled, but I was far too knackered to participate. I was hormonal and in need of alone time. The group activities had knocked me out.

Underneath the exhaustion, I was feeling depressed, and I wasn't sure why, but I couldn't stop crying. I believe part of it was that the visits to the temples can release a lot of stagnant energy within us, and simply being in Egypt itself can have that powerful effect. The other part of it was that I was frustrated that no one could see I was hurting inside. Part of me wished others would have sensed I needed support and reached out to me, but I knew that wasn't the way the world works. I would have to express myself more if I wanted people to know what I was going through.

I was feeling abandoned and forgotten about. I felt that no one would notice my absence or check in to see how I was doing. Part of what triggered me was that I had a one-on-one healing session confirmed, but when I inquired about it later in the afternoon, I was told it wasn't scheduled and they had forgotten about me.

My thoughts continued to get darker and darker. I thought I may as well just go ahead and die. Life had already been enough of a ride. I felt like there was something wrong with me. I felt like I would never excel at anything. If I couldn't even find my place in spiritual communities, then what was the point? I felt like throwing myself overboard, and drifting away down the Nile, never to be seen alive again.

Perhaps the only way to ease the pain was to dive even deeper into the depths of my emotions and heart through Mother Ayahuasca. At least I would feel held by the Divine Mother.

Part of these feelings, I knew, were rooted in the deep pain and emptiness I experienced in childhood from the sexual abuse and emotional neglect. The trauma still lingered within my being, longing for release. I knew part of my journey here would be to work through some of it, but I didn't feel like I had the support I needed. Perhaps I should have reached out for support, but in times like these, my tendency was to isolate and shut down. Communicating and opening up to others just didn't seem like an option. I felt it would only lead to more pain and a lack of understanding.

I sobbed myself to sleep.

The next morning, my period started, and I praised the gods. I felt more grounded and connected to my body. The girls were kind to me at breakfast, saying they missed me at the sound healing session. They told me they didn't disturb me because I reminded them of a wise, old sage, and knew when I needed to take time for myself. I always found it hard to believe anyone missed me. I still felt raw and fragile, wanting someone to save me from myself, but I knew that I was the only one who could do that. I had to work on not being such a master at concealing my pain, if I ever wanted to feel like I was truly seen by the world. It was time to come out of hiding.

We were fortunate enough to have insider access to Sekhmet's tomb, a sacred place normally blocked off from public viewing. A guard led us in groups of three, giving each group a few minutes to commune with her and experience the transcendental effect of being in her tomb, in her presence, gazing into her eyes. The message that I received from her was to be bold about who I am and to trust in my divine perfection.

It was not long before all of us started having emotional breakdowns, left, right, and centre. One of the group leaders, Maya, came to the room that I shared with Lara, bursting into tears, feeling that she wasn't doing enough to make the trip run smoothly, that she was failing at organising her first retreat.

I hugged her and told her I'd had my own dark night of the soul, and she wasn't alone. It was reassuring to hear and a helpful reminder that we were all dealing with our own challenges.

Lara's response to the overflowing tears and general chaos, was a simple "Blimey," which sent the three of us into fits of laughter. Blimey, indeed.

The rest of the afternoon was called off and a day of relaxation and down time was granted. Lara had a spray bottle she would use to cool herself off with. She knew I loved the sound it made and how sensitive I was to certain sounds—some of which could put me in an almost euphoric state. She gently sprayed the bottle near my ears for a few moments.

"I could die," I told her.

"Oh blimey, I don't want to kill you!"

Lara was delightful company, and I couldn't have asked for a better roommate. We laughed and shared stories with each other for the rest of the evening, secluded in the nest of our cabin as we continued to sail down the Nile, heading into Aswan the following morning.

Aswan, the land of Isis, was an exceptionally special place. The coral sun rose in the sky as we entered the land at dawn, singing, chanting, dancing, and embracing. I felt the nourishment and sacredness of the land as we ventured further. I had a sense that my prayers were being answered. My energy was lighter, my thoughts clearer. Something deep within me was shedding, and with that shedding, I grew closer with the girls, more intimate in my connection with the sisterhood.

After visiting Isis Temple and spending the afternoon on a boat ride around Elephantine Island in the setting sun, I had my healing session with Christine. She told me that she admired my pensive nature, but that it could sometimes come off as aloof. She understood that it came from my feeling that I needed to guard myself before I could feel comfortable with those around me. Her remark echoed Scarlett's, about the two conflicting sides of me. One side reflected the true essence of my being—open, warm, inviting, and loving. But then there was the other side that built a protective barrier and kept others at bay. She said that could be unnerving for people because they couldn't read me due to these conflicting energies.

Christine told me that she didn't feel anything in her solar plexus, the main feeling centre, and how that is often the case for women who have been sexually abused. They are cut off from their feelings and experience a sense of detachment from their bodies because of the trauma.

The following evening, after another three-hour sail and three-hour drive to our hotel, we made it to Cairo. The view from our bedrooms was the trio of The Great Pyramids of Giza. It was a surreal feeling to be in such close proximity to one of the most ancient and sacred sites in the world, a place I had dreamed of visiting since I was a little girl. We spent the first evening on the rooftop of the hotel, blessed with a display of fireworks as we smoked shisha and nibbled on an assortment of pita, falafel, hummus, and baba ghanoush. Christine had apparently planned it so that we would arrive on that day specifically to see the fireworks over the pyramids.

Early the next morning, we ventured out to visit the pyramids under the burning Egyptian sun. We split into small groups and explored on our own. I felt claustrophobic climbing down the sharply steep ladders into some of the tombs, but my intrigue led me down further. Each rung of the ladder felt like a step further into an entirely different world. It was almost as if the ladder itself contained its own magnetic field, propelling me deeper underground. The further below I went, the less willpower I seemed to have.

I wandered with two of my girlfriends through the desert. We laid down in the sun on the sand, taking in the spiritual high. We danced and sang and touched the stones of the pyramids until we had had our fill and were burnt to a crisp. We spent the rest of the afternoon exploring the streets of Cairo and shopping for jewelry.

On our final day, after enjoying another Egyptian breakfast on the rooftop, I set out with a group of girls to visit the Great Pyramid of Giza—the largest and oldest of the three pyramids, and the oldest of the Seven Wonders of the Ancient World. It was a long, steep climb up the narrow ascending passageways to reach the King's Chamber at the very top. About twenty people were allowed inside the room at once, so it was fairly crowded when we entered.

Inside the King's Chamber stood a granite sarcophagus. I learned from one of the guards that it was believed to serve as a healing or hospital bed. I leaned over the sarcophagus, touching my skin against it, feeling the energy. The guard was friendly and made an effort to connect with each of us individually when we mentioned that we were a sound healing group. He said he wouldn't allow the next group of people in so that we could be alone in the chamber to work our sound healing magic. It was a miracle that he allowed us the private time in there that he did.

We stood side by side inside the healing chamber, holding hands. We started humming and chanting until a song seemed to land. We sang "We are healing. We are healing all," and in the midst of our singing, I began to experience convulsions. Something like this had never happened to me before, even when on psychedelics. Orbs of light surrounded us. I started sobbing and my body wouldn't stop shaking. Simultaneously, I felt like a heavy weight had been lifted off of me. It was the most transcendental experience of my life, even with all of the ayahuasca work I had done. It felt euphoric and transformational, like a true rebirth of the soul.

As our singing naturally came to an end, we transitioned into ecstatic dance. It was like we had entered a portal of light that extended across the planet, reaching across the planes. One girl played the Native American flute, another the chimes. Meanwhile, another was deep in conversation with the guide, and it appeared as if they were floating above their bodies, communicating telepathically. I felt their spiritual connection and saw the way that they were looking into each other's eyes, as if the meeting had been pre-ordained. I felt like I was on ecstasy as I witnessed in awe everything going on around me.

When we finally stepped out into the daylight, tears continued to stream from my eyes. We had entered into one void and came out into another. About an hour later, I heard the news that Notre-Dame was burning down, along with other mosques around the world at the very same time. Although a shock and a tragedy for many, many others chose to perceive this as a sign of resurrection in the form of the Divine Feminine rising.

Notre-Dame held the energy of both light and darkness, in that it was steeped in a history that suppressed women's roles in society. Things were shifting; outdated structures were crumbling. I saw it as not without meaning that it happened right around the same time as our Divine Feminine celebratory parade in the most powerful spiritual vortex on the planet.

That afternoon and the next day, Harry bombarded me with messages, bringing to a halt a welcome period of silence thus far on the retreat. It was as if he sensed the rise in my light and power and was reacting to it, trying to pull me back down with his darkness. He was giving me a hard time over issues I can't even recall in retrospect. His energy felt disturbingly abnormal, even frightening. I remember thinking on the plane home that until I found another place to live, I would have to guard my energy, as it seemed like he was feeding off me.

When I arrived back to the flat, Harry hardly asked me a word about my trip. Instead, he ran a bath for me, expecting that afterward, I would join him in his bedroom to make love. As I waited for the bath to cool down, I started taking a few things out of my suitcases. Minutes later, Harry entered the room, demanding to know why I hadn't yet bathed, going on to tell me how disregarded he felt that I wasn't paying enough attention to him. I knew he was looking for a reaction, which is precisely what I was avoiding.

I took a bath, and when I finished, I calmly told him I wouldn't be sleeping with him because of the way his energy was. His eyes widened as he abruptly jumped out of bed and ran after me. I tried to lock myself in the bathroom, but he forced the door open. He screamed in my face, grabbed my shoulders, and shook me, his eyes wild and demonic. I yelled for him to get off, but he wouldn't stop. He shoved me into the sink, bruising my knees. I fought to push him off, but the tug of war and screaming went on for about five minutes. He tried to throw me into the bathtub, which broke in the process. I finally managed to escape his grip and ran out of the bathroom, hyperventilating and sobbing.

I ran into the spare bedroom and threw on my healing shamanic dress. As I tried to leave, he attempted to stop me, and I screamed, 'HOW DARE YOU? HOW DARE YOU! You monster! Don't come near me!'"

His face twisted, just as I had described—like a monster, a face of pure evil.

He raised his arms to block me, but I ducked under them and ran barefoot downstairs into the garden. He got the reaction he wanted, but could anyone blame me? I had to fight back. I had to save myself.

I couldn't catch my breath when I made it downstairs, and I wondered what to do. I couldn't go back up there again. I called Scarlett. After three rings, she picked up. Noticing the tone of my voice, she could tell something had gone wrong.

"Samara, what happened?"

"Harry just attacked me. I don't know what to do."

"Samara, you and Harry…"

"Do you have to go back up there at all?"

"All of my things are still up there. I'll have to. At least I need to get my wallet and a pair of shoes. I ran downstairs into my garden right after it happened."

As we were speaking, Harry appeared at the garden door, standing there silently, watching me like a predator. There was nothing I could do but let him watch as I paced barefoot on the dewy grass, making a plan with Scarlett.

"I think we should see each other sooner than next week. I have some time tomorrow if that suits you."

I agreed.

"I would like you to stay with a friend tonight."

"I'll just go to a hotel or something. I don't want to impose on anyone."

"No, I really want you to stay with someone else."

"I'd rather be alone. I'll be okay on my own," I murmured in between sobs.

"Please call up a friend and make an arrangement. Get whatever you need upstairs and then let me know once you have figured something out and you've left. Okay?"

I agreed and called one of the friends I'd made in Egypt. Afterward, I gathered my things and told Harry not to come an inch near me. He knew he had made a grave mistake as he followed me around the flat, desperately trying to plead with me.

I ended up having a sleepover with two of the girls I'd recently become close with. One of them gave me an energy healing, which was helpful, but didn't stop the shortness of my breath. I was still totally traumatised and in shock, as if an energetic knife had pierced me.

As I sat there with the girls, candles lit all around us and incense burning, I couldn't stop rocking back and forth. One of my friends pointed out that it was probably something I did as a child, when I had no one to hold me. I recalled that was what happened when I was deep in my ayahuasca journey in the jungle, where I rocked back and forth, crying like a wounded animal. It was my way of self-soothing. When I finally went to sleep that night, I dreamed the dream I had of Harry when we met, the dream where his face turned into a lion and he was snarling, his fangs ready to rip off my face.

The next afternoon my new friends and I sunbathed on her rooftop before I ordered an uber to 113 Sumner Place. I was still having difficulty breathing and my hands were still shaking when I arrived. Scarlett and I embraced at the door.

I sat down and stared at her, my hand pressed to my forehead, communicating through my eyes. Scarlett sat with me in my pain for some time.

"Some welcome home, huh?"

"I've been experiencing shortness of breath since it happened. It feels like a shooting pain in my heart. I'm just shocked that he would try to hurt me. I didn't expect that, even from him."

Scarlett looked at me sympathetically. "Walk me through what exactly happened. You sounded really scared on the phone."

"I was."

I paused for a moment to remember the sequence of events.

"He expected sex pretty much immediately upon my return. He came charging at me when I told him that I didn't plan to sleep with him. When I ran into the bathroom to try and shut the door, he pushed his way in. He grabbed me by my shoulders, shaking me back and forth. A screaming match ensued. The bathtub broke. My knee got bruised. He didn't even look like the same person. It was as if something else, something demonic, had entered his body. I eventually broke free and ran to the spare bedroom to throw on my shaman dress. He tried to stop me from leaving, but I ducked under and ran barefoot to the garden, and that's when I called you."

"I'm so sorry, Samara."

"I am too. It really hurts."

"At least now it makes leaving him easier," I said, offering a weak smile.

"Yes, I suppose that is true. Where do you think you will be staying tonight? Certainly not at the flat?"

"No, I won't be going back there when he's around. I'll find a place to live, and in the interim, whenever I have to go back to the flat, he can stay at his family home for the night. For the next few nights, I'll be staying with the friend I was with last night."

"Good. I'm glad you have them at least."

"Me too. I am very grateful for their support."

Scarlett sat with me for a while longer, holding space before gently asking me how the trip had been, despite the harrowing return.

"It was a special experience. It took some time to adjust to being around so many other people. Having so many activities planned was a lot to handle. But by the end of the ten days, I became close with mostly everyone. Sound healing sessions on the Nile were magical, as were the healing sessions we were able to do in the temples, tombs, and pyramids."

"I'm glad to hear you made some new friends and you seem to have more of a support system here now. How are you feeling about everything now?"

"Raw. Confused. Scared. Anxious."

Scarlett nodded in understanding.

"What are you most confused about?"

"I'm confused about my perception of reality. What's real? What's not real? Is there one truth, or many different truths? It's something I thought about in Egypt. Is this really who Harry is? I saw this really dark side of him, but I have also seen sides of him where he is genuine, light, and really seems to love me."

"It is who he is. There is light and dark within all of us, though, so of course he has his moments where you would see otherwise. I guess it's about determining what you are willing to accept – in him, and in yourself."

"I just wish I wasn't so confused all the time. Everyone seems to have their act together more than I do."

"No one really has their act together. We all try to pretend we do. Perhaps that is a truth you can find some peace in. There is never a right or wrong answer. We can only make choices that feel right to us in the moment."

"Well, I think it's safe to say that after this incident, the right choice is to move out. What he did isn't acceptable in my book. This was the final straw."

"I would have to agree with you there," Scarlett said.

"I still have no idea where I'll live, but I'll figure something out."

"I am sure you'll find something, so try not to worry about that too much."

I gazed off in the distance for some time.

"I feel a sense of emptiness in knowing this is really a final goodbye with Harry. Losing a lover, someone you have been with for some time, feels like losing a part of yourself."

"It can feel that way. Each person we encounter brings out different qualities within us, and when those connections end, that part of you that emerged while you were with that person seems to die with the process of letting go."

"Why is life such a never-ending struggle?"

"A question for the sages," she replied. "Things will improve though. Just focus on keeping your head above the water for the time being. Life will shift and change again. Things are especially volatile at your age, discovering yourself and grounding in the truth of who you are, attempting to find a sense of stability. It is meant to be an experimental time of life, so try not to worry so much that you don't have it all figured out by now."

"As much as I like to experiment, part of me is just longing for stability. I'll try to stay positive. I'm just feeling defeated right now."

"That's understandable. Let yourself feel whatever you need to feel, so that it can eventually clear and be processed. Running from how you feel will only make the process more difficult and it will eventually catch up with you."

"If I wasn't 'in my feelings' before, then I certainly am now. I feel like that's all I ever do – feel. And sometimes the intensity is too much to bear."

"Especially if you've lived a life of numbing yourself out to not feel pain, I can imagine it would be catching up with you pretty heavily now. And therapy, on top of your own personal life circumstances, brings a lot to the surface. It's not surprising at all that you're feeling this way."

"I just wish I had a safe place of my own to process all of this."

"It's probably best you're around people for some time. It might be healthier for you. Sometimes we need people to share our experiences with. That's part of life. I don't think you should isolate yourself right now."

"I guess. I just think it will be easier for me to fully heal when I've moved out."

We sat together in silence for the remaining moments, sitting in the depth of my feelings. I was still completely out of breath, and my hands hadn't stopped shaking.

"It seems to be time. Please do take very good care of yourself this week. Shall we see each other the usual time next Tuesday?"

"Yes, I'd like that."

I paid her and got up to leave.

"Goodbye, sweetheart."

"Bye, Scarlett. See you next Tuesday."

I walked down the spiral staircase and called an uber to drive me back to my friend's place. The sun was shining, but there was a light drizzle.

As I was waiting for the car to arrive, Scarlett stepped out of the main door, and suddenly, she was there, right in front of me, like a radiant angel in the sunlight. She approached and kissed me affectionately on my right cheek. Then, she stepped back slightly, taking her time to gaze deeply into my eyes before gently kissing my left cheek, her hand softly resting on the side of my face.

I was so stunned and delighted that I stood frozen, taking a moment to come back from the dream made reality. It was so unexpected, so magical, that when it was over, before Scarlett walked away, all I could manage to mutter was, "Thank you." She smiled and, without another word, set off down the street, emanating divine grace. I watched her walk away, feeling as though I were floating above my body, as she opened her black umbrella and vanished into the distance, like a bittersweet mirage.

The car arrived a minute later, and as we drove, I reflected on the connection Scarlett and I had been experiencing. It wasn't unrequited love. It was the highest form of love – pure and innocent. That kiss was the most romantic and tender I had ever experienced. The feel of her lips still tingled upon my cheeks.

I wrote to Scarlett the following afternoon to express my gratitude.

"Thinking of you. Thank you for yesterday, angel."

She replied, "You're very welcome, Samara. I hope you are feeling a little better today x"

It did uplift my spirits, but I was still hurting from what I experienced with Harry. I spent the remainder of the week sleeping at my friend's and was fortunately able to sleep at the flat over the weekend, as Harry spent it at his other house.

A girlfriend of mine from Egypt came over Friday night whom I had been flirting with throughout the trip. She noticed the African mask I bought in Egypt and remarked that she was surprised, as it seemed like such a masculine object for someone who radiates such feminine energy.

We made out for a while in my flat and then continued making out on the front steps into the early morning. She wanted to go further while we were inside, but I was halfhearted about it, with my interests obviously being elsewhere.

The next day, we went to a kirtan with a few other girls from Egypt, where the leader sings a mantra, and the audience repeats it. It is a powerful form of meditation, and a single chant can last up to about thirty minutes. I mentioned to a friend that I was still experiencing a shortness of breath, and she recommended a healer, whom I visited the next day.

I had an intuitive craniosacral therapy session with her, where she shared the messages she received while performing gentle bodywork. A message that came to me in a dreamy state was, 'It's time to breathe a sigh of relief and let yourself off the hook.'

The healer told me that I was working on building strength and foundations as I went through an initiation. She said she saw a vision of me with my inner child, sitting cross-legged across from each other, simply staring. She told me I didn't need outside validation for happiness, as it was all within me. I left the session feeling more grounded, like I could finally breathe normally again.

Even with the healing, it felt like the bleakest day I'd experienced in a year. Harry had been my main support system, even though he wasn't much support. He was all I had, and now, what would I do? I felt utterly alone in the world, completely groundless. I still felt safer with him than I had during those years when I was lost in Thailand and other parts of Asia, with no one at all. I had grown so much with him, more than I ever had before. He was my first true intimate lover. Parting ways with him wouldn't take away from how much I'd miss him and how much we loved each other for a time.

Monday evening my reaction was the opposite, moving from my heart to my head, not wanting to get caught up in the memories, the nostalgia, the perhaps false sense of love. I had to be logical and see the situation for what it truly was. I should have been celebrating my path to freedom, not grieving the loss of my entrapment. As a coping mechanism, I still wanted to see the best in Harry. I had to stop being naïve.

I dreamed of Scarlett on Monday night, twice. In one dream, we were outside in a garden laying on a towel in the sunshine. She told me how much I remind her of herself. She leaned over and lightly touched me, kissing my cheek. I attempted to kiss her on the lips, but she stopped me, telling me we weren't allowed to. She told me she feels the connection but, 'half the time it's the moon' and it hurts her because she doesn't know how I feel, or how she herself should feel.

On Tuesday morning, I woke up hearing 'Olly Olly Oxen Free,' a catchphrase usually used in children's games of hide and seek. A call to come out of hiding and out into the open air, to be seen. Come out, come out, wherever you are. An interesting synchronicity as the day prior I had the song, 'You've Got to Hide Your Love Away,' by the Beatles playing in my mind. I came to find out before heading to therapy that it was national lesbian visibility day. A sign from the Divine to come out, come out, wherever I was, wherever we were?

I arrived to 113 Sumner Place in a sulky state about my life. It seemed that it would take more time to heal from Harry than I anticipated. Scarlett asked me how I was feeling and how things were progressing. I told her that even though I was not turning back after what happened, I was still nostalgic for the times we had together that were happy, and how it was a deep bond that was difficult to break, even with all of its challenges.

Scarlett asked me what I wanted from her again.

"That's a big question. I can't really give you an answer."

She was smirking at something, and I told her that her smirk was making me laugh. Scarlett tried to control her facial expression and told me, "I shouldn't be smirking in here."

I told her, "It's fine, I smirk all the time."

I recounted my experience over the weekend of kissing a girl from the Egypt retreat. She asked me, teasingly, if it had turned romantic.

I shyly replied, "Maybe."

She smiled and affirmed, "It is, then." I wondered if she knew I was only saying it to make her jealous. Whether she was or not was impossible to tell, as her poker face remained perfectly unreadable.

After we said goodbye until next week, I walked away lifelessly, feeling flat and uninspired, even after seeing the light of my life.

Chapter Twenty-Four – The Devil Knows How to Seduce but God is the Grand Seducer

I met up with Luciana, the woman whose house I stayed at for the ayahuasca ceremony, for coffee. She wanted to hear about my trip to Egypt. I also told her about Harry attacking me and that I was looking for another place to live. As fate would have it, she was looking to rent a room in her flat in Marylebone. She showed me photos and I signed the rental contract that day.

The next day, as I was in the process of packing up my things, Harry returned to the flat to pick up some papers for work. He said he would only be in for a minute, so I agreed. I was about to head out to get more boxes anyway. He offered to bring me to a storage and moving facility, then back to the flat.

When I returned to the car, he blocked my way and said he'd only give me a ride back with all my heavy boxes if I 'French kissed' him for ten seconds. I told him to fuck off, but he got aggressive and forced me to hug him. His touch physically hurt my heart. I found my own way home, seething in rage. I moved my things to Luciana's the next day.

Luciana was interesting and full of stories, and I figured that would be a good distraction. Her childhood and life had unique parallels with my own. I enjoyed living with an older woman. We spent the first few days living together going for walks through Regent's Park and around Marylebone, where she showed me all the secret spots, bars, restaurants, and cafés that I couldn't miss. Her beloved dog accompanied us everywhere.

On Friday evening, I received a message from my friend Vighnesh that I had met in the autumn at the meditation school. He asked if I was free to get together and

we agreed to get a drink at sunset and then hang out in
Regent's Park. It was a warm spring evening.

We met at Clarette and sat at the downstairs bar on
pink plush velvet stools, surrounded by stained glass crests.
Neither of us were feeling like a cocktail and as the wine by
the glass menu was limited, we decided to order a bottle of
the Nuits-Saint-Georges 1er Cru. We ordered a charcuterie
and cheese board to avoid stumbling our way to the park.

Hardly any time was wasted before we found
ourselves immersed in deep conversation. The pupils of his
eyes were so large, his eyes so deep, that I felt as though I was
being vacuumed into them. There seemed to be no distance
between us, just as it had been the first time we met many
months ago, which, given everything that happened in the
interim, already felt like a lifetime ago. Meeting with him
again was like meeting up with a long-lost friend. I didn't
hesitate to dive into the details of my life. I explained the
confusion I felt regarding my relationship with Scarlett and
what happened with Harry the day I returned from Egypt,
how we had recently separated, and that I spent the last week
hardly able to breathe.

"Samara," he said, "You're letting all these other
people get in the way of your own peace and joy. Choose to
find peace despite the situations you find yourself in. Don't
get dragged into the drama around you."

"That's true," I replied. "I guess it's just easier said
than done when you find yourself so invested."

"That's the problem. You've invested yourself too
heavily in these people without investing enough in yourself. I
never needed peace because I never knew about war."

"That's beautiful."

"Everything happens in your life to make you more
clear. What's been happening for you is nothing to stress

over, and it's a waste of time for you to feel you made a mistake. Your soul called this in as a learning experience. Since we saw each other last, your eyes are so clear."

I took a sip of wine and gazed into his eyes.

"Tell me everything. I'm your mirror," he said.

"I feel I am very much surrendered to God. And have no idea where I am going, so I am just living. And that's the way it has to be now," I said.

"Yes. I was talking to Him, to God, about you. And he said that I need to protect you. He said that I need to protect you from you."

"Why protect me from myself? Does He think I'm going to self-destruct?"

"I don't know yet. Anyway, it's super interesting to talk to you. I know every person's script. You don't need no friends, my love. Yes, I knew this from the beginning you don't need anyone. This is it. I know the script, anyway. Sometimes I dream about life like a movie."

"Yes," I said, "you know the script. And I think I am beginning to understand it too."

"I just want to be a free bird. I think that is all I ever wanted," I told him.

"I know. That is why I gave you wings. You are such a cool thing. I am very special to have someone like you. Even when I talk to you, I heal so much faster. Wow – I feel your energy right on."

"Ha! Perhaps it's the balmy late-spring evening, the delicate wine, the company of two near-strangers who feel as if they have spent lifetimes together."

"No, it's more than that. It's different. When I feel you, I feel like a baby. I feel like I find myself when I feel you. I feel loved. Some very strange way. I feel like we know who we are. I feel I love you. Unconditional love. So special in my reality, pure like a kite in the sky."

We spent another hour in conversation, feeling as if our souls were speaking to each other above our bodies. After finishing the wine and nibbling on our hors d'oeuvres, we walked to Regent's Park and found a lovely spot beneath a tall weeping willow—my favourite tree.

"What does truth mean to you? Do you think there are many versions of the truth?"

"Though we all have different perceptions, there is ultimately only one truth. Your own truth cannot be so different than mine. Because every individual truth leads to one common universal truth. Devotional service. A devoted service. To the Universe. What is your help to others? You help yourself to the max, and then you give up yourself and help others. Because that is the bigger self, when you start to become a true devotee of the Universe, you became a 'sharman.' Share, man. You and I are like petals of one lotus flower, sharing one sun, one moon. Jesus, he sacrificed everything. What you and I sacrifice, wow. I feel a lot. I feel Jesus in my heart. Wow, how beautiful is this love. He is the biggest love."

"Sharman. I may want to train as a shaman one day. Sacrifice, yes. I think I am coming into deeper acceptance of the concept of sacrifice lately, and trusting that whatever is meant to be, will not pass me by. It's better to release our control issues, do what we can do, and let everything else flow in the way it was always meant to flow."

An ivory white swan glided past us on the lake, turning its head to take a long hard look at the two of us, as it carried on its way.

"You cannot train. You have to invent, your own. It's for real. There is no winning or trying to get to the finish line by a certain point, and don't worry about success. It has to be creative. The creativeness has to belong to you. It doesn't belong to society. Creativity does not belong to the fans or anyone else. Your creativity is in you. So, no one can say you are a good artist or bad artist."

"Amen to that."

"Why does Planet Earth exist?" I asked Vighnesh.

"Remember Jesus. The answer is not to eat the fruit of knowledge but for it to come as it is. To be the king of the kingdom, not the kingdom which has boundaries. To love. To dance. To help. To share. To respect. That's why we are on Planet Earth. Our bodies are borrowed. Other planets are so perfect they don't need bodies unlike Earth. Earth is covered with the illusion of duality but that can be overcome by opening up the third eye. Your third eye is wildly open, which is why when you tell me about what you have been dealing with, I think, 'fuck this stupidity.' But forgive like Jesus did, because they are blind baby. They don't know what they doing. That is why Jesus said last – 'Forgive them father; they do not know."

I spoke to Vighnesh about temptation, and how this can sometimes lead us off track in life, but are we ever actually led off track? Everything that happens leads us into greater awareness, just makes us clearer, as he commented earlier. It is all part of the Divine orchestra, and we are just dancing to its melody, flowing to its beat, skipping to its rhythm.

"Roles," he answered, "just remember they are all playing roles, and underneath the mask is just God in human form helping to bring you into greater awakening. Any temptations that feel not of God are still part of the plan. God is not absent from anything."

"The Devil knows how to seduce, but it is God that is the true grand seducer," I said.

We sat for a few moments of silence.

We continued to speak for hours that seemed timeless. If my heart wasn't devoted to Scarlett, I thought that perhaps there would have been a time and place for us in the future. He expected nothing from what he shared with me. It was pure, honest sharing from a man with a heart as open and vast as the night sky. I considered him as a great teacher.

After I returned to the flat, Luciana was out, and I blasted some music and had a dance party. Vighnesh wrote me telling me, "Drink some water now. Your internal organs need water. Now." I drank some water, and then he asked me what I did when I got home. I told him I had been dancing, and he said, "I feel like an investigative girlfriend hahaha."

I said, "Don't be a jealous clown."

"I love feeling jealous," he said.

"I wish I could feel it sometimes."

He said, "Oh poor girl. You've never been in love then. That's why I love this feeling."

I said - 'You can be in love and not jealous.'

He replied - 'Well, that is also true, but I definitely prefer the first one. Which is full of life, like a river which flows and a tree full of flowers and fruits and the dry season comes the roots never lets the tree to die and hold it tight until it rains again.'

His last message to me that evening was 'And hey, even the whole world don't get what you do, you're very strong. You're the number one for me on this planet. So grateful to the Universe that you showed up in my life. Thank you for being such a beautiful person and making me feel so positive. Goddess who walks this Planet Earth. It is impossible to put your spirit down. I send all my wishes and love to you. You just make someone's reality, really, really nice.'

I replied, "You're such a sweetheart. I love you, too. Good night."

He had a point about jealousy. Why hadn't I felt jealous with any of my previous boyfriends? If I saw Scarlett with someone else, I would most definitely feel like a green-eyed monster.

The next morning, I woke up from yet another dream involving Scarlett. We were playing a real-life game of chess. It was almost like hide and seek. It was a bit scary, and each move felt life-altering. We were standing on a black and white checked platform floating in the sky. If one of us made the wrong move, we would fall to our death. A line came into my mind – "There has to be something for everything." And then afterwards I heard – "No, there doesn't." Maybe I had to give up my desire for control. Some things just are.

Luciana came into my bedroom, gossiping about celebrities she was acquainted with and their recent relationship drama. I was bored hearing about people I didn't know. I kept my eyes on my book, but that didn't stop the chatter. Perhaps I should have said something, but I didn't want to seem rude.

"Would you like to go to a flower nursery later to pick out some plants with me?"

I agreed, and we spent some time exploring more of her secret spots in Marylebone. She had many interesting stories to tell, and most of the time I was entertained. She had a hilarious habit of mentioning someone's sun sign whenever she talked about them, as if it explained everything about that person.

"Jake is head-strong, direct, and stubborn. He moves through life with a beautiful confidence but tends to be short-tempered and impulsive. Aries." And then it was all supposed to make sense.

After our afternoon excursions, a friend of mine from Egypt asked if I wanted to accompany her and two other girls to a polyamory party on Saturday. I agreed.

The party was a gathering of people that slept together and engaged in open relationships. I felt like a queen. Men were bringing me drinks from the bar when I hadn't even asked for them, and I was enjoying flitting around like a butterfly, reveling in the newly single life and remembering what it was like. My friend told me that a guy I'd been chatting with was interested in me and wanted to kiss me. I figured, why not? I kissed him first, and we indulged in a passionate make-out session in front of everyone.

We exchanged numbers and he told me he was a professional cuddle therapist. He had a girlfriend but wanted to take me out on a date and show me some of his favourite spots around London. I told him I would see about that. Kissing him felt exhilarating in the moment, but afterwards I felt a sense of emptiness because it had no meaning.

On Sunday, Luciana and I went to the farmer's market. It was a lovely time, but I got roped into spending the whole afternoon with her. I would have to put up some stronger boundaries if we were to live together, as it was starting to feel like my personal time was being infringed upon. The social life I had been experiencing since Egypt was refreshing, but also a big adjustment as I was used to having a lot of time to myself.

Later that evening, I received an email that looked like it was from my mother. Her name popped up in my inbox, but as I started reading, I knew something was off. My 'mum' appeared to be telling me that Harry and I should be mature and work things out, that relationships fail, that people get back together all the time, and that I should give him another chance. It didn't sound like my mother. It had Harry's energy all over it. I clicked on the name to check the email address. Sure enough, it was not her email. I realised that Harry had created a fictitious account, posing as my mum, in a desperate attempt to convince me to get back together with him.

I had blocked his number, but the next day, he called me from a different one. I nearly hung up when I heard his voice but waited to hear what he had to say. It was mechanic and sounded like he was reading from a script. He tried to convince me to go out to lunch with him so we could discuss things, but the requirement was that afterwards, we would have to have sex.

I told him he was completely out of his mind. He insinuated that he was going to blackmail me about a secret I once told him. He said that if I wouldn't agree to his proposition, he would continue drinking and couldn't be held accountable for his actions, and then added that he had already 'made contact' with some of my friends and family.

Although mind-blown that he had stooped that low, I paid it no attention. Whatever consequences might arise from his actions, I would deal with if they came up. I did my best to not let him get to me and focus back on the light. With everything going on lately, I'd had little room to get lost in reverie about Scarlett – one of the few pleasures left in my life. I decided to write her and tell her what a gift she was to me and that I adored her.

I showed up to therapy on Tuesday feeling pissed off because of Harry, despite my best efforts. He called me again that morning and when I heard his voice, I immediately hung up, not wanting to make the same mistake twice.

"Thank you for your message yesterday. That was so lovely to receive," Scarlett told me cheerily, smiling sweetly like an angel.

"You're very welcome," I said.

I filled her in on Harry's blackmailing scheme and how he impersonated my mother to convince me we should get back together.

"I hate him!" I told her, seething.

She smiled with a noticeable glint of pleasure as she acknowledged my passionate frustration.

"You're enjoying this, aren't you?" I asked her.

Scarlett wasn't used to seeing me express anger. She seemed to find this side of me amusing.

She pursed her lips and didn't reply.

"And on top of Harry's nonsense, I'm not sure how happy I feel about my new living situation," I added.

"Why is that?"

"She's talking my head off! I can't catch a moment of peace."

"Sounds like you're going to have to put up some boundaries," Scarlett teased.

"Yeah, well, she's a step up from Harry," I said dryly.

Scarlett let out a cackle. Her laugh was beautiful, my favourite laugh in the world. I could never tire of hearing that laugh. It's a memory of her that remains vivid, as clear as day in my mind.

"I'd say she's several steps up from Harry," Scarlett said, humouring me.

"I guess we shall see. What am I supposed to say, 'Do you think you could stop talking for a while and stop coming into my room to gossip to me about people I do not even know?'"

"Yes, more or less," Scarlett said.

"I don't want her to take offence and then feel like she can't talk to me. Hopefully she doesn't think I'm anti-social, but that's just how I am. I tend to shut away to have my private time."

"Try not to give it too much thought. Just tell her that when your door is closed, that means you don't want to be disturbed. You're paying her rent, so you don't have any kind of obligation at all."

"That's true. I just don't want to make things awkward between us. I guess this is a good example of my avoidant behaviour when it comes to confrontation."

"So, tell me more about Harry impersonating your mother, and about the blackmailing? That really is nuts. Even I'm surprised at that move."

"I feel like I'm seeing a totally different side of him. I'm really seeing what a maniac he is. It's like the veil has totally been lifted. He's not even trying to pretend anymore to be anything but my abuser."

"I wonder if something has been going on with his medication. I remember the first few months when we were seeing each other how volatile he was as he was coming off the meds and switching the dosages around."

"That's a good point. Well, if I'm ever in contact with him again, perhaps I'll ask. It does seem uncharacteristic of him to be this over the top. It really is like I'm dealing with another person, like he's possessed or something. I don't know what to believe. Anyway, some lighter news is that I went to a polyamory party over the weekend."

"Oh yeah? What was that like?"

"It was a house party, nothing too wild. I didn't stay very late, though, so I'm not sure how things went after that. Lots of open conversation about sex. One guy was interested in me, and we ended up making out. He asked to take me out on a date."

"I thought that's not how polyamory parties worked," Scarlett said.

"What do you mean? Him asking me out?"

Scarlett nodded in response.

"Well, I guess he liked me," I replied.

"I'm not sure if I'll see him though," I said. "I can't really be asked."

"It's probably best that you take some time to heal after just ending things with Harry."

"Yes, it was just a spur of the moment thing, and my interests are elsewhere anyway."

I didn't explain nor did Scarlett ask what I meant by that.

"I had a fascinating dream about us a couple of nights ago. We were playing chess, but not on a board. It was like the entirety of our lives was the chess board. My moves would always alter yours, leaving me uncertain of what you wanted or which direction you would take. It felt like the world's most intricate, masterful game of chess—like a lifetime of hide and seek. Olly olly oxen free, but eventually, there comes a time when it's necessary to stop hiding and set oneself free."

"It sounds like a statement to the power dynamic going on between us," Scarlett said.

"How do you mean?"

"Well, it's like how you say it's difficult for you to open up about your emotions because you feel that I'm not transparent enough with you. And so, the power play going on is that you hold back if you feel I'm holding back."

"Yes, well I always feel that you are hiding something. It sometimes feels like I'm having to dig under layers of concealment to find the truth. I know you say you feel that way with me too sometimes, that you encounter walls, but it is difficult for me to fully open up about myself when I don't know enough about the other person, even if this is therapy."

"Ahh, so it's like 'I'll show you mine if you show me yours' kind of thing?" Scarlett asked.

"Yes," I laughed, "that sums it up quite well."

Scarlett had a way with words. She knew exactly what to say to make me go just a little bit crazy.

"If I feel you're not receptive to me when I open up about my feelings, then I retreat. I guess, in that sense, there is a power dynamic going on. My reaction to being met with rejection is that I withdraw."

"Samara, I haven't been rejecting you."

"I'm just saying that's how it feels to me. I don't like this one-way communication so much. Although this is the way therapy is set up, it's not natural for human beings to get to know each other and fully open up when there's no back and forth and mutual sharing."

"Although the focus does have to remain on you, as much as you may want to avoid that sometimes, there still is an energy exchange between us. Sometimes the unsaid is more powerful than the spoken word."

"So you can see my reasons for loving you despite not really 'knowing you,' to use your words. The truth of what I feel is beyond the knowing, you see."

Scarlett, quite appropriately, responded to me with silence.

"So, going back to Harry, although I'm pissed off with him right now, I intend on working on forgiveness. I don't want any resentment towards him draining my energy. And I'll always be grateful that he helped teach me to stand in my power, because I had to learn to assert myself with him. There was so much going on under the surface, spiritually speaking, and so it was not without purpose."

"There is something to learn from every relationship. Every person reflects a part of us, so the issues you faced with Harry would likely have surfaced with another lover as well.

She looked at the clock.

"It's time to end. Work on those boundaries this week. If you keep avoiding it, it'll continue to escalate, so you may as well speak up sooner rather than later."

"I shall try my best. Goodbye, dear Scarlett."

As I walked home, I reflected on the wisdom of Scarlett's silence. The song 'Enjoy the Silence,' by Depeche Mode came to mind. It seemed that Scarlett's way was to show love, rather than tell it. It could be seen in her actions. I wondered if my words ruined the essence of what existed between us. Breaking the silence brought us back to reality, and it was there that the dream could be broken.

Chapter Twenty-Five – Hidden it May Be, but it Will Come Out When the World Is Ready for Me

I spent the rest of the week in solitude. Luciana left for Hawaii for a ten-day yoga retreat. I needed time alone to digest everything that had happened, so her timing was perfect. I didn't see that I could sustain my life in London much longer. The agony of seeing Scarlett, yet not being able to have her in my life as intimately as I would have liked, was becoming too much for me to bear.

I had felt like London was becoming my home, more than anywhere else had been, and I wanted to make it work, but I couldn't find a way to stay. The search for my home seemed never-ending. I thought about leaving for Sri Lanka for the summer, yet the pain of leaving London, leaving everything behind, was also too much to bear. I just felt stuck and unsure of what to do.

Though I knew it was best for me to stay detached from Harry after everything that happened, I still felt like he was my anchor to my life in London, like my anchor to life in the world. Would a new destination really fill the void inside of me? I didn't want to jump into making a decision just yet.

I decided to write Harry a long email. I had a lot to say and I needed to get it out of my system. I hadn't had a chance to address the hurt I felt. It seemed like something I had to do to find peace in the aftermath of the attack. Aside from expressing my pain, I also reflected on the beautiful moments that we'd shared, and I told him that he was a great teacher to me in many ways, and that I was sad that he wasn't there for me in the ways that I needed him to be.

On Saturday, I went to an ayahuasca ceremony. I hoped for clarity about which direction to take in my life – whether to move to Sri Lanka and help a friend out with his hotel and partake in a yoga teacher training, whether to move to Peru and study and train in shamanism, or whether to stay in London and study psychotherapy.

After the ceremony, I realised it was futile to ask the plant spirits what I should do, for that was my own decision to make. I purchased two small bottles of ayahuasca to micro-dose with, and I looked forward to experimenting with that over the coming months.

Sunday evening, I met a friend for dinner in a French restaurant in Marylebone. I had another ayahuasca session planned for the following night and I could taste the ayahuasca at dinner and for the remainder of the night – a signal of the intensity of what was to come on Monday evening. Even the dreams I had on Sunday evening felt like they were DMT induced, more trippy than usual, perhaps because earlier that morning was my first experimentation with micro-dosing.

The ceremony was with a shaman I worked with from the jungle. During the ceremony, I ascended outside of this realm and felt like I was in the land of Nirvana, where different spiritual beings and ascended masters joined me. Everything was vibrant, alive, in high definition, as I floated and buzzed out of my body amongst the stars, communicating with star beings from other dimensions who sent me vibrations of unconditional love and peace. My temperature was fluctuating from shivering and very cold to perspiring and boiling hot. I sobbed and laughed intermittently throughout the five hours of the ceremony.

I was finally able to release what had transpired with Harry and make peace with it. All of the sorrow from the breakup came flowing out of me like a waterfall, and it was a beautiful emotional purge. My history of sexual abuse came up again in a clear way. I came to the understanding that it started at an age where I would have not been able to make sense of it, an age in which I would have repressed it. I was spared the visual details, but the claircognizance of it told me everything I needed to know.

I didn't get much sleep, so I showed up to therapy the next day drained and raw from the experience, but I still felt like a flower blossoming with Divine light, healed from all I had experienced the night before. Also, a bit of sleep deprivation was nothing to deter me from meeting with my beloved.

"That's a beautiful dress," Scarlett said to me.

"Thank you. I just returned a few hours ago from an ayahuasca ceremony."

"You do look exhausted."

"I'm not surprised. It was an intense healing and I spent most of the evening sobbing, but also laughing at the beauty of life, that with each human tragedy, there ends up being a light at the end of the tunnel. It's just a matter of being able to recognise it."

"What came up for you that led to your sobbing?"

"First, just releasing Harry and making peace with our ending. And the sexual trauma from childhood came up strongly, just this crystal-clear knowing. There was also a peace that came with it, like I could finally put the past to rest."

"Did you get an idea of when it started?"

"An earlier age than I care to mention. It's no surprise that it remained deeply buried until the moment I could no longer ignore what was seeking to be seen."

Scarlett sat with an air of deep empathy, and I felt grateful for how well she grasped the gravity of the situation.

It felt like the room was charged with too much sorrow. I wanted to lighten the load for us both energetically.

"Can you distract me?" I asked her. I wanted to run out of the room, anything to avoid sitting in the silence of what I'd just relayed to her.

"I'm just going to sit with that," Scarlett said.

After some time of us sitting in silence and digesting my emotions together, as a team, Scarlett spoke again.

"It's not always so good to distract ourselves."

I nodded. Nonetheless, Scarlett decided after we had sat in it, that she would grant me my wish.

Although the details are hazy, she relayed a tale about Indian maharajas and their interactions with British colonials. It was very funny, and I was impressed at her storytelling abilities.

"Where did you get your sustenance from in childhood, if not from anyone in your family? Was there someone you had a close connection with? For example, a grandparent or an aunt perhaps?"

"From within...but sometimes that wasn't enough," I said, gazing deeply into her eyes.

"It's the unspoken from you that conveys the most," Scarlett said.

"I feel that way about you too."

We both smiled and there was a soft, tenderness lingering in the space between us.

"What in the unspoken about me says the most to you?" I asked her.

"It's in your eyes. The way you look at me tells me more than words ever could. It's also simply your presence."

"The mirror's reflection runs both ways," I said.

"Dear Samara..."

"Scarlett..."

We gazed, and gazed, and let all of the words that could not be spoken reverberate throughout the silence.

"What do you want from me?" Scarlett asked me.

Again, the question that I hadn't been able to transparently answer.

"I don't know…" I replied, trailing off.

Of course, I knew, but I couldn't bring myself to tell her what I truly wanted after the past recent rejections. I wished I could be honest, as I had been many times before about my feelings for her, but I was reaching my breaking point.

"You know we can talk about anything in here, right?" Scarlett asked.

"On paper, yes, but unfortunately it doesn't end up feeling that way," I said.

"What do you mean?" Scarlett asked.

"Well, some subjects feel like forbidden territory, and we can't technically talk about everything if we can't talk about you. And if you don't trust me to open up more, I can only go so deep with you."

"I do trust you," Scarlett said.

"Do you? You haven't seemed to trust me much in the past. I'll spare you some examples."

"I trust you more now than I did previously," Scarlett said.

"Yes? What changed?"

"Just little things you've done over time, your actions."

"I see. Well, I'm glad to hear that."

"You know I'm very fond of you," she said. "Maybe a little too fond."

"I'm very fond of you, too," I told her.

We gazed at each other affectionately for some time until Scarlett asked me what I was thinking about.

"Your eyes," I replied unashamedly.

"My eyes..." Scarlett repeated, unable to hide her slight discombobulation at my directness.

"How are you feeling about Luciana's absence?"

"I've been isolating aside from the ayahuasca ceremonies, but I think that's what I needed. Luciana will return in a few days."

"It's not healthy to isolate so much from the world, Samara."

"Maybe, but I needed to recharge in solitude. Luciana was giving me no space."

"You'll need to assert your boundaries when she returns, or it's going to keep surfacing."

"If it persists, I'll try and find a way to address it with her when she's back, but for now, I'm soaking in all of the introspective time until her return."

"You can be too serious at times. I think you have to allow yourself to experience more joy. If I wish anything for you, it's not so much spiritual growth, but that you experience joy."

Scarlett's heart was in the right place. Maybe I could trust her more, let go of my control issues, and just enjoy the process.

"Perhaps you're right. It's been such an intense year and I've been trying to make sense of it all. I do need to find a way to have more fun. It's still very raw and I guess I'm impatient to have more clarity so I can lay all of this to rest."

"Sometimes we can only think about a subject so much before we run ourselves in circles. Remember that all things work themselves out in time. Sometimes that's all it comes down to – divine timing."

"Hmm, yes, easier said than done for an impatient soul like mine. You are part of the equation in my overthinking. I often don't know how you're feeling, what you're thinking, and all I am able to do is guess."

"I feel the same way about you," Scarlett said.

We looked at each other, acknowledging all that had been said.

The session ended and I bid Scarlett farewell. She kissed me goodbye on the cheek and my heart fluttered like a butterfly. I noticed her looking after me as I continued down the spiral staircase.

Outside, I ran into Marc, the other patient in the building who had asked me for a coffee.

"You are stunningly beautiful," Marc said, without reservation, the moment he saw me.

"Thank you, Marc. It's so lovely to see you again. It's been a while, hasn't it?"

"What are your plans this afternoon?" he asked me.

I was caught off guard, and struggled to come up with an excuse, then told him that my day was open.

"Well, how about that coffee you once promised me?"

"I don't see why not. I know a place just a few streets down. Shall we walk there?"

"We shall," Marc replied.

Rather than sitting in the café, we decided to take our coffees to Regent's Park. We sat on the grass and delved into a deep conversation. It felt like I was on round two of therapy for the day. I filled him in on my recent struggles with both Harry and Scarlett, sparing no details (I sensed he was a good listener and a natural empath), and told him about my relocation to Marylebone and the experience I was having there since my move.

"Thank you for feeling safe enough to share all of that with me. I feel honoured," Marc said.

"Thank you for listening. I don't open up to everyone like this. I sensed you were someone I could trust. That's a rare find these days."

"Is it okay if I touch you?" Marc asked me, reaching to touch my knee.

I smiled and nodded, unsure of how I felt about it. I didn't want him to feel rejected.

When he took his hand off of my knee, I looked at him questioningly, wondering his intent.

He said, "I felt you needed kindness."

"I think you may be right. Thank you for that. I've been letting this monkey mind of mine run amuck lately, but my heart has been skewered in the process. Both seem to be out of balance."

"You're really compelling, you know that? I see your strength, this power on the outside that shouldn't necessarily be there. I feel it should be on the inside and taken out when needed. Softness is your true natural state, and that's what should be on the outside. It's healing. You're a healer in your natural state."

"Thank you for really seeing me, Marc. I think I need these reminders of who I really am. It's hard not to build a protective shell when the world can be so harsh, rarely honouring our softer, more vulnerable sides."

"It feels like you have a fear of your power. There appear to be these two sides of you."

"It's not the first time I've heard that, about the two sides of me. About the power, you may be right. I wouldn't have come into my light if I hadn't experienced the depths of darkness, so I honour it as much as I honour the light, for all of it is God. God is life. And I love life, and at its core, life is love. There's love in the darkness and there is love in the light."

"That's a beautiful way of looking at God," said Marc.

"I feel it's the only way of looking at God," I replied.

"I wish that there wasn't such a negative connotation around the word God due to the influence of religion, or tragedy that happens in this world," he said.

"I hear you. I feel like I'm constantly defending God these days. People ask, 'Why does God allow such suffering in the world?' The simplest way I can explain it is that God gave us free will. It's not God necessarily God who causes suffering; it's the choices we make as human beings. But it's also far more complex than that. There are so many layers, beyond our comprehension — like the path the soul a soul chooses for this life, the lessons they need to learn, the ripple effect of those choices, and how they fit into the grand divine plan of love unfolding."

"Right, and it's like, we have to learn through those experiences. I know it's been a rough time, but I can see where you are going, and all I see is beauty ahead."

I gently patted Marc's knee, smiling warmly at him in gratitude for his kindness. We lay down together in the sunshine in silence for a few minutes. I mulled over his insight, and I then told him it was time for me to bid him adieu. I thanked him for a lovely, unexpected afternoon and mentioned that perhaps we could meet again sometime.

Chapter Twenty-Six – I See You, and in a lot of Ways, I See a Mirror

It was the morning after the Scorpio blue moon, and boy was I feeling it. Everything was electric in my body, mind, soul. I hopped out of bed and skipped out the door into the late morning May sunlight.

I bought a juice and a croissant and headed to Regent's Park to start off the day. I found a spot on the damp grass, letting it soak into my bare legs and peach-colored sundress, feeling the coolness of every dewy blade against my skin. I stretched out on a sarong from India and reflected on the last week I'd spent in solitude.

I'd be seeing Scarlett the next morning, and I was full of revelations to share with her. I knew something was about to shift, for better or for worse. Would this week's session be consistent with last week?

I'd had a dream that the two of us were walking in a labyrinth of shrubbery and Scarlett had said, as if she'd had an epiphany, "Another piece of the puzzle fits!" I replied, "Another piece of the puzzle? Scarlett, it's a jigsaw!" And that was all the dream had to it.

I had another dream that felt more prophetic. Scarlett looked at me and said something about heart pain. I woke up and my heart physically ached. It felt like it needed to be realigned. It felt like an ominous warning of what was to come, urging me to brace myself, because it was going to hurt. It was going to hurt deeply.

Who knew what was in store? I would just have to wait and see.

I thought about the way Scarlett walked – so deliberately, so aware of each move. I had never seen anyone walk that way. It was a special sight to see. I thought about the way she listened, her super-sonic hearing, whenever someone neared the room. Sometimes I wished there wasn't so much that I loved about her. I wondered if there were any things about me that she daydreamed about. Did she like the way that I walked? Did she like the way that I talked? Did she like the way that I thought?

I wished she were right there beside me on my sarong, the light rippling across both our bodies, shading and sunning us as one electrified beam of energy.

I realised that this beautiful feeling, of being so alive, so in love, was only being experienced by me. I didn't have my lover next to me to dote upon, to share this love with. There was a sadness in that.

I decided that tomorrow I would commit to expressing my love to Scarlett again, without reservation. It was therapy, after all, and it was supposed to be about me. If it was important that my feelings be heard, well then, let them be heard!

In the past week, I'd gone to yoga and Pilates classes, as well as a Chinese acupuncturist. On my first attempt at going to a yoga class, I unintentionally ended up in a Bikram class. On one hand it was great, as I sweat out toxins for probably the first time in months (I was usually rather idle and avoided breaking a sweat at all costs), but on the other hand, I felt irritable. I felt out of place, and I didn't know the positions the teacher was calling out like a drill Sargent. I stood still in the midst of this chaos like an alien dropped in from outer space.

As for the acupuncture sessions, I felt grateful towards Luciana for introducing me to this wonderful Chinese acupuncturist. She had been helping me to get my Qi energy back in order. She said my chi was very low, as well as my circulation, probably a result of Harry draining my energy. I felt like I was being taken care of by a Chinese grandmother which was healing in and of itself, as I was feeling more like an orphan than ever these days. She told me I needed to sleep more and think less. I also felt that a lot of stuck emotions were rising to the surface to be released, so it was no wonder that after each of the sessions, I felt like crying my eyes out.

I'd also reflected on the entirety of my relationship with Harry. As much as he may have disappointed me, hurt me, abused me, I still needed to grieve him, and grieve myself, and let go of the part of me that was attached to him.

In a strange way, Harry felt like family to me. I felt lonely, abandoned, and deeply sad to be left on my own. Who did I have if not him? I wasn't just grieving him, but all that he symbolised. I was grieving my father. I was grieving myself. I was grieving every wound I'd allowed to be inflicted upon me. I was grieving the loss of my girlhood. I was grieving the loss of my innocence. I knew things in my life would never be the same.

By late morning, the sun was beating down on my skin and warming me from the inside out. All shadows had danced away with the clouds. And speaking of shadows, it seemed to be such a thing for Scarlet, as if she loved to dwell in the land of shadows more than the land of the light.

I started to wonder, was I really as similar to Scarlett as I thought, or was I just mirroring her? And considering that she was meant to mirror me, what could the mirror, then, be? The key to mastering my shadow was to stay true to my core self, allowing my essence to shine without changing for others.

The real challenge was discovering who my core self truly was. I was seeking to uncover the original self.

A stunning red-haired woman in an elegant turquoise dress caught my eye. With a black straw sun hat and piercing azure eyes that sparkled in the light, she smiled at me knowingly before continuing on her way, likely sensing my gaze.

Her beauty captivated me, and I thought about how men never seemed to have the same effect on me. Perhaps I had always been more on the homosexual side of things. I knew we were all on a spectrum, but perhaps I had not paid enough attention to my love for women? It wasn't until I fell in love with Scarlett that I realised there was perhaps more to the story. I'd been having more homosexual dreams lately. I could no longer deny that I was very much into women. And that thought excited me.

I remembered how, as a child, I was basically obsessed with boobs. I couldn't get enough of them, and that never changed. After my mum saw my childhood painting that I told Scarlett about, I wondered if I still carried a sense of shame. Did I internalise the feeling that there was something wrong with me? Yet, we can only deny our inherent selves for so long before it inevitably catches up with us.

And that was what seemed to be happening to me — in my dreams, fantasies, experimentations, even earlier memories of telling my friends it was just for 'practice' before 'the real thing.' A woman's beauty captivated me far more than a man's. I was intimidated by women, but never with men. If a woman touched me, it was electric, but if a man, I looked away. Perhaps there had been signs all along I hadn't recognised fully until now.

The intensity of the love I felt for Scarlett was a foreign experience for me, incomparable to anything I'd ever felt for men. Women excited me. With men, at least so far, I was left wondering if something was missing.

Harry called me several times from a phone in Curaçao, where he was apparently hiding out. I didn't pick up.

He continued to add random friends of mine on social media, sending new requests out daily. And even though he blackmailed me, used and abused me, there would still be those times where I would miss him and the love we had, or at least the love I thought we had.

I headed home to catch up with Luciana, hear about her trip, and get out of my own head. Although it was well past mid-day, when I walked through the door, she looked as if she had just gotten up and was brewing a French press.

"Hello, sleepy head! Welcome home," I told her.

"Thank you. It's good to see you. The flight was excruciatingly long and the trip itself was intense, hardly leaving me any time to rest. Yoga retreats are serious business."

"I can imagine. I hope you had time to do other things. Time at the beach? Any leisure time to shop?"

"Hardly. I felt like I was a little girl in school again, getting reprimanded if I was a few minutes late to the six am classes."

"I'm sorry to hear that. I hope you at least enjoyed the yoga itself. How was the company?"

"It did whip me into shape. I'd really like to keep up the routine, so I don't lose momentum. The girls on the trip were closer to your age, but all really lovely. I'd like you to meet some of them who live in London. I think you'd get on well with them."

"I'd love that. I'm open to meeting new friends, especially anyone disconnected from the circle I shared with Harry."

"Yes! Speaking of him, how have you been coping?"

"We had one email exchange which gave me a bit of closure, but I have moments of sadness and moments where I miss him. It may have been a negative attachment, but it was an attachment, nonetheless. I'm doing my best to not remind myself of the happier moments so that I can make this healing process a smoother journey."

Luciana pressed down the top part of the French press, poured us both a cup, and we sat down across each other at the coffee table.

"Everyone can see your power but you, you know that, right?"

"Funnily enough, Harry of all people told me that most."

"I'm not surprised. I'm sure he knew how willing you were to give your power away to him. On some level, perhaps he wanted you to recognise that in a strange way."

"My thoughts exactly," I replied.

It was helpful to be around Luciana, to hear her perspective as an older woman, and to witness the way she went about demanding respect, just by her energy. She helped me realise that I deserved much more than I was permitting myself.

By the time Luciana and I finished our coffee and conversation, it was about dinner time. I felt a strong need to retreat into my bedroom to digest all that we'd spoken about. I spent the rest of the evening reading in bed before drifting off for an early night of sleep.

I awoke with the sun the next morning, feeling a surge of anxiety. Nonetheless, I got myself dressed, and prayed for the best.

"Hi, my darling," Scarlett greeted me.

Knowing that Scarlett rarely had the time for niceties, I jumped right in and started telling her about my dream.

"We were in some sort of a maze. Suddenly, you exclaimed, "Another piece of the puzzle fits!" I laughed, and said, "Scarlett, we're not dealing with a puzzle here. It's a jigsaw!"

We had a shared moment of laughter.

"It reminds me of the chess dream that I had."

"I think your jigsaw dream shows progress, because a puzzle is something you work on together. It's a team effort, whereas a game of chess is individual, working against your opponent."

"It felt like, in the dream, we were mirroring each other. You were playing a game, and I saw it as a game. I was playing a mystery, and you saw it as a mystery. I think I needed to see things from your view, and you needed to see things from mine."

"Do you think I see our interaction as a game?"

"Sometimes I feel that way. It's almost like you intentionally trip me up and confuse me."

We sat quietly, our eyes locked in silence. I recalled how she'd once mentioned a 'gamey' side of me, suggesting that I sometimes step back and don't fully engage. But I couldn't help but wonder if that was more a reflection of the games I sensed she was playing with me.

Did Scarlett want to hear me sing her praises just to push me back into despair? One moment, I felt brave enough to stand in the strength of my feelings, and the next, I was discouraged and defeated. This was the part of me that believed she was playing a game, perhaps only wanting to hear my compliments, breadcrumbing me with a shred of hope, only to bring me right back to square one again.

"I think this environment feels too stiff, too professional. It's hard for me to really relax here," I said.

"I think you're so affected by your environment because you lack a concrete sense of self."

"Maybe I'm not supposed to have a sense of 'self,' though? What if I'm designed to be this way, to reflect the environment I'm in. What if that's the point?"

"I believe that with time, as your boundaries become stronger, you'll be able to reflect without absorbing and reflecting back. You'll be able to express yourself without reservation, regardless of the company you keep. Until then, I believe what you need, before you get to that step, is unconditional positive regard."

"I think you're right. I need to love and accept all parts of myself before I can truly stand in my power. Why is it that I think so little of myself, always bending to what others expect of me rather than being who I truly want to be?" I asked.

"Those feelings are to be expected as a survivor of childhood sexual abuse," Scarlett said.

There were only minutes left to the session, and I felt an urge to tell Scarlett how I felt for her. I couldn't get the words out, however, and so, the session ended. I walked out of the room with my chest tight, feeling like I might explode if I didn't speak up.

I headed down the stairs, not ready to leave the building. I walked into the waiting room and plopped myself down on one of the leather chairs in the corner. I lingered in the shadows, waiting for her to descend the stairs. Nothing was stopping me now. When I heard Scarlett say goodbye to the receptionist and confirm our next appointment, I knew it was my cue.

"Scarlett, may I speak to you for a moment?" I asked, emerging from the shadows.

She motioned for me to follow her out the door to the steps. What did I even plan to say?

"I don't know if I want to continue therapy."

Scarlett looked at me like she didn't have time for my after-session shenanigans. Could I blame her? I had time in the session.

"Well, you need to let me know because I just scheduled you in for next week."

I had been hoping she would ask me why. Why wasn't I wanting to continue therapy? What was upsetting me? She offered me nothing of the sort. I was at loss for words but struggled to come up with a response.

"I just don't know if I can continue seeing you. I can't make a decision now. Can I let you know in a couple of days?"

She agreed, albeit reluctantly, kissed me on the cheek, and we parted ways, walking in opposite directions. As I walked home, tears silently streamed down my face.

Chapter Twenty-Seven – The Jester Who Lost Her Jingle

I left for Paris the next morning, feeling melancholic as I waited for the train to arrive. The song 'Fade Away,' by Trevor Something came to my mind. The lyrics seemed to perfectly describe what I felt was happening with Scarlett and the back and forth dynamic that always left me hanging, questioning, confused. I would try and try, but like a flower perhaps not ready to bloom, she wouldn't open up. Emotions were often held back; sometimes, I felt she truly cared, but other times it seemed I was nothing more than a source of irritation. She would only engage in her puzzle-like game when it suited her, leaving me wondering where I stood, as if I was only a source of amusement. Every time I would try to get to know her and grow closer to her, I would be held back, and then she would 'fade away,' as the song goes.

I sat at a window seat. The tickets were fully booked and so I had someone seated to my right as well as two others across from me. I found it challenging to be surrounded by people in such close proximity given the state I was in. Tears streamed from my eyes despite my attempts to stall them.

Scarlett had become my whole world, and so without her, what was the point? I used to always be able to hold on to some kind of light. My unwavering faith in God and in the Divine would always be enough to sustain me. But when Scarlett became the embodiment of the Divine for me, and I realized that my love for her made my emotional world more volatile and turbulent than ever, it was as if it made me question the very reliability of the Divine. If I couldn't depend on the consistency of Scarlett, could I depend on the consistency of the Divine? I was ashamed to admit to myself that even my faith in God, of all things, was wavering.

I even felt like a failure to God for my lack of trust in the larger plan at work, but I was in no place to find solace in anything. I figured God would have to understand, if he loved me unconditionally, and if he was the one that made me, then he also created me this way – to have these thoughts, to have these feelings, to have these experiences. Even if I couldn't see it now, I strived to trust that it was part of what was happening *for* me, not *to* me.

Yet, I was now at the point where absolutely nothing felt right or okay in my world. It brought to mind a poem I wrote recently, called 'If the Angels Were Crossed.' The last verse went, 'If the angels were crossed, and the summer possessed frost, how would I say, that I wasn't okay.' The whole poem, in truth, was about me expressing that if circumstances in my life had been different, then I might be more functional. But because of the reality of my world, I had to pretend everything was okay, that I could function, when really, all I wanted to say, was that I wasn't okay.

I felt utterly disconnected from everything, as if I were trapped in a never-ending dark tunnel. The faint hope that I would eventually find the light, if I just kept holding on, was fading, growing dimmer with each passing moment. Without Scarlett, nothing felt exciting anymore, nothing had any meaning. Life was starting to feel like an existential crisis, and I could see why my father so loved Nietzsche, because at least when you relate to his philosophy, and take it on as a truth, you are no longer setting yourself up for disappointment or heartbreak because you don't have much hope in the first place anyway.

Life could be moving all around me, but I just felt stuck in suspense – the hanged man holding me hostage, not letting go of his grip on me; the sandman, capturing me in his hourglass of time. My wish at that moment in time, was that I could just slip into the abyss, dropping down like an anchor into the depths of the sea, into invisibility, just like any other barnacle attaching itself to a coral reef.

Indeed, I knew it was true what Scarlett said about childhood sexual abuse often creating feelings of unworthiness, of feeling unlovable, and feeling as though my sexuality was my most important source of worth. And I supposed it was the recent realisation of that, the true toll that it had taken on me, that was the most crushing, the most difficult to grapple with. I had lost my joie de vivre, like the jester who lost her jingle. How I longed to paint the world in colour, but the colour and vibrancy inside of me seemed to have died. My joy was gone, my natural playfulness, evaporated into thin air. I felt as if too much had happened to ever be able to return to a state of innocence, a state of normalcy. Life would never be the same again, and I felt as though I had been robbed.

Harry was just the icing on the cake of everything that had always been there – all of the hurt, all of the pain. He merely brought it all up from under the surface. My distrust of human beings was stronger than ever and yet, I felt so low, so desperate, that the idea of going back to Harry crossed my mind several times, because at least his conditional love felt better than nothing at all. I suppose that just gave me an idea of how desperate I was for any kind of true loving sustenance, any kind of nectar to cure me, even if that nectar had seeds of poison in it. I would rather go back to living with his manipulation to feel any sense of love, or at least acknowledgement of my being on this planet, at least someone that wanted me around, even if it was just to play with me. At least I would then serve a purpose for someone. Anything to take away the pain that was beginning to feel like a prolonged nightmare. I longed for someone to just lift me out of the darkness and back into the light, to come and nurse me back to health and vitality.

I knew all these intense emotions were coming up so strongly because I was at my wit's end regarding the back-and-forth confusion between Scarlett and me. Sometimes she would be there, ever-present, and other times she would shut me out completely, like a castle's fortress raising its drawbridge and sealing everything off.

At this point in our story together, I felt that I had wasted a year on her, pouring all my energy into a fruitless love. I felt like a fool. Maybe I really was totally off-base, living in a delusional dream world, seriously needed help, and couldn't even tune into my own heart or truths. Perhaps my whole world was a lie, and I was living in a state of destruction that I didn't want to admit to. I told Scarlett the day before that I struggled to love myself in the way I sometimes see others love me. If I didn't have them as a mirror, I think I might have hated myself into oblivion. I was at ease loving and accepting others for exactly who they were, but when it came to myself, that was an entirely different story.

I made it through the train journey and stepped off into a grey and rainy Parisian afternoon. I managed to get a taxi to my friend's apartment in the sixth arrondissement. The ride was about thirty minutes, so I sat back and let my destructive thoughts fester. Hopefully I would at least get it out of my system before seeing my dear friend.

My birthday was just around the corner, but this was the first year I had zero desire to celebrate it. Honestly, what would I be celebrating? I had achieved nothing and felt more alone than ever before.

I paid the driver and exited the taxi, meeting my friend on the third floor. We warmly embraced each other; it was a relief to feel the warmth of another human being. We decided to go for a stroll and have a late afternoon lunch. We found a classic French bistro where we swallowed up several hours of time over two bottles of wine, steak frites, and escargot. My spirits were somewhat lifted by the time we left, after I explained the hell I had been going through over the past year since we last saw each other. It was good to talk to an old friend who knew me since my early teenage years. The copious glasses of French red wine helped, too.

We spent the rest of the weekend in the same fashion – sharing stories, eating beautiful French food, drinking beautiful French wine, going for walks through the rain. It was a temporary ease to my loneliness, but when I arrived back in London, I was again back in my misery.

To add to my troubles, Luciana was still not respecting my boundaries, and nothing was ever good enough around the flat. There was always a complaint to be had about something.

To the best of my ability, I followed all her instructions of how to keep the flat spick and span, but I couldn't keep up with her perfectionist standards. She would nag and nitpick about everything.

I felt pretty set on bouncing out of this country by August, when the contract I'd signed with Luciana was due to end.

I was going through a severe depression that didn't seem like it would be going away any time soon. It was all just sandcastles in the sky, floating on by.

Unable to do anything but wallow, I spent the day watching the clock and fretting with anticipation about the next day and moment of truth with Scarlett. I felt like I either needed to stop seeing Scarlett, so I wouldn't be going through this vicious cycle of confusion, or I would keep seeing her if she could have an honest conversation with me.

I thought of the email I once wrote her when I said I was unsure of how we were to continue working together as my love would just get in the way. I wasn't kidding.

On Tuesday morning, upon waking with the sunshine, I felt a shimmering ray of hope. I said a prayer that today would be better, that the following week would be better, that at least I would have a sense of clarity going forward. I resolved to maintain confidence, trusting that the courage I was embracing would help me manifest what I truly desired. Like gazing up at a bright star in the night sky, I resolved to keep the faith.

I thought about the concept of faith, that faith is a strong belief in something that is not evident to others. It's about having faith in a dream, in a vision, that is only visible to your eyes. You are the only one who can see it, and so you must have faith in yourself, to be the only one that can believe in it, with utter conviction. It takes a great deal of strength and courage to stand up for what you believe in, especially if it's just believing in yourself in the face of adversity, strife, opposition.

And if I were to give up on that, it would feel like I was giving up on myself, and so I had to hold on to my dream like a precious gem that I never would part with. I had to hold on to my strength to carry me through the darkest of nights, lighting my own torch through the thick and dense fog to find my own way, even though at times I felt like a blind woman walking without a cane.

If I could manage to ride the waves of my own passion and continue to believe in what I held most dear to my heart, perhaps one day, I would prevail with grace and dignity, inspiring others too, to never give up on their dreams. Just because the golden egg was not yet upon my fingertips, did not mean that it would be that way forever. Would I choose

to see the world as a prison or my playground? That choice
was solely up to me, and the recognition of that, was perhaps
my greatest power.

After my personal pep talk, I decided to take a long
walk to therapy. I figured it would be grounding for my soul..
The day was warm and sunny. I wore a long, golden sunflower
skirt, a deep orange tank top, a brightly coloured matching
tangerine and lemon shawl from Sri Lanka, gold hoops, and a
long, loose French braid. I hoped the colours of sunnier days
might lift me further out of my funk.

As I grew closer to 113 Sumner Place, my heart beat
wildly. My sense of optimism was dwindling quickly. By the
time I reached the fifth floor, I felt nearly frozen, and for good
reason, because Scarlett's expression was closed off. I didn't
feel any warmth. Even so, I had to stick to my plan, or I'd go
through another week of misery.

"Hi Scarlett," I said, as I walked past her to the leather
chair.

"Hi, Samara," she replied in a weary voice.

"Have you given some thought about whether you
want to continue therapy?"

"I have, but I haven't decided yet. There are some
things I wanted to discuss with you first."

Scarlett looked at me, waiting.

"It's not enough for you to just be my therapist. I have
too much love for you to feel satisfied if our relationship can't
progress. So, I'm at a loss of what to do. I'd like to continue
working with you, but it's becoming unhealthy for me. I'm
feeling depressed."

"You do seem depressed. Samara, but if I were to be
your friend it wouldn't work, because therapy is supposed to
be one-sided, focused on you."

How could I not focus on her when I was in love with her? Scarlett acted as though she didn't understand what I meant. I wouldn't be sinking into a depression if I had just been seeking a friendship with her.

"I understand that the relationship is meant to be focused on the patient and I'm not asking you to tell me your life details. I know that would be a distraction, but there needs to be more openness."

"It's up to you whether or not you want to continue. It's not easy work or a fun process. I mean, what do you want to sit in a shitty place like this with me for?"

"It's not that I'm afraid of the process of working through my own stuff; I just want more from our connection. I can tell you from my own experience that the constriction of our roles certainly isn't doing me any favours. We seem to be on different pages regarding the matter. For the time being, I'll plan to continue until August, when my rent contract with Luciana is up, and then take it from there."

"I think it feels constraining to you because of a lack of trust. You don't trust that people are consistent in how they feel about you."

"Yeah, I can agree with that. But I've never felt a consistency with you."

"Samara, sometimes you'll be all over me, and then the next session it might be a different story."

"And that is exactly how I feel about you, Scarlett. You've spoken my exact struggle with you."

Scarlett and I spent a few moments in silence, both seeming exasperated at the roadblock we'd hit once again.

"I have always been consistent in my feelings toward you," Scarlett said. "I see who I want to see, and I come because I want to see you. You're not actually thinking about me or considering me when it comes to your feelings for me."

"How can you say that I'm not thinking about you? And how should I control the feelings that I have to make them more considerate of you? Aren't we allowed to feel what we feel?" I asked Scarlett.

"Samara, you're a lost little girl," Scarlett said cruelly, dismissively, and just like that, the pandora's box of my feelings slammed shut once more.

I felt stunned, as if I'd been slashed straight through to the heart, the pain cutting me deeply. The coldness of Scarlett's tone froze me to the chair. The Doors lyrics, 'You're lost, little girl,' were the only sounds I could hear. The rejection stung, but what hurt even more was knowing that all she saw in me was someone she considered to be lost. It made me feel as if she didn't know me at all.

"I want you to be in a relationship with *a man*…," Scarlett continued.

I didn't respond. How could I respond?

For the rest of the session, she spoke to me in a somewhat gentler tone, but the damage was already done. The rest of the time was trivially spent, I guess in an attempt to ease the tension. My birthday was the following Tuesday, and I said I hadn't yet decided if I would be coming in but would let her know by the end of the week. I was much less inclined to come in for therapy on my birthday after the dreadful session we had, but figured I would give myself a few days to mull it over.

When the hour finally was up, I left and walked down the spiral stairs in a numb state, wondering why I had even decided to continue therapy if this was how she was going to make me feel, only adding to my sense of worthlessness.

Chapter Twenty-Eight — The Thought of Your Existence Will Always Bring Light to my Being

Why am I allowed, to feel the weight of all these clouds? I asked myself, as I woke up the following morning with pangs of pain in my heart, exactly like Scarlett had told me in my dream. At least now I saw the truth and had to accept that Scarlett didn't feel the same way about me. I would try to take her advice and make the therapy sessions solely about me. I hoped the rejection would help me move on from my romantic feelings for her. If seeing her turned out to be too painful, I would take the plunge, cut the cords, and end the sessions.

I lay down in a sunny patch of grass by a bed of yellow roses, wishing that the nature would help absorb and dissolve my sorrows.

Self-care and self-love would be the doctor's order going forward. I needed to love myself more, and so the love I had been pouring on to Scarlett, I would now strive to pour onto myself.

Regarding my birthday, the only thing I wanted was to be with the person I cherished most, which was Scarlett, but I felt I needed space after our last session and therefore should make other birthday arrangements.

Luciana would be a great distraction from my focus on Scarlett. We decided to spend our birthdays together at the Soho Farmhouse. I wrote to Scarlett that I wouldn't be there for the following session, and she wished me a happy birthday for next week.

Luciana and I planned a weekend birthday gathering to see *A Midsummer Night's Dream* at the open-air theatre in Regent's Park. Friends and family came over beforehand, and I made a playlist for the occasion. We ate cake and drank champagne. It was a warm, balmy, summer evening and turned out to be a lovely time.

As Luciana's birthday was in close proximity to mine, we drove up on Monday morning and decided we would spend two nights, for both her birthday and mine, and would return on Wednesday. The ride up took about two hours. Although it ended up being rather cold, grey and rainy for late June, Luciana, her beloved dog, and I still made the most of the circumstances. It was surprisingly empty compared to the usual occupancy, so we didn't party much. We had a couple of cocktails on Luciana's birthday and didn't even drink on mine. It was a healthy birthday – yoga classes, bike rides, walks in the rain with the dog, lovely food. I really couldn't complain. Although I was feeling residual pangs of pain in my heart, at least I ended up doing something rather than sitting in my bedroom wallowing in self-pity.

When we returned home, we had the same issues as before regarding intrusion upon my boundaries.

On Saturday evening I came home to find Luciana watching one of her favourite tv shows that I despised. I casually mentioned that I was thinking of taking mushrooms in the park with a girlfriend of mine the next day.

"No, you're not," she snapped.

"Why not?" I asked.

"I don't want to be around drug takers," she said.

"You must be joking?"

"I don't want to be around that kind of energy." She added, "You're already spaced out enough as it is."

I couldn't imagine what she meant about not wanting to be around 'drug-takers,' when we had gone to several ayahuasca ceremonies together. In fact, that was the nature of our meeting. Psilocybin was also a healing medicine in its own right. It's not like I'd just told her I was going to be shooting up heroin in her flat.

"Okay...that's nice. Thanks," I said.

"Taking drugs is stupid and I don't allow it when people are staying at my flat."

"When I say I'm potentially taking mushrooms tomorrow, you do know that it will be out of the flat? I won't store them here, nor will I be tripping in here, either."

"It doesn't matter. You can take them once you leave here and the rental contract ends in August, but I'm not allowing it before."

"It's not up to you to decide what I do in my personal business, particularly outside of the flat. You don't have any authority to tell me how I should live my life just because I'm paying rent. And you were telling me stories about how you were taking MDMA at your birthday bash a year ago, and how you once rented a room to someone who snorted cocaine all day. So how can you tell me that you want nothing to do with drug takers?"

"I don't want that energy in my life, *now*. I really need to be looking after my health."

I retreated to my room. The time to leave had come. I tied up my hair like Violet Baudelaire and opened my laptop. I did a quick search for flights to Colombo. I didn't even have time to tell my friend I was coming. I'd just tell her once the flights were booked. The invitation was already open as we had talked about my coming for months.

First thing in the morning, I told Luciana that I was moving out. She told me she was thinking the same thing, so at least we were in harmony there. She agreed to cut the contract short, and I told her I was leaving that very same day. I booked a reservation at a hotel near Hyde Park for the next five nights as I sorted out where I would ship all of my things and made sure I had enough time to say goodbye to people I would miss. I packed up my things, we had an awkward goodbye, and I felt relief at getting out of there.

I hadn't had time to think about the fact that leaving London also meant saying goodbye to Scarlett, potentially for good. Once I checked myself into the hotel and made several elevator rides with the bellboy and saw the luggage and boxes covering every square inch of the room, I broke down. I was physically, mentally, spiritually, and emotionally exhausted.

I wanted to tell Scarlett that Tuesday would be the last time we would see each other. Words I never cared to utter.

Scarlett called me a few hours after receiving my text message that I was leaving the country. I told her mournfully that due to a series of unfortunate events with Luciana, along with a need to change things up in my life, I would be moving out of the country on Thursday that week. She asked me where I was going. I told her Sri Lanka and added that the sandman had visited me and told me that my time here had run dry. She responded with understanding, yet a feeling of mutual sadness ran through the telephone line. The phone call ended with her sending me her love, and we said we would see each other in a couple of days.

Once we hung up the phone, the tears started to stream down my cheeks. It felt like I was losing myself in knowing that I would potentially never see Scarlett again.

The next day I went to get shipping boxes. I had no idea where I would be sending my belongings, but at least I could pack and give myself another day to figure out where I should ship everything. Sri Lanka was the next stop, but it wasn't a final destination. All I knew was that I had to get out of London.

I wrote a goodbye note to Scarlett that I would give her the following morning. I decided on a small gift as a thank you to her for being with me throughout my journey.

I woke up the next morning feeling melancholic, almost to the point of being numb. I had shed a waterfall of tears in the last couple of days and I felt like I was on autopilot, going through the motions. I dressed and went down for a coffee in the hotel's café. After finishing my coffee, I decided I would walk for a while and then catch a taxi when I grew tired. I just had to keep myself moving.

In the taxi over, I listened to 'Yesterday and Today,' by Yes, a song that had always reminded me of Scarlett, and I burst into tears once more. I even had a vision of us naked by the seashore as I listened to it, just like in Scarlett's dream. That's where the song seemed to transport me to – a place of unrestricted freedom and purity we might never reach.

When I entered that old Victorian house for the last time, I went to use the loo close to the second receptionist on the first floor. When I came out, I bumped into none other than Harry.

"What are you doing here?" I demanded.

"Oh! I didn't think you'd be here. I intended to get here before your therapy started as to not disturb you. Just wanted to drop some things that came by post for you, as I had no other way of reaching you."

The receptionist in the back handed me a pile of letters and magazines, and I thanked him.

I looked at Harry suspiciously, indicating that I knew he was full of shit and that he knew I would be there at that time. I told him I was moving out of the country.

"What! When? Where are you going?"

"I'm moving to Sri Lanka."

"Well, I'd like to see you before you go, if you'll have me?"

"I'm leaving Thursday," I replied.

"That's in two days!"

"Yes. My time has run up here."

"It's the end of an era! I don't believe it."

"Yeah, well, I won't see you again, so goodbye."

We shared a quick hug goodbye, and the receptionist informed me that Scarlett was ready to see me. Perfect timing.

I ascended the bird cage elevator for the last time, taking in every detail around me, hoping to store everything about this place in my memory bank for as long as I would live. So much had happened in here. It would have a place in my dreams forever.

I saw Scarlett's lanky figure towering over the door as I turned the corner – another vision that would remain etched in my memory.

"So this is it," I said solemnly, sitting down in the brown leather chair.

"What a sudden change. So, you're leaving the country? How soon again?"

"On Thursday. I've hardly had any time to process it myself. It all happened so quickly."

Noticing the pile of letters in my lap, Scarlett asked, "What is that you have there?"

"Guess who I ran into downstairs?"

Scarlett waited for my response.

"Dear old Harry. He pretended he didn't know this was my usual therapy time. He didn't know I was leaving the country, so I just told him. His timing was perfect, managing to catch me just before I left. I wouldn't have even told him I was moving continents had I not bumped into him."

"So, what was it that he gave you? Post?" Scarlett laughed.

"Looks that way. And a few letters from him, it seems."

"You can open them now if you'd like."

I started to open one but thought better of it. Why would I waste one precious moment of our last session with Harry's interference? I tossed it to the side.

Our ending couldn't have felt more sombre and unfinished. Scarlett looked sad, and for once, it felt like her defences had really dropped. The air between us was filled with melancholy.

"Tell me, what happened, Samara?"

I told her I could no longer live with Luciana and about our fight over mushrooms.

"I thought you were going to take a break from psychedelics," Scarlett said.

I'd been drinking ayahuasca perhaps two or three times a month.

"I was planning on taking a break from ayahuasca, but I'd never experienced a proper mushroom trip."

Scarlett didn't press further. "I'm sorry things didn't work out with Luciana."

"Well, my best friend lives in a colonial hotel they've converted into their home on the beach, so I'll live with her, her boyfriend, and her mother."

"Do you plan on just spending time meditating at the beach?"

"Asha signed up for an intensive yoga teacher training programme, starting about ten days after my arrival, so I've decided I'm going to join her on that. Another friend is opening a hotel and said he could use my help with my background. I need a safe place to fall for a while, and hopefully that will be the place."

"I have something for you," Scarlett said.

She took a neatly folded white tablecloth napkin from her bag and walked across the room to hand it to me. As I unfolded it, a sparkling, teardrop-shaped crystal pendant lay in the center, holding a thousand shimmering reflections.

"Scarlett, it's beautiful. I adore it," I said.

I walked across the room to hug her.

"It's for protection. You can rub it with lavender oil or sea salt to cleanse it. It's funny how I came across this for you."

"Tell me, how did it come about?" I asked, my mood temporarily lifted out of my gloom.

"I was thinking about a goodbye gift I wanted to give to you, and I just sort of magically found this one and forgot I even had it. When I found it in my flat, I knew it belonged to you. It was really strange."

"Huh, that is strange. Maybe it belonged to me in a past life."

"I brought something for you too," I said.

"Samara, you've given me enough already. You shouldn't have."

"It's only something small, I promise."

I gave her an iridescent abalone shell and inside of it was my goodbye note. I wrote her that I couldn't say goodbye to her without leaving her with at least one last piece of writing from my heart. I thanked her for everything, for helping me to grow, and for being such a pivotal part of my journey. I told her how much I adored her despite the rollercoaster ride we had been on at times. I finished the note saying I would always be with her in spirit and that the thought of her existence would always bring light to my being.

"This is beautiful, Samara. Thank you. I love all things from the sea."

Scarlett and I gazed at each other with love for some moments until she spoke again.

"Is there anything else you'd like to say to me?"

I looked at her directly, and said, "I think I've said all I can say."

"Yeah," Scarlett nodded.

Tears, for the first time in all our time together, slowly started to roll down my cheeks. I didn't hide them. We started to go through a recall of all that we had delved deep into over the year.

"I think you have a distorted sense of self because of your childhood with your family, and that your perception of yourself doesn't reflect who you truly are. You are much lovelier than you think."

"Thank you. I hope you're right."

"You have a beautiful energy, Samara."

I smiled and kept looking at her in silence, allowing space between the words.

"I don't always feel this way with patients, but I think there's hope for you. You've grown a lot," Scarlett said.

I looked at her as if to say, 'gee thanks.'

"You have," she replied.

"It's a hard goodbye," I said with melancholy.

Tears continued to stream down my face and Scarlett looked down, as if it hurt her too much to witness my tears.

"I'm actually quite sad," Scarlett said, seeming surprised by her own sense of loss.

We sat in our sorrow together until the last fateful minute ran dry, and the sandman came to collect us from our time. We embraced one last time. As we let go of each other, fissures cracked open in my heart, and I felt as if I could collapse and die rather than take a single step away from her. Yet somehow, I managed to move, letting my eternal love for her carry me home.

All I could do was sit in the chaotic mess of my hotel room and weep in my misery. The agony was immense. On top of that, what was I to do with all of my belongings? To ship everything to Sri Lanka seemed too extreme. I knew it wouldn't be a long-term move. I couldn't think logically with my emotions so out of control.

Music entered my mind again, and this time it was 'Pale Blue Eyes,' by The Velvet Underground, that played its rhyme. After listening to the lyrics, I concluded it was all about an impossible love, or at least seemingly impossible, with every barrier and obstacle imaginable standing in the way. It was about everything we had, but couldn't keep. She was everything that couldn't be mine, but the saddest part was that it wasn't necessarily a problem with her, but the world. A relationship seemingly wrong in every way, but somehow right, that somehow just clicked.

In a world pure and strange, where rules were no more, as one of my poems I once wrote for her went, we could be together, and sacred convergence would burst flames forever. But the reality was that we were not, and I was doomed to be haunted by her pale blue eyes. The confession to my sins was that everything inside of me hurt, and if we could never be together again, I would rather hold onto that, even hold onto all of that hurt, because what I felt for her was a love that couldn't be exchanged for any cure. It was a heartache that would last a lifetime, if we were doomed to separation. That much I knew, which made the agony that much greater.

I decided to open Harry's letter. It was mainly an apology and a reminder of joyous memories and the love he had for me. He said it was the end of an era with my leaving him. I think it was the 'end of an era' comment that hit me hardest as I continued to wail. I needed something, someone, and so after two hours of going back and forth, I called him. He heard what a wreck I was, and he insisted I let him help me. I couldn't say no. He was still my emotional security blanket, and I ran back to him seeking solace from the pain.

We went out for sushi, and I continued to cry as he offered to help me with my shipping problem. He must have presumed leaving him was the source of my tears. I let him hold me as I cried, seeking any kind of refuge, just as a drug addict will take anything to ease the pain of the empty void. In my unstable state, I decided to spend the next two days with him before I left the country.

Harry said all the right things to ease my pain. He told me, 'love is harmony, and harmony is stillness in motion.' He asked me if I had ever had my heart broken like this before, thinking my heart was broken because of him. I told him no, but that perhaps the heartbreak was exactly what was needed to crack me open.

I found forgiveness in my heart for Harry and once again, looked at our relationship through rose-coloured glasses. I had a positive last couple of days in London before heading off to Sri Lanka. Harry's wife even came over and welcomed me to the family, telling me how distraught Harry had been over me in our months of separation (as far as I was concerned, we were still separated), and told me she would like me to meet the children next time I was in London.

Although deeply uneasy at my core about what was transpiring, I allowed myself to rest in a kind of ignorant bliss, clinging to anything familiar—no matter how toxic I knew it was—before heading off into the unknown again. Harry offered to keep my things at his place, our old place, until I knew what to do with them. At least it would give me time, if nothing else. Being with him those last few days in London made me feel like I at least still had some sort of security blanket in the world, should everything fall apart.

Chapter Twenty-Nine – 'What the Fuck'

Early on a Friday morning, I arrived in beautiful Sri Lanka, to a glowing, tangerine sunrise and swaying fern coloured palm trees over lush, fertile land.

The plane came to a halt, and I walked out the passenger door at the rear taking in the balmy, sea salt air, feeling the first rays of the sun's warmth upon my skin. My friend Asha's driver was waiting for me in the arrivals. Though his English was scant, we bonded over smoking hashish on the three-hour drive to the south, listening to trance music with the windows rolled down, letting the warm breeze flow in. Despite the emotions simmering just beneath the surface, I was in a light, carefree mood by the time I reached my friend's colonial hotel-turned-home in the early afternoon. I hoped this feeling would last, and I would be able to let the anguish of London be washed away with the sound of the crashing ocean waves in this slice of paradise on Earth.

I was thrilled to see my dear friend Asha, her delightfully spirited mother, Lola, and all the familiar characters had grown to know over the years. The teardrop of India was a world in and of its own, everything operating on its own frequency, its magic palpable. Its raw beauty was not only visible in the landscapes of thick, overgrown jungles, lush rainforests, arid deserts, tropical beaches, and verdant rice terraces and tea plantations, but perhaps most of all in its inhabitants—both people and animals.

The first ten days I unwound by smoking, drinking, partying, and swimming in the turquoise seas. I blacked out from drinking and smoking too much hashish on the very first evening. I ended up being put to bed by Asha's mum with no recollection of what happened the night before – a not uncommon occurrence for parties on the island. There was a saying among the crazy local expats – 'We're all here, because we're not really *there*.'

Asha's family's former hotel, now converted home, felt like living in *The Grand Budapest Hotel*, its originality, creativity, quirkiness, reminiscent of a Wes Anderson film. Voodoo dolls adorned the gold-painted walls, a vintage Coca-Cola machine stood left of the kitchen bar, which was strictly for all-day coffees, and haunting jester masks hung above the doorway. The floor was covered in black-and-white checkered tiles, my bedroom had brick walls, an en-suite French tub, and a mermaid's mirror in the bathroom. I hung the crystal pendant Scarlett gave me over the draping mermaid hair.

Asha and I turned up stoned to the yoga teacher training. My teacher was from California and took her role very seriously. Rules, code of conduct and expectations were drilled in on the first day and I found myself in a state of anxiety. I was physically unprepared, hardly having practised any of the positions that were already supposed to be learnt by the following morning at five am, and also emotionally unprepared, in the sense that I was still too heartbroken to care.

Asha and I strolled home and soon bid each other goodnight—she headed upstairs to the second floor, and I made my way toward the beach. I needed a moment to lay on the sand and process what I was about to get myself into. With days starting at 5 am and ending at around 8 pm, how would I have any time for reflection and contemplation? Not to mention always having to be around people. But maybe that would be a good thing for me – perhaps I needed to get out of my mind and into my body. I had come this far and decided I would try my best to get through it.

The first three days of yoga were brutal. I nearly quit by day four, and because I was feeling so defeated, I got back in touch with Harry sooner than I had planned to. I was clinging to what I thought was safe, familiar, even if it was abusive. I told Harry I was about to quit, and he convinced me not to. I thanked him for his encouragement, and I said I would do my best. We stayed in contact and decided that he would come visit me in August. We would stay at Asha's for a week and then go travelling around the country – visiting the tea plantations, a surf spot and beach village on the east coast, and we would conclude the trip with a safari. We talked about my return to London in October. It wasn't Harry I missed or couldn't live without. It wasn't London itself, either. It was Scarlett.

She still consumed my every thought. I thought that I could manage to live with Harry again in order to see Scarlett again. I viewed going back to Harry as a temporary solution until I would move elsewhere. I would at least land myself where I needed to be again.

By the second week of my yoga training, I felt more confident about my place in the programme. I bonded with a couple of the other girls, enjoyed feeling strong in my body, and I was looking more fit than ever. I felt the yoga was opening channels in my body that were begging for emotional release. Asha and I started getting high each morning just before 5 and would have our second and third hash joints during the lunch break. The long days were challenging but I found solace in knowing that I was becoming more present in my body.

On weekends we spent time in the 'Ivory Tower,' where Asha's mother reigned. Champagne and rosé were always in flow, and there was never a dull moment. One evening, we had a few of Lola's expat friends over and must have gone through twelve bottles of wine, with hashish joints in constant flow. Everyday stories one might hear on a regular basis would be about people having their arms chopped off by machetes, English expats with legless drivers, black magic spells, and commonly orchestrated swingers' parties.

When my body could take no more alcohol, I floated down from the ivory tower like a genie in a bottle with thoughts of Scarlett swirling through my mind. I heard the eerie melody of the creepy bread man, whom I always mistook for the ice cream man, as he drove through the streets late at night. It was like something out of a haunting horror film. The sounds reminded me of the child catcher in *Chitty Chitty Bang Bang* driving his candy van to lure in children and trap them in cages. It was just another of the unique sounds that would always remain etched in my memory when my thoughts would travel to the land of Sri Lanka.

I fell asleep that evening with the last sounds of 'Love Action,' by The Human League playing away. The lyrics spoke of resigning to the experience of being in love, because when you know, you know, and there's no point in denying it. You may as well accept it rather than fight it. You mustn't stop 'fighting the good fight'—you have to keep pushing through, even when there's no sign of hope on the horizon. It was a call to simply accept the madness of my love, and let it be what it was.

Yoga classes continued to the end of July, and I took my alcohol consumption down several notches. At the end of the training, each of us was expected to teach an hour-long yoga class with our own theme. I decided the theme of my final yoga class would be balance. The month of yoga (and reiki) training taught me discipline and the value of time for oneself. One piece of advice our yoga teacher left me with was to know my worth and to not let people take advantage of my gentleness.

Asha and I became YTT yoga teachers at the beginning of August, and I was left with more time on my hands to contemplate all that had transpired with Scarlett. I was still deeply heartbroken and missing her terribly. I remembered one evening when I was out for sushi with Harry and had had therapy earlier that afternoon with Scarlett. I was thinking about my favourite blue button-down blouse of hers that she was wore that day. As we sat there, I thought of all my favourite outfits of hers, especially that white dress she wore one summer, forever engraved in my memory. And with that thought, the song 'My Favorite Things' from *The Sound of Music* started playing in my mind. I laughed aloud, sharing an inside joke with the Divine about 'girls in white dresses.' Harry had asked why I suddenly burst out laughing and I just shrugged him off, lost in my sweet melody of love.

Harry was due to arrive in less than ten days and I no longer felt prepared for it and wondered what I had been thinking. He didn't fit in this new world of mine. I felt distressed about how I would please him and everyone else in what Lola referred to as our 'commune.'

Harry was being sketchy about a woman he'd gone to dinner with, saying there was nothing going on between them but later admitting there had been flirting. He was pressuring me into confirming I would move back to London or else he would have to dispose of all my things. Still, I tried to remain positive. My focus was to get back to London and see Scarlett.

Since yoga ended, I had too much to ruminate on. I was starting to feel the darkness creeping in.

In the days before Harrys' arrival, I tried to keep up with yoga, swam in the sea with the sea turtles, went to the spa for Ayurvedic Shirodhara treatments, and spent time writing, reflecting, and smoking myself into oblivion. Asha was never a fan of Harry, understandably, and I told her about my apprehension regarding his visit.

When I descended into my mermaid's chamber later that afternoon, I figured it was now or never if I was going to get in touch with Scarlett. I drafted her an email, telling her about my life since I left London. I told her I missed her, mentioned how challenging the yoga training had been but that I managed to get through it and found my niche in restorative yoga (where minimal movement is required), and then ended the email by saying I'd prefer to chat on the phone sometime. She wrote back a day later and we arranged to speak over a Whatsapp call before Harry's arrival.

My beloved and I spoke at a quarter to two, Lankan time. Before calling her, my heart started racing. I had known Scarlett for over a year and, without fail, every time I was about to see her or speak to her, the butterflies would start fluttering. How could that not be love?

I spoke to Scarlett at the beach with the waves crashing in the background. It was delighted to hear her beautiful voice again. I told her all about the island's magic and my experience training as a yoga teacher. Finally, I told her I had decided to move back to London, and that I'd be moving in with Harry again.

Scarlett didn't have much to say on the matter. Nevertheless, she said that if I was coming back and going to be living with Harry, that we should most definitely continue in therapy. I wholeheartedly agreed. Our first session would be at the start of September, on Tuesday, the third, at eleven. I lay in bed for some time after our call thinking about what it would be like to see her again.

Three days later, dear old Harry touched down upon the land of Lanka. He texted me to complain that the driver I had sent for him was nowhere to be found. The driver was there on time, it's just that Harry couldn't find him.

When he arrived many hours later, he attacked me for being a little high, which was my usual state of being those days.

"Darling, I made dinner reservations for us down the beach in a few hours, so feel free to rest until then," I told him.

"Samara, you just don't think of me at all, do you? Didn't you consider I would be tired from the journey? I mean, you had all of this time to prepare for my arrival, and here you are, getting high again."

"Of course I considered that, which is why the restaurant is a few minutes walking down the beach..."

Our dinner ended up being tropical fruits, which he said was all he needed that evening, but the next day he bitched about it. I felt like a fool for allowing myself to believe he might have changed.

I had sex with him for several hours that night, and a lasting orgasm that probably sounded throughout every floor, to the point that tears were streaming down my face, whether from sorrow or some sort of masochistic sexual bliss.

Because he wasn't pleased with the start of his holiday, he told me I needed to "prove my love by giving to him sexually, since verbal communication didn't seem to work out so well between us." His last comment to me before he went to sleep that night, "I can still see the stars in your eyes. They'll always be there. It's almost like I'm one of them..."

The next morning, I told myself that it was a new day. I reasoned that he was probably just jet-lagged, and I would cut him some slack. I was beginning to think I didn't know what was truly right for me anymore. I wish I knew what to do. I wish I knew how to be. I wish I knew how to see.

I brought him a coffee in bed when I heard him stirring in my bedroom.

"What would you like for breakfast? I haven't been eating in the mornings of late, but I have fruits and eggs here. Otherwise, we can get breakfast down the beach," I said.

Harry scoffed.

"Just another example of you having done fuck all since I've arrived."

Despite my efforts—arranging his driver, giving him massages, sex, and anything else he asked for the night before—nothing was enough. Our conversation escalated into a full-on row.

Breakfast plans were off, and he said he was going to go down the street to a corner shop. I said I'd go with him and show him the way, but he told me he didn't need company.

I rolled myself a joint and plopped on the sand underneath a palm tree and wondered what the fuck I was going to do with Harry for two more weeks. I wanted him gone and it hadn't yet been 24 hours. As I looked across the expanse of sea, I imagined Scarlett being on the other end of the body of water.

I walked back inside and found Lola's friend, LT, chilling in the darkness rolling a joint. I threw myself down on the sofa next to him.

"I realised no one ever asks how anyone is feeling around here. No one ever really checks in," I said.

"How are you feeling?" LT asked me.

We both looked at each other and burst out laughing. I kicked up my feet and we sat there together in contemplation as the bamboo blade fan above us fanned us away.

I told him I was going to write a book about this place and asked what he thought it should be called. Without hesitation, he said the title should be, '*What the Fuck.*'

Harry returned after taking himself out to breakfast. I took myself out for a facial.

When I returned home around five, Harry was in better spirits. For the next few days that we were in the south before travelling, Harry decided to partake in 'da high lyfe' lifestyle with me, which probably wasn't the best thing for his mood disorder. We didn't do much aside from lay out in the sun, read, go for walks on the beach, and swim. Though things weren't great between us, they weren't bad, either.

On our voyage around the country, Harry and I travelled to Colombo, Kandy, Nuwara Eliya, Ella, Arugam Bay, and the last stop was Udawalawe for a safari. The start of the journey went well, and I felt that I was learning to love Harry again. We got into a harmonious flow and would look after each other in our own ways. I liked the way he made me laugh. I met people I might not normally have met, simply because he would talk to anyone around. I always really liked that about him. We seemed to be getting into a groove again. I would dream up bedtime stories that I would recite to him each night. He would marvel at my creativity. He would tell me how drawn to my love, my spirit, my energy he was. He would tell me he thought the world of me. He would tell me he adored me. He would tell me, "I love you, Samara," so sincerely that I wondered how I could ever possibly doubt it. I was beginning to feel secure with him again.

Yet, slowly but surely, the misunderstandings and miscommunication began. On our last few days, we camped out in a luxury tent at the safari grounds in Udawalawe. Harry and I hardly spoke the whole time.

The day we returned from the trip, Harry met Lola and some of our friends. We had a party up in the ivory tower and Harry decided to throw a fit, in front of everyone, because I passed the joint to a male expat friend before passing it to him. He announced he was going to go downstairs and not stick around. I had zero intention of following him. I drank to my heart's content for the rest of the evening, and finally descended around eleven pm to the mermaid mirror room.

"Are you able to have a rational conversation now?" I asked him.

"You've had hours to come and check on me but once again I'm the last priority. You're an alcoholic!"

Harry ran into my bedroom and tried to lock me out, nearly slamming the door on my fingers. His face scrunched up like a demon, but he stopped himself from abusing me at the last second, stopping his hands when they were inches away from my neck.

"If you dare to lay a hand on me again, I'll have Asha's father come and lock you out of the gates."

"I wasn't going to come near you. I would never hurt you. I was just trying to get away from you."

I grabbed my bedroom keys.

"You're projecting your father issues on to me, which makes sense of course, because why would you want to make it work with an abusive father. I understand you deeply."

"It's over. Get out," I seethed.

I could have killed him in my rage. He begged on his knees for me to take him back. I had a distinct sensation that something had taken over him. I had already seen too much. This is for the birds, I thought. This is absolutely for the fucking birds. He left, saying he would stay in another hotel down the beach before his flight back to London.

It felt like everything was going wrong and crumbling all around me. Although I was surrounded with friends, I felt completely alone in the world again. I called Harry.

"Samara I fucked up royally from the moment I got here. I should have realised it would be a mistake smoking that hashish and how it would affect my emotional stability."

From the middle of the floor amidst my sobs, I didn't have words to react to the excuses coming out of his mouth. We agreed I would fly out in three days' time.

I felt I had no one else, so I breezed out of Sri Lanka just like I breezed out of London, in a pattern that was becoming second nature in my life. Although I was as eager to return to London, where my heart still lay, a piece of my soul would always be left in Sri Lanka.

Chapter Thirty – 'Why Did You Come Back, Samara?'

Three days and thirteen hours later, I touched back in London. As I travelled by taxi to my friend Sofia's vacant house, where I would be staying for several weeks, I wondered if I was mad for coming back, after feeling such an urge to get out only months prior. I couldn't just keep moving continents every few months when my life went up in flames. I promised myself that I would find a way to ground myself, to stay situated in one place.

Did I think Harry and I would last long-term? Absolutely not, but I couldn't imagine returning to London without him in my life. I wouldn't be living with him the first few weeks, and then we would see how things went. I felt that everything would be okay if I could just see Scarlett again.

After landing back in London, I focused on settling in and processing everything alone. I got everything together for the psychotherapy foundations programme I planned to attend in January. I continued with my daily yoga and tai chi practice. I got a bank account set up. I signed up for a Reiki master level course as well as a sound healing training. Harry kept asking me when he would see me, but I told him I needed space and would see him the following week.

Before I knew it, it was Tuesday, the third of September, and I walked into 113 Sumner Place eager to be reunited with my beloved.

I wore the crystal pendant Scarlett gave me in our last meeting to demonstrate my love for her. My heart was racing, as usual.

Just as I turned the corner, I spotted Scarlett kneeling, searching for something in her bag by the second receptionist's desk.

"Hi there," I greeted her cheerfully.

"Oh! Hi Samara!" Scarlett replied.

We embraced each other.

"The room isn't ready yet, but I will come get you in the waiting room in a few minutes when it is."

She'd told me we would be meeting in a different room this time. I took a seat on the leather sofa. Marc came in and took a seat next to me. We greeted each other hello and he asked where I'd been for the past few months.

"I took off for Sri Lanka rather impulsively. And then a sudden change of plans led me back here. I've come full circle and here we are, meeting again. I didn't think I'd ever see you again, honestly."

"You are delightfully mysterious. Last time we spoke you mentioned that you'd be out of London for the weekend."

As he spoke, I anxiously checked the clock and saw the hand strike eleven. Although I enjoyed speaking with Marc, I hoped Scarlett would arrive soon. I had evaded him for several months before leaving for Sri Lanka because I wasn't interested in him *that* way. I also didn't want Scarlett to see our exchange at all.

"Ah yes, I remember that weekend well."

Scarlett appeared, looming in the doorway. She looked furious, her flecked green eyes gleaming. Without a word, she signaled with her eyes toward the lift—it was time.

"Well, it looks like it's time for me to go. See you around," I said, as I quickly grabbed my coat to accompany Scarlett.

We walked in silence toward the bird cage elevator and stood there waiting for it to arrive. Marc followed us, lingering. I prayed he would just go and leave us be. He finally walked past us in the direction of the second receptionist's desk. I breathed a sigh of relief. Scarlett couldn't even look at me as we ascended to the third floor.

As we entered the room, I realised it was where I first met Dr. Hugo Bourke, who had referred me to Scarlett. It seemed we had really come full circle. The chairs were closer together, making for a more intimate experience.

Scarlett began by scolding me about the way I was living my life. It felt like she was attacking me, but I remained calm and composed. She said she wasn't happy I was back with Harry. How could I blame her? And she didn't even know about the blow-up in Sri Lanka. She only knew that we reconciled before I left London.

"I worry about you a lot, you know," Scarlett said.

I attempted to explain what a difficult summer it had been for me. Scarlett had no sympathy, however, and seemed to think I was the source of the drama. Well, of course I was. It was my life, after all. I needed help navigating the world of chaos I seemed to manifest.

"What's the common denominator here?" she asked, continuing to give me a hard time.

"I know how it looks," I said with a smile. My expression of helplessness seemed to soften Scarlett, and her entire demeanor shifted; she looked amused.

"You were flirting with that guy down there."

"I wasn't flirting with him!" I replied indignantly.

"You were."

"We were just catching up."

"You were sitting very close to him on the sofa, smiling and laughing with him."

"I didn't want him to sit there. All the other seats were taken, though."

"He's just a distraction," Scarlett said.

"I wasn't trying to 'distract myself' with him. I was pleased to see you arrive so we wouldn't have to continue the conversation. You came just in the nick of time."

She looked at me with a dubious expression as if to say she still didn't believe me but was willing to let it go.

"You know, it was a delight to see you downstairs."

"It was for me too, Scarlett," I said.

"How are you feeling?" she asked me.

I was disappointed that the first time we saw each other again, we fell right back into volatility, and I felt like I was being attacked.

I looked her straight in the eyes and said, "I. don't. know."

"Well, we can sit here all day if that's the best you can come up with."

After a few moments, I said, "Sad and frustrated."

Scarlett softened and didn't press me further. Of course, she knew I was hurt. She just wanted me to admit it.

"I see you're wearing the pendant I gave you," Scarlett said, smiling.

"Yes, I think it suits me well," I responded, turning the crystal between my fingers, glad that she'd acknowledged it.

Scarlett added, "It's for protection."

"I remember," I replied.

We smiled at each other, both of our guards down, finally settling into each other's presence again.

"Why did you come back, Samara?"

"I missed London, and Sri Lanka wasn't a place I could see myself staying long-term. I wanted to study psychotherapy, so I've set up my interview for the school you suggested to me."

"I see. Well, it's hardly much academic work the first year. It will be mainly group therapy with weekly lectures and weekend seminars. Just be prepared in group therapy for people to put you on the spot. It won't be like it is in here. People will trigger you at times. A lot of challenges will come forth from it."

"I'm up for the challenge. I look forward to it."

"I'm sorry Sri Lanka wasn't a more peaceful time for you. I Imagined you meditating on the beach, sipping coconuts, basking in the sunshine," Scarlett laughed.

"Well, it wasn't Sri Lanka that was unsettling; it was the events in my life while I was there. I see you are right – we can't just jet off to a tropical island hoping to escape our troubles. They'll follow us there."

"I won't argue with you there," Scarlett said.

"Anyway, aside from Harry's visit which turned out to be a downright disaster, I spent much of the summer smoking myself into oblivion, dancing to some great 80's music, and somehow managed to become a certified yoga teacher. The summer had many high highs and a number of low lows, but such is the way of life."

"You must be really good at yoga now," Scarlett laughed.

"I couldn't even touch the floor with the tips of my fingers when I started, and now my palms reach flat on the ground. I had no idea I was actually flexible, I guess because I'm normally rather lazy, aside from dancing. I love to dance."

Scarlett smiled with loving eyes until she broke her bewitching stare.

"We have to end. We'll only be in here two more times, and then we'll be moving back home."

I smiled at her choice of the word "home" to describe our other room. I stood to embrace her.

"Come here," she said as she opened her arms to receive me.

Without premeditation, I kissed the left side of Scarlett's forehead, just above her left ear, as I cupped the back of her head. It was my way of expressing that I was hers, if she wanted me to be, eternally.

Eventually, we broke our embrace, and as we pulled away, I peered deeply into her soulful eyes before floating downstairs on a pillow of ecstasy.

Chapter Thirty-One – 'She Might Have Died in the End, but Were Any of Those Other People Alive to Begin with?'

Harry asked me to drop by the flat so he could officially introduce me to the children now that his wife had welcomed me into the family. I had met his children once before, but at Harry's request, I called myself Lila so they wouldn't report back to their mum, who wasn't ready for me to meet them.

We spent the day at the park, and I gave them piggyback rides, pushed them on the swings, held their hands everywhere we went, already stepping into the role of step mummy, it seemed. I didn't know if I was ready for it, but there it was. The children were reluctant to leave me at the end of our time together. We had them over to the flat again on Friday, cooked for them, played games with them, and went to one of Harry's squash practices, where I looked after them outside during a long game of hide and seek. I went back to Sofia's house on Friday night to sleep there and spend Saturday alone, needing some space to digest how I was feeling. Things were transpiring with Harry at a rate I wasn't comfortable with.

I felt like he was beginning to push the children on to me, knowing that their presence in my life would make me feel more intertwined with him. I wouldn't want to be introduced as daddy's new girlfriend and have them grow attached to me, only to disappear.

I spent Saturday catching up on journaling and reflecting on my session with Scarlett. It seemed telling that she would react with jealousy and possessiveness about Marc. I took it as a positive omen.

I had never experienced a more dramatic year than the one with Harry and Scarlett in my life. My prior relationships were never like this, and I believed the root of the drama was the fact that I was in a toxic relationship.

I decided to email Harry that I wasn't comfortable with the rapid pace of our relationship. I told him it would take me time to warm up to him again, and that things would have to go at my own pace. I explained that we would have to take a step back in how much time I was spending with the children.

Harry and I had plans the following day, and I wasn't going to cancel, but I figured afterwards I would take some time apart. I showed up to my former flat around eleven, only to find that the children were over and joining us for brunch and spending the day with us. We would drop them back at the house around five, and then have a couple of hours to relax before we went to see a film.

"Did you happen to see my email?" I asked Harry.

"No, darling. I was over at the house with the girls last night. What's it about?"

"Never mind. We'll talk about it later."

It was hard to tell whether he was lying or not. It wouldn't be the first time he pretended to not get a message of mine.

I got through the day without any problems, and I enjoyed spending time with the girls. It wasn't that I didn't want to see them; I appreciated that I was now involved in their lives. It gave me a sense of belonging. But I didn't want the girls to get attached to me, only for Harry and me to split. His youngest, who was five, was already telling Harry she loved me, and I was her new best friend. I was getting attached to both of them, too.

After we dropped the girls off, we meditated, then Harry decided to take a nap. We agreed I would wake him at half past six to get ready. Despite my efforts to wake him, he kept sleeping until he had to rush to get ready. I waited for him, then decided to change my outfit as he finished up in the bathroom. Because I was pulling up my skirt when he was ready, he acted as if it was me that was making us late. He jetted out of the flat, telling me to meet him at the car without waiting for me. I rushed to put on my boots and ran down to where the car was usually parked, but the car was gone, and Harry was nowhere to be found. I called him several times, and he didn't answer. I got a text twenty minutes later saying he had to leave without me because we would have been too late for the film. I wrote him back and told him to fuck himself.

He replied, "You're the maddest girlfriend I've ever had." He added, "I've met a lot of women and I've never met anyone like you. You are full of paradoxes."

Initially, I was fuming. but I took a few deep breaths and decided I was not going to speak to him. Not a fucking word. He wasn't worth my anger. I was done being hurt by him. I rolled up a joint and got on the tube back to my friend's place to stay far away from him until further notice.

I woke up the next morning in a sour mood about Scarlett. I still felt hurt that she wasn't more on my side and was so hard on me our first meeting back.

I almost felt angry at myself for being so in love with Scarlett. Why couldn't I just let her go?

It was Tuesday again, and at five to eleven I was climbing up the spiral staircase to our temporary room on the third floor. I found Scarlett standing there, looking especially striking in a white button-down blouse and black trousers. We greeted each other hello, and I sat down across from her.

"Well, Harry and I had another row, and I don't intend on speaking to him any time soon."

"Oh yeah? What's the story?" Scarlett asked, looking somewhat smug. I explained that he'd deserted me after being the one who'd made us late in the first place.

"How did you feel about that?"

"It reminded me of how much I hate him at times, but then I decided he wasn't worth it. I had a much better time getting high and having a solo dance party at my friend's place."

"Samara, why are you still involved with Harry? I don't understand. I thought you were doing so well without him last spring? Hasn't he proven his character to you over and over again?"

"Of course he has. But he's not all dark. A lot of times I genuinely enjoyed his company, his ability to make me laugh, the way he would encourage me to not take life seriously, and the way he'd encourage my creativity. Maybe I'm too quick to forgive and let it go."

"You think? I can't tell you the number of times you've told me you're leaving Harry and then you end up going back. It's a matter of self-respect. If you respected yourself enough, you wouldn't continue tolerating any of this."

"I want to be free of him, but I feel trapped. I don't have anyone else in the world right now. He was the first sense of home and stability I've felt in years, maybe ever."

"You're not trapped, Samara."

"It's not as simple as you think. I don't have the same kind of support system that most people do. When we met, I was totally alone in the world. My family didn't support me and didn't understand why I was living the way I was. I had to figure out everything on my own. He's the only anchor I've ever had. He's been awful at times, but at least he didn't discourage me from following the path that felt right for me.

When he found me in Bangkok, I was a royal mess – often drinking to the point of nearly poisoning myself, putting myself in dangerous situations where I could've been raped, taking MDMA several times a week, taking lines of coke with a Nigerian drug dealer I'd befriended mid-afternoon. I thought I was invincible, but I was jet streaming to kill myself. Harry felt like the answer. I couldn't do it alone. I needed help."

"I think you aren't giving yourself enough credit for how far you've come since then. He came into your life at a time you needed him, but it doesn't mean that you need him anymore. Maybe you just needed someone else to be there so you could believe in yourself."

"When I moved to Asia without a plan, I felt courageous, open to anything. After being with Harry, I find it difficult to return to the free spirit I was then. Too much has happened. He's created this feeling of dependency in me, and it's weakened me..."

"You have so much life yet to live, Samara, and as you said yourself, what's so wrong with being directionless at this stage in your life? It may not be the path everyone follows, but what if you accepted it was *your* path?"

"What benefit is he bringing you at this point?"

I looked out the window as the heavy clouds slowly passed by, and without thinking, I said, 'I don't enjoy having sex with him.'

I think we were both stunned by what had come out of my mouth. I realised then that I hated having sex with him – I couldn't do it anymore.

"Why are you hanging onto him if you don't love him? There must be something."

Scarlett kept pressing me about my relationship with Harry, clearly dissatisfied with my explanations. I didn't think she would stop questioning me until I was more honest.

"I'm not attracted to Harry anymore. I'm no longer invested in our relationship... because I'm in love with you," I confessed with a sigh of relief.

Scarlett responded with her usual deflection, saying that I couldn't be in love with her because I didn't actually know her and was probably just in love with the fantasy.

"The only fantasy that exists is the one in your mind, because you believe I couldn't possibly be in love with you since I don't know more about you, when in reality, true love needs no reason; it just is."

She didn't argue with me like she had in the past, and her demeanor shifted, as if she were flattered. She seemed more open and lighter. Although we moved on to other topics, something had shifted between us. Even the heavy grey clouds lifted, just as our spirits had, and the sunlight broke, brightening the room. It was a moment I knew I would never forget.

We started talking about how it would feel for me to settle in London for a while after hopping from country to country so much over the past year—though really, it had a pattern my whole life.

"I admit I'm weary at this point. I've been in the habit of running away when things go south. It would do me some good to commit to being in one place for a longer period of time."

It was easy for me to say that now, as I knew that I had no intention of leaving Scarlett any time soon. Travelling had lost its charm because I found what I was looking for.

"Do you travel much?" I asked her.

"Not really. I don't feel the need, and it's ultimately futile since one's head follows them everywhere."

That was true enough. But I also traveled to connect with people from other cultures, to gain new experiences and learn more about the world. It was a spiritual thing. I liked that we were complementary in that way. She was like a rock, settled and grounded in her surroundings, while I was the butterfly that never stopped fluttering.

"I forgot to mention that I've been spending a lot of time with Harry's children, seeing them almost every day lately."

"And how has that been for you?" Scarlett asked me.

"They're absolutely precious, but I made it clear to Harry that I needed more space from him when I returned, and here he is, pushing his children onto me."

"You should speak to him about that before they get too attached."

"I emailed him Saturday night."

We shifted the conversation to the topic of unconditional love.

"I don't think Harry ever unconditionally loved me. I now question if there was ever even any love there at all. If there was, it was conditional. That's not what it is to truly love."

"There's no such thing as unconditional love," Scarlett said, matter-of-factly.

I was stunned by her certainty, as if nothing could shake her conviction.

"Do you wish to elaborate on that?" I asked.

"It's just not realistic – it's not possible with human beings. Love eventually fades, people develop expectations that no one can live up to, and the love becomes conditional."

It saddened me to hear Scarlett's perspective, one that seemed somewhat limiting to me.

"If you really love something, you don't have to have the love reciprocated. You can just appreciate it for its worth. The simple act of loving another is rewarding enough."

Although I would have liked to continue our gentle debate, the clock struck twelve, well past our usual ending time, and Scarlett announced it was time to end.

Relieved to have expressed my love to Scarlett and pleased to have made my feelings known so plainly, I dropped my head between my knees, like a lover collapsing onto a pillow after transformative sex. When I lifted my head again, Scarlett and I simply looked at each other, quietly acknowledging my all-consuming passion for her.

Scarlett's eyes sparkled as she gazed deeply into mine, longer than usual, as if she were trying to hold on to something she saw in me. I walked home with the blissful feeling that everything was okay, that everything would turn out just fine, if I just kept believing.

Chapter Thirty-Two – In the Tides of Your Demise

On Monday, I couldn't shake the feeling that something bad was about to happen. I didn't know what, but I knew that something was coming. And I knew that it had to do with Scarlett.

When I turned the corner from the birdcage elevator and saw Scarlett standing there, I knew my suspicions were correct—today was not going to be a good day. Scarlett wore a grimace, as if seeing me was the last thing she wanted to do. I knew she had something to say. I sat in my chair and remained silent, waiting for her to speak. The air between us was ice cold.

"Look," Scarlett said, frowning.

"This isn't working out anymore, and we're going to have to end things."

I just stared, waiting for her to continue.

"You're not going into your emotions enough and we're not getting anywhere."

I felt the betrayal immediately, like a thousand knives piercing my energetic field. But I hardly flinched. I could have won an award for my poker face.

"You're right. I was thinking the same thing. We aren't progressing the way I hoped we would," I said with a subtle smirk, as if I understood her actions better than she did. It felt like a knee-jerk reaction, a defence mechanism. Still, it hurt me terribly, crushing me like a pile of bricks.

Scarlett looked taken aback, as if she'd been expecting more of a reaction. I was intentional to not give her the satisfaction of witnessing in that moment how heartbroken I was feeling, especially after my confession last session. A million thoughts and no thoughts were running through my mind at the same time. I wondered if I was running on autopilot.

"Yeah," Scarlett said, looking at me with narrowed eyes, squinting as if I was a worm under a microscope.

Her timing couldn't have been more brutal. She was well aware that my interview for the psychotherapy school was a couple of hours after our session.

"Do you have anything to say to me?" Scarlett asked.

"No, Scarlett. Nothing to say."

"Well, what do you think I could have done differently? How could I have improved as a therapist to you?"

"Nothing. You did everything just the way you were supposed to. I was the one at fault, the reason we weren't progressing the way we should have. I should have been more emotional with you. You're right."

"There must have been something I could have done better, Samara. I'm not perfect and I know you must have something more to share about how the experience between us could have been better."

"No, you were fine, really," I said.

We sat there in silence. I was too numb to speak to her, but after some time, I managed to speak up.

"Maybe if you had been less intimidating, I might've been able to open to you more. If you made people feel more at ease," I said.

"How could I have been more approachable, less intimidating?"

"I don't know, Scarlett. That's one for you to figure out. We're very different people in that regard."

"Why do you think Dr. Bourke put us together?"

"You tell me. You're the one with the upper hand here. You know yourself and, apparently, I don't. I only know me, so how should I know?"

I waited for her to continue but she didn't. Maybe, for some reason, she wanted me to address why he had put us together. She wouldn't say it herself. It was something she wanted me to figure out.

I took my phone out of my bag, for the first time in all of our time together and checked the time. I wanted to get out of there, fast. The last place I wanted to be was sitting in that room with her. I had to get away from her.

"What are you, checking the time on your phone?" Scarlett asked, mocking me.

"Yes, that's what I'm doing."

"In a rush to leave?" she asked sharply.

I looked at her and didn't bother answering. I looked out the window, still thinking about bolting towards the door.

"How are you feeling?"

Why bother to ask the question? Scarlett didn't seem to give a shit about how I was feeling. She wasn't thinking about how this would destroy me. But who knew at this point, maybe that was her intention, to crush my ideas of love, to squash me.

She had to know this would plunge me into a deep state of melancholia, especially after I had laid my soul bare to her. It felt like she wanted a reaction, to see me hurt. But it was as if I had an emotional cloak shielding me. In that moment, my emotional cloak – her apparent reason for my termination – proved to be my strength.

"I don't have any words left," I said.

"Well, anyway, I thought about some people I could refer you to, if you wish to continue therapy, but then I decided it's better you look into it on your own."

"Great," I said.

"If you need a logging of our hours together – I don't
know how many we've had together, but you can work it out
– just leave it at the front desk or email it to me and I'll print it
and sign it. It won't be necessary for us to meet again; I'll just
leave it there at the front desk for you to pick up at some
point."

She couldn't be any more ruthless, as if I had
committed the most atrocious act towards her and she never
wanted to see me again.

"Okay," I replied.

"Now, did you want to have a final session after this?"

"No, I don't think there's anything left to be said."

Scarlett nodded in agreement, as if relieved.

The way she spoke made it clear she was only asking
out of protocol. She might as well not have bothered. How
could I see her after this? It was as if a different person had
entered her body and her evil twin was speaking to me. I was
mystified as to what went wrong. What changed? What
triggered her, when everything felt beautiful in our last
session?

It was time to end. I got up from my chair, paid her,
and still hugged her goodbye, as if I was supposed to.

"You're a darling girl," she said, as she released me.

The tone of her last words to me couldn't have felt
icier. I looked at her with eyes that had been betrayed. She
looked at me deeply one last time, almost as if searching for
something, until I turned and walked away.

Almost as if by choreographed cue, as I walked down
the stairs, 'This is the End' by the Doors began playing in my
head. The lyric that I kept hearing – "I'll never look into your
eyes, again."

I held it together quite well, but the moment I entered the flat, I broke down. I was supposed to head straight to my interview, but I needed to be alone and cry before I could think about facing anyone.

Almost as if by a force greater than myself, I headed for the bathroom. I opened the mirror door. I picked up a razor. I pressed the razor to my wrists, sobbing as I stared at myself in the mirror, lost in the depths of my agony.

When I finished, I went to the living room and fell to my knees. I wailed from the depths of my soul, consumed by grief.

I had lost everything, and some silly interview no longer seemed significant. But with an eerie calm, I buttoned up a cardigan to cover the marks on my bloodied wrists and took the tube to the interview, feeling as if I were floating outside my body. I was shaking, feeling utterly numb.

As I moved through the crowds going in and out of the tube, down and up the stairs, people gave way to me. It was as if I had gained a power of invincibility. No one could take anything from me anymore, because everything had already been taken.

I think because I gave such little of a shit how the interview would go, it went fantastically well.

That night, I couldn't be alone in my despair. I stayed with Harry. He ran me a bath and rolled me a joint and I just lay there by candlelight, puffing away in my extreme heartbreak. The joint only made things worse, leaving me feeling even emptier. I tossed and turned in anguish all night, and the next morning, I felt the same as when I'd heard that my father had suddenly died – utter grief, abandonment, sorrow.

I realised Harry wasn't going to make things any better and headed back to Sofia's house.

It was paradoxical that I should be terminated on the basis of 'not going into my emotions enough.' People went to therapy for that reason alone. Therapists normally didn't just give up on their patients for not being as emotional as they'd like.

I had told her one of the most difficult things for a person to admit, that I was in love with her, and then a week later I'm told that I'm not going into my emotions enough. It just didn't add up. And it's not like that was the only time I had been vulnerable with Scarlett. I couldn't imagine many patients read love poems written for their therapists across the room. She herself had said I'd progressed, so what was this really about?

Why would Scarlett have acted so possessive when she saw me speaking to Marc? Why would she have looked pleased to see me wearing the crystal pendant she gave me? Why would she look so uplifted when I told her I was in love with her? How could she do something like this to me, if she actually cared for me? The way it was handled was nothing short of cruel. She knew how I felt about her.

I had so many questions, but I was only stuck with my own experience. None of my friends had seen us together, so they couldn't offer an opinion, and I knew she wouldn't reveal her truth. I would never fully understand what happened with Scarlett. Could it really be over? Just like that? Never to see her again, after all of this?

It was possible that Scarlett dismissed me because she was running from true intimacy. I'd scared her off. Maybe she had feelings for me and decided that it was impossible given the nature of our relationship. She was, or at least was acting to be, the more rational one out of the two of us. And so, before she could let the love live, she shut it down.

Could there be a plan in all of this? Did Scarlett need to make me believe she didn't care for me at all, so there could be a chance for us in the future, once enough time had passed and we wouldn't cross any professional boundaries?

After spending several days analysing what had happened, I was only left with an emptiness, a sense of despair that led me into a great depression. I started having suicidal thoughts. Nothing mattered anymore. She was gone. What more could I do?

After about a week, I moved back in with Harry. I was a mess and needed someone around me. I needed someone to make sure I was eating, someone to make sure I wasn't throwing myself out the window. Even Harry was capable of that, and I found myself clinging to him to feel like I was still alive. Harry knew I was upset that Scarlett had abandoned me because he knew I was fond of her. What he didn't understand was that I was going through extreme heartbreak. He perceived it as childhood abandonment issues coming to the surface, and I didn't stop him from believing that, as I was sure there was at least a grain of truth in that.

Mostly Harry just left me to my own devices and I was left with a lot of alone time to wallow in my misery. Harry started having later than usual nights out – late night massages, work meetings going later than usual. On one evening he attended a company awards ceremony and returned home around one in the morning. He got into bed and started kissing me. That's when I realised why he was so late. I jumped out of bed, turned on the light, and asked him, '*Why* does your mouth taste like vagina?'

"What? Darling, what are you on about?"

I repeated the question.

"Honey, what are you talking about? You know I've been at this awards thing all night. When do you imagine I would have found the time to suck some woman's pussy?"

"You're vile!" I screamed.

"And you're full of shit! Do you really think I don't know the taste and scent of a woman?"

"Are you completely off your rocker? I think you need help. I did not go down on any woman tonight, or any other night. I've been faithful only to you."

"Look, Harry, I don't even blame you. I know I haven't been much of a girlfriend lately, so you're not doing yourself any harm by telling me the truth. So, I'll ask you again, did you go down on a woman tonight?"

"Samara, I promise you that I didn't."

"Swear on your children's lives."

"I'm not going to swear on their lives," Harry said with a guilty laugh.

"SWEAR IT!" I screamed like a banshee.

"Okay, okay. I swear on my children's lives that I was not unfaithful to you tonight."

What else could I do? I had no other choice but to accept his answer. I had no proof. It wasn't even so much that I would've been heart-broken if Harry had fallen for someone else. I was holding on to a hope that Scarlett would realise her mistake, and we would find a way to reconcile things. If that were to happen, I would actually love for Harry to be with someone else. Of course, my fantasy didn't match my reality, and so the weeks continued to pass dreadfully.

I stayed in my depressive hole, going over different theories in my mind, a bottle of wine often attached to my hip. My thoughts turned down a darker road. I started to wonder what Scarlett's true intentions with me might have been. Had she intended to lure me in, psychologically toy with me, entice me to fall in love with her, and once she heard me say the words, "I'm in love with you," completely discard me? Did she just get a kick out of seeing me hurt because she herself was hurt? Is that why I sometimes felt like she was looking for a reaction out of me, that she wanted to inflict pain upon me? Was I just a pawn in a twisted game?

Was I just seeking more of what I had grown accustomed to in childhood? Maybe my whole experience was only sandcastles in the sky.

No theory, no speculation seemed too far out there at this point in my grief. It seemed a lot, even with an imagination like mine, to imagine that a therapist – whose role is to help people, support people, contribute to the role of someone's personal healing – would have cruel intentions, but nothing was impossible in this world.

Another theory was that maybe this was just some genius, yet backwards scheme of Scarlett's to trigger all of my wounds – my abandonment issues, my lack of self-respect, my lack of self-love, in order for me to break apart so I would come back together. Maybe this was actually a clever technique to help me to come into my power.

Or maybe, I was just looking for every excuse in the book, like a victim in front of a gun begging for her life, just to go on believing that she actually, not even loved me anymore, but at least *cared* for me.

I carried on, day after day, having difficulty distinguishing reality from fantasy. This went on for about a month until one day, in the middle of October, Harry again came back to the flat later than he said he would. I heard him quietly open the front door and tiptoe in.

Before he could settle in, I crept out of the bedroom and swung open the living room door. He flew into the air, almost as if levitating from where he sat, gripped by fear and paranoia. Guilt was written all over his face when I interrogated him about what he had been up to, and why he was back so late. I confronted him, saying I knew he was cheating, and he vehemently denied it, even dropping to his knees and pleading for me to believe him—but his desperation only made him seem more guilty. I knew what I knew, but still, I wanted proof.

I told him, "If you have nothing to hide, then show me your phone." He safeguarded that phone as if it was his most precious treasure, only making him it worse for himself. I decided I was moving out regardless of proof. He followed me, shoving through my bedroom door as I tried to lock him out. He came an inch away from hitting me again, stopping himself at the last second. He told me my accusations were insane and asked me if I needed to be 'checked.'

The next morning, I woke up feeling shortness of breath again. I went for round two—or maybe three, I'd lost count by then—to a storage facility to buy moving boxes. I was out of the flat a day later.

When I was safely settled back into the sanctuary of Sofia's house, I reached out to Scarlett one last time, in an attempt to at least find some clarity. I hoped maybe now, after the two months since termination, she would be willing to reveal the truth, whatever truth that might have been.

I wrote her asking if she was available to speak on the phone. She wrote me back saying we ended formally some weeks ago, and that it was better that I speak to my new therapist, and that if I hadn't found one yet, she would think of who might be appropriate. Her message couldn't have been more cold and impersonal.

I had held in too much to be shut down without her allowing me to explain how hurt and confused I was by the way she had terminated me. I had to say something. I wrote:

"I have a therapist. This was a personal thing I need to address with you. Whether you respond it or not is up to you.

My whole world crumbled the day I walked out of your office. The way you left things with me felt deliberately cruel after I vulnerably expressed my feelings to you. The way things ended left me with no closure at all. Whether my feelings go down a well or not, I want to just let you know how utterly confused, betrayed, broken, and abandoned I felt by the way you terminated therapy with me. Your intentional back and forth, hot and cold, inconsistent behaviour couldn't have been more confusing. In fact, no one has ever left me so confused my whole life. I hope you're happy about that. The pain I have been enduring is indescribable.

I always had unconditional love for you, and you weren't respectful with my heart. I broke up with Harry and moved out, and in an effort to move on with my life, I wanted to understand how you could leave things off the way you did with me, so that maybe my heart would feel a little lighter. I wanted to hear if there was something I did wrong, and just wanted to have an honest conversation. I'm sorry if you aren't ready for that."

Scarlett replied:

"Dear Samara, it was never my intention to hurt you in any way. I have always held you in high esteem and sought to help you navigate the complex emotional world you grew up in. It was my understanding that the ending was mutually agreed. I would certainly have been happier if we'd had at least one other session, but that wasn't your wish. I wish you the very best with your new therapist and with every other aspect of your life. My thoughts and regards, Scarlett."

I replied:

"Scarlett, I was too hurt to imagine seeing you again, and it was quite clear that you didn't care to see me, either. Anyway, thank you for your well wishes. Everything works out the way it needs to, I guess, even if we can't possibly fathom it at the time. It no longer feels right for me to stay here so I'm moving to South America. Continuing with my spiritual journey in my own unique way feels more aligned with my nature. I'm not ready to commit myself to anything right now as I've got a long road of healing and self-discovery to go down first. Take care and my love to you, Samara."

And that was that. My decision was made to leave on the following weekend. I had started work with a therapist from the psychotherapy school. We'd had three sessions, and I liked her very much, but explained to her that I didn't feel right staying in London. I was accepted into the psychotherapy school but understood that tending to my mental and emotional health had to take precedence for the time being. It felt like there was nothing left for me in London. Everything had burnt to ashes.

In my remaining days, I said goodbye to the few friends I had, as I continued to weep in my grief, hardly able to get my words out in between sobs. I had a shipping company arriving in two days to ship my eight large boxes and four suitcases to America, so I filled my afternoons with drinking red wine, listening to sorrowful music, weeping, and going through everything from my life in London and packing it away, not knowing if and when I'd ever wear those outfits again. Those stiletto shoes, cashmere scarves, the black Russian fur hat, silky summer dresses—those outfits I had picked out specifically for Scarlett were now part of a life that no longer belonged to me. I was not only saying goodbye to the life I had lived there, but to the person who lived inside of me there.

Chapter Thirty-Three – A Heart Healing of the Soul

There was a power and a grace in my loss. The positive aspect of hitting rock bottom was that I felt I could go no lower. There was a quiet confidence in knowing that nothing could affect me or hurt me, nothing greater could be taken from me, because I already lost what I treasured most. I became content in my misery.

I landed in America at my family house, where I would stay for three weeks, before heading off to the general continent of South America, destination yet unknown. I figured if there were any time to wander again, try and heal my soul in the process, the time was now. It felt like I was back at square one, but there was a beauty in that. My canvas was completely blank.

Part of me wondered if I was mad to be walking away from my life in London where I had a sense of stability for once, but I realised it was a distorted perception of stability. Given that my life had mainly been lived with Harry, it was never stable in the first place. And then I thought – *well, at least I was in therapy, there was some stability there,* but I questioned that too. Was there? It was mainly volatility. Wherever I was going, it couldn't get any more emotionally unstable than it already had been.

Although I felt like a ghost, it didn't mean I wasn't a ghost who didn't still wail several times a day. I guess you could say I was a depressed ghost, with a deep scar ingrained into her impermeable cloak. I found it impossible to believe I would ever feel completely normal again, completely fulfilled in this life, if I had lost the love that made me feel at the zenith of my existence. The sun would never shine as brightly for me again. I figured I would eventually come out of my depression, find a way to survive it, but whether I could ever feel happy again was another story.

I landed in Peru and went straight to the ayahuasca retreat I had been to a year and a half earlier. I intended to stay there for several months, working with plant medicine, in hopes to heal my broken heart. I was in the company of some other beautiful people who came in hopes of healing themselves, too. We were good company to each other and lifted each other up. I was living with and on the medicine in an almost warped version of reality, sometimes having four ceremonies a week.

A couple of weeks after arriving, I found myself a boyfriend—Claude, a shaman in training. After two months of being there, we ended up fleeing the camp together, like Bonnie and Clyde, because we broke the rules and had sex. We didn't care as we did it in the name of love.

Claude decided to accompany me on my travels to Brazil and Colombia. We really saw a future together, until the haze of the medicine wore off. Things were different at the camp. It wasn't like living in the real world. We had a good run in Brazil for the first two weeks, wining and dining, finding satisfaction in materialistic pleasures after nearly starving ourselves on plant diets and living with cucarachas. But then I found myself treating Claude more like a friend, and realised I didn't actually have romantic feelings for him.

We travelled on to Colombia, starting out in Bogota and then Medellin, but by the time we got to Cartagena, I just wanted to be on my own again. Claude and I had a spiritual connection, but it was nothing in comparison to the deeply embedded psychic connection I felt with Scarlett. Claude came into my life when I needed him, when we needed each other, and the relationship had a healing purpose to it, but it was meant to be temporary, a seasonal fling. And so, on

Valentine's Day in Cartagena, of all days, we split up and he flew back to England, leaving me in Colombia alone.

Even though I knew it was the right decision for us to split, I felt totally alone in the world again, and the heartbreak that hadn't actually gone anywhere came back in full force.

I had been drinking heavily since I left the ayahuasca retreat, going from one extreme to another, and I had to get my act together. I didn't want to be on holiday at all anymore. I needed to be alone, in my own flat, in a city where I didn't know a soul, so that I could cry all of the tears I needed to cry in peace. I didn't want to see the sun. I just wanted to be alone in my darkness. I flew to Buenos Aires the next morning.

I settled into a flat that I rented for the next six months from February until the start of August, and hardly did a thing for the first two weeks.

By the third week, the pain hadn't subsided, and I knew I would have to learn to live with it. Step one of my recovery was detoxing. I needed to bring my dopamine and serotonin levels back into balance, and so I vowed to not touch alcohol for at least four months. Step two was to dive into intellectual and creative pursuits, starting with my pen— writing the story of my pain—along with reading, studying Spanish, and practicing yoga and meditation.

I became like a hermit in a cave, diving into my imagination, creating my own world, my own bubble, completely disconnected from any reality but my own. I hardly spoke to a soul; I didn't know what was happening in the world. It was like I had entered another dimension of my own making. Never in my life had I ever been so disconnected from reality. My whole world started to feel like one never-ending LSD trip, or a psychedelic dream that never ended. I was Alice, living in a wonderland of my own creation, and I wouldn't have changed it for a thing.

Everything was amplified: my dreams took on a whole new level of intensity and depth, my intuition sky-rocketed and blew my pineal gland wide open, the way I felt my emotions was sharp and crystal clear. The way I felt sadness was how I imagined Mother Earth must feel – not only a personal sorrow, but a culmination of the sorrows of everyone and everything that existed here, and having to bear that weight all on her own. And in the occasional moments where I felt joy, I felt such bliss that I would weep tears of euphoria, falling to the floor in pure ecstasy. When I would look at myself in the mirror, I would see her, and it would make me feel closer to her, make me feel like she never left me, like she was still within me. I saw her in my own reflection.

This personal retreat and isolation from life was exactly what I needed, a precious gift to myself. I couldn't have healed to a deeper degree if I had gone to the most expensive, well-rated wellness centre in the world. I was reviewing my life in its entirety, as if standing on a snowy mountaintop with God looking down at all the pathways I had taken to get there. I was beginning to feel at least *okay* again.

The first stage of my grief was the numbness, where it felt like nothing could touch me because I was so broken that I could go no lower. The second stage was agony. I tried to commend myself for at least not numbing myself out. My heart was as wide open as the night sky and doing what it was supposed to be doing – feeling. It was functioning properly. It was still beating. I praised that precious heart of mine because it didn't stop working on me. If I was going through anything, more so than a depression, it was a heart healing of the soul.

I hardly spoke to a soul in Argentina because no one could understand my story, no one was hearing me, no one was supportive. I hadn't spoken to my mother in over half a year and when we finally exchanged some words, she told me, "I last got wind that you were in Brazil," just to give an example of how isolated and disconnected I was from her. I didn't feel heard by even my closest friends. It takes a rare person to understand a rare love. Whether it was too unconventional for some to fathom, or too unusual of a tale to be true, or too easily pinned down to transference, I understood that true friends were few and far between so the best thing we can hope for is to become best friends to ourselves. At least I could hear my story. At least I could hear my truth, and so, I told my own tale to myself.

Morning moulded into night, dreams moulded into reality, and a creation began to form – first as seedlings gently sprouting with the first of spring's light, and then came the stems and the leaves, as I re-lived my joys and my sorrows, riding the waves of my emotional terrain.

Three months into my living reverie, I started to have homosexual dreams, often several times a night, for months on end. Maybe the reason some people thought I was hiding something was because I was concealing my own identity to even myself. Perhaps I was trying to conceal my true self, and what had been clouded within my sexual orientation.

There was something that I was working out with Scarlett, in my forbidden love for her. Perhaps it took falling in love with a woman to see that it didn't compare at all to any of my other former relationships with men.

About four months into my isolation from the world, I started to drink again. I got into a habit of having about a bottle of red wine a night, sometimes more when I really wanted to check out. Revelations and self-understandings or not, I was still in agony over the loss of Scarlett. I wanted to numb the pain of my broken heart.

I found myself missing Harry. We video chatted for a day or two and I felt happy to be in touch with him again. I guess any kind of human contact at that point would have been welcomed. I very nearly agreed to moving back in with him in London, but some saving grace stopped me. I remembered that even though I was in despair, Harry wasn't the solution to fix it.

I declared my homosexuality to him and told him I wouldn't be in integrity with myself if I went back to him after this discovery. Harry didn't want to accept it, of course, and the call ended with him wishing me luck on my 'sapphic journey.' Nonetheless, he kept calling and I had to block him again. After speaking to him, I had an intense migraine for days and felt short of breath for nearly a week afterward.

I needed an escape, to remember what it was like to feel a sense of hope. And so, as I continued to express my own tragedy through the written word, I also consumed every tragic love story I could, in hopes to find company in the thoughts and feelings of other heartbroken souls. I revisited Shakespeare's *Romeo and Juliet*, followed *by Love in The Time of Cholera* (which felt tragic despite its happy ending), but ironically enough, what proved most helpful in taking me out of my slump was a rather realistic novel exploring politics and how the concept of truth is distorted in what the majority of people call 'reality.' The characters had an unwavering drive to keep fighting for what they believed in, which helped me trust and believe in myself again.

After feeling completely lost for months in my isolation and personal rehab, I realised that although I didn't want to return to London to be with Harry, I still wanted to return to London. I was weary of my wandering lifestyle, not having a home, not having foundations, not having a support system. I wanted structure in my life, and I still wanted to study psychotherapy.

I flew back home in August for about a month, only to repack my bags once again and come full circle, for the *third* time's return to London. Third time's a charm!

Although I thought I was prepared to face London again after a year away, I fell apart shortly after landing on English soil. It hit me like a ton of bricks that this would be the first time since living here that I wouldn't be seeing Scarlett, that I didn't have Harry meeting me at the airport like he usually would, and that I was truly on my own this time. In a sense of desperation, once I arrived with my luggage to the Airbnb, I called Harry in tears.

Everything went surprisingly well for the first two weeks. I felt a strange sense of homecoming in returning to my past, in spending time with someone from an older generation that I felt more connected with than my own. Harry and I listened to sixties music that we both loved, conversed in our dysfunctionality like old times, walked through the beautiful autumnal air. Everything seemed bright and positive again, and I began to wonder if we were meant to go through hell and back, heal and grow in separation, only to come back together again.

Thankfully it didn't take long for me to come to my senses. On the day I visited the flat where we had lived together, all the memories of trauma, sadness, and depression came flooding back to me. I was no longer the girl I had been with him. After all the heartbreak and pain, I had become a woman—a woman who could no longer fit into a girl's shoes. I was beginning to understand how necessary my months of crying in Argentina had been, as those tears led to my transformation. I just hadn't realised it until the moment when I entered the flat and knew I no longer belonged there.

The girl that had lived at 138 was no longer in existence. She left, and maybe even died, when I left for South America. I sobbed even harder with that realisation. She was dead. She was dead. She was dead.

I rushed back to my temporary flat before Harry returned to his and wrote him an email, kindly explaining that I needed a fresh start and that he could no longer be a part of my life.

He called me several times that evening from a blocked number, pretending as if he hadn't seen my email asking him not to contact me. When I picked up and briefly repeated what I had said in the email, he sent me a spew of attacking messages that hardly even made sense.

It wasn't long before Harry showed up at my new flat, pushed past me, and dumped bags of my things that he had kept, still assuming I would come back to him someday. He called me every sour name under the sun one might imagine, adding his own creative flair. He screamed in my face that there was another trunk of mine in the boot of his car. I told my flatmate to stay with the landlord, but she joined me to make sure I was going to be okay.

At the car, he kept screaming and shoved a trunk toward me. It wasn't mine—his luggage tags were all over it. I insisted it didn't belong to me and that I didn't want it. He pointed to the top, where he had tied a pair of my knickers, and shouted maniacally, 'Those are yours!'

A crowd began to gather, and some guys asked if I was okay. Before I had a chance to respond, Harry ran across the street through the traffic with this trunk of his, screaming that he was going to throw it down the stairs to my flat. All I could do was run after him again, weaving through the moving cars, worried there might be an explosive in the thing. With the way he was acting, I believed he was capable of anything. My flatmate tried to take the trunk, but he swatted her hand away, calling her a cunt and a bitch, and telling her she would never be happy. I grabbed the trunk from him and told him I was going to call the police. He screamed in my face with that well remembered demonic expression. The guys from the street gathered as a means of protecting us. They asked if they could be of service at all, and I told them to just make sure he stayed the fuck away from me. Harry scurried off and I went inside, shaking like a leaf.

I called the police. I was no longer the girl he had trapped and controlled for his own selfish purposes. The girl who had been broken down, believing she was beyond repair, who thought she couldn't trust herself—that girl had transformed into a woman.

When I took this radical step of empowerment, my driving motive was to protect myself, but I hadn't imagined that actual justice would be served. I wondered when anyone in the past had ever sought to protect or defend me.

Harry was put on bail conditions by the police to not enter my street nor contact me directly or indirectly until a future court date. He broke the order a month later when he contacted me via Whatsapp under a different name, calling himself 'Time.' Time tried to tell me that it was all a big misunderstanding.

I told him I wasn't interested in his explanations and that I wanted nothing to do with him. A few days later, he called and threatened to blackmail me with sexual photos if I let this go to court. I informed the police, and he was arrested for intimidation and stalking. After his first hearing, he faced charges of harassment, assault, and stalking, to be addressed at a future court date.

As I worked with the detective, my sense of empowerment grew. It took me fully removing myself from

Harry, with the law between us, for me to realise the extent of his cruelty. To some degree I felt like I needed Harry, but all he did was hold me back from my potential.

The initial shock of knowing this was going to court with Harry threw me for a loop and I spent a number of nights distraught, often wondering if I was making the right decision. In the end, I realised I had nothing to mourn and everything to celebrate. Justice is always served, even if we don't see it when we want to, or in the way we expected.

In the aftermath of the crime, I reflected on how much I had grown. Ultimately, I didn't resent Harry, because I needed to grow through the challenge. From a higher perspective, everything unfolded exactly as it was meant to in my Divine play.

I reflected on just how beautiful life is, how life goes on after love, with love, before love, and that it's always there, waiting to be appreciated for its beauty and splendour. I realised that my heartbreak didn't have to be a sad ending, for it allowed me to transform into a person who was much more self-loving and self-respectful. I was continuously changing, and therefore I knew I was still living.

Even though I had been brought into the depths of sorrow, every moment of it was worth it in the end. I needed my heart cracked open to find my inner strength. Scarlett gave me this gift and her sudden exit from my life was a blessing in disguise. Even though I felt like I had died when she terminated our relationship, I was beginning to feel seeds of life sprouting in me again.

Was I alive, or was I dreaming? Was it a crime, or was I healing? Divinity, or just a feeling? Was I living in a fantasy world of my own creation because of my own childhood trauma that made it easier to dwell in *that* world rather than *'reality?'* Or was I touching upon the truth of what love is all about – perhaps simply a fantasy land in and of itself, that we are meant to get lost and submerged in, only to realise that we won't drown, and we will find our way out into greater depths of our soul's evolution. Why else would dreams be dreams if they weren't a little fantastical? Dreams are the nectar of life, and we are allowed to drink up as much of that nectar as we may please.

And speaking of my own dreams, I was no longer concerned about what my next move would be, or how everything was going to ultimately work out. I realised it was perfectly okay to not have a clue. I still had my own secret dreams, but I had learned to simply flow in a state of existing, living in the now and finding a sense of balance from that place.

I no longer needed others to validate my own truths, my own beliefs, my own dreams. I had been looking for someone else, something else to believe in. The only thing I wasn't believing in was myself. I was putting my faith in everything outside of myself, but not what was within me. Throughout the whole process of falling in love, breaking apart, and slowly coming back together, I learned that I no longer needed anyone else to believe in me because for the first time in my life, I believed in myself.

Likewise, I learned to own my power. I didn't have to change myself to appear a certain way to others. I learned to embrace and own the darker aspects of my nature, and to feel safe showing the parts of myself that were not always so 'nice.' I learned that true freedom is dropping the mask. We are not free if we are always wearing a mask.

Dare to dream. Let the dreamer in you dream dreams the rest of us have not ventured to explore. Push logic to the side, push the mind out of the way, and allow the heart to lead. Trust in your heart. Trust in your feelings. Trust in the light inside of you.

This was a journey of love, into love. What I learned was how to love—fully, completely, unashamedly, and unconditionally. Whatever her intentions may have been, Scarlett assisted me in my quest to understand unconditional love. Her legacy will remain with me as a light that never goes out. I'll find my way through the Garden of Eden.

Epilogue – Café Gloucester Road

As I approached the café Scarlett suggested on Gloucester Road, my heart began to beat wildly in anticipation and trepidation. Would she be surprised? Would she be angry? Would she be the one to surprise me, always somehow seeming one step ahead? The musings came to a halt as I spotted her through the glass window, sitting there nonchalantly, as if she lived on that couch. I wondered if she was intentionally trying to paint that picture of aloofness. It was late afternoon on a Tuesday in September. The numerology of the day happened to be 666.

I turned the corner and entered the café, attempting to ease my heart rate and breathe deeply as to appear more relaxed than I was in truth. I paid for the flat white and started walking over to the back corner, attempting to balance the filled to the brim coffee without spilling it. My attempt at a graceful approach was in vain as a noticeable amount of coffee splashed onto me and the floor. She had been looking down at her phone, and I think she noticed it, though she made no comment about it.

Looking somewhat flushed and rather disheveled, I placed the flat white on the table and took a seat on the green suede chair next to her. I kissed her hello on the cheek.

"Come sit next to me on the couch!" she said.

Interesting start, I thought. Was she flirting with me? We had never sat in such proximity before. Already, we were entering foreign territory. She wore a white, low-cut summer dress I remembered from many moons ago.

Without a word, I moved the coffee next to her on the wooden table. She moved my bag for me, and we embraced. It had been three years.

"You look well. Your eyes are clear," she told me.

We exchanged niceties for the first twenty minutes, unsure of how or where to start. We both knew we were beating around the bush. She could hardly bring herself to look at me, her gaze pointed in the direction of the glass window on her left.

She started mumbling about the concept of time, how it's an illusion, how it's not linear, and how it's occurring at many different levels simultaneously. Somewhere in the whirlwind of her streams of consciousness, she attempted to convey how that was related to us. It seemed important, but I struggled to grasp precisely what she was hoping to get across to me. It was always like that – riddles, parables, speaking in third person, reading between the lines. Nothing had changed.

As she spoke and I listened, the rain started pelleting down from the skies. It rained so hard that we both felt the compulsion to stop and stare, surrendering to the words of nature, listening to the rumbles of thunder.

"I'm not articulating this very well. I feel like I'm doing all of the talking here."

"I'm still getting used to you again. I mean, we haven't communicated in three years."

"You know we've been communicating all this time," she hissed, and I knew I couldn't deny her words. I was just surprised she was openly acknowledging the telepathic communication that had gone on all this time. Did that mean I wasn't crazy? That it really was a mutual feeling that we were nearly always in contact, that she was very much aware of what had been going on with me?

"So, how are you, really?" I asked her.

She looked at me directly, just for a moment, before quickly averting her gaze.

Still struggling to find the words, she placed her head in her hands as if hiding something.

"Discombobulated," she blurted out, as though the word had finally surfaced, identifying the feeling amidst the fragmented pieces that refused to align.

I leaned back on the brown leather couch, drawing myself closer to her as if to hold space.

"What's weighing you down?"

I could tell she was burdened by something, her nonchalant demeanor merely a facade. In truth, it seemed she was carrying a heavy weight on her shoulders—just as I had been.

After a long silence, during which she hesitated, grappling with what to say and what to leave unsaid, she finally spoke.

"A choice."

"A choice..." I repeated.

Don't therapise me,' she commanded, firmly establishing that a boundary had been crossed regarding how much she was willing to reveal. It felt as though she was now more unguarded than she intended to be, pulled out of her preoccupation with her own thoughts and the weight of whatever this 'choice' was.

My point, of course, was not to 'therapise,' her, but I knew all too well that explaining that would have been to no avail. Her defences were up. The door had slammed shut on any traces of vulnerability that had begun to emerge, almost as if there were little beings that existed within her hoping to pop out and see the light of day, that were now being shut back in. Out again was the unraveling of Scarlett's mask. Hello old friend, lovely to meet you again. The dark twin had arrived.

"Samara, what *was* it about our relationship?"

I didn't know how to answer her. I didn't know what she was looking for. I didn't know what I should share. Should I dare, or would she act, once again, like she didn't care?

"I don't exactly know how to explain it, but it was more about the connection."

I recognised that familiar feeling of being put on the spot, compelled to address the unspoken elephant in the room between us. She may have been, as she put it, 'doing all the talking' earlier, but it had nothing to do with the heart of the matter. All of that seemed to be left up to me, but I was used to that role. And I didn't really mind it, either, someone had to do it, but I hoped this wouldn't be another incident about the entire relationship having to do with *my feelings,* rather than considering hers in the equation, and that it takes two to tango, or we wouldn't be sitting in this very café.

It was at this moment that it seemed as if everything and everyone else that existed in that café, had disappeared and dissolved into a hazy, vaporous fog. Time was standing still, the intensity was rising, and all that was left in the room was something else entirely, something that could only be born in each other's physical presence. It was as if a third child had been born. I had almost forgotten what this sensation was like. It was a blue moon occurrence, and blue moon occurrences must be savoured.

"You have no idea how much you impacted me." She looked at me directly, her eyes widening, the emphasis in her voice unmistakable. She said it with such intensity, as if willing me to truly understand, to grasp the depth of what our connection had 'done to her.'

"Well, you weren't the only one. You deeply impacted me too."

"You freed me. You set me on a completely different path. All my relationships have changed. The way I connect with people is different now. My entire life is different. You profoundly changed my life."

I could hardly believe how much she was revealing. What changed? Why was she now coming out with all of this? She had said she had changed, but why wait three years, I wondered.

"There was a time when you were going to leave. Why didn't you?" She asked me.

"I couldn't. The work was in the relationship itself, you see. Some part of me knew that. What unfolded between us and what bloomed in its own unique way was the work. Remember when you wrote me that 'what it is to love' was what we had to work with next? Well, you certainly hit the mark. That's how it had to be. It's a profound spiritual connection."

"It's definitely something karmic between us."

"I don't know if karmic is the word, but it does feel like a past life connection. You know that as well as I do."

"Maybe you'll understand it one day and be the one to come back to me and say, 'I get it,'" she said.

"Sometimes we have to accept the divine riddle," I said.

"There were times when I didn't know what to do with you, or how to move forward. I was really challenged and completely stumped. I felt like I was failing you. You were my most challenging patient."

"That's because you were restricting yourself to seeing it only from a psychotherapeutic lens. I saw it more expansively – from a spiritual and metaphysical perspective. It didn't need to make sense. It was about embracing illogical truths. I saw that, but I saw that you weren't yet able to. And that's where our friction came into play."

"In my twenty years of being a psychotherapist, you were my most frightening patient. I couldn't figure you out."

"I was lost in it all too, Scarlett. We both were. I think it didn't make sense to you because it wasn't just about me. It was about you, too."

"Coming here today, an opportunity came in unexpectedly, and I thought to myself that I wasn't surprised something like that would come up on the day I was seeing you, as if our meeting sparked it."

"We're catalysts for each other," I stated.

"I met someone recently, and he reminded me of you. The energy was similar to what you and I have, not quite as intense, but the vibration was very high, and it was almost too much. I really see your potential, Samara. And I see you have the ability to go further than me spiritually, and that I won't be able to keep up with you."

I sat there, listening, absorbing her words. It felt as though she had been holding on to these thoughts for a long time, as if so much had been bottled up and was now pouring out, much like the torrents of rain cascading from the skies.

"Our connection really scares me. I'm scared we have the potential to go too high together and I would lose myself in it."

"What do you think is going to happen, Scarlett?" I asked, a trace of amusement in my tone, as if to suggest that engaging with me wasn't some cataclysmic event. It felt like she was assigning me an extraordinary amount of power—seeing me as some kind of deity capable of entirely altering her existence, or even erasing it altogether. I couldn't quite grasp why she thought this way.

She looked at me with a half-smile, seemingly aware of how it might sound, but beneath it, I could see the grave expression that read as genuine concern. I felt like I had to take *her* back into reality, out of this overplayed fantasy in her head, and help to ground her.

She was one of those rare souls who seemed to have the capacity to move between realms and dimensions, to see beyond the present moment. At times, there seemed to be a real fragility there, but then I would be utterly confused when I would be slammed by the dark twin.

I wanted her to understand that she would continue to exist and be okay, that life would go on, and that I didn't hold the kind of power to annihilate her—or at least, I wouldn't use it even if I did. She was acting as though I had the ability to push her over the edge, when all I really wanted was to love her.

I then supposed if anyone should understand the effect I had on her, it should have been me, because it was a two-way mirror. The difference was that I wasn't scared of it. I thought it would enhance, rather than destroy. I didn't think it would be the ending of us. I thought it would be the making.

"Do you remember that crystal I gave you? I felt as if it belonged to you. I felt like I had to give you something."

Every single step she took towards me seemed so absolutely thought over, so carefully crafted. I wished she would allow herself to act more freely, to escape the sense of entrapment, unless it was somehow all an elaborate act.

"Of course I remember it. I cherish it deeply."

"I had never given anything to my patients before. I still feel like I have to give you something. I just can't figure out what it is."

I had a few ideas, and it wasn't something tangible.

It was at this time that Henry called.

"Sorry, I just have to take this," Scarlett excused herself.

"Sure."

"Hi Henry…I'm with Samara now. Can I call you in a few hours? Yes, yes. Okay, good. I'll speak to you then. Bye, Henry."

Who was Henry and why was he aware of my name?

"So have you severed ties with Harry?" she asked me.

"Yes, well, you know there's a restraining order in place, so that's been effective since last spring."

"Have you heard from him since?"

"No, he's on a restraining order."

"Yes, well that doesn't mean anything and hasn't stopped him before."

"No, I haven't heard from him," I assured her.

"I'm married, by the way," she said casually, almost flippantly.

"But, we're estranged… well, not estranged," she said, with a dismissive flip of her hand, "but we've been separated for many years. He's with someone else now," she added, as if to reassure me that any romantic relations had ceased to exist.

"Right, was that Henry, then?"

"Yes…" she replied, smirking as she humoured me, clearly noticing the green-eyed monster now flickering in my gaze and erupting in my heart.

So, she was married all this time. Harry and Henry. Samara and Scarlett. Quite the quartet. Separated or not, why would he be calling her when he must have known that she would be with me? How much did he know? The way she had said my name made it sound like Henry knew all about me. "I'm with Samara," was like a code that told him everything. If they were separated, why did he still seem so evidently *in the picture?* Were they even separated or was that also another fabrication of the truth? All this time I had been on a lonely road tour, thinking that she too was fully single, independent, solitary, but I was the only one that had been the wandering hermit. Another major bomb dropped at Café Gloucester Road, but they just seemed to keep coming.

Noticing my contemplative expression since hearing the news of her marital status as a wife, she spoke again. Discreetly and again in third person, she described in cryptic form the reasons why we can't work, the complications involved, the fact that she has children who are slightly older than me, and how that would look... I was more forward.

"I think you need a little more faith," I told her simply, cutting to the chase. It felt almost like she wanted me to cut through all her excuses and take the lead and insist that none of those trivial details ultimately mattered. If there was love, there was love. She kept resisting but I felt that she wanted me to keep persisting.

"We can't be *friends*, Samara..."

I explained, "It's not as insurmountable as you think. We just have to get used to being with each other outside of the setting in which we once knew each other. It will happen naturally. We don't have to put a label on it. It's a very unique relationship. All we can do is see how it unfolds."

'No, we don't have to put a label on it..." she said, but then continued resisting.

Scarlett then brought up the termination of our therapy, asking what it left me with.

"You broke me," I told her, with utter honesty.

"I'm sorry for hurting you," she said.

"Well, what's done is done. The rest is in the hands of the Divine."

The Indian summer sky, which had shifted from pouring rain to blazing sun, had now begun to darken, as if the curtains were slowly being drawn on the day.

"You should read the four quartets poem by T.S. Eliot. Particularly the last part – "Little Gidding". I think you're ready for it."

I knew from our history together that whenever Scarlett would suggest something for me to explore – whether a film, book, or poem – there was always a deeper reason behind it, something that directly applied to our relationship. She just couldn't bring herself to say it outright. She did explain how it was to do with man's relationship with time, the universe, the Divine. The poem asks the question – 'what is reality?' And it says – to be conscious, is not to be in time.

As we parted ways on the day, she offered to give me a lift home, which I accepted. Naturally as one might imagine, my hopes were utterly revived. My heart hadn't felt such peace and relief in years, as the truths that long remained hidden had finally been unveiled. The weight of the tension from our shared history felt lifted from me. We could finally begin a new chapter together, a whole new genre.

One week later, as I was walking home from a yoga class, I happened to run into her on the street. I seized yet another blue moon occurrence and followed her into the shop on the corner to say hello. I felt confident in the new dynamics of our relationship and where we had left off.

"Hi there," I said cheerily.

She turned around, but what I was met with wasn't the same Scarlett I had encountered in the café just a week earlier. Her eyes were gleaming and possessed, as if she had been waiting for me, as if she knew I would be there, at that moment in time, and wanted me to follow her into the store.

I froze in the coldness of her icy stare. Our encounter was brief. Feeling unwelcome and acutely aware of avoiding the trap of her old patterns that once disempowered me, I simply told her to take care of herself and walked out the door.

The next day, she blocked me by telephone. As she had done so many times before, she left me with yet another mystery to unravel. History had repeated itself – I had been discarded once again. The only question that remained was – who was Scarlett, anyway?